The Blood Stone

JAMILA GAVIN

The Blood Stone

JAMILA GAVIN

EGMONT

To Iain and Jan Mackintosh, with love

First published in Great Britain 2003
by Egmont Books Limited
239 Kensington High Street, London W8 6SA

Text copyright © 2003 Jamila Gavin
Cover illustration copyright © 2003 Bryan Patterson

The moral rights of the author and illustrator have been asserted

ISBN 1 4052 1252 7

1 3 5 7 9 10 8 6 4 2

A CIP catalogue record for this title is available from the British Library

Typeset by Avon DataSet Ltd, Bidford on Avon

Printed and bound in Great Britain by the CPI Group

Contents

❖

Acknowledgements

I cast the net wide when I went trawling for information for the background to this book. Sometimes an odd comment or snippet of information gave me just what I needed.

For their trust, I must thank John Irving, Judy and Derek Brooke-Wavell and Kate Kavanagh, for lending me precious books. My immense gratitude to Elizabeth Foster-Hall, Matteo Legrenzi and Donald Sassoon for their advice, insight and knowledge of Venice, not to speak of my extensive reading from books by, among others, Goethe, Jan Morris, H.V. Morton, 'Rough Guide' and Zoffoli and Scibilia's *Vivavenice*. For his invaluable and wide-ranging knowledge about India, Afghanistan and the Middle East, I must thank Dilawar Chetsingh in Delhi, whose many comments and suggestions have undoubtedly enhanced this book, and also Ibn Battuta, Francois Bernier, Jean-Jacques Tavernier and Niccolai Manucci for their contemporary accounts of travelling in fourteenth and seventeenth century India. I pay homage to Homer. I give thanks for the poetry of Muhammad Iqbal, Shanfara, and ancient poetry in praise of Shiva, and to my nephew, Justin Neville-Kaushall, for his wonderful poem which concludes the book. To Geoff Brett, I am grateful for his ever-patient help with my meagre computer skills. To Elisabeth Moody for editing and guiding this book through to the end with intelligence and perception. To my publisher, editor and agent, Cally Poplak, Miriam Hodgson and Jacqueline Korn, who had to wait far too long for it – but were ever patient – my love and appreciation.

Finally, perhaps I should salute Geronimo Veroneo, a jeweller from Venice who went to India, was briefly attributed with having designed the Taj Mahal, and who died obscurely. I give him a story.

Jamila Gavin

❖

Who are you drifting in my moonlight,
Restless, silent as petals,
Wafting like perfume?
Perhaps you are a jeweller.

❖

Geronimo's chair

Filippo was born eight months and thirteen days after his father, Geronimo Veroneo, left for Hindustan. For years, he didn't understand the word 'absent'; didn't realise that it meant not present, not here, away. Geronimo had been present for him ever since the day he was born. Did not Filippo have a memory of lying in his wooden cradle, and of the faces which would swim into his blurry view, loom over him, rock the cradle and move on? Mama he could identify blind from her smell and touch, from her voice and mother's milk. And apart from his eldest sister, Elisabetta, who bathed him and changed him and often laid him in his cradle, he knew his brothers, Carlo and Giuseppe, and their younger sisters, Sofia and Gabriella. Their faces glided above him in an endless procession of smiles and scowls, tickles and tears, raucous bickerings, and gentle croo-crooings like pigeons as they squeezed and kissed him. And, of course, there was Papa.

His face too, often loomed over his cradle. Even after

Filippo's baby eyes had strengthened and his sight became sharper and clearer, he knew the face which gazed down upon him, sometimes smiling, sometimes sad. Was it not in his father's liquid sea-green eyes that he first saw his own reflection; saw his own baby arms punch the air uncontrollably and grasp the finger pushed into his fist? And was it not Papa who played with him in the middle of the night, making him squeak and chortle, so that Mama would sit up startled in bed and look into the cradle at her side, and wonder what it was that entertained her baby?

As Filippo grew older, and his utterings and gabblings turned into speech, he didn't tell of what he saw because he thought that's how things were. Papa was every bit as here as the rest of them. After all, his boots were by the kitchen door, his tools in the workshop, his books in the cabinet and his clothes were in the closet. Filippo liked to climb inside the closet and stand among his father's jackets and tabards, and wrap himself into his thick woollen cloak. He knew his father's smell as much as his mother's.

But most of all, in the parlour, was his chair.

It was the largest chair in the room: high backed, broad armed, and covered in warm mustard-yellow linen. No one had ever sat in it except his father, Geronimo. Not even his mother, though Filippo had often come in to find her standing before the chair as if silently conversing with it, or kneeling on the floor with her head in its cushions, her shoulders shaking with tears. If ever he tried to climb into it, someone would come and scoop him away with a laugh but saying firmly, 'No, baby, no. That's Papa's chair. Mustn't climb in Papa's chair.'

For everyone else, 'Papa's chair' was the ever-empty chair, but for Filippo it was 'Papa's chair' because he often saw him sitting there, and because Geronimo's old dog, Forza, slept most of the time at its feet.

Once, soon after he had found his feet, Filippo came staggering up to the door of the parlour. For a while no one's attention had been on him so, with the thrill of disobedience, he had slipped away, and made a beeline for the open door. He had paused. Forza lay as usual near his master's chair with his head on his paws. His tail thumped gently.

Filippo expected any minute to hear a shout of reprimand, but none came. He crossed the threshold.

Somehow, the sounds of the house seemed to die away. He no longer heard his sisters quarrelling, Rosa, the cook, clattering her pans, the liquid whistle of their pet canary, nor the heart-beat tick, tock, tick of the clock in the hallway.

There was only the light.

The shutters of the parlour had been closed against the heat of the summer sun, but threads of intense white light penetrated the slats and patterned the wooden floor before him. They fell in bright stripes across the face of his father, sitting in the chair. Surely it was all right to climb into Papa's chair, if it was Papa himself who sat there and held out his arms to him, who drew him on to his lap and bounced him on his knee?

When his mother, Teodora, found him missing and galvanised the household into a search, he was finally discovered curled up fast asleep in 'Papa's chair'.

Chapter One

❖

A marriage arranged

It is the feast day of Santa Perpetua. For the first time in many winter days, the icy air which had swept down from the Dolomites is softer. The morning sunshine is warm and bright.

The younger daughters of Geronimo Veroneo are walking through the alleys and lanes of Venice on their way to the Church of Santa Maria Formosa. Somewhere behind is their younger brother, Filippo, straggling as usual. Perhaps he's stopped to look at a conjuror, or listen to a street musician, to stare at a newly arrived cargo of spices and silks from the Orient, or slaves from Africa, shackled and ready for selling. Maybe he's just stopped to admire the way sunbeams shimmer on the surface of a canal. There is always something to distract Filippo.

Leading them is Geronimo's wife, Teodora Veroneo – or is she his widow? She has bowed to social pressure, and now, for decency's sake, dresses as a widow entirely in black, her head and shoulders shrouded in a heavy black veil.

Year after year, she resisted being called a widow, insisted her husband was alive. 'After all,' she had argued, 'until I hear he is dead, indeed until I have proof of it, why should I not assume that he is alive? Besides, I feel it here in my heart that he's alive,' and she would clench her hands to her heart and beat her chest, as if willing his heart to beat too – wherever it was. 'Do you think I wouldn't know if he were dead?'

So she continued to wear ordinary clothes in the colours she loved – sky blue and cherry red, spring green and sunflower yellow. After all, she was still young and full of vitality, almost more like a sister to her family of five than its mother. She attended the religious feasts and masked balls, and enjoyed the festive carnivals. In the beginning, a message from Geronimo would come from time to time, brought by a traveller or merchant. But gradually, as the years went by – six years, seven years – no further word came, and more and more voices questioned whether her husband was indeed alive. She stopped going out and stopped wearing bright colours. She turned to dark green, nut brown and dull maroon, and so, by degrees, she surrendered to common opinion, especially her son-in-law's, Bernardo Pagliarin, and faded to black.

'Mama, is Papa dead?' whispered Sofia, her younger daughter, when Teodora put her to bed.

'No, no! He is not,' she said, kissing her almost vehemently. 'He is not.'

'Then why are you wearing black now?' demanded Filippo.

'Because everyone else thinks he is and Signor Pagliarin orders it.'

'Why do you have to do what he says?' muttered Gabriella.

'Because he is our guardian while Papa's away. I will wear black to appease him, that's all. But I know Papa will return. It may take twenty years – but he will come back. I know it. So pray, little ones, pray and pray. Light a candle in church and pray for his life, and believe, just believe as I do.'

It is now twelve years since Geronimo Veroneo set off for Hindustan and never returned. Such situations are not uncommon in Venice. It is a city of adventurers, seafarers and merchants. They follow the silk and spice routes to North Africa, Arabia, India and China, and are often away for months if not years. Some run out of money, or are shipwrecked on some foreign shore. But yes, it's true, others never return, falling victim to pirates, slavers, hostage-takers, illness, natural catastrophe – or perhaps just do not want to.

Geronimo Veroneo was a jeweller, because his father had been a jeweller and his grandfather and great-grandfather. But in his heart he was an adventurer. Over and over again, Filippo and his sisters demanded to hear the story of how their father had met a Portuguese merchant, Antonio Rodriguez, who offered him a passage on one of his ships to Arabia, leaving in a month. How their father had leapt at it. 'He had dreamed of it all his life,' sighed their mother. 'I suppose he feared that with age creeping up on him fast it would never be possible again.'

Geronimo's goal was Hindustan. Rodriguez had told him about Hindustan: a land which abounded with diamonds as big as duck eggs, and rubies and emeralds which were to be found in great profusion. His ships were leaving in a month and he offered Geronimo a place on one, the *Santa Anna*. He couldn't refuse. There and then Geronimo decided to go.

Teodora had dreaded that day. She knew her husband's restless nature, and had always feared something like this would happen. How she had raged and wept alternately. 'But what about us? How can we live without you? Who will run the business?' she had pleaded.

Then he had dropped the next bombshell. He told her, almost casually, that he had arranged for Elisabetta to be married.

'Elisabetta? Married? Are you mad? To whom? When? Why didn't you consult me?' Teodora had exclaimed, furiously.

The children sighed at that part of the story, and shook their heads wisely, commiserating with their mother's outrage. This was no way to arrange a marriage.

Elisabetta, barely fourteen, was the eldest child. She had been betrothed to the son of a respectable family in the city, almost from the cradle, but the boy had died of the plague in an epidemic some time ago, and they hadn't yet found another to take his place.

He had met Bernardo Pagliarin drinking in the tavern that night. 'You know of him, don't you?' beamed Geronimo.

Bernardo Pagliarin. Yes, Teodora knew of him. Everyone knew of the Pagliarin family and how they made their money.

A slaver. She had shaken her head dumbly. 'I can't believe you would do this to your own daughter.'

'No, no, no, no! Maybe a few slaves perhaps, but he deals mostly in metal, timber, furs and cloth . . .'

'And weapons too,' added Teodora.

'He is much respected in the city,' continued Geronimo, earnestly. 'He has money and influence, and is even close to the Doge. And . . .' he paused for effect, 'he's a widower. NO WIFE! You see, it was impossible to resist. I may never get such a chance again – nor might Elisabetta. You would have called me mad, to give up the opportunity. We made a deal. I would go with Rodriguez and undertake some transactions for Pagliarin. He would marry Elisabetta and be guardian to the family while I'm away. Teodora, my sweet little mare,' Geronimo had soothed her, 'I have trained my boys well. Carlo is nearly as good as I am, and Giuseppe – what a gift he has been blessed with, our Giuseppe! He will be a master one day. As for you, my dear wife – where would I be without you? The whole of Venice knows of your jewellery designs. Cardinal Trovaso only commissioned me to make his ring because you would design it. It's for you and your talent that they come to my workshop. Why, you hardly need me at all, and with Signor Pagliarin's influence and standing in the city, I know I leave you in good hands.'

'Leave us under the control of a man like Pagliarin? Call that good hands?' Teodora turned a passionate face to him and entwined his fingers in hers, as if she could bind him to her. 'Let me tell you, Signor Veroneo, my dearest husband, I have very bad feelings about this. I beseech you to think again.' She examined all the lines and contours of his face like a cartographer studying a map, and saw he was adamant. 'Can nothing change your mind?' she had asked.

'I know this is too swift for you to fully comprehend, but believe me, Teodora, this is divine providence – God's will. *Carpe diem! Carpe diem!* Seize the day. I must follow my destiny.'

'Destiny rubbish,' exclaimed Teodora, who was always a very down-to-earth woman. 'You are a man of free will. It's up to you to make your choice. Don't bring destiny into it.'

'No, it was destiny, I tell you. He was right there, drinking in the tavern. We saw him home.'

'You mean he was drunk!' Teodora had stopped raging and,

for a brief while kept quiet, hoping that a drunken pledge would mean nothing by the morning. This was typical of her husband. He was so impetuous, generous, trusting and foolhardy. He never believed the worst of people – only the best. How many times had he been tricked into parting with his money? How many times had he allowed their designs and ideas to be stolen, because he blabbed too much in the taverns? Yet he never learned. And now, someone had talked him into parting with his own daughter just because he wanted to go and see the world. All she could hope was that all would be forgotten by the light of the following morning.

But the next day, a messenger had called round asking Geronimo to present Elisabetta at the house of Bernardo Pagliarin.

He liked her. Of course he liked her. She was beautiful, with a neat comely figure, apricot skin, rich dark auburn tresses and the same blue-green eyes of her father, set like aquamarines in her sweet, madonna-like face. Elisabetta had no say – what girl ever did? Dutifully, she had accompanied her father to Pagliarin's villa on the Rialto, the Villa Maravege, her anxiety mingled with curiosity, but when she saw the rich man's home, she was awestruck.

It was a three-storey house with courtyards and orchards, arches and pillars, cool marble floors and balconies overlooking the Grand Canal, furnished with carved ebony furniture, Persian carpets, gold and silver-wrought tableware and sumptuous wall hangings. Would she be mistress of all this, and a veritable team of servants too? A few days later, she accepted his token of a gold-set diamond and ruby encrusted ring, with matching pendant. Teodora found them rather crude and tasteless.

So Elisabetta was married to Bernardo Pagliarin and Geronimo prepared to sail away to the east.

'Don't be angry, dear Teodora, *cara mia*, my sweetheart. I'll make a fortune.' He had drawn her into a reassuring embrace. 'It's my chance to make money, get rich. Then we can get away from Rio San Lorenzo, move from this canal, this stinking fondamente, to a healthier district nearer the Grand Canal. Imagine it! And you can have all the dresses you want, and we can have our own gondola – a proper one – with velvet-lined seats and our own gondolier who will sing love songs to us on a summer's night. And while I'm away, Signor Pagliarin will guard over you. With such a man of wealth and influence, what more can you ask? I have promised to take messages and goods on his behalf to the Great Moghul, Jehangir. Jehangir.' He repeated the name as though just the magic of the sound could transport him to India, to the fabulous court of the Moghul emperor who was titled the Conqueror of the World.

No sooner had Geronimo Veroneo sailed off for Hindustan,

than Bernardo Pagliarin rapidly asserted his command over the whole family.

Teodora pauses and glances over her shoulder to see if her younger children are keeping up. Sofia and Gabriella, arm in arm, heads together, are whispering and laughing, their cheeks flushed and eyes dancing with secrets and shared confidences. How innocent they are. She lifts her black veil and they catch their mother's impatient eye, throw back their heads and laugh out loud as she urges them to hurry. And where's Filippo?

The bells of Santa Maria Formosa are already ringing out for mass and, as they round the corner into the crowded square, they glimpse Elisabetta and Bernardo and their tribe of children, waiting for them outside the church. Four of them are theirs, and the three older ones, two boys and a girl, are Bernardo's from his first wife. The step-children stand by, sullenly, determined to be apart.

Elisabetta looks impatient, and imperiously waves her gloved hand at her mother and sisters. 'Come on. We've been hanging around for you like a pack of vagabonds.' She frowns.

'Sorry, my dear,' Teodora apologises to her eldest daughter, embracing her with a kiss. 'Sorry to have kept you waiting, Signor Pagliarin.' Her son-in-law, unsmiling, takes her hand and puts it to his lips. 'We took rather longer preparing ourselves this morning. Giuseppe is not feeling too well. He and Carlo have stayed home.'

'Don't concern yourself, Signora,' he coldly reassures her as he kisses her gloved knuckles. Every time he performs that simple mundane courtesy, she shudders. There's something about him . . .

But Elisabetta interrupts tersely, 'You know how slow my sisters are, Mama. You should have got them up earlier, and I suppose Filippo's running wild again, as usual.'

Teodora reddens and opens her mouth to scold her daughter for her impertinence, but seeing Bernardo Pagliarin's indifferent expression, changes her mind, and says nothing.

Gabriella and Sofia look at each other amazed. Was that really Elisabetta? Talking so rudely to Mama? Their eyes shift accusingly to Bernardo Pagliarin. Will he tolerate this?

Tolerate it? He positively indulges it. He puts his arm around Elisabetta's shoulders and begs her not to get so perturbed. 'Don't frown so, my little pussycat, otherwise the lines will become permanently engraved on your exquisite marble forehead.' And she leans into him and purrs.

Just then, Filippo comes tearing out into the piazza, his cap at a tilt, his shoes and stockings muddy and scratched, his face shining with excitement. He rushes up to show them something caged in his hands. 'Look what I found!' he cries.

'What, what?' Elisabetta's tribe cluster round squealing. Gabriella and Sofia too nudge and jostle, crying, 'Show us, Pippo, show us! What have you found, little brother?' Despite themselves, the sullen step-children, too, can't help wanting to see and try to shuffle forward imperceptibly. Even Elisabetta leans forward. When they are all bending over close, Filippo's fingers fly open and there sits a beady-eyed crab, its claws waving with outrage at its sweaty incarceration. He swoops it towards them, and the children stumble back, screaming. Then he tosses it mischievously to Elisabetta, shouting, 'Here! Catch!'

Elisabetta screams, 'No!' but the crab sails through the air and, because she makes no effort to catch it, it lands on her velvet bosom. For a moment, she lashes out in a frenzy, losing all dignity, until Filippo takes pity and sweeps it away.

'You idiot!' Elisabetta slaps her young brother across the face.

'Ow, Betta,' protests Filippo. 'I didn't mean to . . . that hurt!' And it did. Sofia notices his eyes fill with tears. The step-children snigger.

'Of course it didn't, you cry-baby,' retorts Elisabetta stiffly. 'I hardly touched you.'

The younger sisters reach out hands to comfort their little brother, but he pulls away furiously and dashes off.

'Filippo!' Teodora cries after him, but he turns a corner and is gone.

Sofia and Gabriella grab each other's hands and hurry on into the church. 'What is it with Betta? I don't like her any more,' hisses Sofia.

'She's a bully,' mutters Gabriella furiously.

'She always was,' agrees Sofia. 'I pity her children.'

'We'd better say a special prayer for her.'

'We'll pray to Santa Anna and Santa Monica.'

'If she goes on this way she'll go to purgatory.'

'Mama,' says Elisabetta, 'we think Filippo is becoming like a little heathen. He needs some discipline. He's thoroughly spoilt. Carlo isn't severe enough with him. We think he should live with us, don't we, Signor Pagliarin?'

'It does seem like a good proposition,' murmurs her husband, taking her arm.

'He needs a father's strong hand. You're all too soft with him – he's just a spoilt brat. Bernardo and I would soon make a man of him.'

Teodora is silent as they walk up to the great doorway of Santa Maria Formosa. She wonders why they would want to take a 'little heathen' into their household. Surely not out of the goodness of their hearts?

'Signor Pagliarin and I have been talking,' Elisabetta

continues. 'We also think it's high time Sofia and Gabriella are married, don't we, Signor Pagliarin?'

'We do indeed, my little pigeon, and we would like to discuss all these matters together with you, Signora Veroneo, in a day or two, when it is convenient. I have one or two proposals to put to you.' Bernardo Pagliarin stands aside, and with a sweeping bow ushers Teodora into the church.

Chapter Two

❖

To the island

Filippo ran and ran. His throat was choked, his eyes were blurry. It wasn't the pain of the slap that made him cry, but the humiliation. 'I hate Betta, I hate Betta, I hate Bernardo, I hate Betta and Bernardo. I hate Mama, I hate everybody.'

He plunged into the shadowy maze of canals and alleys, running up and down steps of little bridges, bursting into busy sun-filled squares and marketplaces, weaving in and out of geese and mules, traders and ragamuffins, troupes of entertainers and flocks of nuns. Then he disappeared again into further sunless lanes, criss-crossed overhead, roof to roof, with washing and flower pots, twittering bird cages and women calling to each other. He muttered, 'I hate everyone. I'll run away to sea, just like Papa. I'll go to Egypt, Arabia and Hindustan, and never come back. I might go on to China. Then they'll be sorry.'

He reached the Rialto bridge which arched over the Grand Canal, and stopped in the middle. A brisk wind struck his cheeks and made him clutch his collar close round his throat. It chilled his anger. He looked down at the reflections fragmenting, like his thoughts, on the choppy water.

Something had changed in the family. Not today, not yesterday. He wasn't sure when, but something had changed. A sense of secrecy hung in the house. Mama would abruptly stop talking to Carlo when Filippo entered the room. His sisters had become like twins, preferring their own company, and had even made up their own language that no one else understood. Elisabetta, who once had been as much a mother to him as Teodora, had become arrogant and proud, and hardly came to see them any more. Carlo was just so busy all the time, he hardly had time for him. Filippo felt left out.

Only Giuseppe was the same: gentle, distant, disconnected; almost as though, since his last terrible fever, he was floating above the affairs of the world like an angel. If Filippo grumbled to him about anything, he would just turn his soft tranquil eyes on him and murmur, 'It's just the way things are in the world, little brother. It's all a part of the tapestry of life.'

Yet, it was the name Pagliarin that he would catch before a conversation stopped, the name that brought a frown to the brow. Recently, Bernardo Pagliarin had been visiting the house more frequently, interfering in their affairs, questioning their finances. It was him that Teodora and Carlo would be discussing in low voices, with anxious expressions.

Below him on the whipped-up water, pontoons of gondolas reared and tossed like wild horses longing to break free of their tethers. The sails of barges billowed and flapped as boatmen heaved on their long oars and zigzagged their way across the busy thoroughfare.

Filippo headed for the fish market where he hoped to find his best friend Andreas and, as he ran, he concocted plans in his head. I've had enough of home. I'm going to ask Andreas if I can live with him. I'd rather be a fisherman. Then I won't be bossed around by Carlo and Mama, and I won't be slapped by Betta and her stupid husband, and jeered at by their idiot brats.

He reached the square. His eyes scoured the market place for Andreas among the hundreds of baskets and crates wriggling with eels and squid, crawling with crabs, prawns, sea-spiders, and glistening with silvery, slithery, scaly fish. Not seeing him, he turned and walked across to the water's edge and stared along the sweeping curve of the Grand Canal, hoping to spot their boat with its little sail, which sometimes looked no bigger than a man's shirt flapping on a washing line. Gulls wheeled, screeching over the fish market like spirits in purgatory and Filippo screeched with them. 'Ayeii Ayeii! Ayeii! Ayeii!'

'Pippo! Hey Pippo!' Andreas had been ashore all the time and now spotted him.

Filippo wiped his running nose across his sleeve, and dashed the tears from his eyes before turning with a mocking laugh. 'Hi there, you fish-stinking moron. Where were you? How yer doing?'

Andreas ran towards him, leaping over crates and baskets to reach him. Though bare-footed and bare-armed, this Greek boy, with his pale grey eyes and his tough, black-as-an-African body, weathered by wind and salt, hardly ever seemed to feel the cold. They flung arms about each other as if it were two years rather than two days since they had seen each other.

'Good that you came, *mio amico*! You OK? What's with the eye, man?'

'I bumped into something,' muttered Filippo, furious that his bruise was so visible, and unwilling to say it was his sister who caused it. 'Here, fight me, fight me!' Filippo grabbed two sticks from among the crates and tossed one to Andreas. '*En garde!*' he shouted, and they leapt around thrusting and striking their make-believe swords together.

'Stop, stop! I've got to go home,' gasped Andreas. 'Grandma's waiting for her vegetables. Know what? Papa's going on another long fishing trip. We may even get to Crete!'

'*We?*' echoed Filippo.

'Yes! Isn't it great? He's taking me – my first proper trip. I've never been further than Spalato before. We'll be away days and days, maybe weeks.'

'Oh!' Filippo felt bereft. Another change. Now even his best friend was abandoning him. He felt his throat tighten with envy and despair. Andreas would be out on the open sea exploring the world, while he was cooped up in the workshop, day in, day out, bending over precious stones till his eyes ached. He was forever polishing, grading and sorting jewels for scabbards, for the hilts of swords and daggers, for belts, brooches, pendants, necklaces, bracelets, snuff boxes – and even clothes. Wealthy dukes and merchants and their ladies liked to have jewel-encrusted jackets and waistcoats, bodices and skirts. I'm just their slave, he often thought bitterly. Filippo, fetch this, Filippo, fetch that. He wasn't being fair, he knew that. They all worked hard in his family. But it was worse for him, he thought, because they loved it and he hated it. He'd rather work hard as Andreas did, fishing out in the lagoon.

'Wish I could go with you,' Filippo muttered.

'Wanna come?' Andreas panted, flinging down his stick.

Wanna come? How cheerfully he said it. How easy it sounded.

'There'll be room in the boat. I'm sure of it. We're going in the *Galatea*. This was their two-masted fishing boat. 'You and me are the same size as one of my brothers. Only Pedro and Vasilis are going. Let's ask Papa.'

Stefano Georgilis was a short but mighty broad-backed man, with muscles like twisted rope, and a face as lined and rugged as an old tree. His jet-black hair, spangled with silver, flowed to his shoulders, and his thick dark eyebrows had a life of their own, rising, falling and twitching over his deep-set black eyes. He straightened up from his fish crates as the boys rushed over to him, with Andreas shouting, 'Hey Papa, Filippo would like to come on our trip with us. Can he?'

Stefano put his hands on his hips and jerked his head derisively. 'You some kind of gentleman of leisure now, eh?' he bellowed at Filippo. 'Haven't you any work to do? What would you do on my boat, eh? Sit in the stern and look at the dolphins? You think I'm a gondolier? Do you know how to rig sails, read the currents, navigate by the stars and toss the nets, eh?' With every 'eh?' he lifted his shoulders and raised his bushy black eyebrows. 'What you been up to then?' He had noticed the bruise round Filippo's eye. 'Fighting again?'

'He bumped into something,' said Andreas.

'Eh!' Stefano jerked his chin forward as though to say, pull the other one. 'Come on you,' he tugged Filippo's ear affectionately. 'As you've time on your hands, you and Andreas take this stuff home to the island, but come straight back again, do you hear? And maybe I give you some cuttlefish for your mama, eh?' He knew Teodora needed their black ink, which she squeezed out of their bodies and used for her drawings and designs.

Lugging a crate of fish and some bundles of vegetables, the two boys headed for the water. It was just a battered little flat-bottomed boat, squashed in among larger sailing boats and barges which had been bringing their produce into the market. The boys unlooped the rope which tethered the boat to a pole, and jumped in. Taking an oar each, they pushed and prodded their way out and rowed towards the open lagoon, which stretched away across the expanse to where sea met sky.

Andreas had been rowing across the lagoon since he was seven years old. Now that he was twelve, his arms were muscular and his shoulders broad. He proudly boasted that he could do the Rialto to the island in half an hour, that's if he didn't dawdle to watch the ships coming in from the Adriatic.

Flurries of sea breezes whipped up the green waves, sculpting them into minuscule mountain ranges with ridges and contours. In the distance, huge sailing ships with fluttering flags, their masts taller than any tree he had ever seen, flapped their white sails while their decks and yard arms crawled with the little figures of sailors. Filippo watched them pass, silent as dream birds, beyond the green waters of the lagoon into the grey-blue seas of the Adriatic. One day, he vowed to himself, one day . . . I'll go to sea and see the world, and I'll come back a millionaire – just like Marco Polo! *Il Milione*! That's me.

A tall-masted ship was, at that moment, dropping anchor,

waiting till there was a place to dock at the Piazza San Marco. It was a sailing ship from Alexandria; its crew were African, Arabian, English and Spanish.

'There's the *Fidelis* back again!' yelled Andreas.

'Let's go closer! Let's ask!' cried Filippo urgently.

Andreas was used to his friend insisting, 'Let's ask!' He knew why Filippo was so keen to row to the ship. He was always hanging round the piazza watching the ships come in, asking all and sundry for news of his father. It had become an obsession, and he was used to him rushing up to any recently arrived travellers disembarking on the quayside, to ask over and over again, 'Has anyone come from Hindustan? Does anyone know of the jeweller, Geronimo Veroneo? Can anyone say if he is alive or dead?' So Andreas obediently changed course, and the boys pulled hard on their oars, and approached the huge painted prow carved like a gaudy golden-haired mermaid, from whose neck churned out a great clanking chain with an anchor on the end.

The boat sat low in the water, heavy with cargo. The deck was milling with all kinds of people: Venetians returning home, Syrian merchants, French envoys, English, Dutch, Jewish and Portuguese dealers, traders, travellers, soldiers, and merchants of every race and colour. They leaned over the side of the ship scanning the faces of boatmen, who had rowed out from the islands, calling out their prices to take anyone who was keen to get to dry land as quickly as possible. More and more craft came scuttling towards them, and soon Andreas and Filippo were caught up among the yelling, touting locals, whose jostling boats tipped and bucked in the wash.

On deck, an Arab and a European shouted and flicked whips as they herded a consignment of African slaves. They were being made ready for ferrying to the slave market near Piazza San Marco. Chained and manacled together, they clustered nervously on the deck, not daring to do more than shuffle their stiffened limbs in case the overseer's whip should crack across their backs. Only their eyes were alive, blinking into the bright noon sun and staring across the lagoon with awe at the city they had come to. It was a miraculous city of marble, brick and stone, of statues and fountains, of glittering palaces and giant churches which, defying their weight and solidity, rose out of the water.

'Oi!' Filippo cupped his hand to his mouth and yelled up. 'Anyone heard news of Geronimo Veroneo, the jeweller, last heard of in Hindustan at the court of the Emperor Jehangir?' He repeated his call again and again till he was hoarse, rowing round the ship to make sure he was heard. At last someone yelled down, 'Never 'eard of him! Now get lost!'

As the boys rowed away, heading for the island, a single

figure, standing aside from the babbling passengers, limped casually across the deck from the far side and shaded his eyes at the departing little boat. It was hard to tell his race or nationality; he was burned black by the sun, yet his eyes were light, and he wore leather boots in the European manner beneath long oriental robes. For some minutes he watched, until the boys and their boat were just a speck. Then, with an unconscious shrug, he turned away to hail one of the boatmen. Jerking and bumping, they lowered him by basket into a barge, with just a cloth bundle strapped across his back, and soon he was being ferried across the lagoon towards Venice.

It was twelve years since he'd been here. He no longer knew anyone in the city – but he had a name of one of its inhabitants.

Chapter Three

❖

Encounters and confessions

'Why weren't you at mass?' It was Carlo who confronted him, when Filippo crept back into the house hoping not to be noticed just yet.

'Mama was running short of ink, so I went to the fish market to see if there was any leftover cuttlefish,' Filippo explained inventively, plonking down the bundle Stefano had given him when he and Andreas returned from the island. But he couldn't look his brother in the eye.

'Hmm.'

Filippo, stinking of fish and streaked up to the elbows with black mud from the island, could tell that Carlo didn't believe that's all he'd done. He saw the dark round bruise on his face where Elisabetta's ring had caught him when she slapped him.

'Have you been fighting again?'

'No, I have not,' protested Filippo. 'I just . . .' Hating to admit it was Elisabetta, his inventiveness failed him. 'I just . . . bumped into something.'

'Hmm,' said Carlo, but didn't pursue it. 'Just as well you're back. I can make use of you. Mama and the girls have gone to the Pagliarins' after mass, but Giuseppe's not feeling good again: his fever has returned. I've sent him to bed. You can finish off his job. I need to get it done today. Take off your boots and come to the workshop. I'll show you.'

Filippo went to the kitchen where Rosa, the cook, grumbled at him for bringing so much muck into the house. Giorgio, the kitchen boy, smirked and held his nose. Filippo put up a silent fist to him. Was there no one who wouldn't pick on him, he thought, self-pityingly, as he kicked off his boots and snatched a piece of bread from the baking tray.

'Get away with you!' scolded Rosa.

Ducking a swipe from her, Filippo dashed out of the kitchen and down the passage.

On his way to the workshop, he passed the parlour. It had been some years now since he had seen his father. Growing up had been a busy affair. Once he was old enough to play a part in the household, snatching time to go out with his friends, he had almost forgotten his infant encounters with Geronimo. But now, he had seen him three times in a month. He was about to mount the stone steps up to the workshop, when he glanced through the parlour door. There he was again, in his chair, just sitting there, looking at him.

Filippo leaned weakly into the wall, staring. The clock ticked. His thudding heart seemed to stifle his ears and choke his throat, but still he stared. His father seemed as yellow as his chair; so transparent, that he could see through him to the weave of the linen. Only his eyes still swam with the green of the lagoon.

'Pippo, is that you?' rasped his brother's voice from above, dry with fever.

Briefly Filippo blinked upwards to Giuseppe's room at the top of the next flight of steps. When he looked back to the parlour, the chair was empty. His father had vanished.

Filippo dashed up two at a time to his brother's room. Giuseppe was lying very still, his face flushed and his eyes closed. As he breathed, he seemed to rattle like dried flowers.

'Beppe?' Filippo whispered. 'Are you OK?' Suddenly, he forgot all his resentments about being bossed about by his elders, and was full of concern. If he feared Carlo's authority as oldest brother, he adored and worshipped Giuseppe.

Giuseppe's eyes opened ceilingwards. 'Mary Mother of God, you stink like a fishwife.' He tried to turn his head, but it hurt. He shut his eyes again. 'Close the blind,' he muttered. 'Too much light. My eyes hurt.'

'But Beppe, it is closed,' said Filippo, looking at the slatted blind, with the pale brown canvas flapping loosely in between.

'Come on!' called Carlo, from the workshop beyond. 'Don't bother Giuseppe. Let him sleep. Sleep is the best physician.'

'Beppe?' Filippo knelt by his brother and whispered in his ear. 'Have you ever seen Papa?'

'Of course I have. Before you were born,' he muttered.

'No, I mean after he left.'

'What do you mean? Dreams? Yes ... sometimes ... I dream ...' His voice trailed away as he sank into a restless, groaning sleep.

Quietly, Filippo left his sick brother and hurried on to the workshop.

'About time, slow coach,' chided Carlo. Then without stopping what he was doing he said, 'You didn't get into another fight with Matteo and Federigo, did you?' They were Elisabetta's step-sons.

'Nope. The idiots,' snarled Filippo.

'They're bigger than you. Don't chance your luck,' advised Carlo.

'They're mean. I hate them. Anyway, they're usually too busy fighting each other to go for me. I don't know how Betta can bear being a mother to them.'

Carlo grunted, and though he didn't say anything, Filippo knew he felt the same.

'Carlo, I want to get a sword,' declared Filippo.

'Absolutely not. Mama forbids it.'

'But why? Matteo and Federigo have swords.'

'They're much older than you, and taller. You'd be tripping over it, you little shrimp. You know that, now shut up and get on with your work.'

'Will you at least teach me, then? Teach me to sword-fight?'

'No. You're not old enough.'

'But I need to be able to defend myself. I had to run for my life the other day, through the ghetto, when I made that delivery for you.'

'You'll have to make do with your fists. Next year, maybe. Now get on with your work, I want this gold hammered very thin.'

Filippo obeyed with a sigh and the two brothers bent over their tasks, each concentrating in silence. Filippo wanted to ask Carlo if he had ever seen Papa since he left, but he changed his mind. It sounded stupid, and he didn't want to be laughed at.

As he worked, his mind drifted to Andreas's island. How he loved it there, loved that muddy black shore. They would go beachcombing for objects washed up in the tide, collecting pebbles and shells and old moulded glass, which in Filippo's opinion were far more beautiful than the rubies, diamonds and pearls so treasured by everyone.

There were voices down below.

'They're back,' Filippo looked up stiffly. Three hours had passed, and the sun was dropping lower and lower. It would soon be time to light the lamps.

Feet pounded up stairs. Gabriella burst into the workshop. 'We're back!' she gasped.

'We heard you,' replied Carlo dryly. Then he saw her face. 'What's up Gabri?'

'Mama wants you downstairs.' She looked about to cry and rushed off.

Carlo rubbed his hands on his work apron before taking it off. 'You carry on, Pippo.'

Filippo carried on till it was too dark to work any further, then he went back to Giuseppe's room. Giuseppe was lying frighteningly still in the darkness, but he opened large gleaming eyes when Filippo crept in.

'Beppe,' he whispered, kneeling by the bed. 'Will you teach me how to sword-fight? I mean properly, all the moves and their names and everything. I want to learn.'

Giuseppe smiled. 'You're a bit young for a sword, Pippo.'

'I know, I know, and I'm not asking for a sword yet. I'm asking if you'll teach me how to fight, when you're better, of course, so that when I'm ready for a sword, I'll know how to use it. Please, Beppe. Say yes.'

Giuseppe groaned, and pressed the temples of his forehead with both hands.

'Oh Beppe, I'm sorry! Are you feeling so bad?' Filippo reached forward and touched his brother's brow. 'Jesu Maria!' he exclaimed with alarm. 'You're like a furnace. I'll fetch Mama.'

'No, no! Don't do that. Just get me a drink, my mouth's on fire.'

Filippo had taken up the water jug, when Sofia burst in. He turned jerkily, slurping water over the rim of the jug. 'Look what you made me do, Sofia!' he muttered with annoyance. 'What's up, anyway?' Sofia too was crying.

She flung herself down beside Giuseppe, burying her head in the sheet.

'What's up, Sofi?' gasped Filippo, staring from his weeping sister to his feverish brother, not knowing who to attend to first.

Giuseppe raised himself up on one elbow, grimacing with the effort.

'Sofietta? What's happened? What is it?' he asked, reaching out a hand to stroke her hair.

'Bernardo! He's told Mama he wants me to get married. Gabri too, both of us. He says it's time – and that he knows two families who are interested. He's asked Mama to declare all the family assets so that he can put together a dowry for us both. Oh I don't want to, I don't want to. Neither does Gabri. He can't make us, can he? He's not our father. I never want to leave home. I never want to get married, I'd rather be a nun.' She heaved with sobs.

'No you wouldn't,' muttered Giuseppe, patting her head.

'What's it to do with Bernardo?' hissed Filippo furiously. 'It's not his business.'

'He says Papa left him as guardian, and that if Papa were here, he'd be doing the same thing.'

'Which families has he in mind?' asked Giuseppe quietly.

'That's the worst of it,' wept Sofia, 'the boys are friends of Federigo and Matteo.'

'Those pig-dogs!' shouted Filippo, in disgust.

'Oh, where's Gabri? She's as upset as I am. We don't want to leave home.' And Sofia ran from the room.

Giuseppe flopped back exhausted on his pillow. 'Give me that water, Pippo.' But before Filippo could pour some into a cup, Giuseppe was asleep again. Why didn't Giuseppe get well?

Filippo crept out of the house, once again feeling helpless and excluded from what was going on. Helpless in the face of God, who seemed to do his own thing no matter what, and excluded from the decision-making of his elders, whose behaviour often left him confused.

It had been a strange day. He'd been slapped by Elisabetta, run off without his mother's permission, not gone to Mass, lied to Carlo about looking for cuttlefish, and now Bernardo had upset the whole family with his proposal to marry off Sofia and Gabriella. Above all, there was the matter of his father.

He hadn't planned to go as far as the church of Santa Maria Formosa, but somehow he drifted there. He pushed open the doors and stepped into the echoing gloom. The smell of incense hung heavily in the air. Facing the main altar, he dropped to one knee and crossed himself rapidly, then turned to the side aisle where the confessional boxes were positioned against the south wall. He had timed it just right, for suddenly, the curtain of one of the boxes was swept aside and a supplicant shuffled away.

Filippo took his place kneeling on the cushion. Crossing himself behind the curtain, he pressed his mouth to the grille.

'Good day to you, Father,' said Filippo politely.

'Is that you, Pippo?'

'It is, Father.'

'Why didn't you come this morning with your family? You caused your mother a lot of pain.'

'Yes, well . . .' Filippo muttered uncomfortably.

'You want to confess to me?'

'Yes, Father.' He sniffed loudly. 'Forgive me, Father, for I have sinned,' said Filippo, twisting his cap in his hands.

'God will forgive you if you open your heart and truly repent. What sin have you committed?'

'I hate Elisabetta.'

'You HATE your sister?' sighed the priest. 'Hate is a dark sin. I think you should rephrase that. Perhaps she annoys you.'

'She's so bossy, and she slapped me today.'

'Hmmm . . .' The priest smiled. He knew all about it, because Elisabetta had earlier confessed to slapping her little brother.

'What did you do to annoy her?'

'It was only a little crab – a baby, Father – yet she screamed as if I'd thrown a viper at her.'

'You threw it at her?'

'Well, it was only a joke. She didn't need to slap me.'

'What may be a joke to a twelve year old, may not be so for a young woman who treasures her dignity. You must promise to apologise to her.'

'Must I, Father? Can't I just apologise to God and say a few Hail Marys?'

'Indeed you cannot. You haven't offended the Good Lord because you threw a crab, you've offended him because you *knew* when you threw the crab that it would upset your sister. I'll ask you to say three Hail Marys and two Our Fathers for your bad intention, but you must promise to apologise to her, then come back next week and tell me. Now, what else have you done?'

'I sat in Papa's chair.'

'Oh! Is that not allowed?'

'No.'

'Well, say another three Hail Marys and one Our Father for disobedience.'

'Is that it?'

'Yes, Father.'

'*In nomine Patris et Filii et Spiritus Sancti*, I absolve you of your sin.'

'Except . . . Father . . .'

The old priest sighed. He was removing his stole but paused. 'Yes?'

'I suppose it doesn't make any difference if Papa *asked* me to sit in his chair?'

'He asked you?' The priest looked startled. 'Filippo?' He tugged back the curtain. But the confessional box was empty, and he just saw the boy's shadow flitting through the doorway and out into the fading light.

Chapter Four

❖

Unwelcome news for Bernardo

Bernardo Pagliarin sat brooding in his favourite walnut Bologna leather chair in the arched veranda overlooking the Grand Canal.

The sun was hotter now, and he was loosely dressed in a fine silk robe, girdled with a twisted tassel. He watched the reflections of water wavering on the pillars, and casting green shadows in the alcoves of the arches, which would protect him from the full glare of summer when it came.

His pale, peculiarly slender fingers draped over the carved armrests. The index finger of his right hand moved obsessively over the wooden curve of the arm, which had been chiselled like the body of a bird; it caressed the rippled feathers, and his manicured nail probed into its cuts and ridges, which tapered intricately down to an eagle's head.

Although his public image was that of a strutting, self-important kind of man, who held his chin too high and looked down his thin nose, in the privacy of his chambers, he could seem to hunch over to half his size and look strangely like a rat, especially when he was mulling over a problem. It was the way his whole rather pallid face seemed to be drawn by some centrifugal force; dragging down his brow, narrowing his eyes, sucking all his being into the thin line of his nibbling mouth as he chewed the inside of his cheek. His thoughts gnawed at him, gnawed his guts with avarice and ambition, gnawed with fury over the possibility that one of his plans could be thwarted.

He had just received a foreigner straight off a ship, a cringing man with a limp who looked like a vagabond and said his name was Rodriguez, bringing news from Hindustan. The fellow told him they'd met once, but Pagliarin didn't remember – and didn't believe him. He was always being plagued by people trying to curry favours with him, or remind him of some invented favour owed. Everything about the man was indeterminate. His race and creed were unclear, his eyes were neither blue nor brown, his hair was neither brown nor black, but something darkish, reddish. He spoke Italian with a Portuguese accent, French with a Spanish lilt, and he knew only a smattering of Venetian words. Even his clothes were a mixture. A North African burnoose, over thick, broadcloth breeches and footwear which was neither boots nor sandals, but just a foot covering of sacking. And he had an indefinable smell about him, spicy yet sweet, which somehow added to his lack of substance. No sooner did Bernardo decide the man was a Turk or a Persian than he changed his opinion and thought he was a European: Dutch, German or French. He changed his mind again and thought he could be a Slav or a Kurd – there was something about his high cheekbones and his curving nose. Perhaps he was Semitic, an Arab or a Jew. But finally, he concluded that his visitor was most likely a mixture of several races and that he was definitely not a Christian. Instinctively, Bernardo feared him.

It had taken the man, Rodriguez, many months to arrive, what with one thing and another, and the news he brought displeased Bernardo greatly. After questioning him, Bernardo paid him off brusquely, with a warning to say nothing to anyone – he didn't want the man's news to become well-known – and ordered him to leave Venice within twenty-four hours.

As soon as the fellow had been let out of the back door, Bernardo tugged a satin bell-cord three times, and instantly, his secretary appeared. 'I want that man followed. Watch who he speaks to, and make sure he leaves Venice and,' he added softly, 'I don't care how. Oh, and send a boy to Signor Martinelli, requesting he come and see me urgently. Now!'

So Bernardo Pagliarin sat in his chair. He chewed the inside of his cheek obsessively. His brain seethed with questions. Why hadn't he already known this information? After all, he had spies everywhere, even abroad, to protect his interests. He prided himself on knowing most things. 'Knowledge is power' was Bernardo's motto. He always wanted to know what his rivals were up to, whether little or big. What were his neighbours doing? Why did the Cavalli family suddenly have money to buy a new villa? To whom was the Manucci family going to betroth their daughter? How high a dowry was part of the transaction? How did Pedro Del Conte get promoted to being a Cardinal? What deal had Signor Bossi made with a French merchant in Cairo? He had a spy here, a spy there. Some were small fry, such as a gondolier or a sailor, a family maid or a kitchen boy, like Giorgio, in the Veroneo household. Others had more status, like a prince's private secretary, a ship's captain, a clerk in the government, or even someone in the establishment of the Doge. He hired burglars when he wished to obtain private documents or personal letters and, from time to time, an assassin to eliminate an enemy.

So how could he not have known about something so central to his own interests? And how disturbing that he should be told by someone not in his employ, of no reputation, who claimed to be a merchant of sorts; an intermediary – a middleman. Pagliarin had snorted sceptically. The whole story could be a pack of lies just to get money. The man was definitely not to be trusted. He knew that sort – the kind who liked to run with the fox and hunt with the hounds. However, this news, if it was true, came at a bad time. His business was in trouble.

The man called Rodriguez left the household of Signor Pagliarin, pulling his travel-worn robes around him, preferring to walk the alleyways rather than take a gondola. Before he turned the first corner, he knew he was being followed, but for a while, he limped slowly and awkwardly, giving anyone who cared to notice the impression of being painfully handicapped.

This allowed Pagliarin's man to follow him with ease – almost boredom – up and down lanes, over bridges, across market piazzas and round in circles again.

Every now and then, Rodriguez stopped, as if he were lost. He looked around in a bewildered sort of way, studied the position of the sun, and even asked for directions. But really, he was checking his pursuer and formulating a plan, for although he gave the appearance of being a stranger, he knew Venice backwards. He had walked it many times in the past and, with his extraordinary memory, recalled every calle, fondamente, piazza, marketplace and the entire canal system. He knew the city as well as any Venetian. That was why he was so good at his job. Pagliarin didn't know that he had sent an amateur to trail a professional.

Rodriguez, along with all his other skills as a merchant, a seaman, an envoy and a freelance messenger, was also a spy. He hated the word, and preferred being called an agent. A hired assassin, a gun-runner, a slaver and a mercenary militia man, he was willing to undertake most tasks for a fee. He had been away – as far as China – for some years, trading, bartering, acting as a go-between. He came back to Hindustan and joined the court of Jehangir as an adviser. That was when he heard about his old friend, Geronimo Veroneo, and when he heard the other rumours too.

Rodriguez entered the Campo San Polo. Here there was a confusion of alleyways, steps and fondamentes all leading in different directions. He limped his way along the Calle Cavalli, over a crooked bridge, under the portico and, as neatly as a thread into the eye of a needle, slid into the Calle Stretta, the thinnest of alleyways. With sudden speed, he ran to the end of it, turned right and right again, then backtracked till he reached another bridge and, with unexpected agility, leapt down the steps on to a fondamente, and continued at a great pace until he reached the arch of the Del Angelo bridge and merged into its shadow. He stopped again, and listened.

His trained ear knew the difference between the footsteps of ordinary passers-by, and those of someone looking with an urgency bordering on panic. He leaned back, removing his reflection from the water. Above him, he heard an intake of breath and a spit of frustration. Pagliarin's spy had lost his man. The penalty would be severe. He ran this way, then that. His footsteps receded, returned, and finally receded for good.

Rodriguez slipped off his hooded travelling cloak, and stuffed it into his pack. He pulled out a wig and a cap, donned a pair of leather boots and, with a few rapid adjustments, was dressed now in Venetian garb. He stepped casually into the open, a different man with a different name, walking briskly, almost limp-free, and disappeared into a maze of alleys.

Teodora had been given a week's notice. Bernardo Pagliarin wished to call to discuss the matter of dowries for her daughters.

Of course, Teodora had been assembling a marriage chest for each of her girls ever since they were born. They now each had plenty of good linen, Egyptian cotton, Brussels lace, boxes of silver cutlery, tableware and Venetian glass. They also had a few good pieces of jewellery which Geronimo had set by for them, enough to satisfy most families of their rank and class.

But Bernardo had sneered, 'A drawer full of knives and forks will not suffice. You are not peasants. We don't want anything that will discredit you. I am looking for dowries to the value of ten or fifteen thousand florins.'

'Good heavens, sir,' Teodora had protested. 'We haven't got that sort of money.'

'I can decide that. I want to know all the assets of the business and expect you to display every single precious stone in the workshop when I next come.'

Teodora had swept her hand across her head, a gesture she always made when she was angry. Who could possibly stand up to Bernardo? If only Carlo had succeeded in being acknowledged as head of the household. He had tried when he reached the age of sixteen. He had applied to the authorities to have himself declared their guardian instead of Bernardo. After all, he was now a master jeweller, he had been admitted into the guild, and could support the family. In one respect, Geronimo had been right: Carlo was a fine craftsman, and Giuseppe was learning fast. With their mother's wonderful designs, they were attracting more than enough business to their workshop. But Bernardo had friends and influence. He fought the case and won. How bitterly Teodora remembered Geronimo reassuring her exultantly that Bernardo was close to the Doge.

It was early evening when Bernardo called. Unexpectedly, he brought Elisabetta with him, and also another, a jeweller and diamond dealer from the Rialto district carrying a large leather bag.

'Meet Signor Martinelli,' intoned Bernardo Pagliarin without apology.

Signor Martinelli was a bloated, puffing sort of man with a flabby brow on which clustered drops of perspiration, who simpered when he bowed and held Teodora's hand a little too long when he kissed it.

'Just so we have a clear understanding of what is what,' explained Bernardo with an unfamiliar smile.

Was it for Signor Martinelli's benefit that Bernardo was unusually affable? He had brought Turkish shawls for the girls and a beautiful Russian fur-lined muff for Teodora. He slapped Carlo on the back, tweaked Filippo's ear, and enquired solicitously after Giuseppe. When he heard that the boy was still unwell, he offered to send round his own physician. He didn't notice, or simply ignored, the sullen expressions around him. The way Sofia and Gabriella politely accepted the shawls then escaped on the pretext of attending to Giuseppe, the barely disguised hostility in Carlo's eyes, and Filippo's swift recoil at his touch when he ruffled his hair.

Without being asked, Bernardo took it upon himself to wave Signor Martinelli to a Tuscany chair, while he himself – and a sense of astonished outrage filled the room – casually sat down in Geronimo's chair.

Teodora winced, and turned her back on him to stare

out of the window. Even Elisabetta looked uncomfortable, and moved away as if to distance herself from her husband and sat in a far corner. Filippo looked at Carlo. Would he do or say anything? His brother stood as cold as a statue. The only sign of his anger were his fists, knuckles white, clenched at his side.

Old Forza gave an unhappy sigh, heaved himself to his feet and hobbled off. Rosa brought in a lamp and set it on the table with a thump, making her feelings quite clear, then with a snort of disapproval went out again. As the shadows swung with the flickering flame, Filippo swore he saw a faint figure standing behind Bernardo.

'Papa?' He wasn't sure if he said the word out loud. The figure looked up. He had an impression of green brimming eyes, then Bernardo positioned the lamp and slung his legs up on to the table – the ultimate affront – and the figure vanished.

In a cold voice, Teodora asked Filippo to bring them a carafe of wine from the cellar, while she produced a tray of her best Venetian wine glasses from her cabinet.

Carlo refused a drink, but Bernardo and Signor Martinelli toasted each other, and gulped down glass after glass. Sitting in Geronimo's chair, Bernardo became effusive and talked seamlessly. In a drawling voice, he commented on the more than usual filth in the canals and thoroughfares, how he hoped they'd seen the end of such inclement weather, and how the war with Austria was affecting his business.

Signor Martinelli appeared content to listen and drink, his body seeming to expand even more, until he overlapped the chair in which he was sitting.

An hour passed and, just when a weary Teodora thought that perhaps this would be merely a social call after all, Bernardo paused in mid-flow to sniff some snuff and sneeze, and then asked Teodora kindly to lead them up to her husband's workshop and display all his assets and jewels as he had requested. He directed a nod towards Elisabetta, a prearranged signal it seemed, for rising to her feet she turned to Filippo and murmured encouragingly, 'Let's go find the girls and play cards. They're only going to discuss boring old business,' and she herded him from the room.

Carlo took up a lantern in one hand and his mother's arm with the other. 'Very well,' he said coldly. 'Please follow us upstairs.'

They climbed the dark stone steps and entered the workshop, a long, rectangular room with three tall arched windows which, in contrast to the darkness of the lower rooms, let in as much daylight as was possible, giving maximum light for the draughtsmen at work on drawings and designs.

Now it was dark, Teodora lit some more lamps. Carlo went

to his father's bureau and produced a roll of documents containing sketches, plans and business accounts, which he laid out on the worktop. Then, extracting from his waist a great bunch of keys, he went to a cabinet, unlocked several long drawers and pulled out three trays of jewels which he also set before them.

The affability vanished. Bernardo leaned forward like a bird of prey. He angled the lamp over the account book. While he pored over the figures which Teodora had kept meticulously, Signor Martinelli reached for his large leather bag, and took out a sheet of vellum, a writing box with quill and ink, a pouch of tools for measuring stones, an eyeglass, and a small set of scales with a row of brass weights, which he set on the table. Suddenly, with surprising delicacy for so obese a man, he darted from tray to tray, and picked his way selectively through the array of precious stones, his concentration being punctuated by snorts and grunts.

He's like a bailiff, thought Teodora, feeling humiliated.

He put the eyeglass to his right eye. One by one, he examined each and every gem, then measured and weighed them on his scales. Minutes went by in silence, half an hour, an hour, then at last he spoke. 'Yes, yes.' He straightened with an unenthusiastic sigh. 'There is something of value here, perhaps in the region of thirty thousand florins, but not even half the sum you were looking for, Signor Pagliarin.' He poured himself another glass of wine and downed it almost in one gulp.

'For goodness' sake!' exclaimed Teodora, aghast. 'You are surely not trying to marry my girls off to princes. It is already twice the amount we sent with Elisabetta.'

Bernardo turned a chill eye on her. 'You forget, Signora, that apart from the somewhat pitiful dowry I received for Elisabetta, your husband was to pay the rest in kind, by agreeing to undertake certain transactions for me on his journey to Hindustan, and at the court of the Great Moghul. That was in lieu of the amount of dowry I would normally have accepted. Since we must assume that our esteemed Signor Veroneo is dead, may God rest his soul, I feel entitled to some reimbursement for the extra responsibility I have taken for you and your family all these years. As you know, my plan is to take Filippo into my household, and for my sons, Federigo and Matteo, to be apprenticed to Carlo. They need to learn a trade, and it might as well be this one.'

'I beseech you, sir,' Carlo burst out passionately, 'to reconsider. Filippo is just learning the trade himself. It would be damaging to interrupt him now. Take what we have offered and, please sir, refrain from putting my mother through any more of this humiliation. We can't give you what we haven't got, and why the hurry to marry off my sisters? They are still young. They can wait a year or two, and maybe my father will return.'

'And maybe pigs will fly,' retorted Bernardo callously.

'You . . .!' Carlo's hand had gone to the knife at his belt.

Teodora's hand flashed out and gripped her son's arm, 'No Carlo, no!'

Bernardo's eyes narrowed. He strode up to the angry young man till their foreheads were nearly touching. 'Listen to me, you young dog. Don't you ever threaten me, do you hear?' His voice was menacing. 'I advise you not to become my enemy. I do not tolerate my enemies for long. And you can tell that heathen younger brother of yours to prepare himself to move into my household by the end of the month.'

All this time, Signor Martinelli had been prowling round the workshop as if uninterested in the scene behind him. Suddenly he stopped dead before a portrait on the wall. He stared for so long that Teodora noticed.

It was the painting of Geronimo Veroneo.

He is depicted as a man of his trade, a jeweller. He looks out of the painting and almost seems to smile at them. He has a long narrow face, olive-complexioned, and pale green eyes which are strangely vibrant, as if they too are jewels, which have been cut and fashioned by his tools and set into his sockets. He has a drooping red moustache, and his hair would have been seen to be red too, except that, for the purposes of the portrait, he is wearing a formal dark auburn wig. His expression is full of pride and hope.

He stands a little to the right of centre, so that his workshop is revealed in the background with its trays of gems and the many designs pinned to the walls. His tools are neatly lined up on the work bench before him. But it is to his cupped hands that the eye is drawn again and again. Holding it out for all to see is his most glorious creation – the painter has caught it well – a jewelled pendant.

'It's a portrait of my husband,' said Teodora in a weary voice. 'Don't tell me you want that painting too.'

'Not the painting,' said Signor Martinelli, 'but the jewel.'

Chapter Five

❖

The Ocean of the Moon

The jewel. Ah yes, the jewel at the heart of the pendant, a diamond which the family knew as the Ocean of the Moon. It is thirty millimetres high, forty-two millimetres wide, and only three millimetres at its base. It weighs fifty-five point seven Florentine carats.

It is as pure a diamond as any jeweller could wish to see.

Geronimo's father had brought it back as a raw uncut diamond from Hindustan over thirty years before. It was given to him, he said, by a Moghul prince, because he had saved him from being mauled by a tiger during a royal hunt. The painter had caught its vibrancy and lustre.

By the time Geronimo's father had returned to Venice, he had endured such privations on the journey that he felt too ill and unsteady to attempt to cut such a valuable and peerless diamond himself. But he would never hand it over to any diamond-cutter in Venice. He told no one about it, and kept this knobbly-shaped stone in a pot alongside his glues and varnishes.

He did nothing with it till Geronimo was thirteen, and already proficient at grinding and cutting crystals and minor diamonds. Then his father decided the time had come to teach his son everything he had learned at the Moghul court of the great Emperor Akbar. In those days of plague and sudden death, who knew when the Great Reaper might swipe him off the face of the earth, and all his skills would be lost.

So he prepared Geronimo for the task.

For practice, they first worked on raw crystals. The old man taught Geronimo how to grind, just enough to smooth away the imperfections. He instructed him in the art of facet-cutting, of creating smooth, flat surfaces over the face of the stone. It was an ancient Islamic technique he had learned from Afghan jewellers, whom he met at the court of the Great Moghul in Hindustan. They worked for many months till Geronimo had mastered all the skills his father had taught him.

One day, he told Geronimo to go and look on the shelf containing his varnishes. Pushed to the dusty back, he found an old earthenware pot.

'Show me what's inside,' demanded his father, his voice quavering with excitement.

Geronimo had tipped the pot over into the palm of his hand. Out fell an object wrapped in velvet, about the size of a quail's egg, yet weighty.

Geronimo gave it to his father who held it with as much reverence as if it were the relic of a saint. He unwrapped it.

'A diamond?' Geronimo was awe-struck.

Even an untrained eye would have gasped at the size and the brilliance, but to a jeweller, it made the heart beat even faster. It was as if an unformed moon lay on his palm, and that all it needed was the right eye and the right tool to transform it into a heavenly body.

'This is one of the finest raw diamonds that has ever been in my possession,' he whispered to Geronimo. Even in the court of the Great Moghul, Akbar, where diamonds were in abundance, this stone would be remarkable. 'Alas, I was never going to be the one to cut it. Now it is yours, my son. Guard it, treasure it, be the one to cut it. Remember what I taught you. Create your masterpiece. Use all the skills I passed on to you and, one day, teach the craft to your son, and let him teach it to his sons. Let this be the one thing that the house of Veroneo is known for. But wait till you're sure you have the skills and a design worthy enough for cutting the Ocean of the Moon. It must be your masterpiece. Don't be in a hurry. You are young. Never part with it. Never sell it simply to adorn the neck of some ignorant fine lady, the finger of a bishop, or the shoulders of a prince. This diamond is your insurance against ill fortune. Keep it in the family and only let it be worn by someone who really appreciates its rare and peerless beauty. Promise me, promise me.'

Geronimo promised.

For many months after his father's death, Geronimo did nothing. He felt paralysed, uninspired, unsure of his skills, bereft of his master, teacher and father. He continued to work mechanically, because work had to carry on, but it was almost a year before the creative spark ignited again. It was because he fell in love, and suddenly he knew who was worthy of the diamond.

Burning with passion and inspiration, he started work on it secretly, at night and alone, after his assistants had left. His confidence carried him along with absolute surety, as he took up the tools and applied them to the precious stone. He put into practice everything his father had taught him.

Any ignorant or less skilled gem-cutter might have over-ground the diamond: wasted much material, cut against the grain and failed to appreciate the natural shape of the stone. Painstakingly, Geronimo laboured with his father's voice resonating in his head. It reminded him each step of the way of how he should work, as he cut and smoothed and polished its surfaces, using the ancient skills of the Afghan jewellers.

Geronimo gradually transformed the hard lump till it was both rounded, yet hewn with sharp lines and corners. With delicate strokes, he cut the diamond to emphasise its broad flat surfaces to the front and back. He layered other facets up towards its most interesting natural characteristic – a subtly rounded dome.

Every now and then he straightened, rubbed his back, and held up the stone to the light coming in from the window. Its water was so pure that with each passing hour, as the light changed, different moods entered the diamond – now fiercely white, then soft, like snow at evening. The light echoed from surface to surface, casting within it rosy shadows changing to purple, then dark grey, as the day dimmed.

He was determined that with this diamond, he would create a work of art which would, forever, be proof of his genius. It would be not just his pledge to the woman for whom he was making it, but his calling card, undeniable proof that he was absolutely a master jeweller.

The whole effect must be white, he decided. He surrounded the diamond with white stones: white jade, white sapphire, crystal, moonstones and pearls interspersed, to emphasise its whiteness, with contrasting tiny rubies, amber and emeralds, as if remnants of rainbows were trapped within the white water of the diamond. The diamond would be like the ocean of the moon, yet also the dawn. It would be placed into a setting of mother of pearl, and attached to a simple chain of plaited gold.

He finished the task at sunrise one day, having worked feverishly all through the night on the final stages. If only his father could see it. Geronimo was sure that he had created his masterpiece. A work of art which was unique and peerless in the world. He was also sure that no other being in the world was more worthy to receive it on her wedding day than his betrothed and most dearly loved Teodora.

Before his wedding day, he sent for the painter, Francesco da Ponte, and had himself painted in his workshop, holding the Ocean of the Moon.

'Does this pendant exist?' asked Martinelli.

Carlo and Teodora exchanged looks.

Bernardo stepped forward frowning and looked hard at the painting to see what it was that had so engaged the eye of Signor Martinelli.

'Well, Signora,' said Bernardo, his voice full of sarcasm, 'is this just a figment of the artist's imagination, a bit of poetic licence to exaggerate Geronimo's skills? For I have never had reason to believe that he was anything other than a fairly mediocre jeweller. Tell us, please do, whether such a pendant exists.'

'The pendant is mine, Signor,' replied Teodora, calmly ignoring his insult. 'It was my husband's personal gift to me on my wedding day, and I will never, never, never part with it.'

There was a reflective silence, like the pause before a snake strikes.

'Not even for the sake of your daughters?' Bernardo was the first to speak in a soft, cloying voice. 'Dear, dear, dear.' He shook his head pityingly. 'But madam, please allow us to see it. It can only be to your benefit to know its value, don't you think?'

'I already know its value sir, and whatever it may be to you, it is invaluable to me. Please do not persist in asking to see it. It is my property and nothing will make me part from it.'

'Have you ever seen the pendant?' asked Bernardo Pagliarin of his wife that night.

'I have not, sir,' answered Elisabetta. 'The portrait has hung in the workshop as long as I can remember. Its only importance to me is that it is a likeness of my father, As for the pendant, I hardly remember what it looks like.' She frowned, trying to recall it in more detail. 'I have never paid it much attention, though I know that my father used to show it to clients as proof of his expertise.'

'I wanted to see this pendant,' said Bernardo, 'but your mother wouldn't let me.'

'What do you mean, she wouldn't let you?' exclaimed Elisabetta. 'How on earth could she refuse you?'

'Your mother is rather stubborn, as you know.' Bernardo

snuggled up to his wife and pressed his mouth to her ear, nibbling and kissing her. 'Be so good, my little kitten, as to persuade your mother to show it to you. After all, it should be yours one day. If anyone is entitled to have it, it is surely you, hmm?' he cooed softly.

For once, Elisabetta was silent. She stiffened at her husband's side, as his voice murmured into her ear. For once, she felt uneasy.

'You will visit her again in a few days, my little pet, and ask her for it. I dearly want to set eyes on this thing, to hold it, examine it, and see for myself whether it is as extraordinary as it appears to be in the picture. Borrow it. Persuade your mother that you need to wear it for an important function which we are attending at the Doge's palace next week.'

Still Elisabetta didn't speak.

'Do you understand?' Bernardo's voice was suddenly hard. He rolled away from her and sat up. His face looked cruel and calculating in the soft candle glow of their night light.

'Yes, Signor,' answered Elisabetta, obediently formal. 'Of course I'll ask.'

Chapter Six

❖

Night shadows

'"*Strangers, who are you? Where do you come from sailing over the wet ways? On some trading enterprise, or is it for adventure you rove, like sea-robbers over the brine who, at hazard of their own lives, wander, bringing trouble to alien men?*"'

The cooking fire cast dark and red shadows flickering over their attentive faces, as Filippo and Andreas sat outside the fishing hut waiting for supper to cook. While she stirred and prodded her stew, Grandmother told them stories from the Odyssey.

'"*We are the men of Agamemnon,*" replied Odysseus. "*Achaeans driven wandering from Troy, by all manner of winds over the great gulf of the sea, seeking our homes we voyage. Our ship was brake to pieces, for Poseidon, the Earth-Shaker, cast it upon the rocks of your country, but I and my men escaped from utter doom. We come to these thy knees, O Cyclops, if perchance thou wilt give us hospitality . . .*"'

Although the boys knew the story backwards, and had

heard it over and over again, it was still the one they begged Andreas's grandmother to tell them.

They loved to imagine the giant Cyclops, Polyphemus, taller than a pine, with only one eye – a huge one – in the middle of his forehead, who ate men as easily as if they were sprats. Grandmother told it to them, blood, guts and all, and they listened with relish as Cyclops took up two of Odysseus's men and, '*clutching one in each hand, dashed their heads together, until their brains flowed upon the ground and made the earth wet. Then he cut them up piece by piece and prepared his supper, and ate them like a mountain lion, devouring entrails, flesh and bones with their marrow . . .*' And Grandmother would rattle the pot even more vigorously, so that the children giggled with fright.

Filippo's eyes gleamed. Like Odysseus, he too had monsters of his own to fight. He longed to be a warrior with sword and shield, to go to sea in those huge many-oared boats, with their billowing sails and fearfully carved prows, and test his courage against storms and enemies.

Earlier, he had rushed frantically out of his house to look for Andreas at the fish market, and found him just about to push off in his little boat.

'Wait, wait!' Filippo had bellowed. 'I'm coming with you.'

With an oar each, they had rowed in silence, but fast and furious, Filippo pulling as if he were heading for the ends of the earth. He was glad that the wind whipped spray into their faces so that Andreas shouldn't see the tears on his cheeks. All he wanted to do was put as much distance as possible between him and the unhappiness that filled his home. He didn't even glance at the recently arrived ships dropping anchor in the lagoon.

Andreas didn't ask any questions. Night was falling across the water, and he felt worried. It would be too late for Filippo to return home that night, and he wondered if his family even knew where he had gone.

When they were more than halfway across, Filippo began to slow down, and both boys finally stopped rowing, leaning over their oars, heaving and panting with the exertion. Ahead of them, the island lay like the spine of a fish dividing the lagoon from the Adriatic beyond.

'What's up, Pippo?'

'I'm running away.'

'Why, man, why?'

'It's that Signor Pagliarin. My brother-in-law, pah! He sat in Papa's chair. Can you imagine? What an insult to my mother! He sat there with his legs on the table as if we were his minions. He wants to strip us of everything we've got. He wants to take us over. He says Gabri and Sofi must get married – he orders it as if he were my father. They might run away too. Gabri says they'll be nuns and go to a convent. And, worst of all,' Filippo choked over his words, 'he wants me to live with him and Betta. But I won't, I won't. I hate Elisabetta and I hate, hate, hate that Pagliarin.'

Andreas's home was just a creaky little fisherman's shack, built up on poles over the black squelchy mud flats at the poorest end of the island of Torcello. Although Stefano Georgilis had four sons and one daughter, and their ancient grandmother lived with them too, they were hardly ever all squashed up together in their little shack. Stefano and two or three of his eldest sons would be out on fishing trips for days at a time, while another would sleep with their stall over at the fish market near the Rialto, ready to receive the day's catch. Andreas went back and forth in his little boat, fetching and carrying and doing whatever tasks he could, sometimes sleeping on the island, sometimes at the fish market. More often than not, there were only three or four people at a time sleeping in the shack, for Andreas's mother had died six years ago when she gave birth to their little sister, Varvara.

'*After the Cyclops had eaten his fill, he stretched out his full mighty length across the floor of the cave, among his flock of sheep, and fell into a deep sleep. Odysseus wondered whether to kill him there and then, but realised he mustn't, because, not even with the help of all his men, could he have rolled away the vast stone which blocked the entrance of the cave,*' continued Grandma.

'They awaited the bright dawn. On awaking, Cyclops ate two more men for breakfast. With a light hand, he rolled away the stone from the mouth of the cave and drove forth his flock of sheep. Then, like closing a lid on a quiver of arrows, he replaced the stone and set off with his sheep into the hills. Odysseus was left in the darkness pondering how they could escape, and prayed to Athene to help him.

'Soon he began to devise a plan.'

As Filippo listened, he became Odysseus. He began to devise plans. With stars and firelight glittering in his eyes, he thought of ways to take to the seas, wandering about, having adventures, gaining the help of the gods to help him rid the family of monsters, like Bernardo Pagliarin. He dreamed of setting off across the world to find his father; how he would bring him home in triumph and send Pagliarin packing.

The vesper bells of San Marco pealed across the water and, all over the islands, other church bells joined in.

'You go back in the morning, eh?' Andreas's father, Stefano, handed him a bowl of fish stew, 'and I hope you don't get too hard a beating from your brother, Carlo.'

Filippo didn't reply. Stefano sat down on a wooden bench next to him and began to gulp down his own soup, every now and then punctuating his thoughts with 'eh?' After a while he asked, 'How is Giuseppe?'

'Bad,' answered Filippo.

'So you go back and not be another burden to your mama, eh?'

'Finish the story, Grandma! Finish the story,' begged Varvara. But Grandmother said, 'Later, later. Now eat your supper.'

Varvara sidled over to Filippo and sat closely at his knees. 'Do you know the end of the story, Pippo? You tell it.'

'I know it, Varvara, but not like your grandma. Let her tell it. She does it much better than me.'

His eyes lolled in his head and his body felt drained of all energy.

'You sleep here, eh?' announced Stefano, pointing out a mat in the far corner of the hut next to Andreas.

'Will you marry me when I grow up, Pippo?' Varvara adored him.

He gently shook her from his knees. 'I'm never going to marry.' Without waiting to be told, he crawled inside on to the mat and fell asleep instantly.

The night which covers their island rolls onwards across the face of the earth. The moon, like a traveller's lantern, goes too, over desert dunes and glistening oceans, teeming jungles and mountain passes. Here she is whole, there three-quarters and there only half. Tonight over the razor-sharp ridges of the Hindu Kush, she is just a curved sickle. A thin sharp edge in the icy sky.

All living eyes note her position: lovers delight in her, travellers thank her, conspirators plot by her, prisoners are jealous of her freedom, and poets are inspired by her.

> *Much have I roamed, and asked the moon,*
> *Your fate is to keep travelling,*
> *Is it also your fate to reach a destination?*

In the alleyways of cities, moon-striped cats slink. Only the thief, the spy and the soft-footed strangler obsessively avoid even its dim light.

When darkness fell and Filippo had not returned, Carlo went out to look for him. He went directly to the fish market and soon ascertained that Filippo had left for the island with Andreas. He felt furious with him, and swore he'd give the boy a walloping for causing such trouble and anxiety.

Earlier, Carlo had called at the government offices and left an application for another interview to decide the issue of guardianship of the family of Geronimo Veroneo. All the time, he had not been aware of the shadow that followed him. It had been behind him ever since he left home, padding along behind, as noiseless as a stalking leopard.

Taken up with his thoughts, he continued on his way

hoping that the authority would see the justice of him becoming head of his own family. Surely, he was man enough now, especially since he had been welcomed into the Guild of Jewellers? But he knew he couldn't underestimate Pagliarin's powers of influence.

Still unaware that he was being tailed, he called in at a tavern and bought a drink. Not being in his usual tavern, he chose to sit quietly in a corner by himself. At another table, low voices were discussing some gossip. It was to do with Bernardo Pagliarin. But sometimes, low voices can carry just as clearly as loud ones, and Carlo heard everything.

'Bernardo Pagliarin's business is in trouble. A fleet of his ships went down off the coast of Africa. He's lost a fortune. He's trying not to let word get out – he has many debts, doesn't want to be hounded by his creditors.'

A rumour was circulating, they said, though no one knew who had started it. Perhaps one of Bernardo's servants had overheard something and blabbed.

Carlo struck his head with the palm of his hand. He now understood everything. He downed his drink and stepped out into the alleyway. He looked for a link boy to light his way, but seeing none, set off hoping to find one in the next camp. He strode rapidly to the end of one street, and turned left into an alley, narrow enough to bruise your elbows. It was totally deserted. Even had his mind not been on the news he had just learned, he might not have heard anything to alert him, for when the attack came, it was silent, unexpected and deadly. A rope was slung round his neck from behind and, with a knee thrust into his arched back, pulled so tight that all his breath was squeezed from him.

Carlo struggled as helplessly as a fish on the end of a hook. His arms flailed, the blood roared in his ears and eyes, he could neither hear nor see, and though his tongue thrust desperately from his gaping throat, not a single sound escaped his lips.

Just as he lost consciousness, something plummeted from the roof. There was a soft thud, a grunt, and the rope fell loose. Carlo toppled forward to the ground like a rag doll. Gasping and retching, he writhed in agony, trying to regain his breath. He curled up in terror expecting more blows. Nothing came. When he could breathe properly, he rolled on to his knees cautiously, and peered around him, but the alley was deserted. There was no sign of who had attacked him, nor of who had saved him.

With bloodshot eyes, he stared up and down, rubbing his neck and thanking God for his life, over and over again.

Above the rooftops, the moonlight glinted on tiles and windows. A prowling cat leapt silently across the void from balcony to balcony and vanished.

A scent of cinnamon hung in the air.

Chapter Seven

❖

Death was waiting

From then on, Carlo trusted no one. Who wanted to kill him? He was racked with suspicions. Who had known his movements? Who was informing on the family? Was it someone intimate, in the household? Who would benefit from his death – Pagliarin? The name fitted. And who had saved him?

He didn't tell anyone yet of his attack. He wanted to sack all the servants, the kitchen boy, Giorgio, even Rosa, claiming they were spying on them, and that he didn't trust them any more.

Teodora was horrified. 'What's wrong with you, Carlo? What's happened? Why should anyone want to spy on us?' she protested. 'You can't go sacking everyone. Rosa's been with us since I was a girl. I'd stake my life on her loyalty to us. And Giorgio's her grandchild. No, Carlo, don't fall into the trap of suspicion. It will make you like Bernardo.'

But now he found himself wondering why Giuseppe wasn't getting better. Was someone trying to kill him too? Was he being poisoned? Carlo asked his mother to supervise the kitchen more closely, to be the one to prepare Giuseppe's food and serve it to him. He became obsessed with their safety, checked and triple-checked all the doors and windows at night, ordered his mother and sisters never to go out unaccompanied, and he bought another dog, as Forza was no use as a guard dog now.

The new hound was a powerful, dark brown, iron-muscled animal called Moro, which he bought from a trader in the animal market. The dog terrified everyone except Carlo. Teodora was perplexed, and wondered what had happened to make her son so nervous and upset. Still Carlo didn't tell anyone about his attack, but just insisted that they were being spied on. He also kept to himself that the person he mistrusted the most was his own sister, Elisabetta.

When she came to call unexpectedly a day or two later, his suspicions deepened. Usually they saw her once a month at church and she rarely came to her old childhood home, as if it were beneath her to be seen in that part of the Castello district. Did she know about Bernardo's losses? Was she helping him in his plan to take over their father's business? Why had she come so soon and to the house? Was it to inform on them to her husband?

That day, that fateful day, would haunt all of them forever.

It would be a day everyone would re-enact over and over again – especially Elisabetta.

It was the day Carlo was due to take some drawings to the Santa Croce area, to a certain Signor Legrenzi, who had ordered a jewelled chain and wanted to see some designs. Suddenly a hitch had occurred over the cutting of a valuable ruby, and the stone-cutter had asked for him urgently. So Carlo instructed Filippo to deliver the drawings instead, with the message that he would call the very next day. He emphasised how important the drawings were.

It was the day that Giuseppe felt well enough to get up from his sick bed. He had improved in the last week or two. Was this because Teodora had done as Carlo insisted, and had been supervising his food? At any rate, Giuseppe awoke that morning feeling well and suddenly desperate to be out in the world again. Winter had really gone; there was a smell of early summer in the air. The swallows were back, flitting and darting round the roofs. The apple trees had burst into flower and the temperature was rising day by day.

As Filippo was pulling on his jacket in readiness for his errand, Giuseppe called out eagerly to wait. He wanted to accompany him. Teodora disagreed, and the two of them began arguing about the rights and wrongs of going out.

'It's a bit soon, *mio caro*,' said Teodora cautiously. 'You've been in bed for so long. It's wonderful to see you feeling better at last, but you should wait a few days before going out – otherwise you might have a setback.'

However, Giuseppe had seen the sun and, where the slit of their dark brown canal broke into the lagoon, the blue water beyond. Like an opened floodgate, his energy came surging back. He longed to be out.

That day, Elisabetta had called, unannounced, looking very pretty and spring-like, in a bright green dress, with slashed sleeves through which glinted bright golden yellow. She was light-hearted, almost theatrical, as she wandered about her old childhood home. Strangely girlish and sentimental, she hugged Rosa and reminisced about the old days.

Giuseppe was arguing with his mother about going out, and Elisabetta put in her oar. 'Oh let him go Mama, you're too fussy. Look how sunny it is out there, and look how pale my brother is. He needs some apples back in his cheeks. He needs some good sea air. No wonder he hasn't got better next to this filthy, rat-ridden canal. Anyway, he's old enough to make his own decisions . . .' and she continued to argue on his side.

In retrospect, one might wonder why it mattered to Elisabetta one way or the other; wonder why she seemed so forcibly determined to support Giuseppe in his desire for an outing. Was it so that she could have her mother to herself?

Was it so that no one would witness how hard she would try and persuade Teodora to let her borrow the Ocean of the Moon?

Whatever the reason, she took Giuseppe's side so vigorously, that Teodora weakened. Elisabetta didn't visit often, and it was a pity to cloud the atmosphere with a row. So Giuseppe won his argument.

He put on his woollen tabard and fleece-lined cloak, wound round with a broad scarf. 'Here,' said Filippo, taking up his brother's sword. 'Take this too.'

'Not today. I won't need it today,' replied Giuseppe.

'Then can I carry it?' asked Filippo.

Giuseppe laughed. 'You never give up, do you? Here, then. Put on the belt and scabbard.' He helped Filippo to strap and buckle the belt around his waist, and sheathe the sword into the scabbard.

'Hey! It's almost my size. I'm taller, Beppe, nearly as tall as you!'

'Come on!' Giuseppe cuffed his younger brother affectionately and, warmly scarfed and cloaked, he set off with Filippo to deliver the drawings.

A superstitious person might have looked for omens and portents, might have noted that the canary had been strangely muted that day, and that Rosa had dreamt that her statuette of the Madonna had wept real tears. Some might have said it was fate which made them go out that day, but for Giuseppe and Filippo it was a random decision to go along the northern shore. Giuseppe wanted to see the lagoon, which he hadn't set eyes on for over a month. It was a random decision to linger and chat to old Luca, the fisherman, go here but not there, look at this but not that.

Filippo had drawn and re-sheathed the sword a dozen times as they meandered through the streets. '*Guardia!*' he challenged imaginary foes.

Giuseppe yelled instructions. 'Head up. Eyes on your target. Upper body upright. Lower the knees. Keep your weapon low and closer to the hip. Thrust and cut. *Fendente!* (Vertical down.) *Montante!* (Vertical up.) *Tonda!* (Horizontal.) Be ready to swivel at a moment's notice. *Squalembrato, ridoppio, mandritti!* Feet apart! Eyes on your foe!'

Filippo leapt and swiped and plunged. He must have the power of a panther, the grace of a dancer and the strategy of a chess player.

But they moved slowly. Giuseppe was far weaker than he had at first realised.

'Shall we take the Strada Nova, or go across the Rialto to the gold market?' they asked each other. Giuseppe said perhaps the gold market took them too far out of their way, but Filippo said it was much more interesting. So they decided on the gold market.

It was like entering the centre of the sun. Sheets of dazzling gold hung like curtains, resonating in the breeze like the soft clash of distant shields. They examined, criticised and fingered ornaments, rings, chains and bracelets, discussing the quality of the designs, the settings of the stones. They continued along the Ruga di Speziali and crossed over the Rio delle Beccarie, moving nearer to Santa Croce district. Bored with his brother's slow pace, Filippo charged ahead and back again, to and fro like an over-energetic puppy, and swishing his sword at make-believe enemies. Giuseppe stopped often, his heart pounding and his legs feeling wobbly. Mama was right. It had been too soon to go out. But he said nothing to Filippo. There was nothing for it but to keep going.

And so they crossed the Campo San Cassiano, past gossiping women, men drinking peppermint tea, and tribes of children hurtling about like shuttlecocks, on down the Calle Carminati.

None of this was planned beforehand. The only thing that was clear was their aim to deliver the drawings of Carlo's commission to the home of Marcello Legrenzi. Could anyone have predicted that the boys would arrive at the square, the Campo San Pantalon, at exactly that hour? That every step they took was leading them to a fatal encounter?

Filippo had charged ahead again, leaving Giuseppe leaning against a wall for a rest. He had entered the Campo San

Pantalon and stopped to wait for Giuseppe, when he was assailed by a shout.

'Oi, Flippo-lippo!' came the taunt. It was Federigo, Bernardo's oldest son. He and his brother, Matteo, stood with a group of about six other young men – some with swords and knives in their belts – and was that not their own Cook's boy, Giorgio, ducking out of sight behind the fountain?

'Bit far from home, ain't yer?'

'Who's that shrimp?' jeered one of the gang.

'My uncle!' laughed Federigo.

'And mine!' chortled Matteo. 'Where yer goin' mio titchy uncle?'

The boys advanced closer. 'What have you got in your bag, eh?'

'Cuttlefish, I expect,' sneered Federigo.

Filippo went mad at that remark, which clearly insulted his mother, Teodora. He charged headfirst into the boy's stomach.

Federigo went sprawling backwards, winded.

'Why, you monstrous little toad!' Matteo leapt in and punched Filippo in the nose.

With blood spouting from his nostrils, Filippo wheeled away clutching his face, but was immediately apprehended by another member of the gang who grabbed his satchel. As it was slung across Filippo's chest, the force brought him to his knees on the filthy ground.

By the time Giuseppe entered the square, he didn't see Filippo at first, surrounded as he was by the gang, who were now trying to grapple away the bag. All he saw was a group of boys in a tight circle laughing raucously at something in their midst.

He crossed to the far side of a small fountain, wanting to catch up with Filippo as soon as possible, when suddenly he saw one of the boys break away with a whoop of triumph, twirling Carlo's leather bag round and round his head. The circle widened as the bag was flung from one boy to another and then another.

'Give it back!' Filippo's voice wailed like a gull on the wing. Giuseppe stopped and turned. He saw his young brother on the ground, protesting loudly, his face and hands covered in blood.

'Hey!' shouted Giuseppe, stumbling forward. 'What are you doing? Pippo, are you OK?'

'The bag, Beppe, the bag. We must get it back!' cried Filippo desperately. 'Giorgio, help me!'

But Giorgio stayed half-hidden behind the fountain.

Federigo and Matteo seemed surprised to see Giuseppe, and hesitated. 'Where's Carlo? Is he with you?' asked Federigo looking round.

'Nope, he's gone to the stone-cutter. Now give me back the bag,' Filippo pleaded.

'Oh, give it back,' drawled Matteo, as if the whole thing bored him.

But the rest of the gang were enjoying themselves now, and continued to toss the bag around.

Giuseppe ran up to Federigo and grabbed his arm. 'Give the bag back. It's got Carlo's drawings in it. Come on, you've had your fun.'

'Leave off!' snarled Federigo, and pushed him aside.

'You dog!' cried Giuseppe, enraged. 'Don't push me!'

'Don't push me?' mimicked Federigo with a sneer. 'Are you such a namby-pamby that you can't take a push? How about this then?' He thrust Giuseppe's arm in an arm-lock, put a foot between his and tripped him to the ground.

'Who's that?' yelled one of the gang.

'Another uncle!' laughed Federigo.

'A plague of uncles!' chortled another.

'We didn't expect him,' whispered Matteo, uncertainly.

Giuseppe tried to get to his feet, but Federigo stood above him and thrust him back with his foot. 'Apologise for pushing me,' he ordered, his hand going for the knife in his belt.

Filippo saw the action. In an instant, he grabbed the hilt of Giuseppe's sword, and clumsily pulled it from its scabbard with a ragged scraping sound, his arm barely long enough to swish the weapon out in one movement.

Federigo turned at the sound of steel, his own knife glinting in his hand. Giuseppe yelled with alarm, 'No Pippo, for God's sake, no!' He grabbed Federigo's leg. Federigo swiped down with his knife just as Filippo lunged forward with the sword.

There were war cries. Bodies piled themselves on top of each other. Hands clenched into fists, others grasping knives lifted and plunged. Cloaks billowed, caps flew, arms and legs writhed. There was blood, there was jubilation. The sword was wrenched from his hand, and Filippo was hurled across the piazza as if he were no more than an alley cat.

'Give back the satchel!' yelled Filippo, desperately raising his face from the dust as the gang scattered across the square making for the alleyways.

Matteo had the satchel. He spun round with a defiant laugh, swung the bag above his head, and let it fly. It arched through the air like a stone flung from a sling, and landed in the nearby canal with a splash.

Filippo gave a howl of despair. He didn't know which way to turn – to help his brother or rush for the precious satchel. But he saw Giuseppe getting to his feet, so Filippo raced to the canal and threw himself in.

The water was thick with rubbish and excrement, which threatened to hold him in a filthy embrace and drag him down. At first he could hardly make any headway towards the slowly sinking satchel. Then with a huge thrust forward, he grabbed it and pulled it in to his chest.

Gasping and spluttering, he tried to force his way back through the scum to the bank, but felt the weight of his clothes and satchel dragging him down. 'Help me out, someone!' he gasped feebly.

A pole was thrust out to him. He grabbed it, and felt himself pulled through the rubbish towards the mooring steps. A hand hauled him out, leaving him sprawled face down with the satchel clutched to his chest, spitting and retching. By the time he had caught his breath and turned to see who had helped him, there was no one there. Only the pole lay discarded on the fondamente and, despite the stench from the canal, a faint whiff of cinnamon hung in the air.

But all that really mattered were Carlo's drawings.

'Oh no, oh no, no!' He bent his head into his arms. The satchel was full of water – and he could see ink trailing across the parchment.

'Beppe!' he wailed. 'Beppe! The drawings are ruined. Carlo will kill me.' He struggled to his feet, sodden with stinking water and debris clinging to his clothes. 'Giuseppe!' he continued to call, but got no reply. He staggered back to the little campo where a cluster of traders, boatmen and women were gathered round someone lying on the ground. A voice yelled, 'Call a priest!'

'Beppe?' Filippo began to run. Surely not Giuseppe? He pushed his way through the crowd. 'My brother, my brother,' he was screaming. People gave way to him, crossing themselves and uttering prayers as he flung himself down over the prostrate figure.

It was Giuseppe. His face was white as the moon which was rising pale in the blue sky above them. His eyes were open, staring blankly. Filippo touched his face. It was cold. Then slowly, the blank gaze focussed, and Giuseppe blinked.

'Help me, help me!' cried Filippo. 'Can someone help me to take him home?'

'Where do you live, lad?' asked a gondelieri.

'Rio di San Lorenzo in the Castello district,' wept Filippo, unable now to keep tears of terror from streaming down his cheeks.

'Give us a hand,' the boatman said to another, and two men, with many other helping hands, gently lifted Giuseppe and carried him over to a barge moored nearby. They eased him down and laid him on the slats of the boat, motioning Filippo to sit down and cradle Giuseppe's head in his lap. The two standing boatmen then took up their oars and rowed their way down the canal, their blades flipping this way and that like a fluttering heartbeat.

'Oh God, Beppe, don't die, for pity's sake, don't die. What

will Mama do?' Filippo rocked him to and fro, rubbing his brother's cold face with his equally cold hands.

How silently now the boat glided, with just the soft splash of the oars. Green slime streaked down red-brick walls of houses which towered above him on either side. Clothes hung like garlands from one washing line to the next, silhouettes of inhabitants wavered in lamplit windows, moving like shadows, or ghosts. They passed soundlessly through the gleaming eyes of reflected bridges, and it was as if they floated along the river of death. A flight of sandpipers swooped and coiled away among the roofs, while high above a single gull soared in the wind like a watchful soul.

They came into the Rio di San Lorenzo, and one of the boatmen yelled up to an open window to which Filippo pointed. 'Hey there, Veroneo! Veroneo! Someone come, please!'

Teodora's face appeared then vanished. In a few moments, she was alongside the boat, followed by Sofia and Gabriella, their faces stricken with horror at the state of the brothers.

Giuseppe's eyes were wide open when they lifted him out of the boat; clouds floated across their surfaces, as if the sky was entering his soul. They carried him inside.

'I think you should call a priest, Signora,' muttered one of the boatmen softly, 'just to be safe.'

Just to be safe. Confess to a priest before he dies, ask for forgiveness of sins. Just to be safe from a long, long sentence in purgatory, suspended between heaven and hell, waiting for the final judgement on where his soul should spend the rest of everlasting life.

'I'll go,' said Filippo.

'No, Pippo,' Teodora protested, seeing his filthy dripping clothes and his stark face. 'Send Giorgio.' But no one knew where Giorgio was. In any case, Filippo had already gone.

When Filippo returned with Father Luigi, Giuseppe was lying on his bed. They had removed his mud-stained breeches and his blood-soaked shirt and staunched a knife wound they had found between his ribs. He had lost a lot of blood, but his eyes were still open, as if he dreaded to close them and lose sight of the world.

The family drew back. The priest approached, and took out his phial of holy water. He sprinkled it over Giuseppe's forehead, '*In nomine Patris, et Filii* . . .' then signalled the family to leave so that he could hear his confession and give him final absolution.

Clustered outside the room, no one spoke. The girls clung to Teodora, weeping into her skirts, while Teodora herself stood rigid, as if turned to stone.

By the time Carlo returned, his brother Giuseppe was dead.

'No one helped him! Not even Giorgio!' sobbed Filippo.

'Though someone pulled me out of the water with a pole.'

'Did you say Giorgio?' whispered Carlo. 'Was Giorgio there?' But Filippo had fled downstairs.

Geronimo sat in his chair staring at him. He looked older. Was that grey hair tingeing his once rich red curls? His skin was more yellow, and wrinkled liked parchment. It stretched over his cheekbones and into the hollows of his face, which was surely thinner and had become gaunt. The criss-cross lines on his brow were deeper. They extended down his temples, and merged with more lines, which flowed like tributaries from the corners of his liquid eyes. Those eyes, somehow more dark green, as deep as the bottom of the ocean, now held Filippo's eyes in a desperate pleading gaze.

'Papa!' howled Filippo, and flung himself down beside the chair, gripping its arms. Forza, the old dog, gave a deep sigh and buried his nose into his paws.

Chapter Eight

❖

Remorse

Returning home after a funeral is the hardest part. Returning to the spaces once filled by Giuseppe, seeing his bedroom just as he left it, his clothes and boots, his fishing rod and net, his sword slung on a hook, his sheets of music and the lute propped in a corner, and the piles and piles of his wonderful drawings and designs of jewellery scattered like fallen leaves on table and floor and every surface. A room so full of him, yet so empty.

The funeral guests have departed. Teodora goes up to her bedchamber to change out of the long black satin dress she has worn for the ceremony. Elisabetta follows. She needs reassurance and seeks forgiveness. She feels guilt and remorse for Giuseppe's death. She thinks she will suffocate with anguish. Most of all, she needs to be loved, for never has she felt so unloved. But Teodora moves like a sleepwalker, like one in a dream afraid to wake up, and she seems barely to notice her daughter's presence.

Her mother had refused to lend her the pendant that day, the day Giuseppe died. 'No, Betta, no, I can't lend you the pendant, but I'll show it to you.' Teodora had opened a secret panel in the wall of her bedchamber and unlocked the hidden safe. When the jewel case was opened, Elisabetta had gasped. It lay there on black velvet, the diamond pendant in the painting, the Ocean of the Moon, so white, in a universe of its own. It seemed to float like the moon on a black night with its entourage of stars. When Teodora lifted it from its case and the light of day struck the diamond, it seemed to sing.

Her mother delighted in seeing it again. 'Look at it. Touch it. Here, let me put it round your neck . . . there . . . how beautiful. You complement each other so well.' Then she had hugged her, kissed her beloved eldest daughter and wept with emotion. She begged Elisabetta to understand why she couldn't lend it. 'My darling, my dearest daughter . . . Don't you see? Everything of your father is in this stone. It has his life and soul in it, his genius, its very design was his way of showing his love for me. And I have vowed never to wear it again till he returns home.

'He didn't make this to be a mere adornment on the neck of some fine lady – not even you, my darling. If Geronimo is dead, then I know that the essence of him is here in this pendant. It will stay here, locked in its case till he returns or till I die.

Afterwards . . .' she shrugged as though she had hardly contemplated afterwards, 'it must be retained by his heir as an example of the workshop of Geronimo Veroneo.'

'That means Carlo gets it,' Elisabetta had retorted, recoiling from her mother, and she suddenly visualised it round the neck of Magdelena Ceruspini, that scrawny pale girl betrothed to Carlo, who was barely thirteen years old. They had agreed to marry when she was sixteen. The thought of that chit of a girl wearing the pendant made her stomach churn with jealousy. She wanted to say, 'Why should Magdelena wear it and not me – not even once? Is that fair?' But instead she wept bitterly.

Her mother had tried to comfort her, put an arm round her. 'Look, my sweet. Wear this necklace.' She took out another from the jewel box. 'It has such pretty diamonds and rubies. It too was made by your father. It's just as beautiful in its own way. He gave it to his mother, your grandmother. She would be so happy, may God rest her soul, to think of you wearing it. Please, my little kitten. Understand why I can't let you have the pendant.'

But Elisabetta had recoiled, petulant, almost enjoying her revenge by refusing to understand, as her mother begged her to do. She had flounced away in a sulk and, from the chamber window, had watched resentfully as Giuseppe and Filippo headed off together down the alleyway, laughing and joking. Now she would have to return empty-handed to face Bernardo's displeasure.

Thinking back over that scene now, Elisabetta is filled with shame and remorse. She had confessed it all to her priest. How futile! It had all been for nothing. Giuseppe had died for nothing. He would never have gone out that day if it hadn't been for her and, what was worse, it was her step-sons who had helped to bring about his death.

Bernardo said it was an accident. 'That undisciplined wretch Filippo started it all. He drew a sword and wounded Matteo. Federigo reacted in self-defence. It was unfortunate his knife cut an artery.' He spoke callously, unmoved.

'You're only trying to defend Federigo!' Elisabetta had wept passionately. 'He and Matteo have always gone looking for fights with my brothers. You've known it, but never stopped it. It was almost as though they were waiting for them and knew they would come. Matteo said he thought it would be Carlo. So he did know, didn't he? Did Giorgio tell them? I can hardly look Rosa in the face, knowing that her grandson is in your pay. Oh what would everyone say, Mama and Carlo, if they knew he spied on them? And I blame myself too. Beppe wouldn't have gone out if I hadn't taken his part and argued against Mama. If only I hadn't gone. I wouldn't have gone if it hadn't been for you wanting the pendant so much. Oh God, why did Papa ever create such an object? And why were you so keen to see it? Now look at the calamity that has befallen us. You and I are as much to blame. We killed him too.'

With a bellow of rage, Bernardo had stepped forward and struck Elisabetta a blow which pitched her to the ground. 'How dare you include me in your blame? You stupid little guttersnipe. Do you think you and your good-for-nothing father don't owe me? I, who could have married nobility. I, who took you, a common tradesman's daughter, and made you my wife when I could have married no less than a countess, had I chosen to? My wife! Huh, some wife! And what have I received in return? Nothing. Not even the transactions your father promised me in Hindustan. No, little madam,' Bernardo bent forward over his wife lying huddled on the floor, and grasped a handful of her hair. 'You owe me,' he hissed. 'For I now consider the Ocean of the Moon to be mine in lieu of payment by your father. And in due course, I will have it, along with everything else.'

Elisabetta watches her mother undressing, just as she used to when she was a child. Item by item, she removes her funeral clothes. The skin of her arms and neck is so white, as translucent as marble. Until she covers herself once more in another simpler black mourning dress, she is like one of the statues in the church, full of folds and movements, yet utterly frozen.

Every now and then, Elisabetta reaches forward to offer help, but Teodora ignores her and will not catch her eye. Never has Elisabetta felt more unloved. Her sisters avoid her, Carlo is distant, as if he didn't trust her, and Filippo hates her. She remembers how her mother and father had loved each other – still did – even across the void. Bernardo didn't love her like that, no more than he loved his spaniel. He had worn her like an ornament; just used her. She knows that now, and is racked with wondering, does anyone love me? She thinks of her children. Her own were sweet little darlings, but it was always to Nanny they ran, so she didn't know if they loved her or not. Her step-children were indifferent. Tears of self-pity well in her eyes. She tries to show she is sorry, tries to glean some crumb of forgiveness, but her mother is remote and so withdrawn into some dark place with her grief, that she hardly seems to know she is there; so Elisabetta slips away in despair.

Teodora hears her daughter leave. She hates herself for feeling nothing. In time, and it would take time, she would start to feel again, even if it was only the grinding, deep pain of sorrow. In due course, she would comfort her daughter.

She stares at her image in the glass. For the first time, she can accept the wearing of black and mourn for her son, in a way she has never been able to for her husband. She still cannot accept Geronimo as dead.

Chapter Nine

❖

A man from the east

Filippo had been working alongside Carlo for hours. His neck was stiff from bending over the workbench for so long. He straightened with a sigh and Carlo, working alongside, said, 'Take a breather, Pippo.' He spoke softly as if still in the presence of the dead, for voices continued to be low and hushed in this sad household, as though Giuseppe were lying ill, but alive, and in need of the utmost quiet.

Filippo pushed back his stool. The grating sound it made on the floor seemed almost obscene. Any breaking of the silence seemed like an offence, a sacrilege. But the silence itself was unquiet, its breath shallow with fear, suspicion and resentment. Mistrust had entered the household. Each one of them lived in dread, feeling at the heart of a conspiracy. The girls clung ever more closely to each other's company. They all knew now of the attempt on Carlo's life, knew he could never walk down a street or an alley, without wondering if an assassin lurked round the next corner, or trailed him across the roof tops ready to drop silently upon him like a hawk on to its prey.

Rosa had fretted and wrung her hands, for Giorgio hadn't come back after Giuseppe's attack, and she couldn't explain why he wouldn't have tried to help his young masters when they were attacked. She felt caught up in the tangle of suspicion, even though Teodora had wept across her knees like a child and reassured her that she trusted her as if she were her own mother.

With each of them isolated in their own fears and sorrows, Filippo's thoughts fled to the island across the dark rippling sea, to the mud flats gleaming in the moonlight, the resting place each night for hundreds of seabirds, to where upturned boats sprawled like exhausted swimmers. Open-eared shells hummed with the sound of the greater ocean which lay beyond the lagoon.

Andreas, his father and brothers would be leaving in a few days. Filippo could hardly restrain himself from fleeing this house of dread to join them, and escape the prospect of being taken into Pagliarin's household. His mind was with them all the time. He wondered if they could see his phantom hanging around, watching and longing, working alongside them while they stored the fishing nets and ropes, and stocked the boat with pots of curd and sour cheese, dried meat and fish, figs, olives and dates – enough provisions for the many days at sea.

Here, in the heart of the city, it was nearly time to light the lamps. Shadows gathered in the dark alleys, beneath the bridges, and spread like a dark stain along the winding canals. The last of the sun blazed in a thousand glass windows all over Venice. Any moment, it would quench itself in the waters of the lagoon, leaving the roofs and domes of the city to the pale glimmering of lamps and candles.

Filippo went out on to their little balcony, which overlooked the canal. He could hear the bells of Santa Maria Formosa and San Giorgio dei Greci ringing out for evensong. Dogs were barking to each other all over the city. Moro snarled under his breath and pricked his ears. Only Carlo was his master, and he still responded defensively when anyone else moved.

'It's all right, Moro!' Carlo muttered, giving his hound a reassuring pat. 'It's only Pippo. Is there anything to be seen out there, Pippo?' he asked softly.

Filippo looked into the night among all the watercraft, the barges and boats, the punts and gondolas, bobbing with lamps as they jostled their way down the narrow canal. 'Nothing, Carlo,' he answered, 'nothing. Just the usual crowd.' His eye swept over the people hurrying along the canal side, the hawkers and beggars, the scattering children and scuttling goats. Their sounds rose and fell reassuringly, except – somewhere – the sound of a flute floated above the hubbub like a moth fluttering in the darkness. But it would be rare not to hear any music – someone singing, a hurdy-gurdy grinding, or a lute being strummed – so no, there was nothing that was worth mentioning. Yet the strange, coiling melody of the flute caught his ear.

Filippo stretched his arms and arched his back. He could see the last curve of the sun as it sank like a golden galleon into the waters of Grand Canale beyond and, hazily, his eye fixed on a gondola emerging out of the shimmering light. The gondolier, standing with his back to the sun, was outlined in gold, as he rowed his boat closer into the dark canyon of the narrow canal on which Filippo lived. Although it was only one of dozens of watercraft to-ing and fro-ing, Filippo's eye never left it.

Back and forth, back and forth, as elegantly as a dancer, the gondolier stepped and flipped his long oar with an easy rhythm, bringing the gondola deeper into the shadows of the overhanging buildings. It carried a single passenger. A strange bundled figure enveloped in some kind of shawl.

Nearer still, it came. The flute-playing ceased. The passenger in the gondola adjusted his shawl with a hand and, briefly, Filippo glimpsed something of his head which seemed to be wrapped in some kind of turban. The east! A man from the east, there was no doubt, and coming to their neighbourhood, perhaps to their own door. And if it was a man from the east, surely . . . Filippo leapt to the only conclusion he wanted. 'Carlo!'

Carlo grunted a 'don't disturb me' grunt.

'Carlo! It's Papa! Papa has come home.'

In the workshop, the stool clattered to the ground as Carlo rushed out to join his brother on the balcony, followed by Moro barking uncontrollably.

They craned over the edge trying to see, but the shadows were too dense for any detail, and the man too covered up.

The gondolier hooked his oar to a mooring and eased his craft to some steps. Money changed hands, the passenger retrieved a bundle, then alighted and walked quickly away down a side alley without even a glance in their direction.

Carlo lightly clipped his brother round the ear. 'Wishful thinking, eh?' He smiled faintly, but he lingered on the balcony and scanned the rooftops looking for shadows which moved. He peered down into the gathering darkness beneath the balcony where their domestic animals clucked and grunted, bleated and mooed in the straw. 'Come on, boy!' He tugged Moro back to the worktop. 'There's nothing there. It's just little brother seeing things again.'

It was completely dark when, an hour later, Moro sprang to his feet, and Carlo saw that all the hairs along his spine stood on end. The hound stood stock still, rigid, listening. The boys listened.

'What is it, Moro?' hissed Carlo, hooking the dog's head into the crook of his arm.

Then came the knock. One sharp rap on the door downstairs. It startled them. Moro burst out into a fusillade of barking. Carlo barely restrained him by the scruff of the neck, and the two brothers made their way below. Teodora, the girls and Rosa had also heard the knock and were already crowded nervously round the door clutching each other's hands, wondering who could be calling on them after dark.

'Who is it?' Carlo called out, without opening the door.

'A messenger from Geronimo Veroneo,' replied a low but urgent voice.

The air quivered with the shock, the gasped breath, the rush of blood, the jolted heartbeat. Was this a game, a practical joke, a mistake?

'If this is the house of Geronimo Veroneo, I have a message for you, but let me in for I must speak with you in private. There is danger for all of us.' The voice was foreign, the words used a mixture of Italian and Venetian, so broken and gutteral that they could only barely understand him. Carlo listened, frozen by indecision.

Then Teodora's anguished whisper broke through their trance. 'Let him in, Carlo, let him in.'

'No mother. It could be a trick. We need proof. What proof

have you?' Carlo's voice came out as a shout. He pulled aside a
grille in the door to see the face of their visitor. 'What proof?
We need proof.'

'This?' The visitor's face was covered and in shadow, but a
hand held up a chain, on the end of which dangled a small
crucifix alongside a figure of San Francesco and a small ring
with an orange stone. 'Signor Veroneo gave it to me for proof.'
His mouth pressed up to the grille. 'Let me in, I beseech you.
Believe me, the danger is great.'

Teodora pushed Carlo aside and looked through the grille.
The crucifix gleamed eerily in the light of the taper which she
held up. Teodora drew back blinking, as though her eyes had
dazzled. 'Carlo, they're mine.' She felt Rosa take her arm.

Carlo once more pressed his face to the grille. 'This is
not proof enough. How did you come by them? Perhaps you
stole them.'

'Geronimo Veroneo told me this was a gift from his wife,
Teodora. The ring too, she gave it to him the day they were
betrothed. How would I know this if I stole it?'

'It's true, Carlo,' murmured Teodora. 'That's my ring. I've
had it since childhood. I would know it anywhere.'

'We have enemies, you and I. Let me in quickly.
Danger, danger.'

'Open the door, Carlo. Open the door,' begged Teodora.

Rosa held up a lamp in one hand and a heavy oak club in the other as Carlo drew a dagger from his belt. 'Filippo!' He jerked his head to the bolt. 'Open it.'

Filippo pulled back a bolt, turned a key in the lock and opened the door, then stepped back.

'"O Son of Odysseus, would you allow yourself to lose possession of your property and the right to be lord over your own house? But I would ask of this stranger, where does he come from? What land does he belong to? Who are his kith and kin and where are his native fields? Does he bring news of thy father on his travels, or has he come on some business of his own?"'

The stranger was tall. He stooped to cross their threshold. Ignoring Carlo's threatening knife, and Moro's thrusting head and bared teeth, the stranger kicked shut the door behind him.

For a moment, no one knew what to do, except stare at the man. Was he the man from the gondola? Filippo couldn't be sure, though he was dressed in the same oriental way as many who were commonly seen coming off the ships in Venice, all wrapped round in a long shawl. A turban enveloped his head and face, leaving only his eyes visible. Brown, nearly black, infathomable eyes. The crucifix and ring swung from his fingers. Filippo watched it, mesmerised. Seconds passed. No one spoke.

The only sound was Moro, rasping on the lead.

Teodora reached out tentative fingers. She touched the orange stone of the ring, drew back as if burnt, then reached out again. 'Rosa!' The strength of her voice was a shock. 'Bring our guest some wine and refreshment.' She turned decisively and walked into the parlour, followed by Sofia and Gabriella clinging to her, one on each arm. Rosa nodded but didn't go, hanging instead around the doorway, unwilling to miss a single word.

Carlo lowered his knife. He waved it towards the parlour, directing the stranger from the east to go in. The man removed his sandals then, barefooted, obeyed.

Teodora had already sat down with the girls clustered at her knee. She sat in Papa's chair. It was the first time she had done so since Geronimo had left. None of them showed any surprise. It was right. It was she who was in control.

Old Forza, sprawled in front of his master's chair, didn't even bother to sniff the ankles of the new arrival. Carlo said with formal sadness, 'We sent many messages to my father, but over all these years we have never had any reply. Could it be that you, sir, are a messenger, and bring us news at last?'

The stranger nodded slowly, 'Yes, yes . . . I am a messenger of sorts.' He unwrapped part of his turban to reveal his face.

Everyone stared unashamedly. He was a lean, gaunt man,

with skin as brown as almonds. His long, curved nose reminded Filippo of a bird of prey. His lips were tightened into a thin line, as if afraid of letting out secrets, but which suddenly parted and widened into a charming smile. But his black eyes surveyed them without communication as if, like a wild animal, he had a completely different process of thought and action.

He loosened his shawl and revealed a long barley-coloured linen coat over linen trousers, travel-worn and stained. From a leather belt round his waist hung a scimitar with a mean-looking edge. His bare feet were blackened, gnarled, and hard-skinned from much travel. A gold ring glinted on one toe.

'Are you from the land of Hindustan?' Filippo blurted out impetuously.

The visitor tipped his head in a strange sideways nod, which seemed to mean yes.

He bowed before Teodora.

'Signora, my name is Sadiqui Iqbal Khan. I am a Musalman from the land of Hindustan. Are you Signora Veroneo, wife of Geronimo Veroneo?'

'She is, sir,' replied Carlo, curtly. 'I am his eldest son, and this is my mother.'

'And you must be Giuseppe?' The stranger turned to Filippo.

'Giuseppe is dead,' Carlo answered mechanically, as if he had had to rehearse the words.

'Sweet Jesus rest his soul,' murmured Rosa, crossing herself twice, and wiping her eyes with her smock.

'This is Filippo, his youngest son, of whose existence my father isn't aware it seems – despite the many messages we sent.'

Signor Khan clasped his two hands to his heart in a gesture of sorrow. 'I regret. Deeply. This news of Giuseppe will bring him much grief.' He brushed his right hand from his lips to his forehead and up into the space above his head, as if he sent a heart-felt message of intercession to God himself.

The Musalman solemnly untwined the chain and gave it to Teodora. 'Signora, I come with a message from your husband, Geronimo Veroneo, may God strengthen him. He also gave me this crucifix and ring so that you would know that what I say is true.'

The chain with the crucifix and ring lay coiled in the palm of her hand. She raised them to her cheek as if their touch was Geronimo's touch. 'Is he alive?' Teodora asked in a clear voice.

'Yes madam, at least, he was when I was freed and left him eighteen months ago. God is great.'

Eighteen months? The family hadn't heard of him in twelve years, yet here was this stranger telling them he had seen him alive eighteen months ago. No one moved or made a sound.

'He begs you to free him. He is a hostage. He is being held

in a fortress in the northern hills of Kabul, by the Afghan warlord, Abdhur Mir.'

'Where are the northern hills of Kabul?' whispered Sofia.

'High in the Hindu Kush – the mountains beyond Hindustan.' He outlined a map on the table with his finger. 'Very high, very cold, but it is part of the empire ruled by the Great Moghul.'

'Jehangir?' Carlo spoke the name as if it burned his tongue.

'It was Jehangir, but he is no more. His son, Shah Jehan, Light of the World, is now the emperor.'

There was the utmost silence. Tears sprang into Teodora's eyes, but quickly dried again.

Rosa began to rock and moan. She threw up her hands, 'Oh Jesu Maria, oh God in heaven, thank you, thank you, thank you for answering our prayers. But we knew it all along, didn't we, madam, didn't we always know that God was listening and preserving the life of our dear master? Didn't I tell you that the early swallow I saw was a sign of good luck? And all those visits we made to the Santa Maria dei Miracoli – didn't I say our dear Lady would be listening and would intercede for us?'

'Where's the wine I asked you to bring for our guest, Rosa?' Teodora interrupted her gently.

'Yes, yes, it's coming!' Rosa smiled her first smile since Giuseppe died, and hurried off to the kitchen.

Filippo and his sisters positioned themselves where they could stare at Signor Khan, as Carlo and Teodora talked and talked, questioning and listening. The girls had their arms draped round each other, and occasionally whispered in their made-up language. Filippo noticed a scar near the Musalman's throat, and another long scar from his right eye down his cheek. Yet, he didn't look like a fighter. Although his wrists were broad, his hands stubby, his fingers tapered as if they were more used to playing a musical instrument than handling a weapon.

'Why did you not just go home, once you were free? Have you no wife and family who have waited with the same longing and despair as we have?' asked Teodora.

'You said there was danger, for you and for us? Why? Who is our enemy?' asked Carlo.

'Where there is money, there is danger. Where there is power, there is a struggle for power. Abdhur Mir will have informed the Emperor's court of my mission. The ransom demanded is quite a sizeable amount. I may have been followed. I hope I have not brought danger to your door.'

'Why would you undertake something so risky for my father, a foreigner, a man who is not of your race or religion?' asked Carlo.

'Because I made a vow.' Signor Khan's face dipped out of the light of the candle. His voice was light, almost singsong. His sentences rose and fell like short musical phrases. 'Your father was ill in prison. He had a great fever. He thought he was dying. He made me promise to find you, to tell you what had become of him. He took my hand and made me swear by Allah. I swore that if I got free, I would find you.

'In prison, he was my great friend. He never gave up hope. If I despaired, he would look at the moonbeams falling on our prison wall and say, "Is the moon still there? Then hope is still there." We were like brothers. No, we were closer than brothers; we were of the same soul. We helped each other to stay alive, promised each other – I him, he me – who gets free first, will find the ransom for the other.'

'You say you left last year. Why did it take you so long to reach us?' asked Carlo.

'It's because I made another promise. I promised myself and my God that if I got free, I would make my Haj to Mecca. Thank Allah for saving my life. Last year, my brother came at last with a ransom. I was freed by the grace of Allah. I promised your father that I would find you and get ransom money. I have been to Mecca and now I am here.'

'Where's Mecca?' Filippo whispered to Gabriella.

'Arabia.'

'Arabia!' The word rang in Filippo's ear, mysteriously magical.

'But I know I have been followed and watched ever since I left Hindustan. Many try to intercept those carrying ransom money.'

'What must we do?' asked Carlo. His voice was cool and business-like. 'How much do you want?'

'Your father says you are a jeweller like him, and that you will surely find something of sufficient worth to make up the ransom equal to about 15,000 florins.'

Teodora gave a bitter laugh. 'Why, that's the amount Signor Pagliarin seeks as a dowry for the marriage of my two younger daughters.'

Chapter Ten

❖

Mistrust

They were just small figures, poised between water and sky. Filippo often thought there must be little difference between fish and bird. How he envied the way they could skim across their surfaces, while humans seemed only able to move with immense effort and struggle. He and Carlo were rowing across the lagoon. He thought how cumbersome their movements were, compared to the gull soaring above, or the shoals of fish darting below. A Muslim from India, a Musalman, had come in the night and told them Papa was alive. Wasn't this the most marvellous news they could have had? Shouldn't they have been shouting it to the world and celebrating? Yet somehow, as they rowed across the water, all he felt was an unbearable helplessness, crushed between the weight of the sky and sea.

At dawn the next morning, Filippo had rushed down to Carlo as soon as he dared, crawled into his bed, urgently gabbling about their visitor who had stayed last night. 'Carlo!

The Musalman, he knows about the Ocean of the Moon.'

They could hear Signor Khan's voice softly calling out the dawn prayer to Allah from the balcony. It mingled with the church bells all over the city, chiming six o'clock matins.

Carlo stifled him with a hand over his brother's mouth and whispered deep into Filippo's ear. 'Not now, Filippo. You can come with me to deliver a commission, then tell me about it. Go. Get dressed.'

The morning sun was still low when they left the house and manoeuvred their boat along the already narrow, bustling waterway Rio di San Lorenzo. They passed the Greek church of San Giorgio where Andreas and his family would come to Mass, and emerged, at last, into the glistening expanse of the lagoon.

Away from the shade of the buildings, it was suddenly hot. The temperature made an unexpected leap. Carlo raised a single mast and unfurled the sail. There was barely a wind to help them along, and the oars were heavy in the languid waters. Everything seemed leaden, and the islands lay like basking reptiles, some lush and green-backed, others just low and brown, full of mud and marsh. Carlo was aiming for a little island, barely inhabited except for a few local people who combed its shore for whatever they could find. Midway across, he paused, letting a light wind which had gathered in the sail billow them along for a while.

'At least we know we won't be overheard out in the middle of the lagoon, unless the gulls are spies too. Now then, what happened?'

'He came in the night,' Filippo at last blurted out his story. 'I thought he would cut my throat. I managed to hide – I can still slide down between the bed and the wall!'

He was referring to the bed in the workshop where he often slept if a visitor took his room. It was built into a niche, like a bunk on board ship, and shielded by a curtain. Rosa had told him to sleep there, so that the Musalman could take Filippo's bed.

Filippo had woken sharply, unsure if he had called out in a dream. His heart had thumped so fiercely he had pressed his hands over his chest in case it leapt from his body. He had lain motionless. Something had woken him; there was another presence in the workshop.

He saw a faint quivering light. A hand shielded a candle. A shadow loomed across the ceiling. Someone was in the room. 'Beppe?' he had nearly called out. Shut up, he stopped himself with plunging misery, Beppe's dead.

He listened, his brain racing as fast as his heart. Carlo? No. Why should Carlo come creeping round the workshop in the middle of the night? Why isn't Moro barking? He barks at everything else. Now when he's really needed, he is silent.

Without turning his head, Filippo could see through a chink in the curtain. Long dark shadows fell like bars through the arched windows across the stone floor. There was no moonlight, but just the faint glow of candlelight wavering round the room.

Whoever it was thought himself alone. The shadow slid across the walls, gigantic, giving the figure a sinister hunched-up look as, steadily and methodically, it moved round the workshop looking for something.

He saw the figure intermittently, as much as his chink of curtain would let him, for he dared not raise himself to see more clearly, but he knew it hovered over worktops, where sketches and designs lay spread everywhere. It went to cupboards and miraculously opened them without a sound; then to the drawers of precious stones, with no need of keys. One by one, each was scrutinised, then meticulously replaced. He was seeking something in particular, but not finding it.

Filippo's terror intensified. The shadow turned towards him. He had noticed the curtained niche. He was coming over to him. The moon caught a glint of metal. A knife? Instinctively, Filippo rolled over to the far side of his bed and silently slid himself down the crack between the bed and the wall, pulling his covering with him, just as he used to do as an infant, when he would hide from Mama. He sensed the curtain held back, a presence hovered briefly, then moved away. A faint smell of cinnamon hung in the air.

Filippo watched from under the bed. Whoever it was moved rapidly across the room as if to leave, then paused as something caught his eye. Momentarily, the candle was raised and the room rotated with the shadows as it was swung round. He heard a muffled exclamation. 'Ah!' Then pouff! The flame was extinguished and the intruder vanished.

Filippo couldn't move. He lay under the bed for the rest of the night, too terrified to move, and waited for daylight. When, at last, the pale grey light gleamed through the arched windows, and the shadows began to fade, he unfroze his muscles and stiffly rolled out.

It was as though nothing had happened, as though no one had come. It could all have been a lucid dream – something that had seemed real, but wasn't. He checked through everything. There was not one detail to suggest anyone had been there. Not one thing out of place or set back differently. He remembered the last sight of the presence, where he had stood and paused, where he had given one short gasp before plunging into darkness. Filippo slowly went to the exact spot. Then he was certain. It hadn't been a dream. Someone had come into the workshop.

In the pale brightening light of day, Filippo had found

himself looking into the portrait of his father, Geronimo Veroneo, his pale green eyes glimmering as if alive. 'Look!' they seemed to say. 'This is what he was looking for!' Filippo's eyes were drawn inexorably to the masterpiece entwined in his fingers. This was what the intruder had seen. The Ocean of the Moon.

'Carlo! He recognised it!' cried Filippo, rocking the boat in his intensity. 'I know he recognised it.'

'Take it easy, *fratellino*. Are you sure it was the Musalman? Did you see his face?' asked Carlo, steadying the boat with an oar.

'Yes. Well. Not exactly . . . it was too dark. I just know. I mean, who else could it have been? If he had come from outside, Moro would have barked, and he didn't. That's all he wants, this Musalman. He just wants Papa's diamond,' cried Filippo.

For a while, Carlo rested on his oars and said nothing.

Filippo too said nothing, fearing to disturb his brother's thoughts. But he was bursting to say more, and finally asked, 'Do you believe him when he says Papa is alive?'

'I don't know. We have only the Musalman's word for it. But if Papa needed a ransom, he would have told him about the diamond. Papa would know it's the only thing we have valuable enough to get him released,' Carlo reasoned. 'On the other hand, yes, it's possible he may have been sent by someone to trick us into parting with the pendant, or to steal it.'

'Pagliarin?'

Carlo shrugged. 'Perhaps.'

'The pig-dog! The stinking piece of . . . How could he do that to us – especially to Mama? I suppose if the Musalman had found it, he would have stolen it from us and vanished into thin air, the low-down, good-for-nothing . . . I could kill him.'

'Shush!' Carlo shut him up again. 'I'm trying to think.'

'He left a funny smell too, sort of like cinnamon.'

'Cinnamon?' Carlo looked up quickly as a swift memory of his attacker in the alley flashed through his mind. He lifted the oars and began to row again, as if by exerting himself physically, his brain would also be invigorated and come up with a solution.

When they reached the island, it was a relief to get wet, jumping into the cool reedy shallows to pull the little boat up on to the shore. There was already a smattering of women and children from neighbouring islands, squelching among the mud flats, competing with the gulls and wading birds for mussels, molluscs and crabs left by the tide. The brothers walked up into the deep shade of the cypress trees and into the wilder, cool foliage of ancient gnarled trees. Soon they left the shore behind and the sounds of other humans, and it was just the two of them.

'The important question to be asked is do we believe our

father is alive? If so, do we give the Musalman the Ocean of the Moon?'

'We can't!' Filippo shook his head, aghast. 'And Papa wouldn't want it – surely?'

'Not even if it means his life?' asked Carlo. 'And what about us? What about Mama? Do our wishes not count? What value has the diamond, if it can't even buy back our father's life? We could never sell it, even if we were starving – we could never look at it again. It would be a dead thing without meaning, and even without beauty. It would become an object of abhorrence to us. Think about it. If we don't give it to the Musalman, Pagliarin will get hold of it. He's determined to.'

Filippo was silent. He dropped back disconsolately, while Carlo walked on with head down and hands clasped behind his back.

'But the Musalman, we can't trust him! He could have cut our throats in the night . . . he could have . . .'

'He could have, Filippo, but he didn't – if it was him, and I'm not sure that it was.'

'But Moro . . .'

'There are ways to silence dogs.' Carlo spoke quietly. 'Facts, Filippo, we can only stick to facts. Who wants the diamond?'

'Bernardo.'

'Who objects to me being guardian of the family?'

'Bernardo.'

'Who would want to save my life from an assassin?'

'We would – and Papa.'

'Or a messenger sent by Papa?' Carlo frowned anxiously. 'We have to make some very swift decisions. We have to choose between trusting the Musalman, who we don't know, or being at the mercy of Pagliarin, who we do know – only too well. We also know that Pagliarin has been ruined. All his ships were lost at sea, and he's up to his nose in debt. All he has left is us, and Papa's business.'

'That's why . . .'

'Yes, that's why he wants to get rid of us, get hold of the business and put in his own sons. Marrying off Sofia and Gabriella is his ploy for getting hold of the Ocean of the Moon and all our assets.'

'What about the Musalman?'

'You're right, we can't trust him altogether. Perhaps he just wants the diamond for himself. We don't know if Papa is alive or dead. But consider this: the Musalman says Papa is still alive, Pagliarin says he is dead. The Musalman asks for a ransom, Pagliarin asks for a dowry. Who would you rather trust, Pagliarin or the Musalman?'

Filippo looked into his brother's face. Suddenly, he realised that Carlo was talking to him man to man, sharing his thoughts and anxieties. A few moments ago he had just been little Pippo, the Benjamin of the family, the baby, but with Giuseppe dead, Filippo had grown up, almost overnight, and filled his shoes.

'Who do we trust? We have a choice,' murmured Carlo, 'or we *think* we have a choice. Perhaps we should say, we have no choice except to choose, but then it is God's will.'

'In that case, I suppose I choose the Musalman,' said Filippo warily.

'Agreed,' said Carlo, putting his hand on his brother's shoulder.

'Does it mean you are going to give him the Ocean of the Moon?'

'No. Yes. Not exactly. Perhaps it wasn't the Musalman who came into the workshop. He wasn't the one trying to kill me and Giuseppe. The boatman told me he had brought him straight from a ship.'

'We can't trust him completely though,' warned Filippo.

'That's why I will give him the Ocean of the Moon, but one of us must go with him to Afghanistan.'

'You?' whispered Filippo.

'You,' Carlo said quietly.

'Me?' Filippo's stomach turned over. 'Me?' He was aghast, then disbelieving. Then he laughed. 'Me? You can't mean it! Carlo, I've never even been to Verona.'

'You're the only one who can,' said Carlo. 'I would go if

Giuseppe were alive to carry on the business. But now, if I went with him, how would you keep things going? You're good, *fratellino*, but not yet good enough. The rest of the trade would make mincemeat of you. And if I went, ran into trouble like Papa and didn't come back for years, what would happen to you all? Pagliarin would take everything. I can still fight my case with the council. I still have hopes of being recognised as the "legal guardian" until Papa returns. My case is even stronger now that we have information that he is alive.'

'But me take the Ocean of the Moon . . .?' Filippo was filled with dread.

'Yes, this.' Carlo put his hand into his jerkin pocket and produced a leather pouch pulled tightly closed with a drawstring. Casually, he tossed it to his brother. Filippo's hands flew open automatically, and caught it. He clasped it to his chest with a gasp of alarm. 'Look at it,' said Carlo. 'You've never seen it, have you, except in the portrait?'

Filippo pulled open the string and felt inside. His fingers closed over something hard and sharp. He tipped it out into the palm of his hand.

The soft light falling through the trees instantly entered the diamond, flashing like a shooting star. It diffused through its crystalline facets, reflecting the pearls, opals and moonstones. It was like holding a constellation in his hands.

Carlo burst out laughing at his brother's look of idiotic astonishment. It wasn't an altogether pleasant laugh, edged with anxiety and fear, and all the burden of responsibility that he had been carrying for so long.

'It's . . . beautiful . . . it's fabulous . . .' Filippo stuttered.

'And you know what, *fratellino*?' said Carlo, leaning forward, his laughter dying away. 'It's a fake. Papa and I made it together. It was his way of teaching me the trade, and also a way to make an exact replica of the pendant for security. I was younger than you – do you realise that? Even Mama doesn't know. He thought it was safer that no one else knew. Papa exchanged the real one for this before he went away. He told no one but me. She thinks this one is the real one. She gave it me to keep in a safer place than her bedroom, ever since Bernardo began pestering her for it. But it was the fake she has had all this time and the fake that she showed Elisabetta. Only I know where the real one is.'

'And you want me to take this, and go with the Musalman to Afghanistan?' Filippo's head reeled as thousands of thoughts streamed through his mind. He was confronted with all his fantasies and dreams, of travelling and seeing the world, of being the one to find his father and bring him home. But suddenly his fantasies were becoming reality, and instead of joy and excitement, he felt as if he had been flung into a black pit.

His mouth had gone dry and he felt sick to his stomach. 'I can't. I can't.'

Carlo didn't respond. He pulled out a flask from his sling bag and swallowed back some water. 'Want some?'

Tears fell as Filippo folded the pendant back into its pouch and returned it to his brother. 'I'm sorry Carlo, I'm sorry.'

Carlo shrugged and, with the same casualness as he had taken it out, dropped it back into his bag. He handed the flask of water to Filippo. 'You need time to think about it.'

Filippo wept, gulped back his tears, but wept again. It was the first time he had let go since they buried Giuseppe. He wept for his brother, wept for fear of the future and what could happen to them all. What was his choice? If he didn't go with the Musalman, he would have to go and live in Pagliarin's household. He wept for his own terror at being confronted with leaving home, leaving Mama, Gabriella and Sofia to go and look for his father – a man he didn't even know.

Through blurred eyes, he gazed across the water to Venice, the only world he had ever known. *O Bellissima*! Suddenly, it had never looked more beautiful. The golden dome of San Marco blazed in the sunlight, like a beacon. It seemed that all the lions of Venice leapt from their pedestals and fountain heads: leapt from the walls and tops of doorways, broke out of the stone city – for what were they doing in a city of stone and water? They seemed to spring across the turrets and palace roofs, as if they would fly back to Asia and Africa, to their desert homes and mountain lairs. Yet here he was, Filippo, so full of brave plans for adventure, reduced to a pathetic coward. Now Carlo would know he wasn't a man after all, just a snivelling boy.

They continued walking in silence, except for Filippo's gulps and smothered sobs. Turning ever deeper into tangled undergrowth, they skirted the walls of a derelict chapel, and came to a small grotto almost covered with trailing vines. A faded wooden figure of a saint was almost lost in the cramped darkness of the rock. Carlo stopped briefly and crossed himself. They paused, each deep in their own thoughts. Carlo handed Filippo the flask of water again. He made no comment, ignored his younger brother's distress, and set off once more. Filippo drank deeply and followed, running to keep up. Gradually, by having to concentrate on his footing and not lose sight of Carlo, he recovered himself.

'But Carlo!' he called out at last.

Carlo stopped and turned round with a faint smile.

'The Musalman is a jeweller too, he said so. He would know it's a fake.'

Carlo's smiled remained. 'Signor Sadiqui Iqbal Khan, our Musalman, is no jeweller – I'd stake my life on it. He won't know. I'm not so naïve as to simply take him at his word. After you had gone to bed, I got out some jewels on the pretext of showing him what our assets were, but I was testing him. He has a certain eye. He can tell an opal from a moonstone, a garnet from a ruby, a crystal from a diamond. But he wouldn't know this fake diamond from the real thing – not this one – even if he held it in his hand to feel the weight. This one is cunning. Grandfather learned the arts from jewellers at the Moghul court, and then taught Papa all the secrets of the trade. Only a true jeweller would even suspect that it wasn't the real thing. But, you're right. You can't go with just the fake. So you will take both – if you can find the courage to go, that is.'

But from his tone of voice, Filippo knew that Carlo wasn't really giving him a choice.

The lagoon was still when they returned to the shore, like a vast liquid canvas with all sorts of watercraft painted on to its surface. As a fisherman cast his net, a spangle of spray arched into the sun, flashed, and was extinguished. Filippo remembered how only two days ago he had been ready to run away with Andreas on that fishing trip all the way to the Greek islands, and perhaps further, to Arabia and India, even to China. He fantasised about being Odysseus, or a great explorer like Marco Polo, becoming rich and famous. Now here he was, barely able to choke back his tears, so scared of leaving home.

'Andreas is going on his first trip ever to the Greek islands in a day or two. I wanted to go too,' Filippo said with an ironical smile.

'Yes, I know,' said Carlo, 'and I think you should go.'

'Go? Go with Andreas and Stefano?' Filippo felt his old excitement surge back.

'It's the best way for you to leave Venice without suspicion. Come on, let's go.'

Filippo could hardly draw breath as Carlo continued, 'We have very little time. We have much to do. It's all up to you, little Benjamino.'

'What about Mama?' Filippo asked in a small voice.

'We will tell her you're going on a short trip with Andreas, but we can't tell her the full truth. Not yet. She'll only get upset. I'll tell her when it's right. The main thing is that Bernardo doesn't get to hear. He would suspect something and stop you.' Carlo waded into the water and gripped the stern of the boat. 'Get in,' he ordered.

Filippo clambered aboard and took hold of the oars. The boat rocked violently, as Carlo dragged it free from the shore and jumped in. Filippo rowed, and Carlo sat in the stern pulling the rudder, but barely noting the direction. His eyes were staring toward the Spinalungi, where a huge merchant ship was slowly easing its way through the gap and into the open ocean beyond.

'So, will you do it?' asked Carlo.

'Yes,' said Filippo tugging on the oars, trying to suppress the terror which still threatened to engulf his excitement. 'Where are we going now?'

'We're going to the ghetto. There's an old rabbi who's supposed to be a surgeon, and good with the knife. There is the matter of how to conceal the real diamond on you.'

Chapter Eleven

❖

A diamond in the skull

The diamond is set into my skull. It dances in my brain, sparkles and gleams as though I have been given another eye. Ever since the old rabbi inserted it into my head, I have been bombarded with strange sensations. I can see forwards and backwards, sideways, up and down with such clarity and detail that even the smallest particles of dust are revealed to me in all their constituents. I seem to see inside people's heads, read their thoughts, even enter their dreams. It gives me the power to understand all the languages of the world, communicate with animals, sing the same songs as birds.

I sit in Papa's chair and feel him all round me, rushing through my bloodstream, making my nerve-ends tingle. He has entered through the pores of my skin like the gentle heat from millions of specks of sunshine pouring through the window and, as my hands spread over the arm rests, I see his hands merge with mine.

I think I may be invisible. Elisabetta has come. She stands

now in the doorway staring at me, yet unfocused as if she doesn't see me. I look into her face, feeling my childish hostility rising up inside me. 'I hate Betta, I hate Bernardo, I hate . . .' And then my diamond-struck gaze passes through the dilated pupils of her eyes. I enter her soul and am shocked. It is a chamber of ice, somewhere down at the bottom of one of those frozen seas I've heard tell of in the north. There, jade green waves swirl and creak as they solidify death-white, imprisoning giant ships within their petrified grip, and squeezing till they are reduced to shreds of timber. She is trapped beneath, in this frozen hell of an ocean – oh poor sacrificed daughter – she too is a prisoner being slowly crushed. I swim towards her and take her hand. I must save her; I must save her. Somehow, we must break free of that icy chamber and rise through the ocean till we reach the surface.

I reach her side. I stand and stare at what she is staring at, and there is Papa, still sitting in his chair.

'Do you see him too, Betta?' I whisper excitedly.

'See who?' Her voice is harsh. She turns and looks at me and her glazed eyes focus. She sees me.

'Papa, of course.'

'You idiot, Pippo!' She raises her hand and though the blow isn't struck, I recoil instinctively. The pain sears through my head, for the wound is still new, hiding beneath my curls and the specially-woven hair stitched over the incision in my skull. I raise my arm to protect myself and just say, 'Don't, Betta.' And she doesn't.

Tears fill her eyes and she turns away, rapidly. 'Where is everyone?' she asks.

Pagliarin hadn't told Elisabetta the news that her father was alive and awaiting a ransom to set him free. But he fretted to know if this news had reached the Veroneo family. His man had been given a merciless beating for losing that beggarly messenger, Rodriguez, who could have blabbed all over the city by now.

He sent out spies, but they hadn't found him, and Pagliarin got no confirmation or reassurance. He found himself buffeted by waves of frenzy and frustration, but one thing was clear: the answer to all his financial problems lay with the Veroneo business. This wretched man could cause havoc with his news that Geronimo needed a substantial ransom to be freed. Pagliarin had to know if Rodriguez knew about all Geronimo's assets, especially the Ocean of the Moon. He must move quickly. So he had tugged the bell-pull and summoned his slave, Pelle. 'Request the Signora to attend me immediately,' he ordered.

'Ah, my little pigeon,' he cooed, rising from his chair to

greet her when she had entered a few moments later. Elisabetta looked strained and formal in her mourning dress. The days when she might have run to him like a child and thrown her arms round his neck had gone since Giuseppe's death, since he had struck her to the floor. Now she only glanced at him briefly, then dropped her gaze. But he drew her fondly into his arms, to soften her and make her more pliable to his wishes.

'Have you had any communication with your family in the last few days?' he murmured into her hair, though he knew the answer. 'No messages?'

'No, Signor,' she replied stiffly. 'Not for a while.' Not for a month, not since the day of the funeral when Mama hardly noticed my existence, she thought to herself.

He studied her face to see if he could detect a lie, but it was listless and passive.

'Then go, my sweet. I'm sure your dear mama would be pleased to see her daughter. You must not lose touch with them in these dark days.'

Elisabetta had draped herself in her black hooded cloak. She also put on a white mask to protect her identity, before stepping into the Pagliarin sedan. As she was gently jogged along towards her childhood home, she pondered on what this new indulgence of her husband could mean. He usually hated her going home. She shrugged cynically. She had no illusions any

more. Her husband rarely performed any action without there
being an ulterior motive.

When she entered the house it was eerily quiet. A new
kitchen girl looked up indifferently from her parsley chopping,
and her '*Buon giorno, Signora*' was practically inaudible. She
discovered Rosa preparing the meal. The house was usually
filled with the sound of her singing, laughing, nagging, and
clattering her pots and pans, but today her lips were pursed.
Even the canary was subdued.

'Where is everyone?' demanded Elisabetta, removing her
mask.

'Why should Rosa know? Isn't Rosa the last to know
anything these days? The man from Hindustan is gone, Carlo is
out, Filippo is somewhere. The girls have gone to church with
your mama to light a candle for your Papa and Giuseppe – but
that's all I know, and no one told me you were visiting.'

'Sorry, Rosa.' Elisabetta was unexpectedly meek, and Rosa
looked at her closely.

'You all right, my little Bettina? She hadn't used that pet
name since Elisabetta married. Suddenly her experienced old
eye noted the young woman's pale cheeks, that she was
thinner and looked less lustrous. The gleam had gone from
her eye, and the usual arrogance had been replaced by a
cowed look.

'What do you mean, the man from Hindustan? What man?' Elisabetta frowned.

Rosa hesitated, and inwardly cursed her loose tongue. She hadn't been ordered to say nothing, yet she knew instinctively that she should have kept quiet, especially to someone from the household of Pagliarin. 'Oh, just a passing merchant from the east with precious stones to sell. He's been visiting all the jewellers in the district.' She waved a hand inconsequentially. 'Carlo saw something which caught his eye, so I expect they've all gone to the stone-cutters.'

'Had this man from Hindustan heard the name of my father?'

'I'm sure they asked him. Filippo never lets anyone who's been within a thousand miles of Hindustan get away without being asked if they have heard of him. Shall I make some rosehip tea, Signora? Were you expected?'

Elisabetta noticed that Rosa had reverted quickly back to her formal title. 'No. I decided at the last moment. I haven't seen you all since Beppe's . . .' her voice trailed away. A tear hung on her lashes, but she blinked it back fiercely and said, 'Thank you, Rosa. I'd love some tea.' While she waited, she had wandered over to the threshold of the parlour and looked through to Papa's chair. She murmured soft words to old Forza who, without even raising his head at the sound of her voice, thumped his tail with gentle familiarity. Then suddenly, there was Filippo at her side, babbling on stupidly about seeing Papa, and she felt her anger bringing her to the point of slapping him.

'Don't, Betta.' Filippo's soft reprimand had arrested her.

Her hand had dropped to her side without striking a blow. She hadn't yet made amends for the previous slap she had given him outside the church, and she had promised the priest in confession to be reconciled with her little brother. She turned to him. 'Pippo?' But he ran away from her, silently, without another word. 'Please come back,' she had called. It wasn't Filippo she was angry with. It was Papa, for having made her marry Bernardo Pagliarin. Papa, who should have known the man was a monster. Papa, who had gone away and left them all to his mercy.

When she had drunk her tea, she made her way up to the workshop. Filippo was there tidying things up. That was not like Filippo, who was always being yelled at by Carlo to keep some order in the place.

'I know you don't want to live with us, Pippo, but I want you to come so much. Just to have some of my own family around me will make me feel less lonely. I'm sorry if I'm a bit rough with you sometimes. Please forgive me. I'll watch my temper in future. We should be friends – just like we used to be.' Elisabetta held out her hands.

* * *

With my diamond eye, I see my sister in her icy chamber, so desolate. 'Oh! Betta, Betta, I can't help you now. There's no time – and besides, I have no power,' I cry inside my head. 'But when Papa is free, he will come and save you, and I will be your friend.' My thoughts flutter desperately like trapped birds – I can't let them out and tell her. The secret is unbearable, but it must be kept.

'That's all right, Betta. I shouldn't have thrown that crab at you,' Filippo said out loud. 'Sorry.'

'We're friends then?' she smiled wanly.

'Friends.'

Voices swept into the house downstairs. Teodora and the girls had come back. Elisabetta rushed down to meet them. Filippo continued his tidying up. Every action now was a farewell; his fingers lingering on surfaces, and holding objects just a fraction longer, as if somehow they could retain the memory of their feel.

The secret was unbearable, but it had to be kept. Even Teodora couldn't be told that, when Carlo rowed him across the lagoon tomorrow to Andreas's island, Filippo would not return for a long time.

Chapter Twelve

❖

A spy of quality

Rodriguez strode along the Riva degli Schiavoni. A keen eye would have noted the slightest of limps, but mostly it was well disguised. He was a foppish sort of fellow, with a sweeping hat in the Dutch style with ostrich feathers flopping and bobbing over one ear. He looked like a foreign merchant, which in a way he was.

He strode about the city with an air of superior respectability, putting about that he was a merchant man seeking to buy Spanish gold. He was indeed buying gold. But only a week back, he had arrived in Venice on a ship, looking like a travel-worn wanderer. He had been announced at Pagliarin's household as a humble messenger, and had stood as deferentially as it was in his bones to do before that jellified eel of a man, Bernardo, with his message that Geronimo Veroneo was alive and in need of a ransom. On that occasion he was there partly as a friend of Geronimo, but partly in the employ of the Grand Vizier in the court of the Great Moghul at Agra in Hindustan.

Rodriguez prided himself on his reputation for being, if nothing else, 'trustworthy'. Any job he undertook, whether it was delivering a message, or murdering a man, he liked to know it had been done well and in accordance with the wishes of his paymaster. He never cut corners, and was unforgiving if others did. That was why he felt so irritated. He had delivered the news about Geronimo requiring a ransom to Bernardo Pagliarin, and Pagliarin had ignored it. Instead of finding enough for a ransom, Pagliarin had paid him off with a measly three florins for his pains, and put an incompetent spy on his tail. So it felt like a job unfinished.

Why? A good agent always asks why. Why wasn't Pagliarin prepared to pay the ransom to release his father-in-law? Without any feasible answers, Rodriguez didn't feel his mission had been accomplished, and the added indignity of being followed raised his suspicions as well as his hackles.

Refusing to be hounded out of Venice, let alone murdered by one of Pagliarin's idiots, he had simply changed appearance, once, twice, however many times it took, to frequent the docks, dens, theatres, marketplaces and wine houses of Venice to wheedle out information. He soon found out that Pagliarin's ships had been lost at sea, and most of his business gone down to the bottom with them. He soon concluded that Pagliarin's plan was to get hold of the Veroneo business and all its assets.

But he was sure there was more to it than met the eye.

As good a secret agent as he was, he wasn't superhuman. Nor did he possess a third eye. How was he to know about a certain Musalman? A city like Venice is a stepping-off point for all directions of the globe, where people of all races and creeds come and go by sea or road – a city of strangers. How could he know of a *particular* man stepping off a ship? That this particular man had shared the same prison cell as Veroneo for ten years? That this particular man had been freed, and come all the way from India to the household of the Veroneo family? A man who was not a spy or an agent, not a trader or a diplomat, not a courier or a soldier, not a representative working for any of the system of networks which spangled across the trading routes between Europe and Asia like a fine spider's web. How could Rodriguez know that the Musalman was just a man on a personal mission, working for no one but himself? How could he have known?

A good agent reacts to changed circumstances, reassesses the options, changes course when necessary. During a delicate nocturnal break-in and search of the Veroneo household, Rodriguez had not expected to find this man, a Hindustani, asleep in bed in the very bosom of Geronimo's family. He had stood over him, trying to decide what to do about him. Who was he? How was he able to charm his way into the household and become their guest? It had to be because he had come to seek a ransom. Rodriguez asked the same question as the family had done: why would a man risk such a long and dangerous journey all the way to Venice, unless it was for something of huge value? True, Veroneo was a jeweller. There were gems, but Hindustan was awash with gems. There had to be something more extraordinary, and he was sure this man knew what it was.

Not for Rodriguez was there a belief in any notions of brotherly love, the undying bonds between friends, even between cell mates. Nor did he believe in promises made which could last beyond the grave. He believed in things you could touch. He believed in money. Rodriguez had stared into the portrait of Geronimo. 'Come on, my friend, what is it you have that the Musalman wants, that Pagliarin won't give?' Should he kill him there and then? But no. It was too soon to kill him. Not until he knew what the man was after.

Rodriguez paused, looking out beyond the fluttering sails and the commercial frenzy of the Grand Canal, then turned away sharply and headed into the Castello district.

Chapter Thirteen

❖

The flute

Somewhere off the Fondamente San Lorenzo the sound of a flute rose and fell among the hubbub of the market stalls lining the streets and alleys. A knowledgeable ear might have detected a simple row of eight notes which were played in variation swaying through whole tones, half tones, quarter tones, and even tones in between. The melody was like a snake: mesmerising, forgettable, and yet instantly recognisable.

Filippo paused and frowned, as he slowly collected together the things that he could not be without, taking care to avoid fierce movements with his head which could send shooting pains through it. He was sure he had heard that tune before. He went over to the window and looked out across the canal. Everything sparkled and danced. It was as if he could penetrate the sunbeams with his eye, count each hair of the cat that idled by, pick out the finest detail in the veins of the fig tree which fanned out across the wall of the garden opposite. But he could not see the player, nor a second flautist who sent an answering phrase.

The melody ended abruptly. Elisabetta suddenly left the house and stood in the street awaiting her sedan, her face mask dangling in her fingers as if she no longer cared whether she was recognised or not. She looked pathetic and desolate. Filippo called out to her, 'Bye, Elisabetta!' But she didn't hear him amid the raucous cries of evening streetsellers, and the yells of boatmen as they manoeuvered their way around each other.

Since it would never have occurred to her to look into the faces of her sedan carriers, how was she to know that these men were not the same who had brought her there – and were not in Bernardo's employ? She didn't look into the face of the man who drew aside the curtains and helped her in, nor those in front and behind who lifted the poles. And she didn't know that someone followed, loping along behind, as they set off at a steady jog. They had turned down a narrow alley which brought them out into the Campo Santa Maria Formosa, but instead of taking the direction for the Rialto district, she was carried deeper into one of the busiest and most crowded parts of the markets around San Zulian, and soon they were in a jam on one of the narrow bridges crossing the Rio Fuseri.

They came to a standstill and lowered the sedan.

Elisabetta peered out, puzzled and irritated. 'What are we doing here? Why have we stopped? This is not the way.'

'We're stuck, Signora. A pack horse has gone down ahead

and held everything up. I was trying to find a way round it,' explained a fellow, not turning round.

With a weary shrug, she leaned back into the cushions, almost glad of the delay for which she couldn't be held responsible. It postponed the return to a household which now filled her with despair.

A voice suddenly quivered in her ear, startling Elisabetta out of her reverie. 'Signora! Don't scream and I'll let you go,' the voice rasped deep into her ear as, simultaneously, a broad hand thrust itself inside the sedan and clamped over her mouth and nose.

She struggled for breath.

The voice was deadly. 'I'm going to give you an explanation. If you understand, nod, and then I'll take my hand away.' The moisture of her panic-stricken breath gathered like a dewpond in the palm of his hand. 'Your father is alive. He's a hostage in Afghanistan,' continued the voice. It was calm and barely audible. Her body stiffened almost to breaking point. The little puffs of shallow breaths almost ceased.

She hadn't known.

'Your husband didn't tell you?' he tutted with sarcastic disapproval.

No, thought Elisabetta with sickening realisation, neither did my brother Carlo, or my mother.

'I will take my hand away, but believe me, Signora, if you scream, I shall vanish into thin air. You will never hear of me again, and you will have to live with the knowledge that you destroyed any chance of helping your father. You will also destroy any chance of freeing your family from your husband's tyranny. Do you understand? Please nod if you do.'

Elisabetta nodded. The hand slackened but stayed over her mouth. She breathed freely.

'Your father needs a ransom. Your husband knows, but is unwilling to co-operate. I wonder why nobody told you?'

Because, Elisabetta howled inside her head, because nobody trusts me. My own brother and mother don't trust me, and neither does Bernardo. Her stiff body suddenly sagged as if broken. She shuddered with silent sobs.

The hand relaxed further, but lay on her cheek, ready to pounce if she cried out. 'If Pagliarin won't pay up, has your family any assets which could be sufficient to have your father released?' The voice was soft but insistent.

'The Ocean of the Moon.' Elisabetta whispered the words into the palm of his hand. His fingers slackened over her face.

'What?' It was as though something dawned on him.

'The Ocean of the Moon. It's a diamond. It's my father's most valuable piece.'

'Does your husband have it?'

Gasping to form words amidst her weeping, she stammered, 'N-no, h-he's never seen it. But he knows of it. He wanted me to get it for him. But M-mama wouldn't even let me borrow it.'

'So your mother has it?'

'Yes!' Elisabetta's voice rose in terror. 'Oh sweet Jesus! You won't hurt her, will you?'

'Uh uh uh!' The hand moved as swiftly as a snake and clamped over her mouth again. 'Keep your voice down, Signora.'

She leaned into his touch in despairing surrender. She didn't care any more. This was an assassin's hand. If he chose to kill her, so be it. She almost welcomed it. She could love death. There was something tender in the way he cupped her tear-drenched face in his hand.

His fingers loosened so that she could breathe again, and trailed lightly, menacingly, down her neck, fragile as a sparrow, pausing over her thudding pulse. 'I am an old friend of your father. I've come to obtain a ransom large enough to free him.'

Elisabetta nodded.

'It seems as if your husband, Signor Pagliarin, has need of the diamond for his own sake. He is ruined, is he not?'

Silence.

'Who is the Musalman who called at the house on Rio di San Lorenzo – a man from Hindustan?'

Elisabetta gasped. 'How did you know? I didn't know of him

till today, and I never saw him. Only Rosa mentioned that a Hindustani jeweller was trying to sell Carlo some precious stones. Carlo will know. But first, he's taking my little brother Filippo over to . . . He's going on a fishing trip with his Greek friend, Andreas.'

The hand slid from her throat to her shoulder. There was a sudden gentleness, a pause, then it was gone.

'Sit back, Signora!' called one of the carriers. 'We're off again.'

'Wait!' The moment was too brief. 'Don't go.' She felt bereft. Her fear had been replaced by a strange need. She pressed her hand to her cheek, where his hand had been, spread her fingers over her nose as he had done. His skin had left a faint smell of cinnamon. She closed her eyes and breathed it in, then put her palm to her mouth and kissed it.

There was movement outside. It jolted her back to reality – guilt. Her hand dropped to her lap, and she rubbed the palm with her shawl as if to remove all contact. Was she mad?

She was being lifted again. She craned out of the window but, amidst the seething crowd, she couldn't identify who had been speaking to her.

'Please . . .' she whispered. Please? She wondered what she had meant. Please don't hurt us? Please don't leave me? Please . . . save me?

* * *

Andreas sang out loud as he rowed down the Grand Canal.

> La biondina in gondoleta
> L'altra sera go mena.
> Dal piaser la povereta
> La s'ha in bota indormenza.

He had come across from the island to do last-minute errands. Apart from fish, they were taking a small cargo of items to sell among the islands along the Adriatic coast. He had to buy more twine for sewing nets, needles, hooks, knives and other metal objects. He was also to purchase a basket of lemons, six fat earthenware jars of olives and six rounds of cheese. They were set to go on the night tide.

The wake of a small thirty-oar merchant ship sent ripples fanning out across the water, making his little boat rock as if it were laughing. He wound his way into the canals that would take him to the metal and weaving districts, and finally, before returning home, he would visit the fruit and vegetable market. He chanted his father's list to himself, going from stall to stall, bargaining at the top of his voice. He kept looking around, hoping to see Filippo. It would be their last chance to be together for weeks.

When he staggered back to his little craft, his muscles

burning with the weight, a man stood nearby piping on a flute. Andreas wouldn't have even given him a second glance, had the man not spoken to him. 'Going on a big trip, then?'

Andreas was taken aback at being spoken to. He couldn't quite see his face. He wasn't a vagrant or an itinerant musician, nor an actor or a street performer. He was probably a trader from the east, though he was dressed in a mixture of styles with his Moroccan leather boots and britches, loosely covered over with a North African burnoose, beneath which glinted a scimitar.

'As far as Crete. I've never been that far before.'

'Ah ha! Crete!' murmured the man and, as if propelled by some force, he turned and just strode quickly away.

Chapter Fourteen

❖

The third eye

The sea breathes and sighs on the mud flats. There is a crackle of flames, familiar faces glancing at each other in the firelight, gentle smiles and soft voices. They eat Grandmother's food and listen to her stories, while she stitches gems into the linings of Filippo's underclothes and cap. She can keep secrets. The jewels are stitched into the hems and seams of his underclothes, while the Ocean of the Moon, the replica that is, is contained within a small, shabby, inconsequential-looking little leather pouch, and hung round his neck along with his crucifix and St Christopher.

'Nurse,' said Telemachus, son of Odysseus. 'Fill me twelve jars with sweet white wine. Close each with a lid. Pour me barley meal into well-sewn skins, and let there be twenty measures of the grain which are bruised barley meal – and tell no one.'

Stefano has been smoking fish all day, enough to see them

through until they reach Spalato, on the Illyrian coast. He knows by then he will have caught a boat load of fresh fish which he must offload and sell in the markets. From there, they will meander among the islands, selling and buying and restocking their stores, until they reach Crete.

Andreas was still at the Rialto when Carlo had rowed Filippo across to the island. For the moment, only Stefano and Grandma knew that Filippo was going with them, and that in Crete, he would meet up with the Musalman and continue with him to India. It was safer that way.

'How will he find you?' Carlo had asked the Musalman.

'I will find him,' came the reply.

> *The eye never has enough of seeing,*
> *Or the ear its fill of hearing,*

His mind wandered deliriously. Flashes of pain seared through his head where an old muttering rabbi had cut a hole into his skull and inset the Ocean of the Moon.

> *What has been will be again,*
> *What has been done will be done again,*
> *There is nothing new under the sun.*

Mumbling under his breath all the time in Hebrew, the rabbi worked all night long, bent over him. He had sawn out a section of Filippo's skull and set the diamond into his head, as he would set a precious stone into its mount. The diamond had been too big to fit the whole of it, so skilfully, he had placed the narrower end into the skull and, getting some animal skin, had enclosed the rest which protruded like a bump, and stitched it to his scalp.

The rabbi wove Filippo's hair and stitches in with each other, and rearranged his long brown curls so they fell naturally over the spot where the diamond had been concealed. His voice droned on . . . and on . . . and on . . . incomprehensible, repetitive, seamless, as though his tongue threaded words like fingers threaded beads.

Suddenly, the words began to glimmer with meaning, springing like opening flowers inside Filippo's brain . . . The Lord said . . . the Lord said . . .

> *I will take away their harvest . . .*
> *There will be no grapes on the vine . . .*
> *There will be no figs on the tree . . .*
> *and their leaves will wither . . .*
> *What I have given them will be taken away . . .*

Filippo could understand. He had been given another ear, another tongue, a gift of translation. He had been given a third eye – an all-seeing, all-knowing eye – which could not be dimmed by hair or skin, which heightened all his senses beyond the threshold of anything he had ever known before.

> *Those destined for death, to death,*
> *Those for the sword to the sword,*
> *Those for starvation, to starvation,*
> *Those for captivity, to captivity . . .*

The words had frightened him. He clasped the rabbi's hand. 'What's going to happen to me?' he asked.

'Meaningless, meaningless, utterly meaningless. Everything is meaningless,' the rabbi muttered, as if he had wandered throughout all time and history, as if he had seen everything there was to be seen under the sun.

'What must I do?' Filippo shuddered.

'Speak the truth, but speak it gently.' His voice nearly died away, but it lifted again. 'Don't judge the present for what will happen in the future.' The rabbi's voice was suddenly clear, as if he had woken from a dream.

When the task was done, Carlo thanked the old man and paid him what he asked. He took Filippo away, speechless and full of terror, and rowed him across to the island.

Filippo didn't sit by the fire with the others. Waiting for Andreas to return from the Rialto, he lay on Andreas's mattress trying to forget the Rabbi's disturbing words. Grandma was telling her stories about Odysseus, as she stitched gems into his clothes.

'*Odysseus handed the Cyclops, Polythemus, a rich dark wine to drink. It was sweet, and he found great delight in drinking it, and Odysseus gave him another cup and another, till the Cyclops fell backwards with face upturned, into a deep sleep. Then Odysseus and his men drew lots as to who would take a club of olive wood, which they had secretly fined down to a sharp point, and plunge it into the one eye of Polythemus while he slept. It fell to Odysseus to do the deed. As when a smith dips the iron axe into chill water with a great hissing, so did the eye of Polythemus hiss as Odysseus plunged it in like a man bores a ship's beam with a drill. The Cyclops raised a great and terrible cry which made the rock of the cave ring all around, and sent Odysseus and his men fleeing into the shadows to get out of the way of the blinded giant, as he flailed around maddened with pain. "Who is it that blinds me?" he cried bitterly.*

' "*No-Man,*" *answered Odysseus.*

'*The other Cyclops who dwelt in the surrounding caves, came running. "What hath so distressed thee, Polythemus?" they cried, and he replied, "It is No-Man – No-Man who is slaying me."*

'You see,' said Grandma, 'Odysseus had told Polythemus that his name was No-Man.'

' *"If no man is attacking you, then you must be afflicted by a mighty sickness sent by Zeus. Our advice is to pray to your father, Poseidon, he will help you,"* and the other Cyclops all returned to their caves.

'By morning, when it was time for his sheep to be let loose to roam the hillside, the blind Polythemus groped his way to the entrance of the cave groaning and moaning, and lifted away the huge stone. He sat himself in its place, with hands outstretched to catch Odysseus and any of his men attempting to escape with the sheep. But cunning Odysseus had already devised a plan of escape. He lashed the sheep together in groups of threes, and each of his men clung to the belly of the middle sheep to make his escape. The last to leave the cave was the ram, bearing the weight of Odysseus.'

Filippo tried to fill his mind with images of Odysseus and his men rowing away from the island of the Cyclops, but he couldn't shake off the dread that filled his soul, and the words of the old rabbi mumbling as he worked.

> *There will be no grapes on the vine . . .*
> *There will be no figs on the tree . . .*

When Carlo had hugged him so close that he nearly squeezed

the air from his body, he had simply shaken his head, too choked with sorrow, and clung to him.

And their leaves will wither . . .
What I have given them will be taken away . . .

'You'll be fine,' Carlo had whispered. 'Here, take this,' and he had slipped a chain with a simple jewelled cross round his neck, to join the pouch with the fake diamond. 'When you meet Papa, he will know it's you, because he gave this to me before he left home. God willing, when we next meet, it will be with Papa. And this, Pippo. It's what you always wanted, isn't it?' He undid the belt at his waist from which hung a scabbard with its sword sheathed. 'It's Beppe's. I know he'd want you to have it. It's still a bit big for you, so don't go tripping over it.'

Filippo had taken it half dumb with gratitude, and yet also with guilt. He couldn't get it out of his head that if he had not swung the sword that day, Federigo and his companions wouldn't have retaliated with their knives and killed Giuseppe. He held the sword at arm's length, as if he could hardly bear to hold it. 'I just drew it, Carlo. I didn't think that . . . I can't take it.'

'It's OK, Pippo. Don't blame yourself. You acted as a brother, instinctively, to save him. It takes growing up for wisdom to replace instinct. Take his sword and be wise, for Beppe's sake. He would want you to have it. You know now, that a violent act will be met by violence. So you will only use it when you have no other choice. We will pray for you every day. Stay safe for Mama.' Then, thrusting his young brother over to Stefano, Carlo turned abruptly and hurriedly took to his boat again.

Filippo had watched and watched, till his brother faded into the purple light of evening and was finally lost from all sight. He didn't put on the belt, but carried the sword almost like an offering, and laid it by his pillow.

'Ah, dear boy!' cried the old nurse to Telemachus, son of Odysseus. 'How could you think of going on such a search – you – who are so loved and cherished? As for him, your father, he is surely dead, far from his own country in the land of strangers. While here, there are those who would seek to lay their hands on your inheritance. I beseech you, stay here. Don't go into that far unknown.'

'My purpose comes from the gods,' said Telemachus. 'But dear, good Nurse, tell no one – least of all my mother, not till the eleventh hour of the twelfth day from now, or she will miss me already and spoil her fair face with tears.'

It is almost night. For the first time in three days, the blazing pain in my head has subsided. The only fire now is the brilliance of the stone set in my skull. I lie staring into the darkness, yet I can see and hear everything. Carlo is telling Mama. I hear them! I hear my mother's stifled shriek of disbelief. 'You've sent Filippo, my little Benjamino? You've handed him over to the Musalman – just like that – without any proof of who he is and whether he speaks the truth about Papa?' She sinks to the floor, weak with disbelief and fear. 'How could you, how could you? How DARE you without first consulting me? How do we know he won't be sold into slavery, drowned at sea, be murdered by brigands? How do you know his body won't be ripped to shreds by those seeking the diamond?'

'I don't, Mama. I don't know.' I hear Carlo's voice. 'I had no choice. I couldn't tell you, Mama. You would never have let him go. Believe me, this is the only way. Pagliarin has spies everywhere. We no longer know who we can trust. I had to be the one to stay. I have to fight my case with the council and win back the power over our lives from Pagliarin. Filippo is a bright lad, he's cunning, street-wise; a survivor. It was a gamble to send him, but one with a chance. His youth will be his greatest protection. And if I had gone, who would there be to fight for Sofia and Gabriella – or for you?'

'He's right, Mama,' I whisper into the darkness. 'There was no choice.'

But Filippo is her little Benjamino. It will break her heart.

She will scream and rail at Carlo; never forgive him for sending her beloved youngest child away into unknown danger. Then he will explain all over again and try to reassure her, and she will have to keep the secret. All she will be able to tell everyone is that Filippo has gone away on a fishing trip with Stefano and Andreas, his best friend, to the Greek islands.

Across the dark lagoon flickering with firefly lights from the prows and poops of ships, Filippo crawled from the shack and gazed out to sea. His diamond eye seemed to enhance the powers of his own two eyes, and he fixed on Andreas and his little boat, pulling closer and closer to the island. He heard his song, ringing through the dusk. He smiled.

It was the eleventh hour, the grey hour before dawn. The tide was up, the moment had come to leave. Stefano woke the boys. The boat was stacked and ready: the nets, ropes and tackle all aboard, and the provisions for the trip stowed neatly away. Filippo had made a bundle of his clothes, wrapped Giuseppe's sword in linen and bound them into a sail cloth. They all assembled on the shore, Grandmother with little Varvara clutching her hand.

Filippo embraced the old grandmother. 'We'll light candles for you, and pray for your safety,' she whispered.

He lifted Varvara into his arms and she clung round his neck. 'Take it easy, little 'un,' he managed to laugh, as a shaft of pain scissored through his skull.

'Bring me a present, won't you,' she cried.

'Just you wait and see!' He set her down with a kiss and, extricating himself from her clinging hands, waded through the seething waves holding his bundle above his head to board the *Galatea*.

He sat in the stern and took the rudder, while Andreas, with his father and brothers, helped to raise the mast and set it into the hole in the crossplank. Then they fastened it with forestays.

'You ready now, eh?' shouted Stefano.

'I can't believe it! You! Coming on the trip! What adventures we'll have!' cried Andreas, his black eyes shining with excitement. He didn't know either. The secret must be kept. They hauled up two square white sails and almost immediately they sprang into life with a spring wind. Soon, they had no need of their oars and, with billowing sails, were cutting through the rosy dawn waters, heading beyond the Guidecca for the open sea.

The fish are singing. Silver shoals skim beneath the surface like darting moonbeams. When the net is tossed the singing turns to screams, as hundreds, wriggling and leaping in their last death throes, are hauled aboard and tipped into vats. 'Don't you hear them?' I cry in anguish. The wheeling gulls, which follow their boat, shriek with delight as they dip and dive and snatch at their meal, but only I can hear them, with the diamond in my head.

They sail down the Adriatic. The wind takes them towards the scattered islands along the Illyrian coast. Stefano knows them well, knows the treacherous shallows, the wicked currents, the hidden rocks that can rip the bottom of a boat to pieces. He also knows on which islands they can beach for the night and so, by hugging the coast, they meander their way nearer and nearer to Greece.

'I can see into your soul, Andreas,' Filippo speaks to his friend inside his head. Andreas is not just the son of a fisherman, he is a son of the sea, a child of the winds, an interpreter of currents, clouds, skies and flocks of birds. He communicates with dolphins. He has no need of diamonds.

Ancient castles and monasteries crouch like eagles on the cliffs and headlands as they pass; home fades, and with it the pain. The voices of his mother, brother and sisters diminish with each day until, by the time they've sailed into the Ionian Sea, and glimpsed craggy forested islands singing in the sun-laden mists, they have almost gone from his head. Only at night, as he lies with throbbing head, and stares up at the constellations, does he see Giuseppe glittering with stars, and is comforted.

The wound is healing, the pain lessening, but still the diamond gleams inside his brain.

'I didn't know the ocean was so wide, nor the earth so high!' he shouts into the wind.

As they journeyed down the coast of Illyria, meandering among the islands, Filippo knew he had never tasted purer happiness than this.

Chapter Fifteen

❖

A dark green prison

When Elisabetta entered the villa, she was greeted by one of their slave girls, Minou. She looked afraid, and as though she had been beaten, as one eye was bloodshot and swollen. But it was not an uncommon sight. Minou was often beaten.

Of all the people in the world, it was Minou to whom she felt closest. How ironic, when she had loathed her at first.

Years ago, on their marriage, Pagliarin had taken his new wife to the slave market to choose a slave to be her personal maid. It was his wedding gift to her.

One of his ships had come in with a cargo of slaves to be sold in the slave market along from the Riva delli Schavione. As they filed off the ship and were paraded around the square, Pagliarin separated out the young girls from the men, women and boys, and lined them up before Elisabetta so she could choose. They had been a motley consignment: Ethiopians, Hottentots, Moors, Russians, and even a few from closer to home like Albania, England and Germany. Elisabetta had walked, arm in arm with Bernardo, while he showed her the finer points to look out for. Did the female have a firm straight gaze, a sign of honesty? Were her teeth and nails good, a sign of robust health? Did she have a strong body odour? A personal maid should be fragrant.

Bernardo had pointed out Minou, an Ethiopian girl. He opened her mouth, examined her teeth and tongue, felt her arms and thighs, looked into her eyes, sniffed her body, turned her this way and that, then set her to one side. 'I like her,' he said. But Elisabetta held back. Even though the girl looked her straight in the eye, as Bernardo required, there was something about her that made Elisabetta feel uneasy; guilty even. She remembered how her mother, Teodora, loathed slavery, had said it violated Christian law. In this girl's eyes she saw such a sadness as if their strange glimmering depths mirrored an ocean at night, seething, fathomless, beneath a dark moon.

'She's too black for me,' said Elisabetta. 'I don't need a slave. I'd rather just have your housemaid, Maria.'

'Have a white girl then. I like the look of this one.' Pagliarin studied a Russian girl. She was broad-boned and strong-wristed, with stubby fingers attached to spreading hands looking as if they could cope with anything. Her dark corn-coloured hair hung thickly in two plaits down to her waist.

She looked straight at Elisabetta with wide blue eyes – filled with hate. Elisabetta said, 'No, no, not her, I don't like the way she looks.' But Bernardo had seen something different in the gaze. 'I like her,' he said. 'We'll take her anyway.'

'What about that girl over there? She pleases me.' Elisabetta had pointed to a thin pale Irish girl, who reminded her of her sister Sofia. But the girl coughed and wiped her nose, and Bernardo wouldn't even consider it.

'No, she looks sickly, and I don't like red hair. No, we'll take these two.'

So though Bernardo had taken Elisabetta down to the slave market to choose her own personal maid, they went home with two girls of his choice, the black-skinned Ethiopian and the white-skinned Russian. He said, 'You'd better have the Russian if you can't bear the thought of a black skin near you.' So Nadya was assigned to her, and Minou was put under orders from the housekeeper.

A slave Nadya might have been, but there was nothing servile about her. She did her work to perfection yet always as if she was in command, as if she did it to please herself rather than her master or mistress. She had her own pace and her own timing. Elisabetta might have admired her spirit, but not when she felt the girl gradually put a wedge between her and Bernardo. Nadya served Elisabetta through a thin, almost imperceptible veil of insolence, which was so subtle and targeted, that only Elisabetta was aware of it. Even her children's nanny couldn't see it, and all universally thought she was a find. When Elisabetta complained to Bernardo, he swept aside her reservations. 'You are just not used to these people, and don't know when you're well off,' he had replied curtly. Elisabetta found herself isolated, engaged in some kind of unspoken power play, in which Nadya skilfully endeared herself to everyone else, while at the same time producing in Elisabetta a sense of being a victim in her own house, instead of its mistress.

But through her increasing misery, Elisabetta was not without guile herself. She had got used to seeing Minou about the place, got used to her black skin, become fond of her quiet disposition, defended her if she was beaten by the cook, or jeered at by the secretary, or kicked by the manservants. Subtly, she manipulated things, requiring more of Minou by bringing her in to help with her dressing and her hair. She began to take her on outings and expeditions to the markets. Soon, she began to rely on her sweetness of nature, and to see her skin as something mysterious and beautiful. She became curious about the land of Minou's birth, and would often ask her what she remembered of her family and village. Skilfully, she enabled Minou to perform all the personal duties Nadya had once done and, without her even knowing it, Nadya was increasingly diverted to duties with the elderly aunt who lived with them. But it did not escape Elisabetta's eye that Nadya was also frequently called upon to carry out tasks for Bernardo such as informing for him on other households.

Soon, Minou was the only person Elisabetta felt she could trust, and to see her bruised battered face filled her with fury and alarm.

'What's happened?' demanded Elisabetta, as Minou took her shawl and mask. 'Who did this to you?' The Ethiopian girl didn't answer, but just cast a terrified glance behind her. Two of Bernardo's men were approaching. They stepped out from under the shadows of the staircase and came to Elisabetta, one on each side. Each took an arm.

'What are you doing?' Elisabetta struggled and tried to pull free. 'How dare you lay a finger on me!' she cried.

Bernardo suddenly appeared out of his study. He didn't even address her by name. He just said, 'Your family has thwarted my authority. The Ocean of the Moon, which is rightly mine in view of all I have done for your family, has not been handed over to me. In fact, I believe it is at this moment being taken by Filippo to Hindustan. I have been lied to and misled. Until your family sees sense and cooperates with me, I am having you incarcerated. They must get that little brat – and the diamond – brought back to Venice.'

He nodded at his men, and Elisabetta was half-dragged and half-carried screaming through the house, and down to an inner room in the cellars she didn't even know existed.

The room was all of stone, cold, damp stone. The floor and walls and window ledges were hard, thick, dumb stone. The floor of the room was almost parallel to the green water of the canal outside, and so the whole room, its walls and ceiling, wavered with constantly undulating green shadows, as if it were itself under water. She had been given a single bed, a chair and a table, but not much else. For the first few days, she cried and shrieked and demanded to be let out, but apart from food being pushed through a flap in the door, no one came, no one listened to her. It was as though she had been buried alive and forgotten.

Then Nadya appeared. To show that he had human feeling, Bernardo agreed that Elisabetta should be attended by her slave, which itself was a torture, for Nadya behaved as if she were now the mistress. Elisabetta even recognised some of her clothes. She had struck the girl in anger. 'How dare you steal my things!'

'How dare I?' taunted Nadya. 'Perhaps if Madam objects, she would care to bring the matter up with the master?'

'Yes!' screamed Elisabetta. 'Tell him to come and face me. Tell him I have concerns.' She had clutched at the girl, shaking her in fury, refusing to let go, until Nadya's shrieks brought two men running. They tore Elisabetta away.

Bernardo didn't come. Defiantly, she refused to eat, but no one cared. Slowly, she got weaker and weaker till finally, having cried all the tears out of her body, she lay on her narrow bed, silent, drained and despairing.

Then one night, she heard a voice whispering to her through the door. 'Madam, madam Signora, please eat, please don't die. Somehow, someone will help you. But you must stay strong.'

'Minou?' Elisabetta rolled from her bed, dragged herself to the door and pressed her mouth to the crack. 'Minou, does my family know what has happened to me? I beg you let my brother, Carlo, know of my plight.'

'I'll try,' whispered Minou, and was gone.

But Carlo never came, nor any message from her family.

In the mouldy damp gloom of her cell, Elisabetta sank into a delirious fever. Never had she felt so forsaken, and she only wanted to die, except when she thought of death, it filled her with terror. She could have accepted death at the gentle scented assassin's hand that had stroked her neck. But here, alone, as if already entombed, to die without the absolution of her soul and the forgiveness of her sins, to die cut off from all love, filled her with utter horror.

Sometimes, she fancied she saw faces looming over her.

Sometimes a hand forced open her mouth and poured water down till she choked. But it was never Carlo's face, or her mother's hand.

Then one day, she opened her eyes to see Minou.

Minou, the sad silent black shadow who brought her meals, her water for washing, took away her laundry, and cleaned out her room. Minou had been sent – the lowest of the low in the household – to see to Elisabetta's needs. How would they know that in her calamity, Minou had become her kindred spirit. Minou recognised that they were both now captives, and did everything she could to bring comfort to her poor imprisoned mistress.

'Carlo knows what has happened,' Minou told her in a whisper, terrified there might be ears listening at the door. 'Be patient, madam. Help will come.'

Chapter Sixteen

❖

The blind that see

*T*here is a land called Crete in the midst of the wine-dark sea, a fair land and a rich, begirt with water, and therein are many men innumerable, and ninety cities. And all have not the same speech, there is confusion of tongues. There dwell Achaens and there too Cretans of Crete, high of heart, and Cydonians there and Dorians of waving plumes and goodly Pelasgians.

Even before they neared land, Filippo with the diamond in his head, heard the thread of sound, a strange mellifulous melody that seemed to emanate from mountainous forests of Crete, teetering on the edge of crags and precipices, which plunged down to the sea. It clung to the talons of eagles as they soared in high slow circles. It coiled itself into the milky mists of dawn enveloping the island. It hooked itself on to the back of the wind which tugged and billowed their sails, and drew them closer and closer into a port. It could have been the song of a siren, as it reeled them in, inexorably in, with its magic powers. It spoke to him of danger.

A port is never still, never quiet.

As they arrived in port, it felt like home to hear so many Venetian voices. Crete was still part of the empire of Venice. But with his diamond eye, Filippo also heard all the languages in the world, and understood them. He read their inside thoughts and their outside communication. He began to wonder if his diamond eye was a gift or a curse. He could cope with the haggling housewives and gossiping servants, wheeler-dealing merchants, coarse-mouthed youths and flirtatious girls; but what about all the agonies and suffering of a dying mother, the wailing orphan, the rejected lover, the abused girl, the lonely old man? What about those who stood on the cliffs staring out to sea for the ship that would never return?

His diamond senses mirrored them all. It seemed he heard not only all the laughter and chuckling and smiles of the world, but all the weeping, and the sadness was unbearable, unbearable, unbearable. Even when he clamped his hands to his ears, or pressed his dark hair over the diamond eye, he couldn't blot it out.

'What's up with you, Pippo? Are you ill?' cried Andreas, catching his friend sitting with his head in his hands, rocking violently, as though he would shake something out of his ears.

'Just a pain in my head. It will go soon,' Filippo reassured him.

They had pitched a camp on the shore near the mouth of a shallow cave. Stefano ordered Filippo to stay and guard the boat and their belongings, as he wasn't too well. The rest of them would go into the town to sell their fish, their fishing twine and rope. He knew that it was here at this port that Filippo was to meet up with the Musalman, and continue his journey to Hindustan.

'Do you mind being left?' whispered Andreas. 'I'll look out for gypsies. They have potions and cures.'

'I'll be fine. Look, I have Beppe's sword! I shall guard the cave and all our belongings, like a dragon.'

Andreas and his brothers set up a stall in the fish market, where they hawked their wares, while Stefano hired a donkey and stuffed its panniers with rope, twine, hooks and knives and went off to sell and barter them at the market.

It was midday when Andreas was sent by his brothers to buy bread, cheese and olives to keep their hunger at bay, and melons to quench their thirst. Relishing his freedom, Andreas took off into the town, barely able to anchor his feet to the ground, excited at seeing so many different things. He had never walked among such trees and groves, and seen such hills. The air smelt of rosemary, basil, sage, and thyme, of pine cones and resin, of grilled fish and burning charcoal. He walked quickly, looking and staring, listening and laughing, feeling that surely paradise couldn't be more beautiful. From somewhere, there suddenly came a sound he recognised. Drifting above the babble of the market, above the raucous Greek songs, Moroccan oboes and Arab pipes, above the chant of sailors as they loaded and unloaded cargo, soaring above it all was the same faint, somehow menacing, winding, melody of the flute he had heard at the Rialto on his last evening in Venice.

Andreas felt compelled to follow it. Its thread of sound tugged him down and round and up and back, winding like a maze among the nets and pots and barrels. It drew him in amongst the little coracles and dhows from the Arabian sea, the sailing boats, skiffs, schooners and trimarans, the merchant ships, gunboats, quinqueremes and slavers, where rigging spangled the skies, and forests of masts clustered like stripped pine trees. He followed it down to a single man, sitting on the steps which descended to the sea; a man dressed in a North African burnoose which shadowed his face. The thread of the tune entered beneath long brown fingers, through the holes, into the body of a small wooden flute.

'Buon giorno, Signor! Fancy you being here!' He was certain this was the man he had met at the Rialto.

The playing stopped. The man turned his head and looked at him without recognition. He was not the same man. Andreas backed away, confused by the hard stare. He felt an inexplicable stab of fear. 'Sorry,' he muttered, backing away.

'Hey, you! Just a minute!' the man shouted in Venetian. He reached out to grab him. Briefly, he held his sleeve, but Andreas shook him free and began to run.

He didn't need to turn round to know the man was pursuing him.

He tried to make for the fish market, to the safety of his brothers' protection, but he took a turning to evade his pursuer, and was soon utterly lost. He ran into alleyways, up steep steps, down streets as narrow as those in Venice, then up again, up, up, up, till, suddenly, there he was above the port. He knew, even though he didn't dare turn to look, that the man followed like a hound used to the chase. He could leap, he could stalk, he could guess the direction of his prey, take a shortcut and get ahead of him. Most of all he could bide his time. The boy would tire, feel compelled to stop, to turn round and check. He would begin to realise that he was going further and further into unknown territory, would hesitate, turn back. The boy would run straight into his arms.

Andreas reached the edge of town. The stone-paved streets had turned to earthy tracks, and he found himself climbing towards a cluster of cedars; the smell of smoke and charcoal indicated people. Perhaps he was nearing the gypsy encampment. He would find safety there.

But he was tiring. His legs stiffened with fatigue, and a stitch burned into his side. He had never known anywhere so steep and hilly in all his life. He was bent double now, barely able to go any further, when he realised he was alongside a walled garden. It had a door. He hesitated and stopped, leaning into the old wood. As his breath calmed down, and the agony of the stitch eased off, he heard someone panting up the hill. It was him, the flute player who wasn't the man from the Rialto. He was coming nearer.

Andreas pushed at the rickety door, fumbling at the ring. 'Oh merciful Jesus, open, open!' The door opened, and he toppled backwards into a dusty yard clucking with hens.

'Who is it?' quavered an ancient voice.

Andreas didn't reply, but slammed shut the door. He looked around, but saw no one at first. He had come into the back yard of an old crooked, higgledy-piggledy shack of a house, with an orange wind-battered tiled roof. It perched on the edge of a cliff, and looked as if, any moment, it could just tip over and disappear into the waves. There must be a way out of here. He looked around desperately.

'Who are you?' the voice called out querulously.

He dashed noiselessly across the yard and ducked behind the goat shed, where a large nanny goat bloated with milk, turned a yellow-slitted eye on him.

'The goat shed's no use. If you want a good place to hide, go into the cold hole, just there beyond the fig tree. I don't use it any more. I won't tell anyone, I love hide and seek,' cackled the old voice.

Andreas peered out. He saw an ancient man, as wrinkled as the surface of the sea, sitting in a large wooden chair, facing out over the ocean. His face was tilted up to the sky, as if sun-worshipping, though his lower body was cocooned in a woollen blanket. Andreas hesitated, looking around to see if there were any other people in the household. No dog rushed out to assault him. No one emerged from the house to see who had come. Only a bony black cat arched its back in anticipation of a stroke, and meandered towards him.

Andreas crept forward hesitantly. The old man seemed entirely alone and didn't turn round to look at him. Perhaps it was the way he held his head upright, so that his ears could catch every sound, that Andreas knew he was blind. Yet the old man seemed to see everything.

'Come here, lad.'

Andreas approached, warily.

He held out a claw-like hand. Andreas took it. He felt the old man sigh, as if the touch of a child had disturbed a hundred memories that whispered through his veins.

'Go. Hide. I won't tell anyone. Can you see where I mean?'

His pursuer rattled at the door. He had caught up with him, and would enter any minute. How did he know?

Andreas saw a square piece of heavy stone just to the right of the fig tree. He dashed over to it and heaved it aside. A cold musty smell of old olives and figs rose from the depths of the storage hole. How deep, it was impossible to see.

He hesitated. 'Go, my boy. Go.' The old man's voice urged him.

There were a couple of footholds dug into the soil. Andreas climbed inside, and by crouching low among the olive pots, just managed to drag the stone back in place behind him, plunging himself into total chilly dank blackness.

A shadow crossed the courtyard. It came and stood between the upturned face of the old man, and the sun. The old man shivered in the shade cast by the silent intruder, and felt the presence of death itself. 'What do you want?' he asked, reaching for his rosary.

'A thousand apologies for intruding on you in this way. May San Parasceva and the Archangel Raphael guide you through the darkness of your life,' the voice spoke without sincerity. 'A boy came this way,' it continued softly in Greek, but the accent was Venetian. 'Where did he go?'

The old fingers threaded the beads of the rosary.

'Do you hear me, old man?' the voice hissed.

The old man turned his creamy sightless eyes on his visitor. 'I have seen no one.'

Even had the intruder not been blocking the sun, the old man would have felt the chill of evil and the tension in the hands that hovered over him. He bowed his head as if expecting execution. Then the full warmth of the sun fell upon him again, as the stranger moved away to search. The old fingers continued to count the rosary beads.

After a while, the intruder came back. 'I helped myself to some of your wine, cheese and bread. I'm sure you don't mind.' His voice was sarcastic and sneering.

The old man inclined his head and murmured the words of hospitality, 'My house is your house.'

'I'll wait. Hiding places are often uncomfortable and only tolerable for short stretches. He'll give himself away sooner or later.'

The old man heard him sit on the large upturned amphora, which lay so close to the cold hole where Andreas was hiding. Then came the winding melody as he began to play a flute. The old man shivered. He knew this was not a song of Orpheus, which would enchant the animals and bring love and hope to humans, but an evil spell cast by a beast who intended to lure victims into his power.

* * *

Filippo had waded into the sea. Swimming further and further out, he had tried to escape the smells, sounds and sights which his diamond eye captured unselectively, torturing him beyond endurance. He got some ease by immersing himself completely, sometimes joyfully swimming down beneath the waves to fingertip the hard rippled sand of the sea floor. He was soothed by the thudding heartbeat of the ocean, the clicking chuckles of dolphins. Schools of fish, as they darted by, made a long singing sound, swift as the shadow of the wind.

Now, so far out that the clamour of mankind had receded to faint ricochets of sound, he surfaced and turned on to his back. The weight of the diamond embedded in his head felt less heavy. He bobbed gently, gazing into the far blue utter emptiness of the sky above. If only he could lie there forever and never have to go back, never have to face the journey that lay ahead of him.

He felt hands clasp the back of his neck. He sank into them as if they were pillows. They were Papa's hands, hands he knew so well from the painting at home. They held his head as if they held the Ocean of the Moon, with great care and pride and tenderness.

'I am coming, Papa. I am coming to bring you home.'

'Coor-lee!' A curlew wheeled overhead. He tuned into its

brain, gliding with it on the spirals of warm currents, its stretched wings feathering the air, spanning the surface of the sea for anything worth eating. It dropped lower, as if drawn by Filippo's diamond eye.

'What do you see?' he asked.

The curlew dipped away towards the shore, and Filippo floated on peacefully, not expecting any answer. But after a while, it returned. He heard its high plaintive 'Coor-lee! Coor-lee!' and with it this time a panting breath, a stuttering cry. Mingled with its call too was the flute's melody, rising and falling. The curlew swooped low, its feet almost rifling through his hair, and then it rose higher and higher and away.

The tune was the same as the one he had heard in Venice. Filippo rolled on to his front, his face low in the water, and faced the towering misty mountains which loomed like gods. His peace was replaced by anxiety. The tune seemed to hook into his brain, tugging him towards the shore. He didn't resist. With growing fear he allowed himself to be reeled in.

Before my feet touch land, a panting breath, a stuttering cry enters my brain. I know that breath. I know that voice and hear it more clearly, rising like a bubble above the rest of the cacophony of the island as it tries to break out of the melodious thread which has entrapped him. Andreas! I know it is he. My best of friends, how could I not recognise the sound of his breath – and how could I not know that he is in trouble?

I stumble ashore and pull on my clothes over my wet body. I find myself revolving like a weather vane, desperately trying to find direction. I am still entwined in the melody which draws me on. Which way do I go? How do I find him? Helplessly, I tumble to the sand, clasping my head, cupping my hands round the diamond beneath my hair, as if I can cut out all the other sounds and just hear him. 'Where are you Andreas?' My voice rises into the steep canyons above. And then I hear his voice.

> *La biondina in gondoleta*
> *L'altra sera go mena.*
> *Dal piaser la povereta*
> *La s'ha in bota indormenza.*

Curled up in the darkness as cold as a tomb, Andreas was singing.

I grab Giuseppe's sword, my sword.

Filippo ran with a life and death sense of urgency, twisting among the market stalls, the donkeys and horses, the children and coffee drinkers. He entered the maze of alleys and lanes, climbing up and up along steep paths and steps, till the town fell away below him, following the song which came from the earth and which no one else could hear. The song drew him up to the wooded plateau and the cedar trees, and the long stone wall with the door.

The door was half-open. It seemed to say, 'Enter.' He hesitated, for at the moment he touched the rusty old iron ring, the song stopped. Silence. Not just that the flute had fallen silent, but the world too. He no longer heard the cawing of ravens, or the prattling of sparrows, the distant shouts of shepherds on the hillside, or the yelling of sailors rising with the spirals of air from the bays below.

He didn't understand. His powers were still new and incomprehensible. Ever since the diamond had been inserted in his skull, he had been overwhelmed by his senses all alive and tingling and receiving. Now, suddenly there was nothing: no sound, no images, no touch, no smell.

The door opened into a courtyard. With the silence of a dream, he seemed to float among the noiseless hens fluttering at his feet, and the old goat with its yellow-slit eyes, whose mouth opened to bleat but made no sound. An old, stained amphora lay upturned and broken nearby, and a stone slab used to cover an olive storage hole had been dragged aside. He put his hand to the hilt of his sword.

A black cat coiled its body round his leg. He saw the old man sitting with his face tilted up to the sun.

'Excuse me sir, but have you seen my friend?' asked Filippo.

The old man didn't answer. His eyes were open, but unseeing. Filippo went closer and touched his arm. It was barely cold, but he knew he was dead.

He backed away full of deathly fear. He peered down into the blackness of the cold hole. 'Andreas?' He could still hear the earthy reverberations of the song, but there was no reply. Had even his diamond eye turned to cold hard stone? Was there no message for him? No clue as to where his friend was, or what had become of him? The silence seemed to stretch out and out and out into eternity.

'At last, we meet again, young sir.' A voice spoke behind him.

Filippo draws his sword with a swish, and turns to find the Musalman from Hindustan, standing in the dappled and fragmented shade of the lemon tree.

He is smiling.

He wants to leave now. He says there is danger everywhere. A boat leaves for Alexandria at sunset. They must be on it. Signor Khan glances at the empty soulless shell of the old man. 'Someone has found out about the diamond. They will do everything they can to get hold of it,' he says.

'I'm not leaving till I find Andreas,' I say, defiantly.

The Musalman steps towards me. I step back, in case he holds me by force. My sword is still drawn.

'He's my best friend,' I tell him. 'My blood brother. We swore to die for each other. I can't go until I find him.'

'Whoever has taken your friend mistook him for you,' he says. 'When he finds out, he'll be back. We must get away from here.'

I stare into the eyes of the Musalman. Why can't I reach inside? Why can't I pick up what he's thinking? It's as though he has walled up his mind, cocooned all his senses in cotton wool so that even my diamond eye cannot penetrate his inner soul.

'How did you know I would be here?' I ask, full of suspicion.

His answer is smooth and plausible. 'I had been watching out for you. I heard of your arrival. No one comes or goes without someone knowing who they are, where they came from and where they are going. I saw you running across the marketplace. You were in a hurry. You didn't even look around for me. So I followed you.'

He smiles, but his eyes are blank, distant and impenetrable. Does he lie? Perhaps it is the Musalman who killed the old man. Perhaps he has just this very minute killed Andreas. He can't be far. I heard his song, right up to the moment of opening the garden door. I look around me.

'Where is Andreas? What have you done with him?'

Signor Khan returns my gaze, but I might just as well be staring into the blank, uncommunicating eyes of wild animals. 'I have done nothing with him. But we should leave now.'

I rush away. 'Andreas, Andreas!' I scour the yard, the olive grove, the orchard of fruit trees. I go right to the very edge of the cliff and peer down at the nibbling goats, clinging to the almost vertical sides. The blue of the sea and sky hurtle together as if to drag me down. I tear myself away with stomach churning, and run into the house. I search every room, as well as the grain store, the dairy, the wine cellars, and the animal sheds, but find nothing and no one.

I wince as the sun strikes my eyes when I step back outside.

The Musalman is still standing in the shade of the lemon tree, looking as if his body might disintegrate in the white hot light.

'See! He isn't here.' He expresses the empty loss with his upturned palms. Is he triumphant? 'He's been taken, I tell you. He's probably already on his way back to Venice. Now come with me, quickly. Let's get back to the town. It's dangerous here.'

'You let them take him, didn't you?' I rage at him. Suddenly

I see a fissure opening up, and I almost succeed in entering into his mind. As I try to prise my way in, I continue raging. 'You knew they thought he was me. You could have stopped them. Why didn't you?'

'My duty is to you,' replied Signor Khan.

'And to my father. Are you really my father's friend?'

The Musalman inclined his head, touched his heart and lips with his right hand and gestured to heaven. 'As God is my witness.'

'If you love my father, as I love Andreas, then you'll understand. I can't just abandon him if his life is in danger. I must look for him.'

But already the crack has closed up again. My chance has gone.

'Does he mean more to you than your own father?' asks Signor Khan. His face is expressionless.

My father's image swims into my brain. I see him sitting in his yellow chair at home. He has always been there for me, perhaps nothing more than a ghost. Yet if he's alive as the Musalman says, then he's waiting for his ransom to be paid, so that he can come home.

'You're right. My duty is to my father,' I reply, but inside I cry for Andreas. Please God, let him be safe. Let him not be lost or dead. O, my innocent friend, if anything has happened to you it will be because of me and my family, and because of this accursed diamond embedded in my skull.

'Your finding him or not finding him will not decide the fate of your friend,' said the Musalman softly, as if it is he who has the diamond in his head and can see inside my mind. 'That has already been decided. But if you delay now, if we miss the ferry, then our enemies may find you, and that would decide the fate of your father.'

In the heart of Telemachus, there stirred a yearning to lament his father. At his father's name, he let fall a tear from his eyelids to the ground, and held up his purple mantle with both his hands before his eyes.

I nod, with lowered eyes. There's no turning back, I know that. Andreas must survive in whatever way he can, as I must too. Finally I raise my eyes to the Musalman, this stranger, who won't show me who he is or what he is. This man, who doesn't share my language, country or religion, is the man I must trust. 'Let us go then,' I say.

They stood at the water's edge. The plaintive call of the plover, one to another, trembled in the evening air. 'Tee-you, tee-you.' The sun was sinking into the waves. Filippo stared at the wine-red sea stretching ahead into the descending darkness. Contained within that darkness was the vast unknown: Africa, Arabia, India and China. He shivered.

Signor Khan took a cloth bundle and unwrapped it. 'When we cross this sea,' he said, 'you will be travelling in the land of Islam. It would be better if you were not seen as an infidel, so I have acquired some suitable robes for you to put on. We have already been followed here to Crete. Let us hope we can evade our enemies.'

Keeping on his inner garments which had been stitched with gems, Filippo removed his outer clothes and put on those of the Musalman: light cotton pyjamas, a long tunic, and a cotton skull cap on his head. He took off the jewelled cross, Papa's cross, carefully stored it with his Venetian clothes, and then rolled everything up along with Giuseppe's sword into the sail cloth.

The Musalman turned to the east, facing Mecca, and fell to his knees to pray. 'O God, O Exalted, O Mighty, O Forbearing, O All-Knowing,' he intoned, touching his head to the ground. 'Thou art my Lord, and Thy knowledge is my sufficiency. Thou didst subject the wind and the demons and the Djinns to Solomon. Subject to us every sea that is Thine. The sea of this life and the sea of the life to come. Subject us to everything. There is no Power, nor Might save in God, the High, the Great.'

Signor Khan looked up at Filippo, still standing there. 'Go on! Pray, pray!'

Filippo fell on his knees. He tried to pray, 'Oh beloved San Cristoforo, bearer of our Lord Jesus, guardian of all travellers . . .'

The pall of night descends.

A small trading boat dimly rocks on the swell of the ocean. They hear the rise and fall of the oars. They move towards it like dead souls. To go seemed like a betrayal. 'Forgive me, Andreas.'

As they pulled away, the Musalman watched the shore receding, and made no comment on the thin sound of a flute fading into the darkness.

Chapter Seventeen

❖

In the eye of a storm

At first there had been nothing but sea and sky with no trace of land in sight. But then a stubborn dark cloud appeared. It clung to them above the hollow ship. The sea beneath darkened and turned black. Then came a shrilling screaming wind out of the west, rushing at the ship with such huge force, it snapped the two forestays of the mast and sent them plunging, tackle and all, into the bilge, while the mast crashed backwards on to the hind part of the ship, striking the pilot. All the bones of his skull were smashed, and like a diver, he dropped from the deck, as his spirit left his bones. Then Zeus came thundering out with bolt in hand, and lunged it into the ship. She reeled, filling with the sulphurous sea pouring in, and the sailors were pitched into the brimstone, shrieking and bobbing about like gulls.

Never had Filippo felt so helpless a pawn. At the mercy of his Musalman, the sea, the sailors on board, and at the mercy of some God, who seemed different from the one he had been brought up to worship, at whose whim he felt all their lives depended. For the voyage had been stormy and terrifying. Struggling with the ropes and great rectangular sails in the whipping rain, with the cargo sliding and crashing, and bleating, baying, terrified animals slipping on the decks. Hardly able to breathe, with the wind hurtling up his nostrils and forcing his own breath back into his body, he had unbuckled Giuseppe's sword and crawled on hands and knees, to join other boys. With wooden buckets they baled water out of the boat, as it tipped and crashed among waves, which sliced about them in all directions like scimitars. Night and day merged into one; sleeping and waking became one continuous nightmare. Behind the simmering froth of black cloud, a white opaque disc drifted in and out of view, which could have been the moon or the sun.

At the height of the storm, his diamond eye had flickered on, as if empowered by the lightning energy of the storm, and he heard Andreas's song.

> *La biondina in gondoleta*
> *L'altra sera go mena.*
> *Dal piaser la povereta*
> *La s'ha in bota indormenza.*

He's alive! Filippo knew it with absolute certainty, and he baled with all his might, as if he were alongside Andreas. He sang for all he was worth, loudly and rhythmically, as if the ferocity of his own determination to survive would force Andreas to survive too, whatever danger he was in.

At times they were blown so far off course, he wondered if he would ever set foot on land again. Then suddenly, as quickly as it had blown up, the storm dispersed, leaving a damask sky.

Falling on their knees, the passengers and crew cried out their thanks: 'God is great, God is good, God is merciful.' Curling up exhausted, among the sodden sacks of grain in the stern of the boat, Filippo stared into the firmament and entered the eye of his diamond to look for his friend.

Andreas was alive. From his dark hole in the ground, he had heard Filippo's frantic cries, yelling his name right up to the last minute.

Cramped in the hard, cold musty earth, surrounded by olive pots and stored meats, Andreas's claustrophobia had grown and grown. How long must he hide here? Who was he hiding from? How would he know when it was safe to come out? Would the old man tell him?

He had waited and waited for what seemed like hours. He thought of his father and brothers waiting for him, beginning to wonder, beginning to fear, beginning to panic. Finally, he could stand the thought no longer, and pushed at the tablet of stone above his head. But to his horror, it wouldn't budge even an inch. He pushed and hammered and pummelled, and finally shouted for help, 'Old man! Old man! Get me out!' But there was no answering voice, and no one came. Exhausted, he had fallen back. His throat was sore, and he was terribly thirsty. Suddenly convinced that this hole was to become his tomb, he began to sing, rocking himself gently, as if he were back in his own little boat crossing the lagoon to the Rialto.

> *La biondina in gondoleta*
> *L'altra sera go mena.*

Over and over again, he sang his song, his head lolling on his knees.

His song had become a croaky whisper, when a fierce shaft of light suddenly struck him. The stone was lifted back. He recoiled behind his sheltering hand. He couldn't see the face of the man who was silhouetted above him, just that he was tall, and menacing, as if Death himself had come.

He heard a faint voice calling his name up the valley. 'Andreas! Andreas!'

It was Filippo. He knew it. He stood up to shout back, 'I'm here!' But as he did, a sack was dropped down over him. Plunged back into darkness, he was hauled from the hole, trussed up and slung over a shoulder. No one spoke to him, and before he could cry out again, he was delivered a blow to the head which thrust him into unconsciousness.

'Stay alive, Andreas, stay alive!' The voice seemed to come from right inside his head.

Andreas was in a boat – in the same storm as Filippo – but heading back to Venice.

Still trussed up in the sack, he pitched and rolled about the deck, striking barrels and sacks and wooden crates as the sailors struggled to keep control. He was used to the sea, yet he vomited all over himself, and was covered in his own stench and bile.

'I'm here, I'm here!' he couldn't help shouting from the inside of his sack, where no one would hear him for the howling storm. 'Oh why won't someone bring me water?' he wailed, until he fell into some kind of oblivion.

From time to time, he awoke. Each time the boat was quieter. His eyes were wide open, staring hard, but there was nothing to see, not even dark shapes let alone any glimmer of light. The ship had survived the storm, but still no one came to him.

At last Andreas heard Venetian voices. He sat up excitedly, punching at the sack.

'Right! Someone get the boy. Let's see where the diamond is.'

They were Pagliarin's men, but they had no intention of returning a boy who might be carrying diamonds back to Pagliarin.

'What are you talking about?' protested Andreas as they hauled him out and unrolled him from the sack. 'I don't have any diamonds. I'm the son of Stefano Georgilis, a fisherman, I tell you. Poor as dirt. We came to Greece on a fishing trip. Why the hell would I have diamonds, for pity's sake?'

Even as he defended himself, it was beginning to make sense. They thought he was Filippo.

They dragged him out of the hold, blinking with the shock of the light. They stripped him, ripped his clothes to shreds, tearing out the seams and the hems, then hurling the garments overboard in disgust. They turned their attention to him, laid him out on the lid of a chest as if they were going to flay him alive, as they had done his clothes, and carve him up with their knives. They ran the tips of their blades over his skin, and examined every single bit of his body; they scrutinised his scars and looked for signs of incision. They peered, poked and prodded into every orifice where a diamond could be hidden.

'Seems to me like you got the wrong boy,' sneered a voice, 'you stupid half-wit.' He held up Andreas's hands and feet. They were rough, callused, weathered; used to boats, oars, rigging and scrambling over rocks. 'Call these jeweller's hands?'

'Slit him open, then we'll soon know,' growled a voice running his knife over Andreas's belly. 'It's probably in his gut.'

'It's obvious this isn't him, you pea-brained idiot, and we can't even take him to Pagliarin,' yelled another voice, furiously. 'I've a good mind to –' And suddenly they were at each other's throats, rolling about the deck punching and kicking as if they would fight to the death.

'Cut it out, for God's sake,' a third, more authoritative voice intervened.

Andreas felt a chill of deep fear. It was the flute-player who had chased him in Crete.

'No point in wasting the boy. He's worth more to us alive than dead. Let's head for Naples. We'll sell him off there. He'll fetch a good price. From Naples I can get a ship to Egypt. I'll soon catch up with them.'

Like a dolphin, in one continuous movement, Andreas rolled off the chest and flipped over the side of the boat. Down, he plummeted; down, down, down, his white naked body shafting through the dark green depths. Better to die in his own element – the sea – than be sold off as a slave to some foreign land.

When at last the storm passed over and everything became quiet, Filippo made his way over to Signor Khan leaning at the side of the boat. For a while, they watched the tipping horizon. He touched his arm, and Signor Khan turned and looked at him with such a hard expression, that Filippo almost backed away. But suddenly, the Musalman smiled, and slapped a hand on his shoulder. 'Ah, my boy, so we have survived our first storm together. I think it bodes well, don't you?'

But Filippo wasn't sure. The smile hung in the air without substance, and the eyes remained like windows which had no interiors. Filippo didn't feel reassured at all.

A voice yelled out, 'Land! Land ahoy!' All heads turned with excitement, the oarsmen paused to look, their oars raised, dripping, above the surface of the sea. Even after years of seafaring, for even the most hardened of seamen, the sight of land was always a kind of affirmation of the mercy of God – a miracle that they could never take for granted. Their eyes gazed at the widening crack in the horizon between sea and sky as an indefinable smudge gradually widened into the solidity of land. The voices, which had been high and harsh and strained with fatigue when out at sea, relaxed and softened, and they joked and laughed and talked about their families. But Signor Khan looked increasingly withdrawn. His fingers threaded the prayer beads around his neck as in a monotonous, dead voice he identified the shore which floated towards them.

'It seems we have missed Alexandria and our Red Sea route

to Hindustan. We have been blown too far north-east to the Syrian coast. We need to get to Basra. We could go to Aleppo, cross the River Euphrates and on via Baghdad, that's the quickest way, but . . .'

'But what?'

'That's what they'll expect us to do. We must cross the desert,' muttered Signor Khan, and spoke no more but just stared out towards the land emerging out of the haze.

As their boat drew nearer and nearer to the shore, a strange hot wind blew into their eager faces. A mysterious wind which carried smouldering grains of sand with the smell of heat – if heat can have a smell. The smell of wild beasts, of untamed earth; of unreasoning, pitiless wilderness, unsoftened by water or trees and flowers. Filippo felt a sense of dread as to what lay beyond the yellow shoreline, with its palm trees like parasols, casting dark sharp shadows over clusters of low mud buildings.

It was a wind that was to accompany them now almost constantly, a wind which came from the desert, and which they were to follow into the desert. It puffed its hot breath into their faces, and lined their nostrils and mouths with grains of sand, even though they pulled their scarves tightly round. It flapped at their garments, it followed them through the gates of a walled town and into the warren of narrow-winding crowded streets, billowing the awnings of stalls and shops. They stopped at a money dealer, and sold some Spanish gold coins in exchange for dinars, before heading for the camel market.

They saw the orange dust first, a thick rust-coloured dust churned up by hundreds of people and animals which were reduced to pale opaque shapes that moved like ghosts. Outlined through the mustard murk the camels towered superior, while round their knees gradually emerged the donkeys and strings of ponies. Baskets of fowl fretted and clucked. Little boys with high, frantic voices ran among herds of goats, keeping them contained. There were the hooded falcons and hawks, the hunting birds, sitting silently chained to their perches, their heads revolving with the sounds, as if they too had a diamond eye in their heads which enabled them to sense everything.

'Allahu Akbar!' The eerie voice soared through the dusk from the top of an impossibly slender needle of a tower, from whose minaret a mullah cupped his hands and called the faithful to prayer. Everything stopped. Everyone turned towards Mecca. Hundreds of people dropped to their knees, wave upon wave of backs bent in obeisance.

Filippo felt himself tugged downwards. 'Do as I do,' ordered the Musalman in a low voice. Filippo fell to his knees and, stubbornly, put his hands together to pray the Christian way, but a hand at the back of his neck forced him forwards till his forehead touched the ground. 'Infidels aren't allowed in this land. Do as I do,' hissed Signor Khan in his ear. 'You can't be a martyr to your religion and save your father.'

So Filippo pressed his head to the ground listening to the conjoined voices calling as one on their god. 'Alliyuah, Akbar.'

'Hail Mary, Mother of God, pray for our sins,' Filippo murmured under his breath, over and over, as if trying to expunge the alien prayer from his senses. Yet, he felt caught up in it, and there was something extraordinary about being part of that one voice calling on Allah, Allah, Allah. After all, he reasoned, it was only another name for God, wasn't it?

The hum of prayer died away, the frenzy of activity started up once again. Now the marketplace was criss-crossed with shadows, long angular shapes of people and animals, flitting and wavering among the flames of torches flaring in the wind. Coming up like molten stars were hundreds of braziers and small fires glowing orange in the darkness, and with them, the smell of cooking to stir pangs of hunger.

Voices mingled in the air. Women's voices, babies and children, bartering voices, voices raised heatedly in argument, voices laughing, voices debating, voices singing and, as Filippo and the Musalman approached a camel dealer, there were the competitive, agitated voices of buying and selling and higgle-haggling. Signor Khan moved from one camel trader to another, then back again, examining camel after camel.

Filippo followed him full of awe and curiosity. He had never seen a camel before they reached this land, except in paintings and drawings brought back by travellers. He had heard how they were perfectly suited to the desert and could go for days without water. They stored nutrition in their humps to survive in a barren desert for days on end. He had never ever expected to see one in reality.

Of all the tens of dozens of camels clustered together, his eye was drawn to one camel in particular. Its aloof stillness in the midst of such chaos impressed him. Its hooded eyes turned, deliberately it seemed, towards him then beyond him, as if saying, 'Choose me . . . if you wish . . . I don't care one way or the other.' He elbowed his way towards it and held out a hand. He hesitated, then touched. Its coat was soft and lightest cream coloured. The texture of its skin and fur, muscle and bone, tingled his fingertips. The camel gave a deep sigh and lowered its head. Filippo looked into its eyes. It wasn't aloof at all, but had eyes as soft as a doe which gazed upon him beneath long curly eyelashes.

'Signor Khan,' Filippo tugged the Musalman's sleeve. 'Look at this creature. This one is good. We should buy him.'

'Her,' corrected Signor Khan who came over to examine the creature. He cupped its large soft mouth in the palm of his hand,

and pulled up its cleft lips to examine the razor-sharp teeth. He ran his hands over its body, feeling its fur, its leathery calluses which protected its knees and chest, its long muscular legs down to its broad flat padded feet. After close scrutiny, he straightened and said, 'You have a good eye, young man. This beast is healthy and, what's more, seems to have a stable temperament.'

'Yes, yes!' the camel dealer agreed, intervening. 'I saw it. I saw how they connected. They are meant for each other!'

After a further hour of arguing, disputing and compromising, money changed hands, and a bargain was struck.

'Ata Allah – gift of God – as the Arabs call the camel. Her name is Zubeida,' said Signor Khan.

Filippo took its reins and ran his hands up its neck. 'Zubeida,' he whispered with a smile.

'You must learn to be the master,' Signor Khan called to him. 'You must show her who's in charge. Otherwise she'll get the better of you. Like horses, they have minds of their own.'

Filippo looked up at her narrow face and sensed a deep melancholy and the patience of servitude. 'I think you and me will get along!'

Signor Khan left Filippo with his Zubeida, and went on to buy another bigger camel as they would need two to carry enough provisions for the journey. He then proceeded, much more quickly, to acquire two mules and two teenaged boy slaves,

Abu and Faisal – one to be keeper of the camels, and the other to cook. Suddenly, they were four.

They worked hard into the night, hauling vast oxen-skins of water, grain, dried fruits and flour, filling the wicker baskets which would be strapped to the sides of the mules. Carpets and awnings were ready to be draped over the camels which, by night, would be rigged up as shelter for sleeping in. Only when everything had been acquired for the journey did they sit round a small brazier, and eat baked bread and roasted goat, prepared by Abu and Faisal.

That night, the night before departure, shouts of poetry and song rang through the night.

> *Many a desert have I walked,*
> *Cutting across the windswept plain*
> *Its surface empty and impenetrable*
> *As a shield*
> *Linking the near to the far at last*
> *I reach a summit, and gazing out*
> *Crouching, sometimes standing*
> *The mountain goats,*
> *Flint yellow, meandering like maidens*
> *Their flowing fur draped as shawls*
> *Graze around me.*

Chapter Eighteen

❖

The desert zone

At the first grey light of dawn, the travelling populace rose as silent as ghosts from the grave, unwinding themselves from their blankets. Filippo had barely slept, what with the grunting of camels and restless kicking of mules and ponies. The first call to prayer of the day ran like a current through the populace. Filippo was getting used to the rhythm of falling to the ground five times a day, but as the light increased so did the activity, and they were almost left behind as, with a sudden burst of speed, the caravan was off.

The warbling wailing of farewell from women and children accompanied them till they reached the end of the town. There the townspeople stopped, their burkas and turbans flapping in the wind. Children and animals leapt like atoms of sunlight. As the caravan moved away into the distance, Filippo looked back at them, watching them diminish into wavery lines, their cries swallowed up in the wind and the silence.

Ahead was a never-ending horizon. They entered the zone

of the desert, heading for Basra, a thirty-day trek away.

They moved at a walking pace across rugged wilderness. Scores of individual groups of traders and travellers, each with their own provisions, formed the caravan of camels, asses, ponies, goats, men and boys, servants, slaves and families. Like a vast serpent, it coiled so far ahead and behind that Filippo couldn't see either end; only its body, rising and falling in great sweeps which crested and curved over the sand dunes.

But even though he was with so many people and animals, Filippo felt the terror and desolation of the wilderness, and he clung close to Signor Khan. He walked at his side, and sat by him over their evening fire.

'You are afraid?' Signor Khan smiled at him. 'Fear is a good thing. It keeps you alert and in touch. You will learn. Of all the places on earth, here you will learn how close to paradise you are.'

'Paradise?' asked Filippo. 'Isn't paradise like a garden?

'The desert is more than a garden,' replied Signor Khan. 'It is a living presence. It is more than life, it is the soul. Here, there are no mosques, churches or idols to remind us of God. To survive, you must understand this. Understand nature, man and beast. Understand that there is only Allah alone between you and earth and sky, and life and death.'

Day by day, as he became more used to his environment, Filippo realised that the desert was not a blank void. It was living and breathing with scorpions, birds, beetles, lizards, snakes, goats, antelope, the striped hyena. There were people too, nomadic tribes; some God-fearing and living by courtesy and trust, others bandits, ruthless and loyal only to themselves, all of whom had wandered the desert for thousands of years. They knew the lie of every hill and dune, every breath of wind, every waterhole and oasis. 'The desert is a generous host and will give you hospitality if you respect it,' said Signor Khan.

They moved with the rhythm of the camels, the steady swinging, swaying plod plod plod of their striding, long-legged, padded feet, their necks extending to inscrutable heads, with their drooping eyes gazing over arrogant noses and curling, disdainful lips.

It took Filippo a while to learn how to sit on Zubeida the camel, how to stay on her hump when she rose to her feet, which she did by first pitching backwards and upwards on to her back legs, then hurling forwards as she straightened her front legs, while he clung precariously to the saddle. But he persisted, even though at first he rolled about and felt as sick as if he were at sea. He watched Abu and Faisal, saw how they cared for their beasts, watered them from troughs of buffalo skin, and gave them leaves of fodder which they carried on the journey. How nimbly they moved around the camels, running up their necks to mount them and guide them into the scrub to nibble leaves and tamarisk thorns.

Filippo looked at the terrain through the eyes of Zubeida. He saw by day, shadows of deepest brown, like the inside of waves, curving to a sharp-edged crest before swooping down into the next wave, scorching out the hollows and valleys, spreading down ravines and canyons, and etching the minuscule contours of ridges and rocks.

With evening, the shadows turned to purple before sinking into the descending night. And always the wind, the ever-present wind, drifting and reverberating among the sand dunes like a weeping soul searching for someone who is lost.

The camel driver said there were Djinns, desert spirits, hanging about ready to create mischief. Sharp eyes were always studying the lie of the land, and noting which way the sand was whipped up, preparing at barely a moment's notice to huddle down if one of those Djinn-driven whirling sandstorms should engulf them.

Sometimes a camel driver would stop and hold up a hand, and Filippo would listen as Zubeida listened, the fine hairs in her ears resonating as they twitched and swivelled. She could hear the lizard freeze on the rock, the snake pause in its slithery track. She could hear the silence which wasn't silent.

Eyes scanned the ridges and slopes, hunters fingered their spears and weapons. Was that a faint rustle of a bandit scout trailing them among the ridges, or a watchful hyena? Was that the footfall of a white-bellied oryx, or the bark of a white-footed fox? Their mouths watered at the prospect of a feast that night if they succeeded in hunting an antelope. Sometimes, riders on horseback would break away and gallop off to hunt, with falcons on their wrists, to break up the monotony of the journey. But all the while, they listened for the murderous bands of robbers who could be shadowing them this very moment behind the line of dunes, waiting for the moment to attack.

Signor Khan mixed with the other traders, yet never seemed a part of them. His routine was to take a stroll before the evening call to prayer. He would walk into the sand dunes till he was reduced to a wavering silhouette, moving along the thin edge of the horizon, his burnoose fluttering behind him. Occasionally, he would briefly disappear from sight, then reappear, like a gull bobbing among the waves of the sea.

The voice of a muezzin would bring him back at sunset. Neither smoking, drinking nor gambling as the other traders did, he crouched outside the tent watching the night sky come up, still as a tethered hawk, his head sometimes swivelling to look or listen.

'I wonder what my father will make of me,' Filippo spoke his thoughts out loud one evening.

'He will love you.'

'Will I love him?' Filippo looked down, as if ashamed of his thought. 'I've seen him all my life, as a phantom, through other people. I feel I've always known him, yet I know you better than I know him.'

'That is a different kind of knowing. We know each other as companions. We have walked a road together, we journey together. The knowledge you have of your father is a blood knowledge, it runs in your veins, it is the marrow of your bones. It is the force which gave you life. Such knowledge does not come through companionship.'

'Sometimes, I dream that I am back in Venice walking along the Lorenzo, and I never want to wake. Sometimes, I wonder what I'm doing here. I used to long to travel, but now –'

'– you wish you were home. The wandering traveller knows that. But it is good to release yourself from all ties, even good ties like home and family. It strengthens you and makes you consider the Self – the experience of oneness – and that, in the end, there is only Allah.'

'Allah is your God not mine,' corrected Filippo politely.

'Allah is Allah.'

Filippo looked up at his face. His voice had been soft, but

there was no expression. It was like looking at a blank wall, which even his diamond eye could not break through. Signor Khan was with his Self, and Filippo felt desperately alone.

The cold forced them into the stuffy heat and choking smoke of the tent, into the sweet smell of the hubble-bubble being passed one to the other by the camel drivers and traders. They listened to the sound of bellowing raucous poetry battles. As the travellers flung verses to and fro between them, competing as fiercely as if they were in a camel race, Filippo would lean drowsily into the bolsters around the sides.

The next evening, when Signor Khan set off on his walk before sunset, Filippo followed him.

He trailed Signor Khan, keeping several dunes between them as he ducked and dived to stay out of sight. What a shock then to peer over a dune and see no one. He clambered down that dune and raced up the next. No one. He backtracked, or thought he did, to where he last saw him but there was no one, and in this kind of sand, deep, soft and sifting, there were no footprints. He decided to return to camp, and scrambled off in what he thought was the right direction. There was nothing but wave upon wave of rolling dunes, like the ghost of an ocean now run dry. He couldn't believe it. He had only been walking a bare five minutes, how could he have gone so far off track? He looked round desperately for a landmark, but the dunes all looked the same. He became aware of the descending chill of night.

It was the night Filippo feared the most. The blackest of black nights fell, there was nothing to show him where the edge of the world was, nothing to reassure him that there wasn't some dreadful void into which he could plunge in an everlasting descent. The howl of scavenging hyenas, always lurking just outside the rim of light and heat cast by the fire, reminded him of what fate befell those who succumbed to the desert. Even the stars looked down with a hard and pitiless gaze, and there was nothing to convince him that he was of any value whatsoever to the universe.

He began to panic. 'Signor Khan, Signor Khan! Where are you? Signor Khan, I'm lost. Come and help me!' He hugged his arms around himself. It was already too cold to stand still. He stumbled about bellowing into the night. It was then, as mysteriously as stars appearing in the sky, that Filippo's diamond eye glimmered in his head and he saw what had happened to Andreas.

Andreas, spread across the back of the waves, his naked body gleaming like surf, was bobbing among billowing dunes – but these were watery dunes of the sea. He was numb with cold, and his strength was ebbing fast. He had been in the water for a day and a night now, sometimes swimming, sometimes lying on his back to rest. He gazed up at the dense blue sky by day, and the canopy of stars by night, his naked body as pale as a dolphin. Perhaps that's what brought the dolphin swimming to him, diving beneath him, chuckling and chortling, clicking and clucking, nudging his body along with his nose, as if he were a toy to play with.

Always alongside him, like a dark shadow, it pushed him ever closer to a lonely bleak island shore, where cliffs rose up fiercely, sharp-edged against the sky. His belly scraped the shore. The dolphin, with one last hooting cry of farewell, left him and returned to the waves.

If Andreas had had the strength to lift his head, he would have seen no Christian spires here, or Muslim domes, just broken marble pillars half-buried in the sand, and stone altars destroyed in the battles between ancient gods. He just heard the joyful cry of a demented woman who, for years, had been pacing the shore, trapped in eternal grief. A mother, staring out to sea, waiting for her husband and sons to return from their fishing trip.

A camel coughed. A shower of sparks flew upwards into the night sky. Filippo laughed with relief. He must have circled the entire camp – it had been just there all along. He ran down the caravan until he saw Zubeida, sitting like a sphinx, her jaws rotating. He rushed towards the fluttering ash as more sparks soared into the sky from the fires being lit all along the train, and a smell of cooking reached his nostrils. 'Signor Khan, Signor Khan!'

Filippo sat beside him exhausted with relief yet still strangely uneasy. Signor Khan responded with a questioning glance, unused to Filippo seeking his company.

'Are you all right?' he asked the boy.

'Andreas is alive. He's alive!' exclaimed Filippo, then lowered his head into his arms and wept.

'God is great,' said the Musalman, offering him his cup of water.

They had arrived now in the region of an ocean of sand which rippled and undulated all around them, with not one sign of a shrub or any kind of life. The sun beat down. Filippo sat staring out into the watery mirage on the horizon. He was feeling lonely and homesick, when his diamond eye flickered with life. Coming towards him out of the shimmering were his sisters, Gabriella and Sofia, arm in arm and whispering to each other and laughing, just as they always did. 'Oh look! There's Mama – Mama, Mama!' She's dressed in black. The rest of her life must be in continuous mourning for ever and ever. Even though

Geronimo Veroneo is alive, Giuseppe is dead, and she thinks she may never see her little Benjamino ever again. Behind her, with a protective hand on her shoulder, is Carlo, though his face is solemn. Poor Carlo, having to be the father of the family and bear all the burdens. Filippo raises his hand to greet him. 'Carlo, Carlo!' He knows he loves him, and he hears his brother's voice entering his brain. 'Stay safe, little Pippo, stay safe and bring Papa home.' Just when he thought they had faded away in the dazzling light, another figure appears, approaching swiftly – small at first in the distance, but coming nearer and nearer and nearer and nearer. Papa? It was he, oh Papa! Filippo staggered to his feet and ran towards the figure with open arms – but suddenly, the figure leaps in height and towers over him. It wasn't Papa – but Bernardo Pagliarin. 'He's coming to kill me, he's coming to kill me, he's . . .'

'Filippo?' A hand shook him. He whirled round. It was Signor Khan. 'Come!' He put a hand to the boy's back and turned him away from the glare of the desert. 'Here, drink this,' he held a flask for him, and Filippo gulped the water. It tasted sweet and cool. Then Signor Khan thrust Filippo's face back and poured some water over his face and into his eyes. 'Never stare into the haze like that at midday. You'll blind yourself – do you hear?'

'Yes. No. I won't. Thank you. I won't. But I saw Papa, and –'

'Yes – the desert throws up phantoms. It can fool even a man born here and brought up on a camel. But don't be fooled. Don't look. Never believe what the mirage shows you.'

Filippo's head and neck ached, and he felt as though his blood was bubbling in his veins. He could neither speak nor see. Then he was sliding, sliding . . . Hands held him, water was pressed to his mouth and poured over his head. His scarf, sopping with water, was wrapped round his head, enveloping his face and neck. What relief. He smiled at its coolness, though within minutes, his burning skin had dried the cotton, and the same hands did it again and again. Then he was being lifted back on to his camel, but this time an arm supported him. As the rhythm of travel started again, plod plod plod, he slid into unconsciousness.

The next time he awoke, it was dark, and he was lying under his blanket beneath an awning with a water bottle next to him. He leaned up on one elbow and drank deeply. He could hear the crackling of the fire, and cheerful voices and a wonderful smell of cooking brought him to his senses and made him energetic with hunger.

'Ah, young sir,' a cheerful voice greeted him. 'You have recovered. I hope it will be a lesson to show the sun more respect.'

As if out of the mirage of his own brain, Signor Khan's face shimmered into focus. He was smiling through those dead eyes.

Filippo fingered the pouch at his neck. He felt the hardness of the stone. It was still there. He returned the smile.

'You have an empty belly, yes?' said Signor Khan. 'We have a feast tonight. The boys hunted an antelope.'

With what relish it was skinned and roasted. Everyone's energies and humour returned. The fire was built high, and the voices blurred with wine and laughter. His appetite surged back at the succulent smells.

Further away down the caravan train, a singer's voice rang out. Signor Khan got to his feet and left the tent. Filippo tried to follow, but was overwhelmed by dizziness. He attempted to stay awake until he returned, but his eyes closed with the heaviness of the smoke and smells. Still weak from his heat stroke, he fell back into a sad sleep.

Chapter Nineteen

❖

The sands of death

'Sand storm!'

Heads turned, camels snorted, mules shook their loads, jingling their harnesses. One minute they were swaying on their way with the slave boys running alongside with the mules and provisions. The next minute it arrived, with such speed and ferocity that they were taken by surprise.

They had been travelling for fifteen days, and were in the longest stretch of the journey between any serai or water hole. It was mid-afternoon. A wind blew up and, simultaneously, the sky darkened to a deep orange.

Voices yelled a warning like a fluttering ripple up and down the train. It came so fast. Frantically, in the whirl of stinging, blinding, lacerating sand, the camels pulled up, floundering and distressed. Their drivers tried to make circles of their animals, for protection. He heard Signor Khan yelling his name. 'Filippo, cover up!' He dropped to the ground and copied what the others did, winding his turban round and round his head and neck, leaving barely a slit through which to breathe. A hand gripped his shoulders and forced him close to the body of his camel. He felt a tug at the pouch round his neck. Filippo briefly clasped the hand, but it wrenched away. The pouch was gone. He struggled to his feet, trying to follow a billowing figure staggering through the stinging sand, but it was rapidly swallowed up in the vortex.

Then, within the storm, he saw a different kind of movement. Shadows streaking through across the blurry landscape, so swift, so silent. Something glinted, a reflection of moonlight on steel. The shadows multiplied, and a dozen or so black figures on horseback came galloping through the spinning sand, wielding spears, scimitars and knives. Filippo would have taken them for terrible phantoms as they whirled into the camp, desert djinns out of a nightmare, but the shrieks and cries were real.

Gasping with panic, he crawled frantically backwards looking for Zubeida. He saw her outline almost lost in the whipping sand. Filippo thrust himself against her body and burrowed down between her front legs. She didn't move a muscle, but continued to sit like a monument. Filippo glanced up the arch of her neck to the overhang of her lips, almost invisible now in the murky gloom. He pressed his face into her rugged fur. The wind engulfed them, and all he could do was struggle for breath, as wave upon wave of sand found its way between even the tightest folds of his shawl, clogging up his nostrils, eyes and ears, and threatening to overwhelm him.

The storm screamed over his head, he had no idea how long. His brain too was in torment. All he could think was that Signor Khan was his enemy. He was only after the diamond after all. He had talked to him of God and paradise, taught him about the desert, yet now he had done what Filippo had always feared he would do: pick his moment and steal the pouch and leave him to die.

His anguish subsided into exhaustion. He felt nothing, sliding into a suffocating delirium. From time to time, he flitted into consciousness and wondered if he was dead, yet his brain was beset with dreams and images.

Carlo was sitting there right next to him. 'You're a good little man,' he smiled.

'My darling Benjamino,' his mother coaxed him.

'Come home soon, Pippo, Pippo, Pippo!' chanted his silly sisters with their laughing faces.

And then, everything darkened; not the dark of an unconscious mind, or the dark of sleep. It was the gloomy darkness of a cell with barely any light, except the one high window through which his hope ebbed and flowed.

'Filippo?' His father was waiting.

Silence, stillness. It was this which finally woke him. He

pushed away the sand from his face, and crawled out from beneath the camel. The howling of the wind had stopped, but so too had the snorts and grunts of animals, or voices mumbling in sleep.

The landscape was transfigured. A high moon cast an ethereal light over the desert, and the same huge star which Signor Khan had said was Venus burned low in the sky like a giant sunflower. Eddies of sand shifted. Filippo began to shiver uncontrollably in the intense cold and, huddling back against Zubeida, waited for the dawn.

When he next awoke, the sun had peaked over the ridge, a vast gaping mouth of fire, getting ready to consume the world. His mouth felt on fire too. He hadn't drunk any water for hours. The blue of the sky was strengthening all the time, and would go almost white with intensity. Filippo ripped aside his head covering and gazed about him. How beautiful! How calm. The sand flowed like silk over the hills and dunes unmarred, untouched, as if nothing had ever crossed its surface since the first day of creation. But still there was the silence. No dawn prayers, no 'Allahu Akbar' to reassure him of a new day.

Zubeida snorted loudly. Filippo rolled away from her great padded hooves, as she staggered to her feet and ambled off. 'Come back!' Filippo tried to shout. 'Come back! You have my pack, my clothes!' But his voice croaked uselessly, and she lolloped away, diminishing into a faint blob.

'Oh Zubeida!' he wailed with bitter disappointment. 'Don't go!' Was she after all just a camel, and felt no loyalty towards him?

He stood up stiffly, cascading with sand, and crawled up the dune to look down on the camp. The caravan train lay like a broken necklace, in bits and pieces across a new landscape. Or that's how it seemed, for the power of the storm had swallowed up the hollows of the dunes, and those animals and traders who hadn't managed to find shelter had been wiped from the face of the earth.

'Signor Khan!' he yelled.

Nothing. Silence.

His panic returned. 'Signor Khan, Signor Khan!' Filippo ran and rolled and crawled and stumbled into the desolation of the camp. He blundered over half-buried corpses – hands, feet, clothes, slippers. He moved from one body to the next, searching for Signor Khan, sometimes touching a face or a hand which, despite the heat, was cold and made him cry out with terror. But he couldn't find him, and now, remembering his treachery, he wondered why he bothered. He had probably made a deal with the bandits and escaped with them.

Filippo crumpled hopelessly to his knees, his energy sapped, his mouth swelling with thirst. Is this it then? Must he die here alone in the desert? He felt the diamond protruding through his skull. What an irony! He laughed out loud. All that – and for what? 'It's here!' he shouted hysterically. 'It's here, you idiots, in my skull!'

Perhaps, he thought, only when the striped hyenas and eagles of the desert have picked me clean down to my skeleton, might someone come across my bones and discover something glinting in my skull. That's if a sandstorm doesn't bury me too deep even for the wind.

He heard a snort. 'Zubeida!' Zubeida had returned for him. He crawled towards her crying with relief. Everyone else had gone, but not his beloved friend. She stood by expectantly, as if to say, 'Move! Move, or you'll die.'

He understood. He must act. He patted and hugged Zubeida, then stumbled around the camp. He was full of grief and anger. How could they just go? Had no one bothered to find him – not Abu or Faisal? None of the people he had walked with and eaten with? Those who had survived the attack had grabbed everything they could, mounted their camels and fled. No one had looked for him. And what of Signor Khan? Bitterly, he turned over empty flasks and ripped sacks of grain, and smashed olive pots until, at last, he found one oxen skin that had been overlooked, and still contained water. He drank in great heaving gulps, and gave some to Zubeida. He then filled as many flasks as he could find. A further search turned up some baked bread, raisins and figs. He bundled them into a single rug.

He strapped the provisions to Zubeida's sides, patting her and whispering to her. 'It's up to you now. This is your terrain. I don't know which way to go. You're in charge.' He hauled himself up on to her hump and weakly tugged the reins. 'Go, go!' And they were off in a gangling lope.

He didn't know how many days they walked alone – four, five? Their pace slowed to an exhausted plod, Zubeida barely able to lift one leg in front of the other. Each day when the heat reached its peak, she had stopped automatically, and though Filippo barely had the strength to set up his shelter, he knew it meant death if he didn't. His lips had shrivelled and cracked, his skin had chapped, his gravelly eyes were in a state of constant irritation with grains of sand. The air scorched his lungs, even when filtered through his head cloth which he was now expert at winding round his head, neck and face. He had barely any water left, though he still shared it with Zubeida, for her hump had shrivelled as her nutrition was used up. He knew that soon, they must both die. Where was paradise now? thought Filippo. Where was Allah?

Zubeida continued painfully, sometimes stopping, coughing, then staggering on with Filippo barely clinging on. And so it was through a semi-delirium, that he saw ahead of him a figure crawling then flopping and crawling again.

'Never believe what you see in a heat haze,' the Musalman had told him. Filippo stared and stared through his hard-burnt crusty eyes. Zubeida had already slowed down in anticipation of setting up the evening camp. Filippo tugged the reins and kicked her feebly in the ribs, 'Go, Zubeida, go!' his voice barely able to rasp out the words. She snorted, and reluctantly tried to canter but couldn't. Filippo's eyes fixed on the figure ahead. It hadn't moved since he saw it, but was now spread-eagled with its face in the sand. He drew nearer and the figure became clearer. This was no mirage. This was real. This was a man.

'Down, down, down!' yelled Filippo in Arabic. Zubeida flopped to her knees with a groan and Filippo slid from her hump to the ground and stumbled over to the man.

It was Signor Khan. Filippo felt a surge of fury.

Even as he lifted the Musalman's head and pushed the water bottle to his blackened mouth, he raged at him. 'I don't know why I'm stopping for you. I don't know why I'm giving you any of my precious water – there's barely any left anyway. You traitor! You abandoned me, and faked a friendship with my father just so that you could get hold of the diamond. I'd be pleased if you died. I hate you, I hate you, I hate you. Where is it? Where is the diamond?' His sobs dried in his throat.

Signor Khan got to his knees and clasped the water bottle to his mouth and drank again till he had drained it.

Filippo backed away from him in disgust and took the camel's reins. Signor Khan raised a hand in supplication. 'Don't go.' It was more a whisper than a cry. 'Just listen to me.'

'First give me the diamond.'

'I don't have it. The bandits took it.'

'Huh! Think that stops you from being a thief too, just because they were cleverer than you?' Filippo sneered. 'I know you took it from me.'

'I did. But it was to save you. As the storm struck us, a scout came galloping back to camp saying he'd seen bandits. They often attack just before or just after a storm when everything is in confusion. There was no time to explain. The storm was already on us. That's why I removed it from you. If you had been caught by bandits, I promise you, they don't waste time – they would have just chopped off your head to get it.'

'So why are you alive then? Why didn't they chop you into little pieces?'

'Listen to me, Filippo. When they attacked, I held it up for them, told them to take it and spare us all. They took it all right, and me too for a while, arguing that I might make a useful hostage, but then they changed their minds and just abandoned me to the desert. They left me to die. It was a gamble I took.'

'Liar! That's some story. Liar! Took a gamble, did you? Huh! That's a good one. You just tried to save yourself, that's all. Why did you abandon me? It suited you, didn't it?' Filippo wept a rasping cry, for there was no liquid left in his body to weep with.

'No, Filippo. I tried to save your father, and you, his son, and the diamond which would free him. And it worked, didn't it? I'm alive, by the grace of Allah, so are you, and the diamond is safe.'

'What do you mean, the diamond is safe? You said they took it,' whispered Filippo, too spent for any further emotion.

'They took the jewel in the pouch, but it was a fake, wasn't it? I presume you have the real one secreted somewhere on your body, no? Or in your bundles of clothes, huh?' He smiled painfully.

Filippo fell to his knees and clasped his head in his arms. So the Musalman had known all along.

The burning wind set his lungs on fire. Zubeida too seemed to have used up her last drop of energy. They hadn't passed a water hole for four days, and he had no idea where the next one would be. So they were all going to die anyway.

'Filippo,' whispered Signor Khan, 'which way was my head pointing when you found me? Do you remember?'

'What does it matter, you villain?' sneered Filippo.

'It matters to me. Just think. Look at me now. I haven't moved. Which way is my head pointing?'

'That way,' Filippo grunted reluctantly, waving his head back in the direction he had come from.

'Isn't that proof that I was not trying to get away from you, I was trying to get back to you?'

For the first time since he had found him, Filippo glanced briefly into his eyes. There was some glimmering. They implored him to have trust.

Filippo shrugged and said nothing.

'Don't give up, boy. Help me on to the camel. See that cliff line to the right? It looks like an ancient gorge. There may be a water hole. We should try.'

Zubeida was patient as Filippo helped Signor Khan up on to her hump and tied him to the saddle, just as he himself had been tied down when he rode for the first time. Then, with renewed strength, Filippo took the reins and set off walking through the canyon and, as he walked, he croaked out a song to keep up his spirits.

> *La biondina in gondoleta*
> *L'altra sera go mena.*
> *Dal piaser la povereta*
> *La s'ha in bota indormenza.*

His voice reverberated among the rocks and the sand dunes, and it gave him confidence. It got stronger and stronger, and soon his sand-lined lungs were blasting out the song, filling his blood with courage.

Signor Khan was right. Towards the end of the gorge, they came across a small water hole. Like animals, they flung themselves down, though the sandstorm had clogged it up and it was just a pool of mud. But still they sucked, filling their mouths with mud damp enough to soothe their tongues and cheeks.

'Come Zubeida, come! Drink!'

But Zubeida stayed where she had flopped on to her knees, staring into the south, as if she were praying.

Chapter Twenty

❖

To seek a daughter

Teodora was walking through the Rialto district. She walked with a purpose, not looking at the stalls or markets as she passed through the camp. She was on her way to Bernardo Pagliarin's house, to the man who was trying to destroy her family. She knew now, Carlo had been right. Pagliarin's business had failed and he didn't care how he did it, but he wanted whatever assets of the Veroneo business he could lay his hands on. Using his power as guardian over the family, he was going to marry off Gabriella and Sofia against their will. It was clear to her that one of Pagliarin's men had tried to murder Carlo, and his sons had already caused the death of Giuseppe. She knew that her own daughter, Elisabetta, had been part of the plot. Not to murder her own brother – Teodora would never believe that – but to enable Pagliarin to get hold of the Ocean of the Moon. Wasn't that why she had tried to persuade her mother to let her borrow the diamond?

How Teodora grieved. To lose a child through death was a tragedy, but death was at least honest. To lose a daughter through alienation and treachery was worse than to have lost her through death. But then she got word that Pagliarin had imprisoned Elisabetta, threatening to keep her incarcerated until the diamond was returned and given to him. Her mother love had surged back with the ferocity of a she-tiger, and now she was on her way to confront her son-in-law.

She arrived at the wrought-iron gates. The gate-keeper eyed her with disdain. No lady of any worth would have arrived on foot, and unmasked. His hand was already raised to send her away when, in answer to his questions, she had replied, 'No.' No, she wasn't expected. No, she wouldn't go away. When she demanded imperiously that he inform Signor Pagliarin that his mother-in-law wished an audience with him, the gate-keeper was perplexed and wrong-footed. Perhaps the signora, he stammered, should send a servant ahead to make an appointment, so that she didn't suffer the inconvenience of being disappointed?

But Teodora insisted she could wait, right here at the gate if she was not permitted to enter the house.

With a sigh, as he anticipated trouble, especially for himself, the gatekeeper dispatched a little Moorish slave boy to give the message that Signora Veroneo wished to see Signor Pagliarin.

While they waited, he thought perhaps he ought to make a bench available for her to sit on.

She sat and waited, a long time. The gatekeeper began to express impatience. Perhaps she wasn't worth his deference after all, if Signor Pagliarin himself could show her so little respect?

'It would be better, Signora, if perhaps you came back another day, but sent word first that you are to be expected,' he muttered. But just then, a liveried manservant opened the main door at the top of the steps. Signor Pagliarin was ready to receive her. Another servant came down to escort her into the house.

She was taken into Bernardo's presence in the drawing room. He was seated in his chair, stroking the carved bird with his long finger. He didn't get up, and barely raised his head. His wave of the hand, indicating that she should sit, was almost insolent. Teodora declined.

'I want to see my daughter.' She didn't beat about the bush. 'I'm anxious about her. I haven't seen or had word of her for two months. Where is she? Is she not in good health?'

'Alas, she is indisposed,' Pagliarin drawled, as if the topic bored him. 'She is not receiving visitors.'

'Indisposed? For two months? Then it must be serious. Why was I not informed?'

'Because – the matter is delicate.' He rubbed his hands as if anguished, and dropped his voice as though he had something of the most secret nature to impart to her. 'You see, she had a brief but fierce fever, which I believe has left her mind somewhat disturbed. Her behaviour became strange and in the end, I was forced to keep her under some restriction – for her own good, you understand. We feared she would do herself some harm.'

Teodora didn't respond by keeping her voice down. 'You mean her mind is unbalanced? I demand you let me see her,' she cried, shrill with indignation.

'Madam, madam, I beg you show some discretion.' A dangerous undercurrent flowed beneath his measured words. 'There are already rumours that your daughter is possessed by the devil. It is really not a suitable moment to cause a disturbance. We don't want the church authorities to become involved, do we?'

'Why not?' Teodora's voice resonated with outrage. 'Why not! I challenge you to call an apothecary, or a priest – a bishop even.'

'And risk the possibility she will be proclaimed a witch?' His voice was deadly.

Teodora fell silent, and he smiled triumphantly. 'She shrieks, and calls out devilish words. She tears her hair and rips her clothes. I could cast her out but she is, after all, my wife.'

Wife. The word sounded like the slice of a knife.

'And I am her mother,' retorted Teodora, with equal vehemence.

'Perhaps,' Signor Pagliarin cocked his head as if just struck by a unique thought, 'perhaps, if you were to give me some notion as to the whereabouts of young Filippo, I could be of more help. You know perfectly well that he has broken the laws of Venice by leaving without my permission, or indeed the permission of the council, especially as he has taken something of considerable value which belongs to me.'

'I beg your pardon, sir!' Teodora's voice was low, but seething with anger. 'If you refer to my pendant in the painting, which so charmed the eye of your colleague, Signor Martinelli, then it is not your property, but mine.'

'Excuse me, madam, I do believe if we were to take this matter to the council, I would be able to argue that, as your guardian, and given the long absence of your husband – be he dead or alive – I am the sole charge and beneficiary of all his goods and chattels, which includes you and your children. My proposition is simple. Return the diamond to my possession, and Elisabetta will be freed.'

'Ah!' said Teodora. 'So, it is as I thought. She is as much a hostage as my husband.'

'Call it what you will,' sighed Pagliarin. 'That is my bargain.'

The sun was brilliantly hot when Teodora left Pagliarin's house, yet she felt icy with despair. As she passed through the slave market, a group of men, women and children were being paraded before would-be purchasers, and she wondered whether she was any more free than they. Her family were all hostages. Only Filippo – she choked on the thought of his name – if he was alive, only Filippo was free. 'Please God, let him be alive.'

He was, she was sure he was, just as she'd been sure that Geronimo was alive, and she refused to despair, even though she would wake in the night shaking with fright and unimaginable terrors. How often she would then go to the workshop and start drawing and designing. Only in her work, and her determination to keep up the business and reputation of the house of Veroneo, could she keep her sanity and her belief in the world. She knew she could not expect any message from Filippo, it would be too risky. She and Carlo had spent long evenings, after they had exhausted themselves with work, poring over maps and trying to gauge how long it would take Filippo to reach Afghanistan and return with his father. Carlo urged her not to expect to see them sooner than six months, perhaps a year. Journeys had to be timed with the seasons, the storms and monsoon, let alone any unforeseen eventualities.

Now she must tell Carlo of Elisabetta's plight, but dreaded the fury of his reaction. There was also the problem of Sofia and Gabriella. She and Carlo had been planning to send them secretly away to Florence where an aged aunt in a convent was to shelter them. But now with Elisabetta being held a prisoner by her own husband, and the threats he held over her, who knew what revenge Bernardo might take if the girls were sent away?

Suddenly, a dark dizziness filled all the recesses of her body, deafening her ears with a great roaring sound, and blinding her. She gasped for breath, but her lungs were choked with a terrible despair and panic that overwhelmed her. The babble of the streets and the cries of the gondolieri faded. She felt the ground tipping under her feet, and desperately reached out for something to hold on to. Just before she lost consciousness, she felt a rushing as of wings and feathers, of the powers of good and evil somehow combining forces all around her, like a whirlwind. She thought she smelt cinnamon, as a hand came round her waist and stopped her falling, before the blood drained from her face and she fainted.

Three nights later, Minou did her rounds of the animal sheds, checking the fodder and water for the cows, scattering grain for the chickens and tipping leftovers from the kitchen into the pig swill. She shook with fear. A man crouched in the dairy, hiding among the churns; a man she had let in through the orchard door. She didn't know who he was, nor did she care. Earlier in the day, a strange, crippled old vagabond had grasped her hand at the fish market, pleading for money, gabbling loudly for her compassion and proclaiming that the downtrodden of the world must stick together. In between the whining sentences loud enough for everyone to hear, a younger, robust voice was interjecting another message which only she could hear. 'Listen carefully. I am coming to release your mistress tonight. You must let me in through the orchard door when you do your usual check of the animals. You will find a package under the Angelo bridge. Collect it on your way back. It contains a drug which you must give to the dogs just before sunset. Do you agree?'

She knew by his killer's grip that she had no choice, but she replied eagerly, 'Gladly, sir! I'll do anything to save my mistress.'

'I thought as much.' The hand released her. 'And, by the way, after you've given the drug to the dogs, whatever you do, don't lick your fingers until you've washed them thoroughly.' Then he vanished.

On her way back, she had passed beneath the Angelo bridge and, just as he had instructed, found a package wedged between two bricks which she had tucked into her apron. But could she be of help? The dogs terrified her; their snarling bared-teethed jaws had often been set on people who Signor Pagliarin disliked or wanted to intimidate, and they always looked on the point of breaking free to attack.

When she opened the packet, she found inside four pieces of honeycomb. But though dripping in sweetness, they had been soaked in a powerful drug. Somehow, she must be brave and make sure each hound was given its portion for the plan to work. The dogs got the household leftovers, usually just thrown into the yard for the animals to fight and snarl over. A hungry dog was an active, craving, mean creature – all the better as a guard dog.

Minou had hung round the kitchen, busying herself. The lamps had been lit all over the villa, as the sun set behind the domes and roofs of the city. Cook was lighting the flares in the kitchen. A bucket of scraps, leftovers from the kitchen, stood outside the door ready to be tossed to the dogs. Marco, the stable-hand appeared. She trembled, as he had taken up the bucket and strode out into the yard, whistling for the dogs. The lean, muscular animals had leapt forward, but Marco carefully fed the leader of the pack first, then the second and third and all the way down in the pecking order. After that, he chucked the remainder into the centre for the dogs to fall upon, battling among themselves for the bones and scrags, snarling and slobbering as they tugged and squabbled among themselves.

When Marco returned the empty bucket to the stable,

Minou had stepped outside like a victim stepping into a Roman arena and swiftly extricated the packet from her apron.

'Minou!' The housekeeper's shrill voice demanded her presence. There was no time to be afraid. She had rushed among the dogs, putting a honeycomb to the terrifying teeth-bared jaws of each one. It was swallowed in a single gulp.

Her job done, she fled back into the house to answer the housekeeper's call, frantically wiping her hands on her apron as she did.

An hour later, night had fallen. The candles were lit. Signor Pagliarin had a group of men friends round for an evening of cards. Nadya attended them, as if she were the mistress of the household. The wine was flowing and the villa echoed with their boisterous laughter.

Minou had fetched and carried and been at everyone's beck and call. Now it was time to check the sheds where the cattle and pigs were kept and make sure their water troughs were filled for the night. How had the vagabond known her routines? She shivered to think that she had been watched so carefully. Was he watching her now as she came out and crossed the courtyard towards the orchard at the back? The dogs were silent. Their silence made her anxious. Surely someone would notice and wonder why the dogs didn't bark? She hurried to the wrought-iron gate which led to the orchard. It was unlocked.

He had opened it without the need for a key and was nowhere to be seen.

The night air rang with the persistent barking of dogs all over the city, but not Pagliarin's. The drug had worked. The vagabond was inside and her job was done.

Minou looked at the open gate. It looked so simple. One step, and she would be free. A false freedom though, she knew that. Where can a black face hide? But she couldn't resist tasting the joy, even if it was brief. She looked at the olive trees with their pale starry leaves glowing in the moonlight. Their writhing trunks seemed to draw her to them, as if she should enter and be entwined in their ancient spirit world. She stepped through the gate, her feet deep in grasses and flowers and, as if doing a slow dance, she wound in and out of the trees, embracing each trunk as if it were her partner.

At last, she sank to the ground and pressed herself into an old trunk to be embraced by it. The stars were studded through the crooked leafy branches. She gazed upwards, entranced, drinking in her brief moment of freedom.

'I hope you didn't lick your fingers,' murmured a voice in her ear. 'Go now, quickly, before you are missed. Your mistress is safe and, one day, will hope to reward you for your loyalty.' Minou was lifted to her feet and gently forced back through the gate, back to her slavery.

She struggled, and stared up into the stranger's face. It was totally bound, Arab-style, so that all she could see were his eyes. Beyond him was Elisabetta, propped up against a tree like a rag doll.

'Please,' Minou pleaded with him. 'I beseech you, take me too.'

He released his grip. Minou ran over to her mistress.

'Madam? It's me, Minou. Tell him to take me too.'

Elisabetta grasped her hand and broke into a high-pitched wail like a young lost child. 'Minou!'

'Sssh!' The vagabond clasped his hand over Elisabetta's mouth and stifled her noise.

'Very well, come on then. There's a boat waiting.' The stranger, no longer a limping tramp, was suddenly swift and powerful. He scooped Elisabetta up into his arms and, with Minou holding her hand and running alongside, he carried her to the small canal which ran along the back of the villa and eased her into a waiting boat. Minou jumped in and took the weight of her mistress, and supported her as they huddled together.

There was no gondolier. The stranger, himself, took up the oar and swiftly rowed them away, far from the villa of Bernardo Pagliarin.

Chapter Twenty-one

❖

Blood stones

Filippo smelt roses and a waft of perfume. His diamond eye sang in his head. It was singing of green shaded gardens, trickling with streams and fountains, where peacocks strutted and trailed their glorious feathers, and bowed their crowned heads at each other, where butterflies danced among the camphor and fruit trees, and birds fluttered in the branches. It was cool, it was paradise.

Signor Khan handed him a cup of camel's blood. After he killed Zubeida, he stripped her of every bit of edible meat and every drop of her body's liquid. Ata Allah.

> Drink from the cup of Jamshed, O beloved,
> Refreshing as the dew of night.
> The glittering stars know nothing of the lily's thirst,
> Nor can the lofty moon see inside thy soul.

He longed to drink, but they were going to die. The hyenas were gathering, howling and scuffling somewhere in the darkness. All the while, the diamond was singing inside his head.

Within the singing diamond, and cooing doves, he heard voices, then the neighing of horses and the grunt of camels. A shade came between him and the harsh sun. He felt a cloth soaked in water pressed to his swollen mouth. He sucked greedily, choked, and sucked again. The water trickled with difficulty down his raw throat. There was a whirl of horsemen, wafting robes and rattle of swords, as the riders dismounted. A fire was lit, and soon there was the smell of burning wood and baking bread.

It was a small caravan of merchants on its way to Basra to deliver a group of Arab horses for delivery to Hindustan. In charge of them was a boy, about Giuseppe's age. 'My name is Mahmud Ibn Masoud,' he said. With an authoritative wave of his hand, he ordered that every care should be taken of them.

Signor Khan, though weak, managed to roll on to his knees and kiss the hem of the the young man's garment in gratitude. 'Blessed be Allah, the Most Compassionate; the Most Merciful. Glory be to Him in Whose hands is the Dominion of all things, and unto whom ye shall be returned.'

They entered the hell-hole that was Basra which, though still in its winter months, was unbearably hot. Like a guardian angel, Mahmud insisted on taking them to his uncle's house where he was sure they would be given shelter and indeed, as Mahmud predicted, his uncle Kassim El Kebir was as kindly and hospitable as his nephew. 'Your house is mine,' he told them. 'Rest here and gain your health and strength until you are fit to travel.'

Filippo marvelled at the hospitality. Kassim El Kebir provided them with new robes, and put a horse at Signor Khan's disposal, and Filippo wondered if they had stepped into paradise. The quiet courtyards and verandahs were no mirage. Their rooms, softly darkened against the heat, with windows open to the air, filtered with cool breezes, and beds with capon-feather quilts to warm them when the temperatures dropped at night. The water, flavoured with lemons and ginger which they were brought to drink, was no fantasy, nor the delicate dishes of rice, yoghurt, dates and couscous which were served to them, until their stomachs would be strong enough to take meat.

They rested in Basra for three weeks. Signor Khan would have left immediately, but Filippo was still weak and traumatised after the desert, and their hosts implored Signor Khan to let him regain his strength.

In gratitude for the hospitality, Signor Khan offered to accompany the merchant's Arab horses on a voyage to India and make sure they were handed over safely to his business partner at the port of Surat, an offer which was taken up gladly. A passage had already been arranged with a Dutch vessel, and two weeks later, after heartfelt farewells and thanks, Filippo, with his bundle of belongings, followed Signor Khan, gently leading the horses one by one up the gangplank on to the boat.

'You will stop by and be my guest again when you return with your esteemed father,' pleaded Mahmud, to which Filippo, who had quickly learned the customs and mannerisms of the Arabs, embraced him, touching cheek to cheek on each side, and murmuring, 'If it be the will of Allah'.

After the violent storm which he had endured between Crete and Syria, Filippo thought he would never want to go on board a ship again. But now, in the furnace heat of the sun, to walk on board the gently-rocking vessel was like boarding a royal barque after the trials and stress of life in the desert.

He stared down into the crystal clear waters, where shoals of fish darted like showers of gold-tipped arrows.

The boat slid down the Persian Gulf. The desert stretched on either side. The white sails wafted like huge wings, flapping and slapping in the steady wind.

An old Dutch sailor who spoke a mixture of Italian and Venetian was curious about Filippo. Why was he making this journey? What was his destination? 'Ah! You're going to the court of the Great Moghul? Never been myself,' he admitted, 'but the stories I've heard would make your hair stand on end. It is a court of fabulous wealth, where princes are balanced and measured on scales and given their weight in gold. Where a click of the fingers can make your fortune, or lose your head. Where fathers blind their sons, and brothers murder brothers, and sons murder even their fathers, to gain the throne of the most fabulous kingdom in the world. It's where people with blood stones go to make good deals.' He cocked a head slyly at Filippo.

'Blood stones? What are they?' asked Filippo.

'Diamonds. There's been more blood spilt over diamonds than any other stone. For all the gold and rubies and pearls and emeralds that abound in that kingdom, it's still diamonds that count for the most.'

Did the old Dutchman guess the real purpose of Filippo's journey? Filippo hadn't told him he carried a diamond. Just that he was going out to see his father. But the sailor tapped his nose and leaned close to murmur, 'Your father is a jeweller, did you say? Ah, jewels are much treasured by the present emperor. If I had a stone – a special stone, like a diamond, for instance, I would try and let the emperor see it first. Yes, I would show it to the Great Moghul first, and only to him. When you enter the city of Agra, you enter a city more beautiful than any place you

will have ever seen, even than Venice. But also more dangerous
– even than Venice. If you want a motto, my lad,' whispered the
old sailor, 'keep your eyes and ears open and your mouth shut.
Trust no one.'

Filippo glanced at his Musalman leaning at the deck. They
were bound to each other now, weren't they, even closer than
he was to his own father? Had they not saved each other's lives?
And yet, he heard the Dutchman's cynical words, 'In this world
there is no loyalty, only power.'

And so, at last, the land of Hindustan shimmered into view.

Every sense came alive, bombarding his body until it seemed
to disintegrate into a million atoms. He was burning, drowning,
freezing, hurting, soothing, wounding and healing. This was
Hindustan. It was where he wanted to be. This was the land
where his father was, but it frightened him. It was as though the
whole of his being was sucked into the eye of the diamond to
the very source of creation. A mountain encircled by a serpent
churned a sea of milk, tugged at one end by angels, and at the
other by demons. He felt the force of the struggle between good
and evil, the struggle which produced the universe. Time spun
on a wheel. Strange and extraordinary gods and goddesses, with
six arms or four heads, who rode on tigers, lions, bulls and rats.
He saw a blue god, a dancing god, carrying a trident, wearing

a tiger skin with snakes round his neck and skulls at his waist. This god had a third eye in his forehead, an eye which could kill.

In his mind, Filippo leapt on a horse's back, and bounded into the sky. He galloped over the jungles and desert places and over the mountains until they came to Afghanistan.

A tall, ugly, stone building reared into a chill sky. It had barely a slit for a window, yet he slid through and hovered over his father. It was him, Filippo just knew it was him, even though all he could see was a shivering bundle of a man, crouched in a corner with his head buried in his arms, trying to hold in his body warmth. As if aware that he was being watched, the bundle stirred, and a single eye peered out from beneath his ragged robes. Then a face appeared, haggard and worn, and aged before time which, for a moment, looked transformed by some glorious light, like a cloud's shadow passing swiftly over water. Filippo wanted to stay, but couldn't, and was borne away by his horse. The prisoner, believing that all he had seen was a phantom of his crazed mind, dropped his head back into his rags.

They were swept towards the west coast of Hindustan and into the port of Surat on a tidal wave of smell and stench, and sight and sound, surrounded by a flotilla of all kinds of sailing boats,

rowing boats, dhows and craft. Some were just planks of wood
bound together with rope, with a piece of cloth for a sail, and a
man, blackened by the sun, and naked, except for a loin cloth,
who rode the surf to go fishing out to sea with just one oar – like
the gondolieri. A vast host of voices rang across the bay,
combined with the screech of gulls and the barking of dogs,
while on board the Arab horses fretted and neighed and pawed
the decks, as though they too feared the great foreign land they
were coming to.

They disembarked and were engulfed by a crowd of hawkers,
vendors, porters, guides, middlemen and innkeepers yelling
their services. Weaving in and out were children: girls and boys,
big, little, toddlers, babies on the hips of older children, wizened
children, gangly children, some nearly adult, some barely knee-
high, who all milled around, jabbering, probing, clutching at
the new arrivals' sleeves and hems and pockets. Faces laughed
at them, stared at them, offered to accompany them, carry their
bundles and even interpret for them. All sorts of languages were
yelled out: Français? Inglese? Portuguese? Filippo hung back
alarmed, yet laughed because they laughed.

'Come with me,' shouted the sea captain, and they ploughed
their way through the throng to a white building just
overlooking the harbour, to meet the official who must first give
them a permit to cross the kingdom on their journey towards

Agra. Already, intelligence had reached the authorities of their arrival, and the horse dealer was waiting there to greet them.

Just as Filippo had his diamond embedded in his skull, suddenly the Musalman was producing documents from hidden places in his garments, which showed he had permission from the court in Agra to go there. Pouches were extracted from pockets, there was the jingle of coins as money changed hands.

Filippo felt his feet tingling. The Indian soil hammered at his soles, reminding him that he walked the same ground his father had walked. He sat on a bench on the verandah of the official's house, while Signor Khan went inside to get the documents, feeling he would burst with excitement and anticipation.

Night was falling fast. The sky was wheeling and clamouring with gulls, parakeets, crows, mynas and kites. In dense flocks, like thousands of atoms, they whirled and danced in the darkening sky. Never had he heard so turbulent a nightfall as this one in India. Even the sky, streaked with red, seemed to shriek out the end of the day, and the sun, as though mortally wounded, plunged into a phosphorescent sea, staining it from green to blood red.

In the brief twilight, a figure rode across the compound and tethered his horse. At first glance, in the fading light, he could have been taken for an Arab, in his burnoose. He sprang from his horse and strode on to the verandah with a bold European walk and, in the swinging light, Filippo saw his skin was white – though weathered and burnished so that if he wore a different dress, he could pass for many other nationalities. He barely glanced at Filippo, looking like an Arab boy, sitting there in the dusk. A man with a lantern stepped out to greet him. Filippo heard his voice and Portuguese accent. 'My name is Antonio Rodriguez. I am enquiring after a consignment I am expecting from Venice. Any news of the *Santa Anna* – has she docked yet?'

As they moved inside, a smell of cinnamon lingered on the verandah.

Rodriguez ... Rodriguez ... Where had he heard that name? After a while the man emerged again, striding out. Filippo watched him mount his horse and ride away.

Lamps were lit but the clamour of sound did not dim. Pipes and drums, bugles and horns interlayered with barking dogs and the ever-whirring of the crickets. Out of that din, he heard the flute. It played the same tune he had heard in Venice and Crete, coiling into the air with the spirals of mosquitoes which rose higher and higher, spreading out across the city like a host of vampires looking for blood.

Signor Khan heard it too. He appeared suddenly in the doorway. Filippo couldn't see his face in the darkness. He didn't say anything, just paused, listened and then went back inside.

When he finally reappeared, he just said in a deliberately

loud voice, 'Right, Filippo, we will be guests of Wazir Ahmed, the horse dealer, until our papers are in order. His man is here and will lead us to his house.'

With true Arabian hospitality, Wazir Ahmed provided them each with new robes and fully-saddled horses. They were given cool rooms leading on to courtyards with fountains and shade-giving plants. It was to take five days before they could be allowed to continue the journey, so the horse trader to whom they handed over the horses showed them the same kind of hospitality they had received in Basra, and opened his house to them until all the formalities had been gone through.

Now that he was on Indian soil, Filippo sensed a change in Signor Khan. His movements were quicker like one ready to flee, then he would stop, look wary, his eyes constantly scanning.

On the third afternoon, resting in his room out of the glare of the sun, Filippo heard the flute again.

It was the same tune, and yet with a variation. As if summoned, a shadow moved silently past his door. Bare-footed, Filippo crossed the stone floor and saw Signor Khan leaving the garden through a small door in the wall. He slipped on his sandals and followed him.

At first he thought he had lost him in the bedlam of the bazaar among the street sellers, hawkers, wandering cows, and strings of ponies. Then he glimpsed him weaving his way through the crowd with extraordinary rapidity, into a warren of small streets. Filippo struggled to keep up with him, trying not to give in to panic at being immersed in strange and extraordinary people: tricksters, jugglers, contortionists, street-performers, dancing bears, snake charmers, magicians, traders and pilgrims and bold unveiled women in swinging skirts and loud voices.

Signor Khan stopped at a narrow alley, and turned into it. Filippo's arms flailed as he forced his way forward, desperate not to lose him. When he came to the alley, it was oddly empty. Only a single cow meandered about nibbling at rubbish, and a woman, an infidel – as Signor Khan called anyone who wasn't a Muslim – laid an offering of marigolds at a Hindu shrine.

Then he saw a pair of slippers he recognised in a doorway.

Chapter Twenty-two

❖

The eye of Shiva

The slippers were neatly placed at the bottom of a steep narrow flight of stone steps that went up into total darkness. Filippo paused indecisively, unsure what he should do or why he was there. He began to climb the stairs, and hesitated. He could see no glimmer of light ahead of him. He turned back and stepped out into the alley once more.

A shrill voice rang out. 'He has the eye!' It was the woman, who had straightened up from her prayers before the shrine, and was looking at him. 'He has the eye, he has the eye!' she pointed at him, her voice rising louder and louder.

People peered out of windows and over the balustrades of rooftops. They came out of their doorways and, within seconds, a crowd gathered and was gathering, getting bigger and bigger. Already, the empty alleyway was teeming with people pushing forward and surrounding him with loud cries and clamouring, while the woman went on shrieking, 'He has the eye!'

Everyone was looking at him. Everyone seemed to know he

carried a diamond in his head. A man swathed in a saffron robe, his hair long and covered in ash, whose forehead was marked with a turmeric-coloured smear between his eyebrows, pushed through the crowd. He clasped Filippo's arm, gripping it in a vice-like grip. He stared into his eyes, a hard unblinking stare. The mark on his forehead seemed to glow as if it were an eye of fire. It burned through Filippo's head and connected with the diamond.

> *Although they seek*
> *They do not see*
> *The reflected eye*

> *Burning in the forehead.*
> *Who knows this circle*
> *Knows the mind*
> *Finds Shiva.*

A strange god danced in Filippo's mind. A god with four arms, his hair writhing with snakes, who danced behind a demon in a circle of flames. In the middle of his forehead was an eye as bright as the Ocean of the Moon.

'Kundalini, kundalini,' the holy man chanted incessantly. Filippo tried to pull away from him, but the man's grip was like steel. The crowd got more excited by the holy man's words. This boy was possessed by the gods, he said, by Shiva no less. He has a third eye; the woman saw it, the holy man confirmed it. People began to fight to get close to him, men, women and children, surging forward with outstretched hands, fingers waving, trying to touch. Filippo struggled to free himself, but the crowds thickened around him, nearer and tighter. Hands and fingers poked and prodded, feeling and holding him. His feet left the ground. He was being heaved up on to shoulders and carried away.

'Signor Khan! Help me! Signor Khan!'

Someone appeared in the doorway. He pulled a musket from his belt and fired into the air, yelling, 'Clear off! Get away! *Vas y! Chulloh!*' The crowd ebbed, but did not release Filippo. Another shot rang out, and he was dropped to the ground. The crowd suddenly vanished as quickly as it had come, except for the woman who still stood, blocking their way and shrieking, 'He has the eye, he has the eye!'

Filippo spun round disorientated, unsure what to do, where to go. A hand gripped his shoulder. He pulled away in terror, then saw Signor Khan, smiling at him with his dead eyes. 'Are you in trouble? Come, let's go back.'

Embarrassed and ashamed, Filippo allowed himself to be led out of the alley through the silent, staring crowds.

'What were you doing out on your own? That was rash, wasn't it,' Signor Khan chided him.

'I'm sorry. I didn't mean to . . . I was just exploring,' stammered Filippo uncomfortably. 'What kind of people are these?'

'Infidels,' answered Signor Khan.

'Like me?'

Signor Khan gave a thin smile and tipped his palms to heaven.

'So, you have a third eye?' Signor Khan looked at him closely. Somewhere, Filippo read his thoughts, somewhere on your person, in your body, you have a diamond as clear as an eye, yet full of fire and water.

Filippo's silent riposte was, And what were you doing, who were you seeing, what were you talking about? What is the meaning of the flute?

'They have powers, these people,' Signor Khan said. 'They see and know things. We don't understand them. They're not like us, these Hindus. The infidel priest was telling everyone you were a disciple of one of their gods, Shiva. He told them you had the third eye, that you had special powers. Perhaps it was the colour of your eyes – who knows with these kind of fellows? They wouldn't have hurt you, but they may have carried you off to a temple to be venerated. It was lucky I was there. They might have hidden you away to be worshipped.' He gave a dry laugh.

An elephant, high as a hill and swaying grandly, came down the street towards them. A cacophony of chanting musicians jogged alongside, beating drums and blowing reed pipes. The elephant's head was painted with blue signs and draped with marigolds. Every now and then, it stopped before the doorways of shopkeepers. Like a priest, it touched their bowed heads with its trunk and blessed them in return for alms. Filippo looked up at the small infathomable eye, at the side of its large, wrinkled head. It bored through his brain. As it passed, it raised its trunk and touched him lightly on his head although he gave it no alms. The elephant-keeper turned round curiously, and Filippo felt that even the beasts of this land knew of his diamond eye.

'The elephant is sacred. The son of their god, Shiva, was called Ganesh, who had an elephant's head,' explained Signor Khan, and he spoke with respect.

They had joined a procession of traders, pilgrims and travellers in a mile-long train of bullock carts, for the seventeen-day trek to the city of Agra and the court of the Great Emperor, Shah Jehan. It was the only safe way to travel across a country so ridden with bandits. Signor Khan and Filippo had their own cart, drawn by Indian bullocks, huge, powerful-muscled animals, with strange humps on their necks and long curving horns which reached so far back behind their heads, that

Filippo was warned not to sit too close to the front of the cart, in case a bullock tossed his head and pierced him.

The man called Rodriguez, riding a black horse, joined the caravan right at its tail end. He had travelled hard to catch up with Filippo and Signor Khan. Once he had delivered Elisabetta and her maid to a safe convent near Verona, he had galloped full speed back to Venice. Here he boarded a ship making for Alexandria, and headed by land and sea for Surat.

Hindustan. This was a country where all life was venerated from the smallest ant to the vast elephant, and yet where life was cheap, tough, headstrong and callous. The Musalman called it the land of infidels, but it had been inhabited for thousands of years before the Musalman even came. The Hindus worshipped gods older than the prophet Mahommed or Jesus, son of God. Filippo heard about it from other travellers on that long trek, when he asked about the rearing stone temples in the city of Ujjain or saw multitudes of devotees plunging into the River Shipra. Extraordinary pilgrims and ascetics, smeared in ash, streaked in turmeric and dung. A man who had been standing on one leg for a year in hopes of achieving enlightenment, or another, who had crawled hundreds of miles on his belly to worship at the temple of Shiva. He was curious and wanted to see the idols and images of the extraordinary gods and goddesses he heard described, but his companions held him back and warned him that the temples were forbidden to non-Hindus. To Hindus, they were the infidels.

And all along the route, tribes of monkeys came out of the forests to bound over roofs and walls, and swing like acrobats from the trees. Overhead, circling high on the currents, vultures drifted with outspread wings.

On their long journey from Surat, Filippo and Signor Khan had been in constant danger of wild animals, poisonous insects, snake bites, disease and the terror of bandits. But when they arrived at Agra, and entered through the gates of the city, Filippo sensed a different danger tingling in his head. They could see the huge palace fort, like a city within a city, brooding on the banks of the River Jamuna, whose blue waters swept by its base. It was to the house of the Grand Vizier that Signor Khan said they were going.

Crowds of supplicants crowded at the entrance of his beautiful marble residence, set like a jewel in delicate gardens. Desperate people, clutching petitions and grievances, surged forward clamouring for an audience or for messages to be delivered to the one man who could intercede between them and the emperor. Guards ran out into the crowd with long sticks, thrashing into them as though they were nothing but jungle grass to swipe away.

Signor Khan and Filippo passed through the gates. Servants appeared with flaring torches, casting deep long shadows across marble verandas as they walked through scalloped arches and pillars, trailing with wonderful climbing creepers and flowers. The scent of night flowers cloyed the air, already thick with the steady throb of crickets. A senior servant greeted them respectfully, bowing with clasped hands, touching their feet and kissing his fingers to the air above. Another held a tray of silver goblets containing rose-scented water, for them to have an immediate drink. Then they were led to apartments, where each of them had their own chamber.

It was sumptuous. Filippo gazed in awe at the furnishings: the carpet-hangings, the ebony furniture, the bed covered in beautiful embroidered satin, while on casually scattered low tables were exquisite lacquered boxes into which he could drop his rings and jewellery – if only he wore such things.

Fresh clothes were already laid out for them. The softest, thinnest muslin clothes which would keep his body as cool as possible in the steadily rising heat and, nearby, in a fabulously tiled bathing area, was a large copper tub of water for him to bathe in, with an accompanying clay jug. They had been expected.

Filippo could never have imagined such opulence. Yet he felt as if he were being softened up, fattened like a sacrificial calf. After he had bathed, instead of putting on the garments laid out for him, he unrolled his own Venetian clothes. As this was a land of infidels, then why should he not be seen to be one too? Even if they made him too hot and uncomfortable, the thought gave him courage to put on his own shirt and britches, stockings and shoes. Giuseppe's sword hung from his belt at his side. Finally, with defiance, he put his father's jewelled cross around his neck. How modest, yet it comforted him. Feeling eyes all around him, he never fingered the diamond set into his skull.

He was ready. Night had fallen. The house was oppressively silent. It was as though it was completely empty. He felt nervous, yet from outside, as if from a great distance, in ripple after receding ripple, he could hear a multiplicity of sounds which seemed to ebb and flow from all ends of the earth. His senses stiffened like the hairs of a cat. He felt eyes watching him. He wondered if he should go out and look for Signor Khan. A servant appeared, so soft-footed that Filippo didn't see him for a few moments. He was dressed in a uniform of long white cotton coat over pyjamas bound with a green sash. On his head was a green turban with a long tail which swung when he walked. The servant put two hands together and bowed his head respectfully. He beckoned Filippo to follow.

He was taken to a light room of many windows where, on heavily-embroidered silk-covered cushions which lined the walls, sat the Vizier and Signor Khan. Two slaves stood behind them waving huge feathered fans.

Filippo made a sweeping bow of respectful greeting. Signor Khan, already in deep conversation with the Vizier, looked up briefly. He frowned when he saw what Filippo was wearing, then jerked his head to indicate that he should seat himself, while he continued his conversation with the Vizier, who hadn't even bothered to look up.

Filippo lowered himself down on to a cushion opposite them. His anxiety and sense of danger had made him strangely bold, almost insolent. He stared unashamedly at the Vizier, studying his oddly triangular face, with dark brown eyes set quite far apart which never quite focussed, a squat nose and a long drooping moustache which reached down to his jawline on either side. His lips and teeth were heavily stained red with betel so that Filippo couldn't help imagining that he had just been drinking blood. His podgy fingers were heavily ringed, he wore several garlands of pearls interspersed with sapphires, emeralds and rubies, and there were even long drooping pearl earrings dangling from his ears. His robes too were threaded with pearls and precious stones and Filippo wished his brother Carlo could see it.

Although a silver tray with a jewelled goblet lay within arm's reach, the Vizier clicked his fingers and summoned a servant to

lift the cup and hand it to him. Filippo instantly despised him.
As the Vizier lifted the cup to his lips, he looked at Filippo for
the first time. For the first time since the diamond was put in his
skull, Filippo found himself staring into a dark soul of the most
evil intent. It was the briefest of glances, then the Vizier looked
away and continued his conversation with Signor Khan.

Three low ebony tables were brought in covered in crisp
snow-white cotton, and set before each person. Further servants
carried in steaming tureens of fragrant rice, meats, vegetables
and yoghurt. Later, a servant offered him a cup of sweet liquid.
He gulped it down. The comfort of the cushions – or something
in the drink – made him feel overcome with sleep. He struggled
to stay awake, but the room blurred and swayed. His eyelids
grew heavier. He tried blinking and shifting himself around, but
it was no use, he was unable to resist the compulsion to lie back
and give in to sleep.

He must have slept for hours. When he woke, the sun lay like a
fierce sword cutting across the floor. He could hear a little
orchestra of sounds. The chittering of squirrels, the persistent
cawing of crows, the high-pitched chattering of monkeys, and a
constant croo-crooing of the doves. A woman sang as she
swept the verandas, and a street seller hawked his wares like an
opera singer.

Filippo sat up, startled. Someone had carried him into his chamber, taken off his clothes and put him into silken nightwear. Panic-stricken, he touched the back of his head. The diamond was there. He shuddered and looked round fearfully, wondering if anyone had noticed his action. Almost immediately, a servant appeared. How closely they watched. Did anyone know? Had Signor Khan looked and found the diamond in his head while he slept? The servant had brought in a silver tray with a goblet and jug. The jug contained guava juice, and the servant poured some out into the goblet and handed it to him. Realising how thirsty he was, Filippo was about to gulp it down, when he stopped short. What if it was drugged like last night, or poisoned even? He felt a sweep of panic, and for a moment stared round the room like a trapped animal.

Then Signor Khan appeared in the doorway, smiling. 'It's safe to drink, don't worry,' he said, as if reading his mind. 'Let me reassure you.' He came over and took a sip from the cup. 'See?'

'I was drugged last night, wasn't I?' Filippo burst out angrily.

'Not drugged, boy,' murmured Signor Khan, 'just a potion to help you sleep after your arduous journey.'

'You should have told me. How long are we going to stay here? I don't like it.' He backed away from the goblet which Signor Khan held out to him.

'Drink!' Signor Khan's voice was suddenly, quietly commanding. 'Remember what you came for. If you wish to save your father, then you must do what I say. Trust me.'

'Trust you?' Filippo couldn't help the bitterness with which the words fell from his mouth. Their eyes met. Filippo paused, as if listening for some inner message from his diamond eye. None came. He felt ashamed of his mistrust. After all they had been through, each caring for the other, each saving the other's life. Could anything now come between them? He took the goblet and gulped down its contents.

'Good. Get dressed. We have an audience with the Vizier in an hour.'

An hour later, having ignored pleas from the servant that he put on the fresh Muslim garments which had been laid out for him, and dressed once more in his own clothes, with Giuseppe's sword sheathed at his belt, Filippo stood outside the audience chamber waiting to be admitted. He could hear raised voices inside. The words and meanings filtered through the diamond. Signor Khan was insisting that there must be no delay. 'We must leave within the month before the monsoon. We must not delay.' Then the bead curtain was being lifted aside and a servant ushered Filippo across the threshold.

Filippo bowed with forced respect before the Vizier, who sat on a low wooden carved chair, attended by his fan-waving servant. He waved a bored hand in acknowledgement, but didn't bother to look at him. Signor Khan, who was seated cross-legged on a cushion nearby, patted a place next to him, and Filippo obediently sat down beside him.

They had obviously been in deep discussion before he arrived, and Filippo wondered what they had been talking about. Signor Khan looked up reassuringly. 'The diamond, Filippo. This is why you have come here, to free your father with a ransom. The diamond you bring is of great value. The Vizier would like to buy it from you. The money you receive in exchange will be more than enough to pay the ransom, so be so good as to show it to His Eminence, and then we can be on our way to Afghanistan within days.'

It was time. How ordinary it seemed. His whole journey had been about reaching the moment when he would sell the diamond for enough money to obtain a ransom, yet he held back. He never expected it to be a mere transaction, as if it was no more than bartering for a basket of eggs.

'No!' Filippo surprised himself by his defiance. This was the wrong place, the wrong person. He heard Signor Khan's dismayed intake of breath. Filippo leapt to his feet defiantly. 'I mean . . .' but it was too late. He had already caused offence. The Vizier turned red with anger and rasped some words out to

Signor Khan to the effect that he was not going to tolerate this insolent infidel.

'Please Signor Khan,' Filippo pleaded with him. 'This was my father's most treasured jewel, which he gave to my mother – our family's birthright. It's not just any old piece of jewellery to sell off in the marketplace for the highest price. The emperor must see it first.'

The Vizier began shouting, 'Tell the boy he should be whipped. Does he not know who he speaks to? Does he think he is worthy to be the dust beneath the emperor's feet, let alone hope to gain an audience with him? He should be thrown to the crocodiles. Order him to hand over the diamond.'

Signor Khan sat stony-faced, listening until the tirade was over. Then he requested words with the Vizier alone. The Vizier nodded, though his lip was still curled with fury at being disobeyed.

'Leave us for a moment, Filippo,' said Signor Khan quietly. 'Go out into the gardens and wander about a bit. Think over your position, while I discuss things further with the Vizier.' He pointed through an open archway which led out across marble terraces to a garden beyond.

Filippo almost ran from the room, followed by a servant hurrying along behind him.

'Watch him!' bellowed the Vizier.

It was like stepping into a jewel. The gardens were laid out in geometric patterns, each with their own scheme of flowers and shrubs. They were trickling with streams, pools, fountains and little bridges. Marble seats were set in shady arbours, and arches of inlaid tiles gleaming with precious stones framed pathways that led into rose gardens. Peacocks strutted and shrieked, and doves fluttered from cupolas which perched at each corner of the square wall surrounding the garden. At first he ran, zigzagging among the flowerbeds, trying to get away from the servant sent to guard him. But the man stayed persistently behind him.

In a far corner near a wall, he saw a banyan tree. Broad-leafed and spreading, it had vast creepers which hung down to the ground, re-seeded themselves, and arched up again, so that it was like some strange palace of pillars. He had marvelled at such trees on their long journey to Agra. He pushed in among their roots and began to climb. The servant, in his crisp white robes, stood helplessly at the bottom, unwilling to follow him, but grunting and gesticulating for him to come back down. But as he climbed, Filippo picked up a sound which drew him upwards. Heard at first from a distance, it was coming closer, the sound of beating drums, jangling bells and high-pitched reed instruments. He had to see what it was. He reached a branch which overhung the wall. He crawled along, and with a brief swing of his legs, landed on the top of the wall, crouching on all fours like a monkey.

He couldn't believe it. They were so close to the centre of the town, so close to humanity. There he was overlooking a broad street, and just a short distance away, he could see the vast rearing red sandstone walls of a huge fortress palace. Coming down the street was a procession in the midst of which was a giant elephant massively decorated and draped in rich cloths, with painted tusks and a bejewelled head. The elephant-keeper sat on his head with an iron-pronged instrument, which he used to prod the elephant's head and control him. Behind him, strapped to its back, was a platform hung with gold-tasselled curtains. The musicians formed the vanguard, followed by uniformed soldiers wielding swords who ran in front and behind the elephant. Jogging alongside were liveried servants, in white garments with bright red turbans and sashes, carrying tall fluttering fans of feathers which they held up to wave and cool the air for the benefit of whoever was inside the curtains.

Filippo felt a surge of excitement. This could only be the emperor himself. He stood up eagerly, disregarding the drop of fifteen or more feet below him. Soon the elephant would be abreast of him, and he would be able to see inside. A curtain was held aside. He strained forward, and then gasped in astonishment. The occupant was no emperor. Just a child — a boy of barely six years old who, though dressed like an emperor in silken turban and jewelled jacket, was bouncing up and down with excitement, like any child.

Suddenly he spotted Filippo on the wall. He shrieked repeatedly and pointed, his high-pitched treble cutting through the air.

Guards with swords drawn broke away from the contingent and rushed over to him. The child continued shouting with amazing authority and, at his command, the elephant-keeper turned, reached over with his iron hook and, as if Filippo was just a troublesome fly, hooked him off the wall by his jacket and dropped him into the arms of the guards.

Chapter Twenty-three

❖

A little prince

His feet hardly touched the ground as two guards, one on each side, gripped his arms, and yanked him away with the sounds of the child's shrill voice still issuing commands.

He was frogmarched through the gates of that great palace fort. Up steps, across courtyards, up more steps, along terraces with forests of pillars, past armed guards and elegant courtiers, whose slippered feet slapped on the marble floors, and servants who ran this way and that, and messengers who waited and clerks who calculated. Up and up they went, reaching rooftops which then had steps leading to more rooftops. He felt as if he were being taken up to the top of the world. He caught glimpses of the city now so diminished below him, where the people were reduced to tiny milling specks and their voices rose like the buzz of bees. Most wonderful of all, as they turned a corner and looked to the north, he saw a great shining broad-backed river, winding blue and smooth as silk, and camels, sharply defined in miniature in the bright clean light, steadily crossing the shallows to the vast plain on the other side.

Here, where the heat and dust and stench of the city were left far below, where the winds wafted through the geometrically patterned marble walls and bees hummed among the cupolas of the highest terrace, he emerged into the blinding light of day.

The terrace was strewn with cushions and low tables, and a great wooden cushioned seat swung from a frame. Bound to an iron ring was a cheetah glistening gold and black, who turned its wild golden head and stared at him with glassy eyes. A peacock strutted along the far wall with its tail of turquoise, green and blue eyes trailing down to the floor. Blindingly-white doves flung themselves into the blue air.

His guards called out. From a room set back from a covered terrace of pillars, a woman appeared, her face covered by a veil. But from behind her shot a small boy, like an arrow from a bow, across the terrace and head-butted Filippo right in the middle of his stomach.

Filippo lurched around, gasping with pain, his arms clutched round him and his eyes filled with tears. 'What did you do that for?' he yelled furiously in Italian.

The boy looked up him with black mischievous eyes and just laughed. 'He's bigger than me, he's bigger than me, but I made him cry!' he laughed in Urdu to his nursemaid.

The guard pushed Filippo to his knees and, putting his foot

to the back of his head, pressed it down till his forehead touched the ground. 'Bow before Prince Murad Bhakhsh, Desire Accomplished, esteemed fourth son of the Great Emperor.'

So the boy on the elephant was a prince, a son of the emperor who he had come to find. Filippo groaned, not just with the agony of his bruised stomach, but as he remembered the words of the old Dutch sea captain who had told him that he could have his head chopped off or be thrown to the crocodiles at the click of two royal fingers.

He heard the click, but it was Prince Murad dismissing the guard who had brought him. He stayed crouched and still, praying hard. 'Oh San Antonio and San Cristoforo, don't let him throw me to the crocodiles.'

A hand tickled his ear. He looked up to find two black eyes peering straight into his. The child had dropped to his knees and was still laughing at him. He put his hand under Filippo's chin and lifted it. Filippo dropped back on his heels while the boy examined his green eyes and felt his dark auburn hair. He took his hand and stroked his skin, calling his nursemaid to see the fine golden hairs on Filippo's arm. He pressed his thumb hard on the flesh of his cheek and enjoyed seeing the red mark appear. Then he was filled with remorse. He stopped laughing and said solemnly, 'Forgive me, O infidel, for giving you pain.' Then he leapt back on his feet and said, 'Up! Get up!'

The little prince grabbed Filippo's hand and pulled him upright too. He circled him, touching, feeling, examining his clothes. He had never been so close to a European before. He felt the material of his shirt. '*Yeh kya hai*? What is this?' He demanded, tugging at the chained cross around Filippo's neck as if he wanted it for himself.

'No, you can't have it. It's my father's!' cried Filippo, pushing it back inside his shirt and, to divert the child, tipped him upside down.

The boy shrieked with laughter; he tugged his jacket and laughed at his britches and footwear. Filippo lowered him to the ground and plonked him back on his own two feet. The royal child stamped a little sandalled foot on his boots to see if it would hurt. Playfully, Filippo lifted his foot as if he would stamp on the little prince's toes, but missed them by a hair's breadth, causing the royal child to squeal with laughter.

'Yes, yes, yes! I like you!' the boy shouted and with a flying leap, landed on Filippo's back, with his arms clasped round his neck, and his heels digging into his side as if he were a horse.

Filippo fell in with the game, and bounced the young prince round the terrace, changing directions quickly to swing him about and make him shriek with laughter.

The questions began. 'What is your name? What country

are you from? How long have you been in Hindustan? Where is your father? What are you doing here?'

All kinds of messages were being sucked into his diamond eye. He understood, yet he didn't understand. Language is nothing without meaning. As a child, the boy was innocent, but Filippo saw a future when the boy became a man, and the man became ambitious and treacherous. He had power, yet no power, but he would die in pursuit of it.

He dropped the little prince to the ground and stood back with a shrug and a twist of the hand. '*Main Urdu nahin bolta hun.*' I don't speak Urdu.

The boy clapped his hands and yelled an order. After a while, a servant appeared with an old man. He was a shuffling bent old white-bearded man in a trailing linen coat and squeaky slippers. Prince Murad pointed at Filippo and issued a command.

'Portuguese?' the old man asked. Filippo shook his head. 'French? Dutch? English?'

'Venezia,' said Filippo. 'I come from Venice, on the shores of the Adriatic in the land of Italy. My language is Venetian, but I can speak some Italian.'

'Ah!' The old man smiled. Perhaps because Italians hadn't fought battles here in Hindustan, but only came as traders or fortune seekers. 'Italian.'

The translator explains that Filippo stands before Prince

Murad Bakash, the youngest son of the emperor, Shah Jehan. Murad has never seen a white boy before. But though the prince is so young, the old man warns him to show respect. Even this young prince can have him beheaded at the click of his fingers. 'I advise you to retreat several steps, lower your eyes, bow your head and cross your hands over your chest,' he says.

Filippo was obeying, but the young prince tugged him back and waved at the translator to translate. So the questions began again. 'What is your name? Which country are you from? How long have you been in Hindustan? What are you doing here? Are you alone? Where is your father?'

They had sat themselves down now on a rug and were deep in exchanging information when a harsh voice rang across the terrace. Filippo automatically leapt to his feet as another boy appeared.

He was older, Filippo's age perhaps. A prince too, there was no doubting that by his rich clothes and his superior air.

'What is an infidel doing here?' he demanded haughtily. Keen to demonstrate his higher status, he strode across the rooftop, kicking aside toys and cushions.

Filippo saw the fear run across Prince Murad's face. He scrambled to hide behind one of the ever-present bodyguards, while his nursemaid clasped her hands and bowed very low before the older boy.

'Bow, bow low,' hissed the old translator. 'This is Prince Aurangzeb.'

Filippo bowed instantly.

Prince Aurangzeb strutted up to him and stood so close, he could count the number of diamonds embroidered into his sandals.

'Who is this infidel? I asked a question. Have you all lost your tongues?'

'Oh esteemed highness, Prince Aurangzeb, the Throne's Ornament, his name is Filippo Veroneo. He is from Venice, a land in the continent of Europe between . . .'

'Shut up! I don't want a geography lesson.' Prince Aurangzeb cut the old man short.

He flipped Filippo painfully under the chin, causing him to look up. Their heads were almost touching.

Filippo stared briefly into Aurangzeb's eyes. It was like looking into whirlpools – a maelstrom. He saw terror and war. Although this boy was dressed in rich clothes of gleaming colours, Filippo saw him become a man, clothed in white like an angel, yet failing to shine as true angels do, and carrying a fiery sword which would cut down anyone who stood in his way. It was the white of religion, but a religion perverted by ambition and thirst for power. With bowed head, Filippo gazed at the hem of the prince's garment; his diamond eye saw it drenched in the blood of his three brothers. This boy would attract the loyalty of those who like to walk with the powerful. He would have a great following, but never love, and become the most powerful in the world. Ultimately, this boy, Aurangzeb, was a destroyer and would eliminate anyone who stood in his way to becoming Emperor, the Great Moghul, King of the World.

'Filippo's my friend,' piped up little Prince Murad.

'No, he's not,' Aurangzeb contradicted him harshly. 'He's an infidel. He can't be your friend.'

Aurangzeb tugged the corner of Filippo's jacket, and flipped his cap to the ground. Filippo stooped to retrieve it, but it was kicked out of his reach.

The younger prince whimpered, but no one dared to comfort him.

'Why are you here?' demanded the bully.

Filippo felt a surge of anger which fuelled his courage. With proud defiance he spoke in Venetian, not caring whether Prince Aurangzeb or anybody else understood or not.

'My name is Filippo Veroneo, the son of the jeweller, Geronimo Veroneo, who was known to the previous emperor, his illustrious majesty, the Great Moghul, Jehangir. He was employed here in the court for six years. He was finally given permission to go home but on his way, he was taken hostage in Afghanistan. That is why I am here. I have brought a jewel which my father created, a pendant, which I wish to sell to pay the ransom for my father. Knowing of your illustrious father's passion for precious stones, my family thought it fitting that the Great Moghul, your father, Emperor Shah Jehan, should be given the first opportunity to see this supreme masterpiece. Perhaps he may desire to purchase it for his own use?'

Filippo had spoken rapidly but the interpreter had rattled alongside, translating almost simultaneously. Filippo ended. He lowered his eyes and crossed his hands over his chest and bowed.

'Give it.' Aurangzeb held out his hand.

'No,' Filippo replied firmly. 'It is for the eyes of the Great Emperor and only his.'

There was a stunned silence. Murad sniffled. Again, Filippo had dared to disobey. Perhaps he had gone too far, been too bold. He felt his fate hanging by a thread. His fingers crept to the rosary in his pocket and he began to thread it through his fingers. 'Sweet Mary, Mother of God, save me. San Antonio and San Cristoforo and all the saints, pray for me.' He waited to hear the click of the fingers.

'You are obviously ignorant of our customs, infidel,' jeered Aurangzeb. 'You don't bargain with an emperor. If you have anything of any worth, it has to be a gift. Tell him,' he ordered the interpreter.'

The interpreter obeyed.

'And tell him, that another of our customs is that he accept my hospitality.' Aurangzeb's voice became suddenly soft and sweet as honey. 'I insist he remains here as my guest.' He then shouted a command to a servant and left with a sweep of his long silk jacket.

Chapter Twenty-four

❖

The eye in the wall

Filippo lies on his bed drained of any ability to move, so enervating is the heat. Only his eyes have life, scanning from object to object, but always returning to the same spot, to a particular tile on the wall opposite.

It is not the only tile on the wall, but part of a frieze that runs all the way round. They are all the same. All are turquoise, with an elaborate coiling design of dark blue and yellow flowers wound round a hexagon, in the middle of which is a small red circle, except that this particular tile is different because in it he has seen an eye.

It had stared out at him from the central circle which, instead of being red, was suddenly blue. He knew it was an eye, because it blinked.

He had sat up startled, sprung from his bed and rushed forward, but the eye had disappeared and the circle was black once more. Filippo had reached up and run his finger over it, but felt no hole or cavity, and no join under his touch. Could it be that he was imagining things, or that it was the heat of the day affecting his senses? Panting with the exertion, he had lain back on his bed.

It is the peak of the afternoon, so fiercely hot outside that no man, beast or animal who has any choice in the matter, is abroad. The white marble terraces of the palace are blindingly white in the Indian sun, and no bare feet dare to make contact with its burning surface. He has stripped off his European clothes, and given in to wearing the cool, thin cotton tunics and pyjamas which have been provided for him.

Filippo doesn't know if he is a prisoner or a guest. His accommodation is fit for a prince: sumptuously furnished with ebony and teak furniture, and embroidered wall hangings. Lacquer-painted vases, large jugs coated in silver, brim with cool drinking water, and there are always dishes of almonds and grapes for him to nibble. A narrow gully of fresh water trickles past his door. Each day he has a set of freshly laundered new clothes, and each evening, his bed is made up with silken sheets, perfumed with roses. Throughout the day, he only has to call and a servant comes to see to his every need. At regular intervals, delicious food is brought to him on silver platters.

He is in a cupola-topped tower of red sandstone, with four windows looking out in each direction through which the winds ebb and flow. Wherever he looks, he sees beauty. The luminous light across the plains – so clear he feels he can count the leaves on the trees from miles away. The winding, shining river flowing below, with the silent boats, and flapping sails. The flat-roofed town crammed together topsy-turvy, yet brimming with life and activity. Saris dry in the wind, children fly their kites, people lift their arms as they say their prayers, unveiled girls – infidels – plait each other's hair. And always, somewhere close or from afar, he hears trumpets and drums, wailing reed instruments and the tremor of sitars, as though the people cannot live without music.

The sweepers swish, swish, swish with their brooms and sing softly, as all day they move through the palace rooms, along the verandas and terraces, and up and down the hundreds of steps. From far below on the river banks, he hears the washermen shouting their song, as they scrub and whirl the clothes down on to the rocks with a ringing slap. Even his guards, crouched for long boring hours at the top of his steps, hum and sing beneath their breath in between puffing on their bidis.

Now he watches the tile obsessively but, so far, the eye hasn't reappeared. He feels observed, spied on all the time. Sometimes at night he awakes, sure that he has heard voices right there in his room. They seem to be inside the very walls themselves. There are spies. There must be spies, secret ears and eyes listening and watching, trying even to overhear if he talks in his sleep. He hopes he doesn't touch the diamond in his head and give the secret away. Perhaps the diamond in his skull is sending him mad. He sinks back on his silken pillows, his eyes half-closed, and the whole chamber sways around him as if he is at sea. Grey-green waves lap the walls, the same waves which lap around Andreas, as he lies half-drowned on a lonely shore . . .

The dolphin had swum beside him, nudging and buoying him along, sometimes rising up beneath him so that Andreas sprawled across his grey, shining back, and was carried to an island. As the rocky shore scoured his belly, the dolphin gently tipped him into the shallows and, with a hooting cry of farewell, swam away.

It was an isolated island, swirled by grey mists, with steep unbroken cliffs, and jutting headlands. An island of another time, an ancient time. Filippo in his palace chamber could see it clearly in his diamond eye. Andreas had been brought to a place where water spirits had once lived in pools, and wood nymphs uncoiled themselves from twisting olive tree trunks, to sport among the groves when fleet-footed gods had hunted among the stars, and beasts – half-man, half-horse – had galloped across the headlands.

When the demented woman on the shore heard the dolphin's cry, she ran down to the water's edge and found the boy unconscious on the sand. She bent over him, her long straggly unkempt hair falling around him. She cradled his head in her arms and kissed his cold cheeks. 'My son, my son!' she had cried, moaning with joy. She rushed waist-deep into the waves with outstretched arms extolling the gods. 'Oh Zeus, Father of all things! O Poseidon, Lord of the Waves! Thank you.' Then she returned to the shore and fell to her knees, trickling soil through her fingers and calling on Demeter, the Earth Goddess. 'Thank you, thank you revered Goddess, who knows what it is to grieve for a child. Thank you for giving me back a son.'

She fetched a flask and filled it from a pool of fresh water fed from a cataract, which fell like a bride's veil from the gullies above and, returning to the boy, tenderly forced it between his rigid teeth and tipped it down his throat. Andreas had opened his eyes to see a ravaged, grief-torn face bending over him, with tangled knotted hair writhing like snakes from her brow. He had shuddered in horror and fainted away.

When he next opened his eyes, he was lying on a bed of moss and dried grass, covered in a sheep skin. A smell of burning wood and roasting fish drifted into the cave, and a soft voice sang.

He had been clothed in animal skins, and beside him lay a jug of water and a plate of olives. Somehow, the woman had lifted him up in her arms and carried him to her cave away from the shore, sheltered in a canyon beneath a sheer rugged cliff. But still, a dreadful fear swept over him.

Andreas crept to the entrance of the cave and peered out. The woman with a writhing head of snakes for hair was transformed. Now she wore a long neat garment of cream cloth, which draped across her chest and was fixed at her shoulder with a bronze clip. Her black, grey-streaked hair had been combed and pinned back in a bun, and her movements were as smooth and beautiful as a dancer, as she bent and stretched over her fire and cooking pot. Although he made no noise, she sensed him watching, and turned a face no longer aged and ravaged and grief-stricken, but shining with joy and smiles.

'My son!' she exclaimed and opening her arms ran forward and embraced him.

Andreas bowed his head and accepted her embrace though did not return it. When she released him, he stepped back respectfully, and spoke in Greek. 'My name is Andreas Georgilis. I am the son of a fisherman. I live in Venice. I am trying to go home.'

But if she understood his meaning, she replied as though he had said something quite different. 'The gods have heard my prayers. The gods have been good. They have returned at least one of my men to me. O my beloved child.' And she had fallen at his feet and clasped his ankles and kissed them.

'I beg of you, kind lady . . .'

'Kind lady?' she exclaimed. 'Why would you call me kind lady? Am I not your mother? Will you not let my ears ring with the sound of music again and hear you call me Mother? Say it, say it!'

'Please . . . Mother.' Andreas spoke the word, feeling a terrible unease and sorrow in his heart.

She made him sit, she made him eat; she served him, kissed him, nurtured him like her own lost son. She kept him by her side like an infant, never letting him out of her sight, so that he felt as much as prisoner of her gaze as if he had been bound in chains.

The days and weeks sped by. He grew stronger and sometimes when they sat together over a meal, she would say, 'O beloved son! Why do you look so sad? Do I not feed you well, and give you good wine? Do I not anoint your body with oil and massage the weariness out of your limbs?' And Andreas would try all over again to tell her that he was not her son, and that one day he must leave and return to his own family who would be grieving for him.

But every time he broached the topic, she became demented again, tearing her hair till it straggled like snakes, and wailing that he must never ever leave her again. Even if he woke at night, he would see her crouching in the entrance of the cave, watching him with eyes as luminous as dark pools.

The luminous eyes gleamed in Filippo's head, even when he slept through the blazing afternoon. He fantasised about escaping and going to rescue his father, but he knew it was impossible.

Little Prince Murad came to play with him late every afternoon when it was cooler. Filippo tried to control his diamond eye, and not see too much into the soul of this child and what his future held. 'Stay in the present; accept the here and now. Don't judge the present for what will happen in the future.' He remembered the old rabbi's words. And so he looked forward to the sound of Murad's high laughing voice, chattering away to his nurse, as they climbed the steps to his chamber.

He came with kites which he loved with a passion: red ones, blue ones, orange, pink and green, attached to reels of coloured string. With shrieks of laughter and great competitiveness, they had launched them into the blistering sky, loosening the strings till they become specks, dancing and fluttering in the high currents of air, each trying to make his fly higher than the other.

Sometimes the translator came too, and Filippo begged for information. 'Where is Signor Khan? Is he still with the Grand Vizier? Does he know where I am? Time is passing. I should be on my way. My father – he needs me to free him,' Filippo pleaded. 'Why can't I go now?' He dreaded the thought that he could be be kept for years and years, as his father was.

But the old interpreter just shook his head and said, 'The monsoon is due in a week or two. Then all travel is impossible.'

'Then we should leave immediately.'

'You can go when the prince allows it.'

'Which prince? Prince Murad? He likes me. He would let me go, I'm sure of it.'

The old man shruged and looked cautious, and Filippo knew that he was really a prisoner of Prince Aurangzeb, though Aurangzeb never came to see him.

'Does the Emperor know I'm here?'

'Hush! Never even speak his name,' he was warned.

It is in those blazing afternoons that he feels most alone, when he lies on his bed feeling in turn bored, helpless and afraid.

This afternoon – another lonely afternoon – it is as though the diamond in his skull has become a furnace, so hot that it could explode inside his head. Outside, the only bird who dares to sing through the heat is the brain-fever bird, monotonously climbing a chromatic scale of eight notes, then dropping down and singing the same ladder of notes all over again. On and on it burbles in an insane repetition, pulsating with the throb in his temples.

Filippo pulls the tall oak screens in front of the windows to shield his eyes from the glare and lies back on the bolster dappled by the gleaming diamonds of light which break through the intricately carved panels.

He sees himself entangled in a conspiracy. Threads of intrigue hook from palaces to forts, from bullock carts to ships, from port to port and oasis to oasis, from village to village and city to city. There is conspiracy everywhere, even in the music, in the beat of the drums, the wail of the pipes, and the oh so silky melodies of the flute. The flute which can be tucked into a pocket and carried anywhere. The flute, in the hands of a goatherd or a sailor, a street musician or a gentleman, translating messages from hundreds of different ragas, which deliver instructions from the alleyways of a city, right into the very heart of palaces. Conspiracy seeps in the walls, sails with the ships, rides with the caravans, and crosses the deserts on camels. It is whispered from mouth to mouth, ear to ear, and hand to hand. He sees it passing through the fingers of diplomats and mullahs, of priests and traders, rajahs and nawabs, sea captains and city officials from Kabul to Agra, from Surat to Basra, from Alexandria to Venice. There is money, there is plotting, there is power, there is death.

Filippo's eye returned obsessively to the same tile. His lids narrowed almost to a close when, barely perceptibly, the black circular centre of the tile slid away and was replaced by blue.

This time, he didn't leap to his feet, but remained utterly still, looking beneath lowered eyelids, so that whoever was watching might think him asleep.

The blue eye blinked – vanished. He heard the softest noise, like nothing more than a faint breeze whispering through the marble-slatted windows. The panel on which the tile was fixed slid open.

The heat of the afternoon hung like a dead weight. Even the fever bird was strangely silent. Someone entered his room. He didn't move. He heard a rustle of silk and the smell of sandalwood. A figure tiptoed into his vision. A slight figure, about the same height as he; a girl, dressed the Muslim way in long flowing tunic and pyjamas, with a fine sequined veil completely covering her head and face.

She lifted a hand and drew the veil partly aside to reveal one blue eye.

He opened his mouth to exclaim, but she put a finger to her lips. Beyond her, the opening in the panel led into what seemed like a black void, yet she beckoned him to follow.

He stepped through. The panel slid shut behind him. In the pitch dark, her hand took his, and she pulled him along, her other hand slapping the side of the wall as they went. She was so fast and sure-footed – even in the darkness – Filippo felt like a boat being carried away on a current. At last, far in the distance, he saw a bright band of light which, as they got closer, he saw came from a narrow slit in the thick wall, but just wide enough for them to squeeze through.

He paused, hesitantly. It was dangerous. What if his guard woke up and found him missing? What if they were discovered? She pulled his arm determinedly, and so he allowed himself to be tugged through to the other side into dazzling daylight.

They were on a small roof like the eyrie of an eagle, so high, so perilous, with no balustrade or wall to stop them plunging a hundred feet down. Below him, other roofs, terraces, steps and balconies spread away in layers to the gardens beyond, shaded densely with trees and bushes, and groves of mango and guava. An ocean of foliage billowed around them flecked with vivid-coloured flowers of purple bougainvillea, orange flame of the forest, and the deep red tulip tree. Glinting through it all was the great shining back of the river, with its soft drift of sailing boats. Suddenly there was a rush of tears to his throat as he remembered Venice. *La Serenissima!* Would he ever return?

He felt disadvantaged. She could see his face, but he couldn't see hers through her veil. Then she spoke four words in English. 'My name is Noor.'

* * *

Her name is Noor. His diamond eye shimmers and refracts the light around his brain. Noor. She is constantly moving; her feet tapping, her head tilting, her fingers and wrists twining in and out of each other. When she speaks it's more like singing, her sentences are musical phrases which have to be danced into existence. 'What is your name?' she asks with flowing arms. 'Where do you come from? Why are you here? What is your father? Have you any brothers and sisters?' She is all tinkling bells and fluttering drum beats, of rising and falling melodies and reverberating strings. In her pink silken tunic and pyjamas, she shimmers like light on water. Filippo is dumbstruck, unable to reply. She stops and faces him. All he can do is to stare. Then she unclips her veil and reveals her face.

'I am white like you.'

Although she is bejewelled with ruby and pearl-encrusted earrings, a diamond nose stud, a gold chain and a string of pearls at her neck, and tinkling glass bangles rising up each arm, she is white like him. She could be one of his sisters, with her creamy white skin, light corn-coloured hair which hang in two long plaits, and her blue eyes.

'*Main angrezi nahin bolta hun*,' he says in Urdu. 'I don't speak English.'

'Ah, but you speak Urdu.'

'A little,' he answers shyly.

'Good. I asked your name.'

'Filippo.'

She rotates her wrists, and flashes her eyes, and stamps her bare feet in a gentle rhythm. She sings a tune to accompany herself. He knows the tune. How he knows that flute tune. All the way from Venice, Crete, across the desert, now here, falling from the mouth of this girl who dances for him. She circles the roof, sometimes going so near the edge, he fears for her and reaches out his hands to pull her back. But she pirouettes away and continues to sing her tune and dance.

'Who are you?' he asks in Urdu.

'Do you like my dancing?' she asks with shining eyes. 'I love to dance. It is my life. Clap for me. Like this. One, two, three open, one, two, three, open.' Her right hand beats the palm of her left hand for three beats, and opened, palm upwards into the air, on the fourth.

Filippo claps.

'One day, I want to dance for the emperor. Of course my father is against it. He has forbidden me to dance, so I have to go to secret places and practise. I know all the secret places in the palace. I know where to peep into the music room where the emperor has his musicians and dancers. I watch them and learn from them. Shall I take you to see? Would you like to see them?'

'Yes, yes! Take me to where the emperor is – I want to meet him,' cries Filippo urgently.

She stamps her bare feet, tips her head and flashes her eyes. 'Do you like me? Do you think I'm good?'

'You're very good but –'

She suddenly freezes into a pose, like a stalked animal, listening. What has she seen or heard? A far-away flute, playing that same tune? She doesn't say, but drags him urgently towards the slit in the wall. They clamber through and she hurries him back down the pitch black corridor. He doesn't see what mechanism operates the panel, but at her touch it slides open and she pushes him into his chamber. Before he can turn round to say goodbye, the panel shuts between them and, once more, there isn't even a crack to show it could ever have opened.

Noor. He repeated the name over and over again. It had the sound of a flute. He could make up a poem about it.

Night fell. A huge full moon rose behind his screen and scattered his chamber with specks of light. Feeling calmer than he had since he came to the land of Hindustan, Filippo lowered the muslin curtains around his bed to keep out the mosquitoes and lay wide-eyed for a long time, thinking about Noor. And thinking, there is a way out of my room.

* * *

The same moon hung over the island, low and huge and tinted with red flecks. It was the first full moon since his arrival on the island. Andreas ate his supper in silence, while the woman fussed and chattered and ministered to all his needs. Every time she passed him, she ruffled his hair with her hands and murmured, 'My son, my lovely son'. Even when he pulled away annoyed, she seemed oblivious to his rejection of her.

Tonight, there was a special speed to her movements, a special brightness to her chatter, as though the full moon had affected her spirits. She handed him a flask. It contained not water, but red wine. Its rich fragrance rose into his face, and she urged him to drink. So he did. Almost immediately, he regretted it, for he felt a paralysis spreading rapidly through his limbs and into his brain. Before he could consider what had happened, he fell into oblivion.

When he woke next morning, he was lying on his bed. The sun was already high, and he could hear 'Mother' outside the cave humming as she combed her hair and pinned it up into a bun, and he wondered where she had been while he lay in a drugged sleep.

After a few weeks on the island, she found the confidence to let him out of her sight, and leave him for one hour in each day. The hour before sunset, she took to signalling that she was going into a certain canyon to pray. He followed her once

– perhaps she knew. He observed her go to a small ancient shrine, hollowed into the cliffs, to pray and perform ceremonies.

While she was away, he was supposed to keep up the fire and stir the pot for the evening meal. But with this one hour of unsupervised freedom, he doubled the speed of his movements, wandering further away: at first, into the nearby woods, then up the hillside, then down to the shore. Each day, he moved faster and went further afield, not forgetting to gather up firewood and always getting back to the cave before she returned. He sped inland, into the wooded canyons down the valleys and up the mountain slopes which tumbled into the sea. There must be a way, his conviction rose with increasing determination, there must be a way of leaving this island. He would have plunged into the ocean and tried his luck swimming away, but he knew the currents were treacherous and the only island he could see hung on the horizon, so far away, that often it was lost in the mist.

With his strength returning all the time, Andreas was moving faster. Soon he was covering two or three miles within the time that she was away. He was even able to cross to the other side of the island, to find out what was there.

The days passed by. The weeks became a month.

The second full moon rose in the sky and, yet again, at supper, she presented him with a flask of wine. This time, he managed to pour it away when she went to stir the embers of the fire. He pretended to be overcome with sleep and slumped on to his bed, but all his senses were wide awake. He sensed her pause over him, felt her hand stroke his brow, then she was gone.

Where did she go? Instantly, he was on his feet and, keeping to the shadows, followed the woman up the steep path. Up and up, through briar and stubby copses, where a swirl of feral goats were startled in the moonlight, and an owl flitted by into the knobbly bare branches. It took over two hours of climbing, until at last they broke out on to a headland where a cairn of stones and an altar loomed up against the night sky, close to the edge of the cliff.

It felt like the edge of heaven. The moon was so full and heavy and low, it seemed to hang beneath them. Sea and sky merged together like one piece of glittering cloth, stitched with silver threads and rippling with jewels. The woman stood in front of the altar and began to sing in a high, passionate, ringing voice. She seemed almost like a goddess, and if she had suddenly risen into the air like a winged being, he wouldn't have been surprised.

She began to dance, coiling round and round the altar, her arms weaving patterns in the air, as she bent and swooped and stretched and twirled. Repeated incantations broke the enchanted air. When her chanting was over, she spread herself out across the altar like a sacrifice, and was utterly still.

A long grey line glimmered on the horizon, and Andreas knew dawn would break in an hour. He must leave. Down the path he went, as fast as he could, slithering and slipping in a hectic descent. Back at the cave, he brushed himself down as well as he could, then he threw himself on to his bed to await her return.

It was clear that the best time to escape was on a night of the full moon – but how?

There were to be four full moons before he could leave; four moons during which he made secret preparations. He used his hour of wood-collecting to scour every nook and gulley and cove and shore, storing away any bits of wood that would serve to make a raft, a boat, or anything on which he could float away.

At last, as if the gods were on his side, a storm brought a small boat to the island. He saw it wrecked on some rocks a little way offshore. He swam out to it and, with a great struggle, buffeted by the churning waves, he managed to climb on to the rock and push the boat free. Then, just as the dolphin had nudged him to land, he swam behind the boat, pushing it forward with his hands till he was able to drag it on to the beach and hide it in a cave.

When she returned, she noticed the scratches on his arms

and legs, where he had cut himself on the rocks. She frowned
and asked him what he had been doing. He just shrugged and
pointed to the rough hillside, as if he had scratched himself
among the boulders and gullies, and she insisted on rubbing oil
on his limbs and soothing his cuts with herbs. For once, he was
easier with her, his heart was lighter. He sensed freedom.

Day by day, he watched the fifth moon of his stay grow from
the thin silver sickle to the huge gleaming perfectly round orb
transforming the landscape. He had thought that, with the
moon reaching its fullness, his happiness and excitement would
grow too, yet through these weeks, he could not but be affected
by the care and love this woman showered on him. In harmony
they had worked together, hunted together, prepared meals,
cooked and cleaned the cave together. Her happiness
transformed her to a laughing, singing, joyful person. He had
even decorated her little shrine which she kept on a ledge in the
cave and garlanded the effigy of a goddess with flowers.

He would have tried to suggest she come with him, leave
this lonely wild island and join the world again, but every time
he even commented about the outer world, her eyes would fill
with tears and her face became frenzied. So he knew that he
must focus on his own purpose and continue his plan to escape.

The moon grew fat and round and perfect as a silver coin.
His boat was ready in the cove. He had patched it with wood

and seaweed and woven grass, and made it sea-worthy. He had made two oars and put them inside. He smuggled in jars of olives, figs, goat's cheese, and an amphora of water.

That evening they had their supper as usual and, as usual, she gave him a flask of wine. He had to drink a little while she watched him so closely, but he asked her for another helping of broth. While she was thus distracted, he tipped the rest away and pretended to fall deeply asleep.

She bent over him and kissed his brow, then left the cave.

He watched her set off up the cliff path, her figure strong and confident, and he suddenly felt confused and sorrowful. Where the path twisted steeply, she turned and looked back, as though somehow she sensed he was watching her. Crouching low in the shadows, he lowered his eyes in case the moon reflected the tears which began to flow, and then she disappeared.

He took the things she had given him, his covering of animal skins, a flint-knife and a clasp of semi-precious stone. In return, he took the rosary which he had always had around his neck, and draped it over her stone goddess. It was his farewell. He turned and, without looking back, ran down to the shore and dragged out his secret boat.

The tide was on the turn, and soon the little boat was being carried out to sea, with Andreas paddling furiously into a sharp northerly wind, his eyes fixed on the receding shore.

At last he stopped rowing and lifted his eyes. He gazed upon the island which had been his home for five months, and thought of the woman who had mothered him. The moon hung great and round and full, wreathed in wisps of white cloud. The headland gleamed under its brightness. It fell upon a figure with arms stretched above her head. He knew it was her. It was as though their eyes met even from that great distance – and he knew that her raised arms were not to worship her gods, but to beseech him to return.

He was transfixed, unable to lift the paddle, unable to wave back or make any sign.

Suddenly, she flung wide her arms, her garment billowing out behind her like wings. She leapt upwards and outwards into space. It was as if she reached for that great pitiless moon. For a brief instant, Andreas thought she had found the power of flight, that she would come in pursuit of him. She seemed caught up on the back of the wind, hovering in the air like a strange bird, before she plummeted, as Icarus must have fallen, and was lost from sight in the gullies below.

Whose cry rent the air – hers or his? All he knew was that he collapsed with horror and remorse into the bottom of the boat, and for a long time could do nothing more than let the wind and currents carry him ever further away.

Chapter Twenty-five

❖

Time is running out

She came again. Noor. Like a whirlwind. And took Filippo away from his prison. She rushed him along black as pitch passages, and high screened galleries from which you could look down secretly on the life of the court. She gave him whispered commentaries. 'This is where the . . . this is where they . . . this is where I saw a man have his head chopped off – right there . . . this is where I first saw . . . this is where the emperor receives ambassadors from all over the world. These are the women's quarters. I suppose I will live there one day. The emperor loves women, but no one does he love more than the mother of his four sons, Mumtaz Mahal. How sad that because you are a male, you will never see her face. I've seen her. She is the most beautiful of all his queens and concubines.'

Filippo saw sumptuous halls and jewel-like chambers. He saw vast kitchens where tens of dozens of cooks chopped and mixed and kneaded and stirred and fried and baked vast quantities of dishes, from where liveried servants ran to and fro in a constant procession of silver platters and tureens. There were the little courtyards of running water, exuberant climbing plants, pots of flowers. Exotic animals – some caged, some chained, among them leopards and lions, monkeys and birds paced and roamed, grunted and chattered. He observed the arrival of foreign diplomats, ambassadors and generals who reported after a battle. Messengers arrived with news and armies set off on campaigns. He saw scholars, poets and musicians. All the world came to the court of Shah Jehan.

Filippo pressed his ear against the wall. He heard something emanating from the stones. 'Noor, listen. I know that melody. I heard it even in Venice. What does that flute music mean? Why do I keep hearing that tune?'

Noor looked afraid. 'We shouldn't stay here long. Aurangzeb has spies everywhere. It's his tune. I know because I listen. I know lots of secrets. Everyone who works for Aurangzeb understands the messages the tunes send. He has spies all over the world.'

Filippo felt everything darken around him. So Signor Khan did know about the flute. He knew the meaning of the melodies and even obeyed them.

'My father says, although Prince Dara is the emperor's eldest and favourite son, it is Aurangzeb who is ambitious, and Aurangzeb who already has people plotting to make him king.

Come on! Let's go quickly. I want to show you the dancers.'

She rushed him away down more passages, and stopped before a long marble screen, carved as finely as lace. 'Look, look!' She tugged him to a stop. He heard music and drumming and a voice singing out rhythms. 'This is my favourite place. This is where they dance for the emperor. Oh how lucky. Uma Jaan is dancing for him today. What good fortune. She is my most favourite dancer. I want to be like her when I grow up.' Noor forced Filippo's head to the marble screen. 'Isn't she wonderful?'

Filippo stared down into the most sumptuous chamber he could ever have imagined. Silken drapes, cushions and brocades covered divans and chairs, rich carpets were strewn across the marble floor. The ceiling was hung with chandeliers of crystal and Venetian glass. The tables and chairs were of ebony and teak, encrusted with jewels, and the pillars and railings looked like solid gold.

But it was not the dancer he looked at, it was the man dominating the chamber. He reclined upon a carved couch, a divan; a handsome man with deep-set eyes, a straight narrow nose and a long shapely beard. Behind him, lavishly uniformed servants fanned him with peacocks' tails, and bejewelled handmaidens sat at his feet.

'Is that the emperor?' Filippo whispered.

'Of course it is,' Noor whispered back, 'but look at Uma Jaan. Isn't she beautiful? Have you ever seen such dancing? She's a goddess!'

Filippo didn't look at the dancer. He knew, his diamond knew, that at last he gazed upon the emperor, Shah Jehan. Light of the World, the Most Exalted Emperor, the Great Moghul! Not raised on his peacock throne, not surrounded by his soldiers and guards, with swords and spears and military might, not receiving ambassadors and diplomats, princes and rajahs, but a man whose eyes never left the dancing girl whirling before him, powerful enough to indulge in his senses and pleasures. He loved beautiful things. He thought himself inviolable.

Filippo felt weak. A searing pain shot through his head. He suppressed a groan and leaned his face against the fretted marble screen. The diamond in his skull seemed to expand; he thought it would splinter in his brain and destroy his mind. He gazed upon the emperor. The old Dutch sailor was right. The diamond showed him sons against fathers, fathers against sons, brother against brother – all thirsting for power, the power of the throne, the power of the emperor. Shah Jehan's fine manicured hands were covered in blood. It seemed there was nothing but death all around, and beautiful things surrounded him like companions of death. It was as if he couldn't bear to have any sight, sound or smell that wasn't perfumed and exquisite and beautiful. It was as if beauty could expunge and justify murder.

'Isn't she wonderful?' sighed Noor in his ear.

The dancing girl's long single pearl-threaded black plait fell straight down her back, when it wasn't flying as she twirled in a frenzied rhythm. 'Yes, she's wonderful,' he answered without looking at her.

'Look! Am I as good as her?' High in the upper gallery, hidden by the screens, Noor began to dance silently, keeping pace with the drumbeat. Her arms coiled about her head, and her bare feet stamped in rhythm. Her eyes and eyebrows spoke a language of their own, blinking and arching, expressing all kinds of passions.

'The emperor loves dance. I do too,' she whispered. 'It's all I want – to be – a dancer. I want to dance and dance and dance.' She moved and stamped and flashed her eyes. 'But Papa says I can't. Papa says I must make a good marriage, and if I dance, no one will have me. But I don't care. I'll die if I can't dance.'

'How can I get to see the emperor and talk to him?' asked Filippo. He felt dizzy and burning. Even if Signor Khan was working for Aurangzeb, he could still get to the emperor first and give him the Ocean of the Moon.

Noor shrugged flippantly. 'What do you want to do that for?' She pulled Filippo away. 'We mustn't be seen,' she hissed quietly. 'Come on, let's go. Are you ill?' She noticed the perspiration running down his face, and his eyes hot and bloodshot.

She took his arm and, somehow, coaxed him back to his chamber. She helped him to his bed, pulled the screens across the windows and made him drink water.

'I have to see the emperor.' Filippo's face was desperate in the dim shadows.

'If your Signor Khan was staying with the Grand Vizier, then he must be in his camp,' murmured Noor.

'I know. I think he is,' said Filippo miserably.

'My father says all the princes already have their followers, and the Grand Vizier is backing Prince Aurangzeb. They all want their prince to be emperor when the time comes. My father says even though they are brothers, Dara, Shuja, Aurangzeb and Murad one day will fight each other to the death, and everyone has to choose whose side they're on. I expect your Signor Khan had to choose. It was always like that. Emperor Shah Jehan himself only took power because he murdered his brother, nephews and cousins. That's what my father tells me. He hears things when one of them is ill, and he is called in.'

'Called in? What does he do, your father?'

'He's a captain in the British East India Company army. I should say was – he's a physician now. They think all Europeans are physicians. He was called in to see if he could help one of the little princesses, who had a wound on her leg which became infected. It produced a terrible fever, and everyone thought she would die. But from years at sea and much travel, my father had learned many tricks of the trade. He knows about bloodletting, the treatment of fevers and how to deal with amputation. He knew how to drain the poison from the wound in her leg, and gave her medicine to reduce the temperature. She survived. The emperor insisted he stay on as a court physician.'

'Physician,' Filippo muttered. 'Can I see him?'

'He's away for three days,' said Noor. 'When he returns, I'll take you to him.'

So Filippo waited. Each day the pain in his head grew more fierce. It seemed his diamond eye was telling him, the time is now, it is time to redeem the diamond, it is time to move on and find your father, time. Because time was running out.

Day by day, the heat became more intense – somehow far worse than the desert, as it didn't even cool at night, and Filippo thought he would soon be unable to draw breath. Sometimes he heard voices murmuring impatiently, 'The monsoon. The monsoon will soon be here, Allah be praised.'

When Prince Murad came to fly kites with him, Filippo stared into the blank, white sky and wondered how they knew.

Even Prince Murad said the monsoon would come any day, but Filippo could hardly believe that any drop of rain could fall from the unforgiving sky.

They were flying their kites as usual, when the nursemaid and their servants, in an anxious flurry, bowed low several times and withdrew to the side. Prince Aurangzeb had come.

'Look brother, look!' cried Prince Murad, excitedly. 'That's my kite! The pink one. My kite's higher than Filippo's! Will you join us? I have another. Here, take this orange one.'

'Do you think I've come here to play silly childish games? Why do you forget you are a prince, not a street urchin? Playing with infidels! Huh!' Aurangzeb snorted his disapproval and remonstrated with the nursemaid in a way which made her quake with anxiety.

The boys began reeling in their kites, but Aurangzeb drew a dagger from his belt and just slashed through the twine. Prince Murad gave a wail of distress as both kites, freed from the string, floated away.

'Why did you do that, brother? Why? That was mean,' wept the little prince. Prince Aurangzeb ignored him, and it was left to the nursemaid to lift up her charge and cover him in comforting kisses.

'I want to see this Ocean of the Moon. I demand it.' Filippo's expression didn't change, but now he knew time was running out for him. How could Aurangzeb know the name of the diamond?

Aurangzeb faced Filippo, standing with his feet apart and his hand resting on his sword. He was in hunting clothes, and had a hawk on his leather-gloved wrist whose head swivelled at the sound of his master's voice. 'It is not the custom in this country to refuse the request of a prince.'

'And is it the custom in this country for a prince to hold a guest as a prisoner?' Filippo again threw caution to the winds. He harangued the older boy, speaking through the interpreter. 'Tell his serene highness, Ornament of the Throne, Prince Aurangzeb, that he is an unspeakable bully, and if I were able to meet him on equal terms, I would break his nose, and bloody his handsome clothes. Tell him to let me go free. I will not let him see the pendant. It is only for the eyes of the emperor.' Filippo raged and swore in Venetian, and didn't care how the interpreter translated.

The old man clasped his hands together and, with lowered head, mumbled off some innocuous words to mollify the angry prince, and save Filippo from being flung off the ramparts into the river to be eaten by crocodiles.

Aurangzeb withdrew his dagger once more and came up to Filippo. He ran its point under his chin. Tiny spots of blood appeared as he broke the skin, then he turned swiftly and left.

Murad came to Filippo's side, his face streaked with tears. 'You are my best friend, even if you are an infidel,' he said earnestly. 'I don't want him to hurt you. Don't make my brother angry.'

Filippo picked up the little prince and hugged him. His head throbbed incessantly. He was ill. The diamond must be removed soon, or he would die. 'You are my friend too,' he murmured. 'Come back tomorrow and bring more kites.'

But Prince Murad didn't come back. Filippo knew he wouldn't. Couldn't. Something was going to happen, something bad. Prince Aurangzeb would not forgive him for answering him back. He held his head in his hands. It was as if the diamond wanted to break free too.

All afternoon, even through the heat of the following day, a great clamour from the palace grounds jarred every nerve in his body. Something big was about to happen. Perhaps the emperor was going to war. He could hear trumpeting elephants and the clash of weapons and armour. A thunderous excitement reverberated through the fort and palace grounds, and seared through his body. He dragged himself from the bed and peered over the balustrade from his upper terrace on the river side. He saw hundreds of men pouring along the bank between the river and the palace walls. All along the rooftops, veiled women found themselves a vantage point. But he couldn't see what they were gathering to look at.

Shards of pain stabbed through his head. He had a fever. Where was Noor? He groaned helplessly, and crawled back to his bed. The usually calming rhythmic swish of the sweeper's broom grated his ears, The room tipped around him as if he were strapped to a rotating wheel.

At last, Noor returned.

He sees her blue eye gleaming through the tile. The panel slides open. She looks concerned when she sees his ashen face, dripping with perspiration. She beckons. 'There is to be an elephant fight,' she says, 'the last one before the monsoon. Everybody watches – even the guards. Come. I'll take you to my father. No one will check you for ages.'

So that's what's going on! They seem to skim at great speed along night-black passageways, which break out suddenly on to upper terraces and rooftops that he's never seen before. Noor is like a monkey, leaping from one wall to the next, or up and down steps, two at a time. Then she waits for him, twisting her fingers, exercising her eyes, tapping out rhythms with her feet – for Noor is never still.

A huge wave of sound sweeps up to them. They are

overlooking an extensive arena alongside the river, a huge ditch beneath the walls of the fort, surrounded by a vast excited crowd. Hundreds more line the rooftops, lean over balconies and cram themselves along the terraces. They are perched perilously along the length of the palace walls. Even the trees sway with men and boys, as they squabble over every branch and foothold.

Filippo is fascinated, and lingers despite his fever. He's seen many cock fights and dog fights and slave fights and even once, a bull fight, but elephants! Yet he feels sad, and is surprised at himself. Perhaps it is their size. He can't conceive of any animal on earth being bigger than elephants, and yet their movements are as silent and graceful as galleons at sea. They look too noble for such savagery.

Two huge tuskers face each other, stamping, pawing and trumpeting with uplifted trunks. Their keepers sit cross-legged on their necks with iron bars and, with raucous voices, prod them into a frenzy.

The crowd falls silent; expectant. There is a thudding of drums and fanfare of reed pipes. Noor says the emperor has arrived to view the elephant fight. He has entered his balcony below them. The crowd bows in respect as they wait for his signal for the fight to begin.

Noor pulls Filippo away.

They continue along passages and stairways. Now they are

descending, down, down, along, along and down, and reach a
door. She opens it. It reveals a small walled garden. The hot air
simmers with fragrant flowers. The fever bird is chanting his
unbearable mantra. Filippo's head is almost bursting.

They come to an arched veranda ahead.

'We're here now,' she tells him softly.

Everything tips around him in waves of darkness.

*He took the sacrificial sheep and cut their throats. Their dark blood
flowed, and lo, the spirits of the dead that be departed, gathered out
of Erebus. Brides and youths unwed, old men of many and evil days,
tender maidens with grief yet fresh at heart; many there were,
wounded with bronze-shod spears, men slain in fight with their bloody
mail about them. And these many souls came flocking to greet him
with wondrous cries, and he was gripped with a pale fear.*

They have lifted me into a cool bed. I lie in a darkened room.
A servant stands nearby, fanning me. For a while, I tune into his
repetitive action. His life is a rhythmic monotony of serving,
complying, obeying, on and on and on, like the brain-fever bird.
And so he fans me but, if he pauses even for a moment, the heat
descends, sucking the breath from my body. He starts again.

Someone enters the room. I look up shocked. I see a
European girl, wearing a full-length fitted dress in the European

manner, with high-cuffed sleeves, and a velvet locket at her neck. Her corn-coloured hair is coiled up into a bun hanging with ringlets.

A man's voice calls out, 'Marianne!'

'He's waiting for you, Father,' she replies.

A voice whispers in my ear. 'Papa's here to see you.'

'Noor? Is it you?' I try to sit up, but she pushes me down.

'Papa likes me to be English when I'm at home with him. He calls me Marianne and makes me wear English clothes. He wants me to be prepared for when he sends me to England. But I never want to go. I can't leave my darling Grandmama. I was born here. This is my home, my country.' She pulls away quickly, as her father enters.

His name is Captain Robert Wallace. He is a pallid faded kind of man. After years of living in India, his once-white skin is like yellowed parchment. Everything about him droops. His shoulders droop, his doleful blue eyes droop, his gingery moustache droops, and even the hand he holds out to me droops from a bony wrist. His clasp is limp, as if he has forgotten the custom of shaking a hand. He smells of sandalwood and tobacco.

'Well, well, well! Fancy meeting a son of Geronimo Veroneo!' He speaks in English, though its accent is lilting like Urdu. He reverts to Urdu when Noor reminds him that I don't speak English.

'You knew him?' I try to lean upon one elbow.

'Yes, I knew him. He was a friend of a fellow called Rodriguez.' The captain gently presses me back on to the pillow. 'Relax, relax!' he murmurs, then sits down in a wicker chair near the bed. 'We Europeans tend to find each other. Not a bad chess player, your father! He often beat me. But it's been many years – five or six. I assumed he had gone home, as he wanted. I was hoping to visit him in Venice one of these days, but the emperor has not yet seen fit to give me permission to leave.' He heaves a deep sigh. 'We must be thankful for what we've got, eh? But then Noor tells me he never got home anyway, that he was captured going through Afghanistan, taken hostage. Is that so? And you are here with a ransom?'

I nod weakly.

Outside, the fight has begun. They yell and clamour for blood. The piercing screams of the elephants ring through the palace, as they charge at each other, their tusks ripping into each other's bodies.

Through a haze of blood, my diamond eye sees death.

There was a thunderous hammering at the door.

Pagliarin's voice bellowed through the house as Rosa let him in, flapping nervously and wringing her hands together with puzzled anxiety.

'Where is she? Where's my wife?'

Teodora appeared. She tried to wave him into the parlour, but he planted his feet apart, with hand on sword, bursting with rage. 'Where is my wife?'

'Elisabetta?' Teodora tried not to give way to panic. 'What do you mean, where is she? Is she not with you, sir? Are you not her gaoler?'

He snorted with contempt and barged past her. 'Where's Carlo?' He pounded up the stairs to the workshop, yelling his name.

'Carlo's out with a client,' she called after him.

'Madam!' Rosa clutched her apron with alarm. 'Dear Lord! What is happening?' They could hear Pagliarin rampaging through the house, barging into every room, flinging open every cupboard and looking behind every drape and screen.

'Rosa! The girls! Where are they?' Every fibre and nerve-end in Teodora's body sent out a warning signal. She didn't know what had happened to Elisabetta, but if her younger daughters were to be protected, she must act now.

'They're down on the fondamente watching that hurdy-gurdy man with the monkey,' said Rosa.

'Here's money.' She pulled a purse from a drawer. 'Take the girls and go to your daughter's house. Please ask her, please Rosa, if she will keep them there until I send for them. I don't know

what else to do. Go, go, before he comes down. Go.'
She thrust the purse into Rosa's hand and pushed her out of
the door.

When Rosa had gone, Teodora prepared herself for
Pagliarin's reappearance. She went into the parlour and sat in
Geronimo's chair. Immediately she felt bolder. She spread her
hands over each armrest. Other hands laid themselves over
hers. What a sweet remembered touch. She tipped her head
up. 'Geronimo?'

Footsteps thundered above her head. They descended the
stairs, reached the bottom. A pause. Silence. Menace.

'Madam.' His voice was soft. Pagliarin seemed to slither into
the room.

Teodora was past feeling fear for herself. Her only thought
was to protect her family – what was left of it. She spoke calmly.
'Perhaps you should take a seat. Carlo will be back soon, and
you can tell us what is happening.'

'My wife is missing. You must know where she is.'

'I do not. But if by God's grace she has escaped from
the prison you put her in, I can only hope and pray she need
never return.'

'Let me tell you, madam, such talk could make you an
accomplice to this crime, indeed to this sin, against God and
his church.'

'You dare to talk to me about sin and crime?' exclaimed Teodora with contempt.

'I do, madam.' He cocked his head and smiled. 'You see, I do because I can. Crime is defined by the powerful and, believe me, I am more powerful than you. No one will listen to you. It is a pity that you disobeyed me. You should have given me the diamond. It would have saved you all this trouble. By the way, where are Gabriella and Sofia?'

'They are not at home.'

'Kindly deliver them to my house by the end of the day.'

'Why?'

'Why? Madam, I think you forget your position. It is not for you to ask why. They are my responsibility, just as you are entirely beholden to me. And I tell you this, if you do not present the girls at Villa Maravege by sundown, you will . . .'

'Never,' Teodora said quietly. 'Never, never, never.'

'Why, you!' Pagliarin's hand flew to his sword in fury. 'How dare you challenge me . . .'

'She dares to, and so do I, sir. How dare you threaten my family?' Carlo stood in the doorway. 'Get out of my house.'

'Your house? I don't think so.' Pagliarin whisked his sword from its scabbard and lunged at Carlo. Carlo leapt aside and drew his dagger.

* * *

I hear the sounds of combat. Elephant against elephant, enemy against enemy, anger for fuel, terror for action, tusk on tusk, metal on metal, as I see the man who will remove the diamond from my skull. I do not know him. He is not of my country or language, yet I have to trust him as I have never trusted Signor Khan.

I lie face down on a table. I see the doctor's tools all laid out. They could be the tools of a jeweller. His slender yellow hand lifts a razor from his work bag. He presses the other hand against my skull, smooths back my hair and begins to shave my head.

The swish and clash of weapons ring out, grunts of pain, wounds spurt blood. The evening sky turns to blazing, furious red, as if night fights day, littering clouds across the heavens like broken ribs.

The sun drags me down with it into oblivion. I see with my diamond eye, for the . . . last . . . time . . .

Noor heard him muttering. 'Carlo, Carlo, Carlo.'

Carlo stood astride his fallen enemy whose dark crimson blood spread across the floor like spilt wine. 'Mama!' Carlo spoke in a calm voice. 'Signor Pagliarin is dead, may God forgive his rotten heart. Go, fetch the magistrate . . .'

'But Carlo!' She wanted him to run, escape, leave Venice,

get as far away as possible, otherwise he will surely be tried and imprisoned, if not executed.

'I'm not going to run. If I did, if I just left you and scuttled away like a coward, you still wouldn't be free from his tyranny. I am not in the wrong. I'll take my chances before the court and plead my case.'

Chapter Twenty-six

❖

When the rains came

Captain Wallace was fighting temptation.

For the first time in fourteen years, he had an incredible opportunity there at his fingertips. He could escape from India, leave the remorseless intrigues of this palace and go home. Most tempting of all, he could take Marianne to England. She could be brought up as an English lady, enter society, find a husband of means and be mistress in her own home.

This diamond was like an answer to a prayer. For years, he had hoped he would find a way to leave. Somehow, as time passed, his longing for England had grown stronger. Sitting on his veranda during the afternoons, it was not the shimmering Indian plain his eyes gazed upon, but inner fanatsies about those soft green Devon hills where he was born, the honey-stone thatched house of his childhood, festooned with wisteria and climbing rose, the garden smothered in summer flowers, the orchards of apples and plums, and the little red-bricked walled garden of vegetables. When he looked at the relentless blue of an Indian sky, he longed for those ever-changing skies of England, the landscape of clouds, the veils of rain sweeping in from the sea, the surprise of sunshine emerging out of a grey day. Instead of the daily train of camels crossing the shallows of the river to and fro, he longed to see the simple English yeoman with his horse and plough, and hear the milkmaid singing in the lane.

Captain Wallace had long ago given up all hopes of return, and reconciled himself to seeing his daughter married into the royal Moghul household, and himself dying in this foreign land. It was not a bad prospect. He knew he lived more grandly than he could ever have hoped to in England. There was no shortage of offers of marriage for Marianne, some persistent such as one from a nobleman, another from a general in the emperor's army, even a prince wanted her for his third wife. But once she entered the harem, she would never see England, and he would never return. Oh England! The closer and more inevitable Marianne's marriage became, the greater was his longing to see England once more.

How different it would have been if her mother had survived. He would have been happy to live on here for a thousand years, if it had meant being near her. He thought of his beautiful wife, Gulrukh Banu, his 'golden-cheeked princess', as he had called her. Her death of a sudden fever had almost driven him mad with grief, for none of his skills could save her. Only their little daughter, Marianne Noor, had prevented him from tipping over the edge, and his wife's mother, Zeenat Begum, who took over, and cared for father and daughter with utter devotion. But this stone – this diamond – could change everything.

Thunder rolled across the sky like a herd of elephants. The rain fell in one vast roaring torrent, as if the heavens had stored an ocean up there and simply released it. The monsoon had broken. From time to time, lightning flashed, hurling scissors of light into the chamber.

Captain Wallace gave a quiet groan. He put the stone on the table and rose to his feet. Silently, he paced the room, returning constantly to stare at it. The diamond sparkled vividly. Fires burned in the facets, rainbows glistened in its clear water. The Ocean of the Moon. Arguments raged though his brain. What did it matter if that Venetian jeweller, Veroneo, never got home? It was each man for himself in this life; each father for his own child. Perhaps this boy could find another way of raising the ransom – this diamond was worth a hundred ransoms. Or perhaps he could just let the boy die. That would be the easiest.

Filippo had been watching him for hours.

At some point in the night, he had woken quietly to find

himself back in his chamber. The rains had cooled the air, released an explosion of smells of earth, water, trees and flowers, and all he could hear was water. Water running, falling, dripping and trickling; the gulleys along the terraces becoming rivers. All his senses were shimmering – except for one. The Ocean of the Moon had been removed from his skull, as if an eagle had plucked out his eye. He felt its absence like a great void. He was less seeing, less hearing, less knowing. He was afraid. He could no longer see Teodora, Carlo and his sisters. He could no longer see Andreas. Without the diamond he could no longer enter his father's prison cell.

His eyes had come to rest on a figure bathed in moonlight, racing as the moon was buffetted among mountainous clouds. The rain fell and fell as if it would fall forever. The figure sat at a small table agonising over an object which he held in the palm of his hand. Suddenly, he was no longer merely Captain Wallace. Within the small dark universe of that chamber, he was a god who would decide his fate.

Filippo watched. Captain Wallace got up and paced the chamber, up and down, up and down. Sometimes he paused to stare out into the night, beyond the watery, wavering flares which quivered to stay alight in the hands of the guards along the palace walls. Sometimes he simply sat, leaning on his elbows with his head clasped in his hands. He paced again, circled the table with the precious stone, stared at the diamond, picked it up, held it, turned it, felt it, brought it to his face, as if it could tell him what to do.

'*Allahu Akbar!*' The first voice of the muezzin calling the faithful to prayer broke through the thudding fall of rain on the hard stone terraces. It mingled with other dawn calls to prayer across the city. Captain Wallace was not a god-fearing man, but this night he had grappled with demons. He went to the window facing Mecca, listening to the voices of the muezzin awakening the city, and felt that someone had peered into his soul.

A brief respite in the rain, and a long thin slit opened up in the night sky. Daylight came seeping through, ravaged and dark, bringing with it a smouldering glow which struck the diamond and made it bleed, before being swallowed up by mountains of grey cloud. The parakeets shrieked and arched into the air. Captain Wallace glanced across at Filippo. Their eyes met. He took up a goblet and came over to the bedside. He cradled Filippo's head and held the cup to his lips. 'Drink.' Filippo hadn't taken his eyes off him.

'*Allahu Akbar!*' The thin high voice reached every ear.

Filippo opened his lips and drank.

The rain had steadied to a constant roar. When he next

awoke it was to a sunless chamber. The air was still cool. For the first time since arriving in Hindustan, he felt he could breathe deeply.

The Ocean of the Moon was in a pouch round his neck.

The monsoon rain was relentless, and Filippo didn't expect a visit from Noor. But to his surprise, a dripping little Prince Murad came hurtling in accompanied by his nursemaid and scampering servants with parasols trying to keep up with him. He had brought a board game with him – a Carrom board.

'Play with me. See if you can beat me. I'm the best!' He set the board on a table and laid out counters, and strikers to flick the counters with their fingers into little bags at the corners. It was like a game of billiards but with finger skill. It passed hours of the day in intense competition. Filippo's head ached, and Murad always won.

It was during a brief lull in the rain a week later that Noor returned.

'How are you feeling? Can you walk? There is a boat waiting. I am to take you to an old Hindu jeweller to assemble your pendant. My father thinks it's safer to see an infidel – he won't gossip to the court jewellers – but he is a master, and will help you.'

Filippo wrapped his Venetian clothes into a bundle.

Noor had brought a deerskin cloak for shelter from the incessant rain.

But as he slipped through the secret panel, he heard the flute playing. It seemed closer. He felt stalked, like a mouse. Someone was watching them after all. Someone who knew every single movement he had made – even his excursions with Noor. At this very moment, they were being watched. He hugged his bundle close to him and hurried after her. Surely, within the darkness of the passageways, no one could see them, or know where they would emerge?

They came to a low door. Noor opened it and with a shock he found they were right down beside the River Jamuna sweeping by with such power. A narrow path led along the bank. She danced from boulder to boulder and rock to rock, on and on for some minutes until they came to a small shore where a boat was moored. A single boatman sat patiently waiting in a thin drizzle, the oars resting loosely in his hands. They climbed inside and, at Noor's command, he stuck out an oar, pushed the boat from the shore and began to row upstream. Through the hiss of the rain and the slap of water against the sides of the boat, the sound of a flute drifted down to him from the palace walls. Filippo didn't look up.

They came to the Hindu quarter. Instead of a mosque an elongated square stone temple, heavily carved with all sorts of leaping and dancing figures, rose from the muddy bank. Men lounged in doorways, smoking on string beds, unveiled women milled about with swinging saris and black-lined eyes. There was talking, arguing and bartering, while mud-splattered children, pigs, chickens and dogs all wove in and out of each other, barely making way for Noor and Filippo as they left the boat and squelched their way into the bazaar.

At last they came to a huge banyan tree. Built into its roots and creepers was a cramped dwelling. They squeezed their way inside, and Noor called out. 'Babuji! Respected sir! We have come at the appointed time.'

They peered into the dark interior. A voice from inside bade them enter. Bending almost double, they eased their way among the creepers and found themselves in a small, earthy space. In one corner was a coconut bed mat with a cloth for a sheet. Set back among the roots was an idol, a dancer with four arms, his leg raised in mid-flow, snakes whirling from his hair and skulls at his waist. In his hand, he held a trident. In the middle of his forehead, he had a third eye.

Filippo felt watched by this third eye. It probed through to the empty place in his skull where his diamond had been.

Seated on the ground before them was the jeweller, an old man with white flowing hair and a simple white cloth wound round his lower body. He was hard at work before another idol, a round plump god with an elephant's head, garlanded with marigolds, before which a stick of incense was burning, filling the tree with a sweet, pungent smell. In the narrow stream of daylight penetrating the tree, Filippo saw his tools – jeweller's tools – laid out in perfect order.

'Sit.' Without stopping what he was doing, the old man tipped his head to indicate the coconut mat. Filippo and Noor sat down cross-legged and waited.

At last, he completed his task, and looked up at them with his hands clasped in a brief welcome. '*Namaste*.'

'*Namaste*,' said Noor, and then speaking rapidly, she explained how Filippo had some gems which needed assembling into a pendant.

'Show me,' said the old jeweller.

Filippo unwrapped his bundle and pulled out his clothes. Reaching for the scissors, he began to unpick all his seams and, one by one, laid out the gems on the cloth before him. The jeweller shrugged and seemed unimpressed by the array of white stones which Filippo displayed before him. The pearls, white jade, crystals, moonstones, with just a few small rubies and sapphires interspersed, were of only modest value. He was used to dealing with bright colourful glittering jewels such as emeralds, sapphires, rubies, garnets, set with gold and silver – and, of course, diamonds. Were there no diamonds? He looked bored.

Filippo took the pouch from round his neck and opened the drawstring.

He took out the Ocean of the Moon and set it among the white jewels. Never had the stone looked more glorious as in the dim light of that banyan tree. Its pure, limpid water seemed to draw into itself all the shades of light and darkness – the very spirit of the great ancient tree.

The old man got to his feet, his hands clasped together as if in prayer. He stumbled backwards, muttering. His body blocked out the daylight, and still the diamond gleamed like the eye of Shiva. He crouched before his dancing god, murmuring prayers.

I take the great diamond, over which so much blood has poured. I have Carlo's drawing and instructions telling me what to do. I set them in front of me. Then sitting before the array of tools and glue provided, I start my work – at last. I am filled with inspiration. Suddenly my hands are my father's hands and Carlo's hands. They hover over mine, guiding me, giving me the surety and skill to assemble their masterpiece – this pendant which must save all our lives. Piece by piece, I take each pearl, nephrite jade, crystal and moonstone, and set them into place. The old man crouches at my side. With gentle intervention, he hands me the appropriate tool, the right amount of paste, and checks the strength of each setting. The moment has come; the final act. I nod towards the Ocean of the Moon and ask him to hand it to me. With the utmost reverence, he takes the diamond up in both hands, cradles it, murmurs prayers over it. He holds it to his heart, his lips, his forehead, then places it in my hand.

I take the Ocean of the Moon and set it like a mighty dome into a temple, so that its light and beauty flows over all the other stones and incorporates them into its light. It is done.

Chapter Twenty-seven

❖

The Ocean of the Moon

They crawled out of the tree. The old jeweller didn't see them off. They left him bowing before his gods, with clasped hands, giving thanks for the providence which had let him hold the most flawless diamond he had ever seen.

The sky was darker, even though it was still afternoon. Flocks of silvery-headed crows added to the darkness as they whirled in a black glistening mass of flapping wings, and their incessant cawing disturbed the other animals. The dogs barked and whined and howled. The little horses, worn out from too much work and over-loading, pawed the dust and shook their jingling harnesses.

They hurried back to the boat. The blue of the River Jamuna had turned slate grey, and the boatman rowed steadily against the current, which he could feel strengthening against the sweep of his oars. It took much longer to make the return journey. As they turned the bend in the river, Filippo heard the flute. Looking up through the veil of rain, he saw two figures on

the ramparts watching him. The flute player was playing the
same raga. They knew. They had been waiting for this moment.

The boatman pulled into the shore, jumped out and dragged
the boat up on to land. The children clambered out.

When he looked up again, the figures had gone.

'Noor,' he whispered urgently. 'Go home. There is great
danger. I can find my way back. Go home.'

She tried to resist, laughing at him. 'Silly boy, you can't find
your way back through the palace.'

'I can. Go, Noor, for your father's sake, go home. I'll be all
right. In any case, you can't help me now. It's me they want.'

He grabbed her arm, and ran her through the gardens
towards her house.

She looked frightened. 'What's going to happen to you?'

'I'm going to find the emperor, then everything will be
all right.'

He plunged back into the palace. He could hear voices behind
him, in front of him; voices everywhere. Whispered, urgent,
determined voices. Footsteps advanced. They were after him.
He ran away from them, but more came from the other side. He
ran through the dark maze of passages, looking for the emperor.
He bumped into the curves of the wall as they twisted and
turned. He stumbled up and down stone steps and on again. But

still the voices kept coming. He saw an alcove of light, and like a frantic, stupid moth rushed towards it – almost to plunge straight over the edge of a low balcony, thirty feet down. Just in time, he clutched the balustrade and fell to his knees.

The footsteps raced towards him. There was nowhere else for him to run. 'I am dead.' He leaned his throat on the top of the balustrade as if it were an execution block and looked down on the music room.

He felt a hand on his neck, saw a glint of metal. A voice screamed, 'Filippo!' The hand at his neck fell away. Footsteps fled.

Filippo hung weakly to the balustrade. He had no more strength. He wanted to simply tip himself over the edge and land before the Great Moghul. He was attended by his four sons – his princes of death. Two of the older sons leapt from their divan, staring up at him with hands on swords ready to draw. So these were Prince Murad's two oldest brothers, Prince Dara, aged sixteen, and Prince Sultan Shuja, aged fourteen. They looked fine in their courtly dress, but their destiny was to fight and lose and die.

Prince Murad was waving frantically, as Filippo was surrounded by guards with swords drawn. 'He's my friend. Don't hurt him, he's my friend!'

Filippo was seized roughly by two bodyguards and hauled away, his feet dragging and bumping painfully down the passageways and steps. When at last he was flung to the floor face down, it was before the emperor himself.

Filippo was sure he faced death. He called brokenly for Carlo and his mother. He begged his father to forgive him for having failed.

He heard Prince Murad's plaintive voice. 'Filippo's my friend.'

Filippo looked up and saw the little prince run across the room and leap on to the emperor's lap as only a child can. He clasped his arms round his father's neck and whispered fiercely in his ear. A guard put his foot to Filippo's head and forced it down.

A further flurry of murmured greetings ran round the chamber as Prince Aurangzeb strode forward. 'Your esteemed Highness! Papa, this infidel is an interloper and a common thief. The diamond belongs to your prime minister. Come in!' Prince Aurangzeb flicked his fingers to summon the Grand Vizier who came in with slippers flapping in agitation. There was murder in his eyes.

What a babble of voices. Filippo was racked with confusion. Without his diamond eye, he no longer had any insight or comprehension. He was just a foreigner, with a limited understanding of what was going on.

The princes were arguing, the Grand Vizier was joining in. But suddenly it was Prince Dara who was holding the attention.

His voice was gentle. It gave Filippo hope. 'The translator has been summoned.'

On a command, a warrior hauled Filippo to his feet, though his head was still forced down so that he did not gaze into the emperor's face. The emperor issued another order. The guard released his hold and pushed Filippo closer. He stood alone.

The old translator came alongside him. The emperor spoke first, rapidly, and the translator turned to Filippo.

'His esteemed royal highness, the Grand Emperor, King of the World, hears that you come from Venice and that you are the son of a jeweller,' he said slowly.

Filippo nodded passionately. 'Yes, yes!' he cried. 'And please will you tell his majesty that I have the most wondrous jewel in the world, the Ocean of the Moon, with which my father created a pendant. We believe it to be his masterpiece. My family wanted . . .'

The slightest movement up in one of the high balconies made Aurangzeb look up, and Filippo did too. He saw what Aurangzeb saw – Signor Khan, his Musalman.

He wanted to yell, 'Why didn't you look for me? Why didn't you even enquire after me? Why did you not send me any kind of message?' He didn't know what to think of him. He missed him, he hated him, he needed him, for who else could take him to his father? But suddenly, his anger evaporated as he saw the expression on his Musalman's face. It was full of fear and unspeakable anguish. Then he was gone.

The Prince and the Grand Vizier whispered to each other, and Filippo struggled to understand the meaning. He faltered with barely the will to continue.

'Go on, go on,' ordered the emperor.

'I am instructed by my family,' stammered Filippo, 'to offer this peerless object to his esteemed majesty, in all humbleness.' Filippo bowed low.

The old interpreter translated. The emperor clicked his fingers. 'Where is this pendant? His majesty will look at it.'

Filippo took the pouch from round his neck. A servant with a silken cushion stepped forward.

'Put it on the cushion,' whispered the old translator.

Filippo opened the pouch. There were sniggers round the chamber. How pathetic. Did this scrap of a foreign infidel think that he could possibly have anything worth the attention of the Great Moghul, who had the finest jewel collection in the whole world? But Filippo carefully extricated the pendant and arranged it upon the scarlet cushion.

'May I present to you the Ocean of the Moon.' He bowed deeply again.

The sniggering stopped. Everyone craned forward to see.

The silence seemed to last forever. Doesn't he like it? Filippo didn't dare look up. The emperor took it up and held it aloft, dangling it from its gold chain. Flames and shadows, reflections and shimmering lights entered the stone and made them dance. The diamond flared like the sun, the pearls and moonstones gleamed with the purity of angels. The whole cosmos was encompassed inside the stones.

'What a marvellous thing!' the emperor gasped at last. '*Subhan Allah! Kya Kehne, la jawab! Yeh toh bilkul kamal ki bat hai.* Unbelievable! I've never seen anything quite like it.'

There were gasps from everywhere. Filippo looked up to see the amazed faces.

'He is pleased!'

'Yes, yes!' He was showing it off to his sons, still talking enthusiastically.

The translator murmured. 'You are fortunate. His illustrious majesty is well pleased. He will accept your gift and declares his intention to give it to his beloved wife, Mumtaz Mahal, when she gives birth to his fourteenth child, if it so please Allah, the Most Compassionate and Merciful.'

The princes gathered round admiringly, all except Prince Aurangzeb. His face was utterly frozen in anger, and Filippo knew then that this jewel, or its value, had been promised to him by the Musalman and the Grand Vizier, that he had some power over them. Did the emperor sense the tension? Filippo didn't dare look.

The Great Moghul turned to his eldest son, Prince Dara, and with a fond embrace, entrusted the precious jewel to him. 'Guard this until the baby is born. Only the queen's beauty compares with the beauty of this creation, and only she must have it.' Then he turned back to Filippo. 'You surely did not undertake this perilous journey from Venice just to give me this jewel. Had you no other business? Who is your father?' he enquired through the interpreter.

And so, at last, Filippo told him that his father, Geronimo Veroneo, was a hostage in the hands of Abdhur Mir and that he desperately needed to raise a ransom to obtain his release.

The emperor listened attentively. He beckoned the Grand Vizier to him. They conferred with each other, though all the time, the face of the Grand Vizier was expressionless. The emperor got to his feet and, with a flurry of servants and waving fans, left the chamber.

Coldly, the Grand Vizier addressed Filippo and told him that the emperor would give him 10,000 gold coins stamped with the royal head. Five thousand of these coins would be sealed into a casket which he would take to Afghanistan to gain the release of his father, the other five thousand was to be kept in the palace with the Royal Treasurer for safe-keeping and could be redeemed on his return.

'Thank you, thank you, thank you!' Filippo repeated his gratitude over and over again.

'You will be escorted by an armed guard of twelve men and accompanied all the way by a trusted courtier, Sadiqui Iqbal Khan.'

As if on cue, there was his Musalman, smiling as he had that first day he arrived in Venice.

Chapter Twenty-eight

❖

The empty house

Teodora Veroneo sat in her husband's chair. Her arms rested on its arms, and her fingers cupped the wooden scrolls at each end. She leaned back into its yellow linen upholstery and closed her eyes.

'Oh my husband, oh my dear husband. What has become of us all? Our family is as dust, scattered in the wind. You and I are apart, and our children have gone.'

The house of Veroneo was empty. The servants had been dismissed. Giuseppe was dead – his loss still ground in her heart. There was no Rosa singing in the kitchen. She had taken Gabriella and Sofia and fled with them to her daughter. Elisabetta had disappeared, Carlo was in prison and could even be executed for the murder of Pagliarin, and Filippo . . . Poor little Filippo – her beloved youngest child, her baby, her Benjamino – where was he? Only faithful, ancient, beloved Forza – Geronimo's dog – deaf and blind but still with a will to live in his old bones, only he remained, his nose on her foot, as she sat embraced by Geronimo's chair.

They set a chair for Penelope, wife of Odysseus, before the fire where she liked to sit. A chair well-wrought, and inlaid with ivory and silver, which a long time ago, had been fashioned by the craftsman, Icmalius.

Here she sat, while her white-armed handmaids cleared away the many fragments of food, the tables and cups from which proud lords had been eating and drinking. They raked out the fires from the braziers, and piled on fresh logs to give light and warmth.

Pagliarin's sons had been round with officers. They claimed the house of Veroneo was rightfully theirs and wanted Teodora to leave. But she had managed to persuade the authorities to give her another three months, to see whether Filippo's mission had been a success. Either he would return with her husband, Geronimo Veroneo, or with enough assets from the Ocean of the Moon to pay off any creditors and restore the fortunes of the workshop.

Good friends of the family had introduced suitors to her. Surely this was the answer, to remarry and find security once more, security for herself and her daughters. She knew she was stalling for time.

Rosa had visited and told her the appalling news of the loss of Andreas. His father and brothers had finally returned home, broken-hearted. Nor could they say what had become of Filippo. The boys were either dead or had been enslaved.

But no one mentioned a Musalman. No one talked of seeing Signor Khan, so Teodora still hoped against hope that he and Filippo had met and continued their journey to Hindustan.

She closed her eyes and leaned into the chair. She felt very little emotion now. Her crying and grieving had long since, like ancient water, petrified into stone. She felt like a cave, all hollow inside and full of underground lakes, yet craggy and hard on the outside. She would be strong for others to cling on to if they needed her.

She felt as if Geronimo stood behind her, that he bent low over her and dangled the pendant, the Ocean of the Moon. 'A priceless jewel for a priceless wife,' he murmured into her hair. But a jewel which had only brought them bloodshed and bitterness.

'Oh dear husband, I am in sorrow,' Penelope cried. 'Such a host of ills has been sent by Zeus against me. There are suitors, wooing me against my will, and those who would devour the house. I take no notice of any of them, but waste my heart away longing for you.'

Rosa had begged her to leave this lonely ghost-filled house, until Carlo's fate was known. But Teodora knew she must stay and fight for its possession. Geronimo must have his house to come back to, and if not Geronimo, then Carlo and Filippo. So long as she had life and strength, she must guard it to the bitter end. She swore she would have to be carried away screaming before she would relinquish their home. Meanwhile, she would at least continue creating designs for jewellery. She already had a number of commissions from clients who knew and admired her work.

Forza snuffled, and his tail thumped the floor as Geronimo's presence filled the room, and Teodora rose from the chair and went up to the workshop.

Chapter Twenty-nine

❖

Dance of the gods

Filippo stood on his little balcony overlooking the River Jamuna. He was no longer a prisoner, but a guest. An armed guard still sat smoking his bidis at the top of the steps but he was there to protect him, not to prevent him escaping. The sky was rapidly clearing of those mountainous monsoon clouds which had kept them in such darkness for nearly three months, and now, like a newly discovered ocean, expanded across the heavens from end to end, a rich, clean, washed blue. Its warmth was innocent, as if the sun never did more than bring colour and heat, light and energy and growth.

How strange, that for all the beauty around him, for all the fabulous marble mosques, and intricately carved stone temples, for all the gold and jewels and finery and unbelievable wealth that surrounded him, he knew the Musalman was right. The more wealth there was, the less truth and trust. Only in the desert with nothing to come between him and his god had he understood his mortality and understood his place in the

universe. But how could Signor Khan believe that, if he himself
was involved in such treachery?

Captain Wallace had come to visit him. He had examined
his head to make sure the wound was healing well, and now he
sat in a chair overlooking the river – the same chair where he
had fought the temptation to steal the Ocean of the Moon. He
had a proposition.

'When you have redeemed your father, and come back to
Agra, would you be so good as to consider the notion of
accepting my daughter as your wife? She would come to you
with some dowry. I have assets in England. Naturally, your
father must agree. But I wanted to know if you were not averse
to the idea first, before I put it to him. You seem to be a young
man of courage and enterprise . . .' His voice continued as if
from a distance.

Filippo was shocked. Marriage, a wife, Noor, me? He was
just a boy, not a man. Suddenly he heard Andreas's little sister
Varvara's voice calling to him, 'Will you marry me when I grow
up?' And his casual answer, 'I'll never marry.' But all boys say
that, don't they? He knew he would, as all his friends would
except maybe one or two, who would go into the church. That
wasn't for him. He wondered if any church would ever seem
better than praying in the desert with only the land and sky.
Could he ever be married to little dancing Noor?

Now he was alone, looking out across the vast plain; across a land that seemed to have no end to it. He had promised Captain Wallace to consider his proposal – but how? What would bring him to any kind of decision, he did not know. 'Mama!' he whispered to himself. 'Mama would know what to do.'

A faint movement behind him, a rustle of silk, a catch of the breath. He turns. There is Noor. Although still coiling her hands and tipping her head, she is quieter and more intense. Her blue eyes seem almost black as her pupils expand to let in the brightness of the light over the river.

'Come,' she beckons him. 'I have arranged something for you. Come.'

He follows her through the secret door and down the long dark passage. Hurrying after her, he runs his hands along the sides. As if diamond dust lingers in his head, his fingers feel and see and speak to every bump and join and crack, and understand their being and their histories. It feels like a farewell to the walls of this palace which have enclosed him for so long. He wonders whether his father has made friends with the stones of his prison, and whether he will suddenly mourn them too when the time comes to leave.

A steep flight of steps thrusts them out into a part of the garden he has never been in before. Peacocks screech and parade, their feathers fluttering out like the fronds of amazing plants. The effect of the rains is to bring the universe into being all over again. The colours and smells have a freshness of renewal like spring in Italy.

They run through the shrubbery towards a small marble garden house with its own elegant cupolas and terraces around it. She leaps up the steps. 'Welcome, Filippo! Go in. I'll see you in a minute,' and she disappears.

Filippo entered a chamber and gasped with amazement. Facing him at the far end, reclining in sumptuous cushions, was little Prince Murad, surrounded by his servants and nursemaid, yet looking like an emperor. He leapt to his feet and shouted, 'Filippo! Over here. I have a place for you.'

Filippo crossed the marble floor, feeling dozens of dark gleaming eyes upon him, for the chamber was full of all the children of the palace, the sons and daughters of princes and noblemen, emissaries and diplomats, scholars and clerks, of elephant-keepers, grooms, gardeners and cooks. And hanging about outside, peering through the windows, were the children of humble boatmen, washermen and sweepers. In rich clothes, neat clothes, ragged clothes, they shuffled and whispered and stared and giggled, waiting for something. No one knew what was going to happen, but Noor had assembled them all.

Filippo sat down on a silken cushion next to Murad, who grabbed his hand and said excitedly, 'It's a surprise. Noor has a surprise for us.'

Presently, four tall solemn boys wearing simple white cotton tunics and pyjamas entered in a line, followed by a single girl in a light green embroidered swinging skirt, and fitted blouse with a veil draped over her head. They sat down on a mat to the side. One boy had a pair of tablas, the next boy a sitar, the next a flute, and the last a drone. The girl had no instrument in her hand, but when they began to play, she sang.

Her voice was like a diamond, bright, hard, clear, deep, sometimes harsh, as though parts of it were uncut, unpolished. It reverberated against the stone and marble, and the criss-cross silver patterens of bright light which fell through the marble-fretted window screens. She was telling a story, and they all knew it. If before there had been shuffling, rustling and fidgeting, now everyone fell silent and still with awe. The sitar quivered on a low expectant note. Noor entered.

She was golden. Her burnished bronze-coloured silken dance sari was bordered with gold. It lined her sleeves, it bound her waist, it fell in flaring pleats at the front. Her eyes were lined with charcoal, her lips reddened. Her palms and fingers were painted crimson, so too her toes and feet. Her ankles jingled with bells. Her hair hung like a golden cord down her back, tightly plaited and threaded with flowers and pearls at the sleeves. She looked possessed, transformed. She walked, yet floated. Ching, ching, ching! The bells at her ankles chimed with every step. She stood before Prince Murad with hands clasped together, and bowed with respect. He waved an imperious hand. 'Begin!'

She began to dance. She was Noor, but no longer Noor. She was Durga, Parvati, Laxmi – a woman, a goddess. Through her, the gods entered that chamber bringing energy, joy, sadness; a hundred expressions of feeling and thought, through gestures and hands, eyes and fingers and feet. She brought the language of the gods, a language without speech. The drum thudded, her feet drummed, the singer's voice grew in passion, as Noor danced about love and desire, rejection and tragedy. Her shining body melted into the gold of her sari, and still she danced.

The drumming got faster and faster, Noor twirled till she seemed to almost disappear in a blur of spinning gold. A final flourish and it was over. The children burst into cheering applause. She was human once more, her chest heaving with exertion, her perspiration pouring down her brow, staining her armpits, the flowers in her hair drooping, her shadow sharply etched across the floor, where her feet did, after all, touch the ground.

She looked at Filippo. 'Do you see?' Her eyes spoke to him. 'Dancing is my life. I cannot leave India.'

Prince Murad beckoned her forward. Noor came and respectfully kneeled and touched his feet, her heart and the air above her head.

'I want you always to dance for me,' he declared. 'Will you, Noor?'

'So long as your highness desires it, I shall always dance for you,' whispered Noor, but she glanced at Filippo, and saw his eyes fixed upon her. They were brimming with light and tears, as if some new door had opened, as if he glimpsed something even his diamond had never shown him.

After the performance, when the children dwindled away, their laughing excited voices dispersing in every direction, after the little prince had been whisked away by his attendants, Noor and Filippo walked in the gardens.

'Your father wishes me to marry you and take you back to Venice. He wants you to be European, a Christian. He wants you to live like a lady.'

'I know,' she said in a low voice. Suddenly, they were no longer children. 'That's why I wanted you to see me dance, really dance. If I was taken away from that, I would die. I would not be Noor. I would be Marianne. What I am here, I would not be there.'

'But once you stop being a child, how can you go on dancing, even here?'

'Do you want to marry me, Filippo?' Her question was unexpected.

Filippo couldn't speak. How could he say that she was the most beautiful, miraculous person he had ever known in all his life, something so special and unrepeatable – as immeasurably precious – even more to him than the Ocean of the Moon? That he could never have imagined such a person as she existed on this earth, that like the Ocean of the Moon, she was a jewel surely not ever to be possessed by him? His feelings were too new, too unpractised. He hadn't got the words, was unfamiliar with the emotions.

'I would only want what you want,' he replied inadequately.

A remnant of the monsoon winds quivered through the trees, and a shower of rain fell scattering across the garden. They ran to the palace and through the small doorway. Without speaking, she led him back along the twisting passageways, across the rooftops and terraces until they reached his chamber. The secret panel slid open. 'Goodbye, Filippo. I won't see you again before you go, but when you come back – I pray that a merciful God will protect you and bring you back – then please –' She faltered.

'I'll come and see you,' he said.

They both lacked further words. She kissed him lightly on his cheek, and dwindled away into the darkness.

Chapter Thirty

❖

A dark road to the moon

It was a fine, cloudless morning in mid-September, when no rain had fallen for three days. Signor Khan came to announce their departure. Although he looked as inscrutable as ever, a little more gaunt perhaps, and anxieties had added creases in his brow, there was a fervour in his eyes, and an impatience to be gone.

Filippo was wary, alert and ready. Whatever Signor Khan's role was, he was still there, still guiding him, still promising to take him to his father. Perhaps he would never get there. Perhaps Signor Khan still had plans to deprive him of the money. But Filippo had no choice but to go on.

The waiting for the end of the monsoon had been almost unbearable. His energy had been storing itself up, and his patience was at bursting point. He, too, longed to be on his way again.

'You've grown taller since we last met, young man,' said Signor Khan.

Filippo smiled. He knew that Giuseppe's sword was now the right size for him, and hung well from his belt. Once more, he wore Venetian dress, his leggings and shirt, his tabard, and his pouch and sword on his belt. He had a longing to be himself, Filippo from Venice, and with the weather being cooler, it felt natural and comfortable to be wearing his own clothes.

Before they left, Prince Murad presented Filippo with gifts. One was a silver dagger with a jewel-encrusted handle which Filippo had already sheathed to his belt. The other was a ruby ring which fitted his little finger. But most wonderful of all was his gift of an Arab horse, a pretty white one, with slender intelligent head, a long fanning tail and dancing hooves.

'Forgive my paltry gift – this is all I have,' murmured Filippo, embarrassed that he could give him nothing but his rosary and St Christopher medallion.

'You are my friend, that is all I wish for.' Murad had leapt into his arms and hugged him till he nearly choked.

The little prince cried when Filippo left, and begged him to return. Filippo was to remember him as he last glimpsed him, all aglitter in his fine clothes, the sun flaring in the sequins and pearls of his wafting silk jacket, his turquoise pyjamas billowing in the warm autumn wind that blew across the river plains.

They were to travel in a convoy of bullock carts, with a

contingent of archers with bows and arrows, and guards armed with pistols, swords and spears. Each cart was drawn by four massive horned bullocks, and each with four armed guards. Alongside too, on horseback, was a further convoy of armed soldiers, who were to accompany them. The money for the ransom was in the middle cart modestly covered with a carpet and surrounded by guards, while the end cart contained their provisions and a further four armed men who were also cooks.

And so they left the capital of the Grand Moghul. They left behind the fabulous grandeur, the music, the sport, the ceremonies. They left behind the conspiracies and subterfuge, except that with the packs of stray dogs that rushed out barking, some to join the caravan for the whole journey, out too came a single rider, who merged himself with the cooks and guards, who sometimes tied up his horse to a wagon and leapt aboard to rest his horse, who amused his companions by playing his flute.

The lengthy bumping ride by bullock cart from Agra to Delhi would take ten or eleven days. But just being on their way once more exhilirated Filippo, and drove all sense of danger and suspicion out of his mind. He sat in a cart with the Musalman, in the middle of their convoy for safety, with their horses roped to the wagon and trotting alongside. Filippo could hardly take his eyes off his gift, his white Arab filly, dancing alongside like Noor. 'I will call her Marianne,' he said.

They lurched along tracks full of holes and ruts created since the rains, spending their nights in *serais* – the traveller's inns – along the way. Sometimes, because Signor Khan urged them onwards, there were fearful nights spent sleeping outside, with the constant threat of wild animals, snakes and scorpions, and being bitten half to death by mosquitoes. But Signor Khan seemed driven by something, surely something more than fulfilling his promise to obtain the release of Filippo's father? He forced the pace onwards day by day by day. 'The monsoon has gone, but we must reach Afghanistan and back to the plains before winter,' was the reason he gave.

Sometimes their road ran through dense forest, twittering, chattering and grunting with all kinds of life. The wagons joined the chorus with their own creaking, crunching sounds of wooden wheels grinding and squelching along paths still soft and muddy from the rains.

Even Signor Khan had to accept the pace of the bullock cart, and to release the pent-up energy and impatience, each day he and Filippo would take to their horses in the early morning, and ride off into the forest to hunt and explore. Filippo marvelled how quickly he and his steed got to know each other. Marianne's ears twitched and responded to every word from Filippo, to every touch of the rein and subtle heel into her flanks.

They stalked after deer, raced after wild pigs, held their breath as families of pea-hens crossed their path. Filippo laughed at bands of monkeys tumbling and leaping like acrobats, squirrels that spiralled up trees and the beady-eyed mongoose slinking through the grass. They kept their distance from the rhino drinking at the lake, and the wild elephants so huge, so silent, as they nibbled their way through the leafy undergrowth. And they never went out after dusk, when the tiger or leopard might be on the prowl.

They had been hunting for small game for a meal, and were on their way back to the convoy, when they heard the rattle of distant gunshot. They pulled up their horses and listened: more gunshots, desperate shouts, and the clash of steel. Filippo's first desperate thought was the ransom. He wanted to charge ahead, but Signor Khan held him back fiercely. 'If the guards can't defend the convoy, you can be sure there is nothing we can do. Don't throw away your life in bravado.'

So they waited, hanging their heads over their horses' necks. Screams of agony rang through the forest as wounds were inflicted on and on and on.

Suddenly it was over. A terrible silence descended. 'Stay here,' commanded Signor Kahn. Filippo obeyed, while his Musalman first walked his horse, then broke into a trot, up the path towards the track and was lost from sight.

Filippo waited. He waited and waited. Hadn't his whole life been one of waiting? Ever since he was born, every day had been about waiting: waiting to grow up, waiting to be tall enough to carry a sword, waiting to be a man, waiting for his father to come home. Every minute of every day since he left Venice, had been about waiting – waiting for each part of the journey to be over, the destination to be reached, the quest to be at an end.

And so here in the forest he continued to wait, within a silence which wasn't a silence. It was as if he was caught up within the breath of a huge invisible being, within his guts and bloodstream, within his heartbeat, within his mind and the decision which was being made about his fate. Although he heard nothing, Filippo suddenly saw people coming out of the forest, rustics and forest dwellers. They came from every direction, and silently gathered around him in the dappled light. And they just stared; some standing, some squatting. They looked like parts of the trees themselves, with their hard twisting muscles and sharp-boned bodies. Half-naked labourers gave themselves no higher status than the women with unveiled faces and babies at their breasts, or the little girls with arms as thin as creepers, coiled round younger children who were clamped to their hips, or the wide-eyed boys, carrying long sticks as thin as themselves.

They all waited and none of them seemed to have any

substance, as though there was no difference between being alive and being dead. He no longer heard the screech of the peacock, nor the scuttering of animals in the undergrowth. The silence of the forest was the silence of Yama, the Lord of the Dead, passing among them on his way to noose those fluttering souls from the dying on the track ahead.

So time slid by like a river. One hour or two? He had no idea, but whenever he looked up, there they were, the people of the forest, still staring at him.

Then, like the voice of silence itself, he heard the flute, the wretched, haunting, menacing, stalking flute, the flute with its secret messages which had trailed him all these months, clung to him like a parasite, gnawed at his confidence, undermined his trust. It echoed eerily through the forest. Filippo sat upright in the saddle. The forest dwellers had gone, vanished away, all of them, every man, woman and child. He looked at the branches of trees, their swirling trunks and tangled creepers, as if he might see them in the barks and the foliage. But all he saw was a pair of red eyes, which remained fixed on him, glowing through the dense, leafy glade. A faint wind rippled round him and there was a brief rustle of leaves. With a sudden burst of panic, he dug his heels into Marianne's side and, with the sound of his own screaming ringing in his ears, he broke into a gallop, and rode as if the demons of hell were after him.

He reached the track. There had been plunder, murder and mayhem. Bullocks and people lay slaughtered, pierced by gunshot, arrows, swords and knives. The wagons were upturned, among which the dogs were scavenging for food and, silently, silently, the hawks and vultures circled in the sky. He wheeled his horse round this way and that, yelling for all he was worth, 'Signor Khan, Signor Khan!'

As if mockingly, the flute still played. With a shout of rage, Filippo left the track on the other side, galloping into the undergrowth in search of that infernal instrument which seemed to taunt him. Twigs scratched his arms and legs, and ripped at the sides of his horse, but still they plunged ever deeper into the forest.

'Signor Khan, Signor Khan!'

Suddenly, he saw a wagon tipped over on its side. The thick teak boxes which had contained the emperor's own coins for the ransom lay broken open and empty. There was no sign of Signor Khan. The smell of cinnamon drifted as faint as evening blossom. He saw the flute.

As if to taunt him, it was placed across a wooden wheel lying to one side. Was this all it amounted to? A pathetic hollowed-out piece of wood with holes in it? He slid to the ground and, still enraged, snatched up the instrument. He held it as if it were a hated serpent. He pressed his fingers over the holes as if he could choke the breath out of it, then with a howl of frustration and anger, he leapt on his horse and clasping the flute as if it were a spear, rode back to the track.

A figure on a horse waited, holding another horse on the rein. At the sight of Filippo emerging out of the forest, he threw up both arms in gratitude.

'Allah is merciful,' shouted Signor Khan.

Filippo galloped right up to him, thrusting the flute up in the air. 'Did you forget this?' he cried bitterly. 'What does it mean? Who are you?'

Signor Khan reached forward and snatched the flute from Filippo's hands and, passionately, broke it across his knee. He hurled the pieces away and bowed his head with eyes closed, as if praying, thinking, considering. 'This is the instrument of Aurangzeb,' he said at last. 'I learned its language of conspiracy from others when I was imprisoned. I lied to you. I have always known about the diamond. I heard your father muttering about it when he had a delirious fever one day, and thought he was dying. He told me about the Ocean of the Moon. It would save us both, he said, if only we could get a message over to his family in Venice. I thought it was my opportunity to get out of my prison. I saw it as a way of making my fortune.'

'I knew it! We all knew you couldn't be trusted,' shouted

Filippo, his hand on his sword, ready to plunge it into the treacherous man.

'Listen to me. Listen to my whole story, and try and understand I am just a frail human being, but one who tried to find a right and good path.'

Filippo fell silent.

'If everything your father said was true, I knew the diamond was worth more than a ransom. It was worth an army. I bargained with Abdhur Mir. I told him about the diamond. He agreed to let me go.'

'How could he just let you go?' demanded Filippo disbelievingly. 'How could he trust you would return?'

Signor Khan ignored Filippo's outburst.

'I went via the court of Shah Jehan. I planned to sell the diamond there, thinking there would be far more than the warlord wanted for his ransom. But I fell into the hands of the Grand Vizier to whom I told my story. He persuaded me that I should sell the diamond to him when I got it. Only then did I realise that the Grand Vizier was part of a conspiracy. He is raising money even now, to pay for armies who would one day fight to overthrow Shah Jehan and put Aurangzeb on the throne.

'It was too late for me to back off and change my mind. One falter and they would have my life. They wanted the diamond, and I knew that I would be followed every inch of the way until I got it, and delivered it into their hands. Whenever I heard the sound of the flute – that tune – I understood its message. I knew they were reminding me that his spies were everywhere. From Venice to Crete to Surat to Agra, they followed me. Only because the storm blew us off course, and we went through the desert, did we lose them for a while. I prayed it might be forever, but there they were again, waiting at Surat.

'But Filippo, it is thanks to you that the Grand Vizier failed to obtain the diamond. I had no power to stop him. I only persuaded him not to have you killed immediately. I knew that sooner or later you would bring out the diamond from its hiding place.

'But you thwarted him, and managed to give the diamond to the emperor as you always wanted. So now he has tried to get the money instead. He nearly succeeded. He would have done, but we were helped, Filippo. Someone has helped us. I followed the sound of the flute meaning to kill whoever was still threatening us, but instead, it led me to the money.' He slapped a hand over two large panniers, apparently stuffed with cloth for trading, and pointed to the horse in tow with loaded saddlebags.

'Who?' The old rabbi's words came back into Filippo's mind.

> '*Beware of your friends,*
> *Do not trust your brothers,*
> *For every brother is a deceiver,*
> *And every friend a slanderer,*
> *Friend deceives friend and no one speaks the truth.*'

Signor Khan shook his head. 'I don't know. Perhaps one of Shah Jehan's own men? The emperor is no fool. But there is no time to waste thinking who are our friends and who our enemies,' and as if he too heard the rabbi's words, he murmured, 'all we can do is trust each other.' He tipped his head questioningly.

'Yes,' muttered Filippo.

They rode hard, and Filippo asked no further questions and, as the sun descended lower and lower, till they were perilously close to nightfall, a dim cluster of glimmering lights in the distance showed them they had reached a small wayside town.

Chapter Thirty-one

❖

Desperate truth

At the small town, they had to wait for another convoy going to Dilhi. It was unwise to attempt to go alone. They stayed quietly in their room. They spoke little. Signor Khan restocked their provisions, hired another bullock cart and took on six armed guards who would ride on ponies alongside. When they finally set off again, it was a further five days until they reached Dilhi, and passed through the outer walls of the city. They were to stay at a royal residence to recuperate before the next leg of the journey.

Signor Khan showed signs of agitation. He wouldn't rest. He spent every hour of the day getting together more provisions and animals for the next leg of the journey. 'Time is running out,' he insisted.

'Dear man,' his host tried to pacify him, 'you have plenty of time to get to Afghanistan before the winter. Stay a few days longer. The boy is sick.'

He was right. Filippo had flushes of fever, his stomach

churned, his mood was despairing. The constant travelling, staying at *serais* where the food was bad or the water unhealthy, had left him exhausted. He was riddled with worms and drained of energy. But Signor Khan was adamant. They must keep going.

So as soon as they could, they were off again; another fifteen days on the road heading for Lahore from where they would make the ascent to Peshawar. To encourage him, Signor Khan took a stick and drew a map on the ground. He showed him that up from Peshawar was a pass into Afghanistan. 'Here is where your father is being held.' He jabbed the earth at a spot in the mountains above the plain of Kabul. 'We must get him released before the winter, otherwise we may be trapped by bad weather and have to wait till the spring.'

Filippo understood the urgency, and never complained when Signor Khan kept moving ever onwards, even though his fever raged and, unable to sit on his horse, he had to lie in the bullock cart. There was now just his father, waiting, waiting, waiting for release. And when his delirium carried him away into strange realms, time past and time future, all merged and mixed. He saw Giuseppe laughing as he taught him to use the sword, and his sisters, Sofia and Gabriella, whispering together. There they were, Elisabetta and the Pagliarin family outside the church in Venice, and he threw his crab, and she slapped his face. And there he was confessing to his priest, and saw

Elisabetta, in that dark place under the icy sea. There was his mother, so loath to give up on life, so loath to give up hope that Geronimo would come home, retaining her youthfulness and strength to keep the family going.

The picture changes and she is being worn down as a rock is worn down by water, and rivulets of lines have appeared in her face, and she sits in Geronimo's chair and he stands behind her with such love in his eyes. Then everything turns to water – and Filippo swims with dolphins and leaps with the flying fish. He is nudging Andreas nearer and nearer to home.

But Noor is everywhere.

She has become the diamond in my head.

When I hunt with the hawk, ride the silken desert with Zubeida, and gallop with my horse, Marianne, she is there. Even when I enter the heart of the lily, fainting with its perfume, she is there. I see Papa in his chair at home. I am the baby, staggering into his outstretched arms to be bounced on his knee. I am running to him now, but he is no longer at home, and I speed across the universe to his prison of thick, high stone walls with a single slit for a window, and the moon shines through. The moon is Noor and she is laughing, and Filippo hammers at the cell door, hammering to be let in. The hammering turns to a drumming and the drumming into

Noor's dancing feet. Did anything matter more than Noor?

'Filippo?' Signor Khan's face bent over him with a moist cloth in his hand which he pressed to his burning forehead. 'Your little white horse misses you. Isn't it time you got well?'

'Noor.' Filippo spoke the only word in his head.

So it was the end of October before they reached the foothills and felt the first faint chill blowing down from the mountains. The air was fresher and smelt of pine cones and woodfires. Different birdsong rang through the air, and bands of silver grey monkeys called Langur with black faces and long looping tails leapt alongside them in bounding tribes, gibbering and chattering, and Filippo felt his energy and health surging back. When they stopped at a *serai*, they were served by very pale-skinned people with light eyes and brown hair. The women wore beaded veils with smiling faces, and the men in round caps and woollen waistcoats with baggy trousers. Not even the smallest request was too much trouble.

But one morning when Filippo rose and went out to wash, it was to find the bullocks and the carts gone. He rushed back into the inn in a panic, yelling for Signor Khan. 'They've gone! The bullock carts have gone.'

The Musalman calmed him. 'I should have explained. I'm

sorry. From now on, the terrain becomes mountainous with narrow paths, quite unsuitable for bullock carts. From now on it's horses only.'

Filippo was deeply troubled and suspicious. Why couldn't he just trust Signor Khan? Surely they had a bond, after all they had been through together? Yet still his doubts crowded his mind. All those questions they had never asked back in Venice. If it was just the money, then why hadn't he made off with it long ago? Filippo was sure there was something else about Signor Khan, something he hadn't been told, some piece that was missing so that he still couldn't make sense of the whole picture. 'You never ever asked me where I had hidden the diamond,' said Filippo. 'Why?'

'I didn't want to know,' replied Signor Khan, 'because I might have been tempted to kill you to get it.'

'Does this money not tempt you?' asked Filippo.

Signor Khan turned away without replying, and Filippo felt ashamed.

They were a convoy of twelve now. Signor Khan had hired porters and mountain ponies to carry all provisions, and six armed men who he paid well to guard them. Saddled and bridled and with panniers bulging with provisions, Signor Khan and Filippo, still with their ransom hidden on their own horses, set off again.

Marianne was far more nervous and often had to be coaxed along. One day, trotting single-file up a mountain track, Filippo glanced at the rider behind him and realised he didn't know him.

When the track broadened sufficiently, he rode on ahead and then, as casually as he could, dropped back and back, until eventually he had scanned all their faces. He didn't recognise any of them, and never looked twice at a man, taller than the rest, his face almost submerged in his turban, who rode a black horse, and smelt faintly of cinnamon. They had all changed again – it must have been at the last village, though it had barely seemed big enough to provide them with such a guard.

'I don't know these men. When did we take them on?' he demanded, pulling alongside Signor Khan.

'Trust me.' Signor Khan had never shown short temper before. But day by day, he seemed more irritable and anxious, and this only increased Filippo's sense of danger, more than the dangers of the lonely mountain paths with precipitous drops and furious rivers.

The higher the altitude, the sharper and colder the temperatures became. Signor Khan urged them on and on. It would snow soon, and then they could be held up until the spring. He had become desperate. He hated everything that had held them up, hated the monsoon, hated the snow, hated the illnesses and, Filippo felt, hated him. Even Signor Khan's love of God had turned to hatred. He no longer stopped to pray, but as soon as they were on the road kept up a relentless pace. And so, in a broken rhythm of stop, halt, wait, and move on again, they made progress inch by inch and day by day.

Lofty highlands now rose on either side of them. The scenery got bleaker, browner, but somehow purer. Filippo marvelled at the great beauty of the ice blue skies, the terraced slopes of vines, nuts and fruit trees, and the slender turquoise domes and minarets they began to glimpse on the distant skyline.

One day, they crossed through a pass, and Signor Khan said, 'We are in Afghanistan.' He got down from his horse, fell to his knees and clasped handfuls of earth to his heart as he prayed. But though they had reached Afghanistan, it only seemed to make Signor Khan more desperate. He was jumpy and nervous and was constantly glancing about him. Filippo noticed that he avoided his eye. Once more, he urged the men onwards like a slave driver, and had long since stopped asking Filippo considerately whether he was fit and able to continue.

They stayed high, in the rugged unforgiving valleys and slopes of the highlands. Far in the distance on a brown dusty plain, they glimpsed the city of Kabul. Filippo saw its delicate minarets and turquoise domes, gardens and orchards, fountains and streams and its sweeping river, sapphire blue in the wintry light. Like a pearl necklace in the background gleamed the snow-covered peaks of the Hindu Kush.

I am rolled up tightly in my buffalo-skin bed beneath the chill stars. I have been woken by the sound of a flute gently pulsating through the darkness.

I lie rigid. Death has come. I think about Noor. I open my eyes and see Signor Khan standing just a few yards away from me. He is talking to someone. I don't recognise the man, though the moonlight is strong and bright. If the man came by horse, I never heard its hooves and Marianne, who usually never fails to neigh and fret at the approach of strangers, stands silently, tethered nearby.

I want to crawl closer and hear what they say, but I daren't move.

Signor Khan throws his hands up to the sky with one gasp of agony, then slumps over a boulder, weeping noiselessly. The stranger backs away, and is lost in the shadows. I watch in horror as Signor Khan rocks to and fro, thumping the stone with his fists. Full of terror, I get to my feet. 'What is it? Have you news of my father? Is he all right?'

He hears me, turns with the swiftness of a cobra. I see his dagger glinting in his hand. Our eyes meet, his full of tears yet burning with fury and grief. He wants to kill. He could kill me now.

'Why don't you?' I ask.

'Why don't I what?'

'Why don't you kill me?

The Musalman shakes his head violently.

'You want the money, don't you? Haven't you always wanted it?' I didn't flinch and my voice stayed steady. 'You should have taken the Ocean of the Moon. I don't know why you didn't take it in the desert when you could have. I don't understand.'

Signor Khan lowers his knife. He stands away from the boulder, tall, gaunt, ravaged.

'I always knew we couldn't trust you,' I say bitterly.

'I implore your forgiveness.' The Musalman puts a hand to his heart. 'I know you haven't trusted me. Why should you? As you say, why did I not steal the Ocean of the Moon?' He spoke fast and quietly, as if there wasn't much time. 'I could have skinned you down to the bone to find it. I knew it must be on your person somewhere. But . . .'

'But?' I hear the hardness in my voice.

'But, I told you.' He is almost inaudible. 'I went first to Mecca on a Haj. I made vows. I am a God-fearing man. I made vows, not only to God, but to your father. I promised to get his ransom. I was tempted. Many times, I was tempted.'

The tears hang like icicles on his unshaven cheeks. He glances round him as if afraid, then he drops to his haunches and rests his head between his arms. He waves me to come close. Hesitating and afraid of him, I sit on a rock just a little way off.

'We are surrounded by spies, so be on your guard. You see, I was always as much a hostage as your father.' His whisper is low but harsh. 'When the warlord, Abdhur Mir, let me go, he kept my son, my own dear son. He let it be known that if I didn't return with the diamond within two years, he would kill him. It is one month over the two years agreed. Oh my son, my flesh and my blood. May God forgive me. I kept my vows, and pray Allah, I meet you in paradise.'

He speaks so quietly that surely only I can hear his words, but there is a swish, a whistle, a drawn breath, a hiss. My Musalman stays as he is, sitting on his haunches with his head in his hands, but now a dagger quivers in his back.

'Signor Khan!' My voice cuts the air, as he slowly topples over.

I leap for my sword, Giuseppe's sword, the sword Carlo said I must only use when there was no choice. I have no choice. I lunge blindly and strike flesh – but I too am struck. My skin is ripped by a dagger tearing through my cloak. A figure leaps at me. He swipes left and right and whirling round screaming like a demon. We hear each other's screams. I make a final plunge and am unable to pull back my sword.

Another figure leaps forward. I see his face briefly in the moonlight. I see a glint of another weapon. I don't know if it's for me or against me, so I throw myself into the black void below. What does it matter how death comes. I have failed.

Chapter Thirty-two

❖

Too late

Filippo was being carried, slung face down like a corpse over the back of a mule. He could hear its funny little hooves click-clicking on the stony path. His father's jewelled cross dangled from his neck, dancing before his eyes, catching the sunlight. He saw from this position a pair of European boots that walked alongside him. Filippo made no sound. All he could think was that Signor Khan and his son were dead.

He felt racked with guilt as he remembered his harsh words. How he had never even enquired who the messenger was who came that night, nor shown pity for Signor Khan's distress. And just at the point when Filippo understood everything, the Musalman was killed.

Bouncing along helplessly, he went over everything from the moment the Musalman arrived at their door in Venice, to his death by a knife on some god-forsaken hillside in Afghanistan. Now it all made sense. Too late, too late. Tears fell to the hard brown track. Only now did he understand the trap

Signor Khan had been in, why he had been in such a hurry, why even his diamond eye had not been able to break through the wall of secrecy Signor Khan had built round himself. It was a wall to keep out temptation. It was all clear to him now that Signor Khan had tried to be a friend – and had been more than a friend. He had taught him, advised him, comforted him, nursed him when he was ill. He had done everything he could while his own son's fate hung in the balance. Filippo thought of all the delays that were to kill his son.

His sorrow finally broke from his throat and he sobbed out loud.

The boots stopped, the hooves paused restlessly, shifting and clicking on the stones. A hand cupped his chin and raised his head. Filippo found himself looking up into a sunburnt, travel-worn face, a European face. It was Rodriguez.

'Did you kill Signor Khan?' Filippo asked in a blank voice.

'I did not. He was killed by Aurangzeb's men.'

'Why?'

'He disobeyed them. He didn't hand over the money, so they took it. He was always your friend.'

'He was like a father to me,' Filippo's head dropped down, grief-stricken.

The mule came to a standstill, and Rodriguez lifted him off. He smelt of cinnamon. 'I'm sorry to have slung you over the back of a donkey like a bale of cotton, but I had no other means of carrying you,' he explained in Venetian, albeit with a Portuguese accent. He smiled when he saw Filippo's stunned face. He hadn't heard his own tongue since leaving Crete. He sat Filippo astride the saddle, but the boy flopped over the mule's neck, and slept.

Filippo next came to his senses in a dark windowless stone hut, lying on a bed of straw. Around him were animals: goats, a yak, and a couple of mules with odd chickens scraping around. Nearby was a jug. Someone must have tried to get him to drink. He sat up on one elbow, and pain shot through his muscles. He ached and hurt all over. He drank – nearly spitting it out when he tasted, not water, but thin yoghurt made from yak's milk. Its rancid taste brought him fully awake. Next to the jug was a flute.

A brown, leathery, weather-worn face, strong-featured and light-eyed, looked in on him, bending almost double to enter. A tribeswoman came to his side, bundled in yakskins, with a woven covering round her head veiling half her face. Underneath it all, he glimpsed heavy silver jewellery, lapis lazuli and amber, round her neck and wrists and jangling at her ankles. She smelt of rancid butter and yak's milk, and when she smiled, she showed a mouth only half full of teeth, and those were black. She held out a bowl of barley soup with bits of mutton floating in it, and encouraged him to drink.

'Where is the European?' he asked in Urdu.

She shrugged and beamed with incomprehension, and chattered on in a language he couldn't understand. Now he had no diamond eye to help him.

He held up the flute. 'What is this doing here?'

She just laughed, pretended to play the flute – peep peep peep – and came over to his side. Without his permission, she began to massage his limbs. Her fingers probed into his tendons, stretched his bones and manipulated his muscles. Under her touch, his body flowed. As if she had unlocked a river, his feelings coursed through his veins. His hopes, his sorrows, his doubts and his love were released. 'Signor Khan!' The name broke from his throat. 'Signor Khan!' How could he go on without his companion? 'Signor Khan!' His voice seemed to echo across oceans and deserts, as he drifted into sleep beneath her hands.

By the next day, his body was alive, restored and totally free from pain, yet it was as though he drifted outside his body. He felt unconnected and without emotion. A shaft of pale sunlight fell through the low door, spotlighting hens and chickens clucking and picking their way to and fro. The light darkened; a tribesman entered. He was heavily bearded with a swathe of turban and full baggy pants. He looked fierce and powerful, but

Filippo was beyond fear. He didn't really think he was going to live much longer. Signor Khan was dead, and he no longer believed his father was alive. There was no longer any ransom.

The man jerked his head, unsmiling, indicating he should get up and go outside. Filippo pulled on his boots and went outside.

He strode up a track, and Filippo knew he was supposed to follow.

They walked all day. Night came. The cold was unbelievable, but the tribesman unrolled yakskins from the bundle on his back, and it was possible to sleep.

By dawn the next day, the tribesman had vanished. Filippo was alone. It hardly mattered. Here in this high, cold, bleak alien country, the diamond was gone, the money was gone, Signor Khan was gone. He had seen the future for Murad and the court of Shah Jehan, and how the Great Moghul would be brought down by Aurangzeb. If he had been abandoned here to die, then so be it. But a track was there. Automatically he rolled up his yakskin and walked down to it. He would follow it until . . . who knows what? Filippo had no idea where he was going. So he walked and sang Andreas's song.

> La biondina in gondoleta
> L'altra sera go mena.

Dal piaser la povereta
La s'ha in bota indormenza.

I have taken the fair-headed maiden
on a gondola, the other night.
Such was her pleasure
that the little dear fell suddenly asleep.

After a mile or two, he saw it: the curving, battle-worn ramparts of the prison fort, perched above him on a great rock. The first snowflakes of winter tumbled heavily through the stark sky.

He climbed the steep slope and approached the huge, scarred, wooden gates. Lounging around outside, smoking leaf-rolled tobacco, with spears propped up against the wall, were guards, scrawny jagged-looking men, with swords at their sides. They stared casually. He might have been a stray dog, for all the interest they showed. Perhaps, Filippo thought, he no longer looked foreign, no longer looked European. His skin was sallow, he was thin and gaunt, and even the greeny colour of his eyes was not unusual in this country, where so many races from east and west had crossed to and fro over thousands of years. Apart from his boots, he no longer wore his Venetian clothes.

'*Chulloh!* Get away with you!' One of them shooed him off like a stray dog.

Filippo spoke in slow, careful Urdu. 'I am the son of Geronimo Veroneo, and I have come to pay his ransom.'

Every head turned. They roared with laughter. One of them, still laughing, disappeared through a small portal within the huge wooden door of the fort.

It was a long wait. Filippo waited fatalistically. At last, the warrior reappeared. His face was blank. He waved him inside. Filippo entered a spacious but bare earthy courtyard, and was taken across to a dark high room and thrust inside.

Propped like a vast doll, in a swirling turban, a long loose tunic which flowed over a mountainous belly, and loose baggy pyjamas, was an older man. His beard was thick and grey, and his podgy face was puckered with old scars. He lounged on a grubby bolstered mattress smoking a hookah, as proud and arrogant as the Grand Vizier, all those months ago. He hardly bothered to acknowledge him, but carried on puffing and smoking and sometimes spitting an arch of betel red into a corner. He didn't look him in the eye. Filippo didn't care. He didn't bow and show respect, even though he realised this must be Abdhur Mir, the warlord.

'I come to obtain the release of my father, Geronimo Veroneo.'

'So what have you got as payment?' the warlord demanded in broken Urdu. He grinned a betel-red toothed grin, though his eyes were callous.

'I have already been robbed. Perhaps by you. Perhaps by followers of Aurangzeb. I have this ring. It must be worth something.' Filippo wrenched off the ruby ring given him by Prince Murad, and tossed it on to his lap. 'Killing me will bring you no further benefit. You have most iniquitously and unjustly held my father here for six years. No doubt he's dead too.'

Filippo's emotions were about to overflow. He wanted to kill this man, if not with his own hands, then to believe that God would condemn him to burn in hell. Just when he was ready to throw caution to the winds, and hurl all his bile and fury at this toad, he heard the old rabbi's voice speaking to him inside his skull, as the diamond had once done. 'Filippo, speak the truth, but speak it gently.'

Filippo halted. There was a pause. The warlord looked up expectantly. Filippo continued, his voice dropping to a clear, quiet, measured tone. 'You have just killed my friend, a good and noble man, a Hadji, who was only trying to fulfil his obligations. You killed his son – wantonly, uselessly. It is not for me to judge you, but Allah will. Such treachery can surely not go unpunished. If there is any God and any justice, you shall be punished, if not in this world then the next and for eternity. I am Filippo Veroneo, and I have come to take my father home.'

The doll, who had looked as if he would explode, suddenly sagged back into his cushions. His eyes narrowed then widened, and his puffed-up red face seemed to drain. He waved a hand, and issued orders. A guard strode forward, grabbed Filippo and dragged him out. He felt nothing – no fear, no sadness, no hope – nothing.

He was dragged down steep dark steps, a door was opened and he was hurled inside. He lay face down on the earth floor, listening to the scuttle of mice and cockroaches, thinking vaguely how strange that the door was not locked behind him.

Someone is shaking me. I look up. A barely human, bedraggled figure stands over me. His hair is long down to his shoulders and quite white, as is his long tangled beard. It is the eyes I recognise, though they seem devoid of sanity. How often have I gazed into those strange greeny-blue eyes of the portrait in the workshop in Venice?

'Father?'

'Giuseppe?'

'No, Father! My name is Filippo. You don't know me because I was born after you left. We tried to tell you . . .'

I get to my feet and fumble for that simple cross around my neck. I unclasp it. 'Look! You gave this to Carlo.' I put it in his hands. He stares at it, his mouth moving, but making no sound. Briefly it lies in his palm. Does he recognise it? The gold chain trickles through his fingers like water as the cross falls to the ground. I scoop it up. He cackles and weeps. 'No, no, no. Not enough.' Now he is murmuring and mumbling incoherently. It is so long since he spoke his own language, that it is broken and mixed up with Urdu. 'The Ocean of the Moon! Did you bring the Ocean of the Moon?'

I sway with dizziness. He reaches out and, though barely sturdier than I, supports and embraces me. We cling to each other as if drowning. I don't answer the question, and he doesn't ask it again. I go to the open door.

There are no guards. I put my arm round my father. Beneath his thin, threadbare covering, it's like holding a skeleton. He is so light, I am almost able to carry him. We cross the threshold. There is no one. No guards. No warriors. No one to stop us. We climb the steps, one painful step at a time. We are not apprehended. We cross a courtyard – horses shuffle in the stables on the far side – and go to the main gate. It is open. No one challenges us as we stumble out, father and son, arm-in-arm. Before we walk away, my father, Geronimo Veroneo, presses into the walls of his prison. He runs his bony fingers over their scarred and pitted stones, then with a great tenderness, he presses his mouth to them, and kisses them. I knew he would.

We walk away.

* * *

So it was done. It was sixteen months since Filippo had left Venice. His father, Geronimo Veroneo, was free. But for what? They had kept him in a dungeon all those years till he was a sick and demented old man, reduced to a wreck in mind and body. Slowly, on foot, they left that hard pitiless place to begin their long journey home.

From a high peak, a man on a black horse, with a white filly in tow, observed the father and son slowly, painfully making their way along the road towards Hindustan. He gently put his heel to his horse's flank, and set off down the hillside towards them.

Chapter Thirty-three

❖

The death of a queen

Sofia and Gabriella leaned over the balcony overlooking the Rio di San Lorenzo. The sun was an hour away from sinking into the lagoon. Birds circled the rooftops, already preparing for the night. Their mother, Teodora, was still bent over a design, which she had promised to have ready for a consultation with an important client the next day. Down in the kitchen, Rosa was moving quietly about between yard and pantry, oven and fire. She didn't sing as she used to. The house was still, with a kind of peace. Abnormality had become normal. They were four women, forced to exist without a male, waiting for news.

The girls observed the last bustle of the day. All kinds of watercraft wove in and out of each other. People gossiped loudly across the rooftops and balconies. Boatmen swore and sang and argued, while hawkers plied their wares.

Working its way round a corner and into Rio di San Lorenzo, Gabriella's eye rested on a boat as it manoeuvred its way through the crush. It was coming in their direction. The boatman rowed steadily, his craft merging into the shimmering reflections of the water. He had two passengers. One of the passengers twisted his body eagerly and looked behind him, to the Veroneo house drifting slowly towards them. Gabriella caught his profile outlined in gold in the setting sun. 'Pippo! Oh Mama – it's Filippo!'

Stools clattered, feet thudded, Moro leapt and barked, infected by their tumultuous excitement. They rushed out on to the fondamente. The boat was pulling in. Filippo leapt ashore and was instantly enveloped by his sisters. But Teodora stood apart. She stared at the second passenger. He still sat in the boat, as if waiting patiently for the family reception to have its full expression, before drawing attention to himself.

'Geronimo?' Teodora's voice carried over to him.

Almost with reluctance, the second passenger turned.

'Mama!' She felt Filippo's arms around her. 'Mama!' His voice was heart-broken. She realised he had grown taller than her. He touched her face, and she saw that he was no longer a child. 'I found Papa. We met, I embraced him, I freed him. I told him about us all. He spoke your name, over and over again. He never ever forgot you. I took him away from that prison, but . . .'

Teodora knew. Geronimo Veroneo was dead.

* * *

'He died a free man.'

Antonio Rodriguez, Geronimo's friend, the man who could pass for a European, a Turk or an Afghan, the man who liked a job well done whether it was to be a good spy, an assassin or a friend, had led them to a trade route through the mountains. There they bargained a place with the caravan train of mules, horses and donkeys, laden with carpets, pashminas, rocksalt and opium. They just managed to get through the pass and down on to the plains of Hindustan before winter set in with a vengeance and driving snow blocked all the passes, and left Afghanistan in its own prison.

Rambling and mostly incomprehensible, Geronimo had questioned his son repeatedly and repetitively, as he was carried by Marianne, his body so shrunken that he was easily enfolded by Filippo who sat behind him holding the reins. His father still called him Giuseppe, unable to comprehend that another son had been born after he left. Patiently, Filippo answered his questions again and again, though his father would forget his answers. 'Have you brought the Ocean of the Moon?' Sometimes he would just repeat the name, 'Teodora. Teodora.'

They only got as far as Dilhi.

One morning, Filippo woke to find his father dead beside him. Geronimo Veroneo had died quietly, as if like a clock, his body had just wound down and stopped.

Filippo couldn't mourn then and there. The light had gone out of his soul. He knew that the loss he would feel would grow and grow into the future, with every year that went by. It would merge and become part of the sorrow he felt for Signor Khan. But now, he was just numb and unable to grieve.

Filippo and Rodriguez carried on to Agra, travelling by day and night, taking Geronimo with them. Better for his father's bones to lie in Agra, near the River Jamuna, within sight of the palace fort. Somehow it felt closer to home and closer to his wonderful creation, the Ocean of the Moon.

As they approached the city, they heard a high wailing like a vast flock of birds at evening. The wailing was a lamentation. Was it for them? Filippo thought illogically for a second. But no, the wailing which rang from the balconies, rooftops and minarets was spreading the news that the beloved wife of Shah Jehan was dead. Queen Mumtaz Mahal, Exalted of the Palace, Mumtazul-Zamanithe, Distinguished of the Age, the favourite wife of the emperor, for whom he had bought the Ocean of the Moon, had died in childbirth. The emperor was crazed with grief and the whole kingdom was plunged into mourning.

Messengers went riding out all over the kingdom bearing

the news: '*The ship of power fell in the whirlpool of restlessness. His heavenly dignity could not keep from lamentation and mourning. The world-discerning eye of the world-conquering king was flooded with tears. The eye of cloud raised a storm, and during that period of one night and day, on account of the torrential rain of wail and lament of the people of the world, the Euphrates flowed in every lane and a river of blood streamed forth from every eye.*

'*His majesty donned white garb like dawn, and all the fortunate princes, illustrious amirs, pillars of the government, grandees of the kingdom and the rest of the people put on mourning-dress. Some tore the collar of the gown and a few, the sleeve of life, on account of the disastrous death of the Queen of Life.*'

There was a small Christian church in the city, with consecrated ground. We found a spot beneath the shade of a pepul tree, and it was here that we laid my father to rest. It was a simple ceremony, conducted by a Jesuit priest who lived in Agra, and was attended by Captain Wallace and Noor.

I thanked God that my father never knew that his wonderful masterpiece, this creation of incomparable beauty, had brought nothing but sorrow and death. How I cursed the Ocean of the Moon. How I hated this land. All I wanted to do was get away from this country, this whole continent, as fast as possible.

'Noor, come with me,' I begged, as later we walked in the gardens along the river.

She held my hands, her eyes overflowing with tears, but she knew her own mind. 'I can't, Filippo. I can't. This is my home. This is where I belong.'

I left Hindustan, feeling empty and bereft, never wanting to return.

Chapter Thirty-four

❖

Reconciliation

Elisabetta walked through the cloisters of Santa Caterina. Rows of pillars cast black shadows across the ancient, footworn flagstones. They swallowed her up as briefly as the blink of an eye, until the brilliant sunshine exposed her just as briefly in the gaps in between. She threaded her rosary through her fingers mechanically, muttering her prayers whenever her mind came back to the reality of where she was. She tried to surrender to the prospect of a life of prayer and meditation. On good days, she saw this as a necessary way to repent. If only she had been a better person, a sweeter daughter, a more loving mother, a more loyal wife, perhaps the disaster which had befallen her household would never have happened. In such moments, she prayed passionately for forgiveness, and promised to devote the rest of her life to serving a higher purpose. She made one pledge after another, to make the necessary sacrifice and surrender her whole being to obedience to God, to join the order of nuns who had cared for her ever since Rodriguez had brought her there. But she could never cling on to those moments for long. Her spirit was restless and tormented and gradually, she felt that the strict, unrelenting discipline of life in the convent, safe as it was, would drive her mad.

Sometimes she left the cloisters and walked into the convent gardens. She often watched Minou, now wearing the habit of the order, toiling silently among the furrows of vegetables. Sometimes Minou would straighten her back, pushing her hand into the base of her spine, and Elisabetta might glimpse her face, and see an expression of total peace, as if her incarceration in the convent had freed her completely from slavery. But if ever she saw her mistress watching, her eyes would fill with tears. There was no other human being she had ever loved as she loved her.

Then one day, a horseman rode up to the convent gates and rang the great clanging bell. A grille slid open, and a voice asked who had called.

'My name is Carlo Veroneo. I wish to see my sister, Elisabetta Pagliarin.'

'Please wait,' the voice commanded and the grille slammed shut.

He passed the time sitting under a tree, watching the soft line of hills glimmering into summer in a blue haze. Lines of peasants in the surrounding fields bent and stretched and swung their hoes like dancers, while high above, little birds swooped and trilled among the orchards. He relished their freedom as he too, miraculously, was free. For the last four months, he hadn't seen the light of day, but had been imprisoned for the murder of Bernardo Pagliarin. The penalty was death, but somehow his mother, Teodora, had pleaded his case and begged for mercy. Some of his wealthy clients also came to his aid and testified to his good reputation, so that day after day, a decision on his fate was postponed. It was only on the return home of Filippo, in the company of a certain Antonio Rodriguez, that the full scale of Pagliarin's crimes and threats had come to light which led to his immediate release.

When they let Carlo in, they took him to an anteroom deep in the heart of the convent. A nun sat in a corner, fingering her beads. A young veiled woman, not wearing the nun's habit, but dressed completely in black, stood at the far end, her back to the doorway. She was thin, and he could see her shoulder blades protruding through the bodice of her dress.

Elisabetta still remained transfixed, not turning round, as if she dreaded seeing her brother, dreaded the hostility and blame in his face.

'Elisabetta?' His voice was soft. 'Elisabetta, I have come to take you home – if you wish it, of course.'

Elisabetta turned, unable to speak. He came forward and

took her hands and embraced her. As she wept quietly on his shoulder, he asked her again, 'Elisabetta, do you wish to return home with me?'

'Yes, Carlo. Yes, I do.'

❖
The shining tomb

It is more than twenty years since these events took place. Andreas hasn't come home, but I can never accept that he is dead. He was so close to getting home when I last saw him with my diamond eye. He was not the sort to die. He is more than just foam on the back of the sea, or sand in the desert. He is somewhere. Every day of my life is a search for him. One day I will find him – or find the truth of what happened to him.

I waited for Andreas's sister, Varvara, to grow up, and I married her. We have five surviving children. Our eldest boy is called Andreas.

But now I am back in Hindustan with my brother Carlo, and though I swore never to return, we are here in the city of Agra. Carlo had always wanted to visit the great Moghul empire, and to pay his respects at our father's resting place.

Prince Aurangzeb deposed his father and is the ruler of the empire, but I shall not go to court and ask for an audience. On our journey from Surat, we heard of the murders, treachery and many dark deeds which, several years on, eventually led to Prince Aurangzeb taking power. My little friend Prince Murad is dead, as are his brothers, Prince Sultan Shujah and the revered Prince Dara. They raised armies and fought each other, as my Musalman said they would. They were outwitted and murdered by Aurangzeb and his supporters. It was also Aurangzeb who was the most ambitious and the most ruthless. We heard of the humiliation and decapitation of Prince Dara, the emperor's eldest and most favoured son, the drowning of Prince Sultan Shujah and his entire family, the betrayal, imprisonment and execution of Prince Murad. I had seen it all as a child, with my diamond eye, and what I saw came true.

However, Aurangzeb did not kill his father. The Great Emperor, Shah Jehan, still lives. They say he is a prisoner in his own palace.

We had heard that after the death of his beloved Queen Mumtaz, Shah Jehan had built her a tomb, which many fellow travellers told us was of unimaginable beauty, and not to be missed.

So now we stand outside the great arched gateway. It is not yet dawn.

There is a sense of immense peace and goodness. The gate-keepers unroll themselves from their blankets and sleepily greet us as we enter the dark green gardens.

Night hangs like a silver-threaded veil, and moonstruck shadows stretch long-fingered across the lawns. The great sky is like a silver ocean. Our hearts stop. The light illuminates something so vast that at first we do not realise that we are looking, not at the sky, but at a dome – opaque, vast, a dome bigger than any I have ever seen. We move silently towards it like sleepwalkers. Carlo hides his eyes as if he has seen a vision. 'Is it really there?' he asks, awe-struck.

He looks again. 'Yes, yes! It is still there.'

But I am silent. I remember Shah Jehan holding my father's masterpiece, the Ocean of the Moon, in his fingers, suspended in the candlelight, so that the gems were filled with air, fire, water and ice. I seem to see it again now, but huge and overwhelming, as if we stand within the moon itself. I too shut my eyes, expecting that such beauty cannot be real, that it will have vanished when we open them again. But it hasn't.

I leave my brother alone to his own thoughts and emotions, and walk through the deep shade of the gardens along the river towards the Hindu quarter where I assembled my diamond within the roots of a banyan tree.

'Filippo!'

The voice is soft, hesitant. I see a shape among the trees. I go towards it and see a veiled woman. Despite her flowing garments, I can see that is graceful and slender. She lifts aside her veil just sufficient to show one eye. The moon glints on a surface the colour of lapis lazuli. One blue eye.

'Noor.'

'I had heard of your arrival. They told me where you were. I always hoped you would come back some day,' she whispered. Her fingers interwtined and her wrists rotated just as they used to do, and when she spoke, she still danced her words.

'Are you happy Noor? Are you glad that you stayed?'

'I did what was right at the time. I would do the same if I had to live that time again. I cannot regret something when there was no other choice I could have made. Now . . .' Her voice trailed away, and her movements became still.

'Did you ever dance for the emperor?' I asked.

'No,' she answered sadly. 'I never did. I was given in marriage within a year of your departure. I only ever danced for children.'

We stare in utter silence, watching the rosy dawn sliding over the white marble of the mausoleum.

'The emperor loved his wife very much.'

'Yes,' I say, and think of the Ocean of the Moon, and how my father created it for love of my mother.

'I must go,' says Noor – and suddenly looks as she did all those years ago, when she was afraid we would be discovered. 'Goodbye Filippo.'

'Goodbye Noor.'

She stretches out a hand and touches my cheek, then is gone forever.

I return to Carlo.

More and more light pours through a crack in the dawn sky. The dome floats, translucent, awakening like a giant lotus, and the four white minarets stand like handmaidens at each corner.

Within the high walls, we can see the tops of the trees and clouds of green parakeets swooping with heart-rending cries as they greet the new day. We hear the call to prayer. The echo reaches us. Long, long reverberations of:

Allahu Akbar
Ash-hadu-alla-ilaha-illallah
Ash-hadu anna Muhammadar-Rasulullah
Hayya-alassalah
Hayya-alal-Falah
Allahu Akbar
La ilahu illallah

We have been standing for three hours. The sun is riding high in an azure sky, the dome is too white, too bright to look at, but still we stand, speaking occasionally in hushed voices. Beyond, we see the glittering River Jamuna, and the fields stretching away to a shimmering horizon. A distant camel train picks its way through the shallows. Life goes on.

Only later, as we rode away from that sad, beautiful city did my brother say, 'We have just seen the Ocean of the Moon.'

Perhaps that's how it should be. A true masterpiece cannot stay hidden, either in its creator's workshop or in the secret jewel box of a queen. Rather, it is an inspiration forever and ever. Instead of the Ocean of the Moon being a gift for the living, it was transformed for Shah Jehan in his grief into this shining tomb.

Whoever has the Ocean of the Moon now, and for whatever dark purpose it has been used, the Taj Mahal, as they call it, will always be a monument to love, and simply represent all that is good in the world. Perhaps even the life of my father was worth it.

I leave this land in peace.

❖

Silence enables us to cross the water,
and to see, again,
faces on the opposite shore
which we collect with clouded eyes.
Only leaves and birds leave no trace.

We are dangerous with what
is never said. And
knowledge blossoms like dreaming, like light
rising to the world's essence –

Too many words without music destroys
sings Orpheus

Forgotten language
divides. Spaces between people die,
like hands wringing in the black
that fall vanish and fall.

You are silence,
one that has known the voice of departure
and will go on singing
until history, like time, loses trace
through water; when Lethe

guides our way home.

Justin Neville-Kaushall